Secrets of Cuniculum

Book One of the Nriv Series

C. T. Berry

Contents

World/City Names and Meanings

Nriv – A small dystopian world where robotics and humans exist simultaneously. This world is made up of five massive primary cities and scattered outlying cities can also be found far away, separate from the governing power of Nriv's ruling system.

Votum – *Vote-um* - (Promise) The capital city among the Five. The largest and most advanced technologically, Votum is a pinnacle of military power and houses the Presidential Candidate.

Nobiles – *Nobe-ee-les-* (Noble) One of the largest of the Five Cities, known for its academic opportunities and scholars. The language and manners of the city's people are exceptionally polite and formal.

Phylidrum – *Phi-lid-rum* - (Water Lover) This city rests near the western ocean. It is famous for its varied artistic contributions and beautiful landscapes. Morality and kindness are strongly valued. It is the only area where *khilange* is available.

Torquent – *Tor-quint* - (Twist) A high-tech city with the biggest subway system and an above-ground tunnel structure that connects a majority of the city's buildings. Many of Nriv's robots are manufactured here. The population is distrustful and unfriendly.

Primus – *Pry-mis* - (First) This city is the oldest and smallest of the Five. It has strong historical significance and is home to several mysterious and dangerous cults.

Cuniculum – *Coon-i-cu-lum* - (Tunnel) An outlying city south-east of Nobiles. A lawless and stuffy metropolis, ridden with crime and run by the Night Tunnel Gang (NTG) that controls the city's underground tunnels.

Carbo – *Car-bow* - (Coal) An outlying city south-west of Torquent. It is a self-sustainable coal-mining metropolis that is poor and environmentally unsafe.

Character Name
Pronunciation

Laeli – *Lay-lee*

Javeer – *Ja-veer*

Kye – *Ka-i*

Malin – *Mal-in*

Bria – *Bree-a*

Khar – *Car*

Lyon – *Lion*

Jace – *Jay-ss*

Dreadon – *Dray-den*

Elina – *E-leena*

Renon – *Ren-in*

Heathel – *Heeth-el*

Mimi – *Mee-mee*

Cair- *Care*

Special Note*

Certain characters will have a very formal use of speech that may come across as stiff. This is a dialect characteristic common among people from the Five Cities. It is also heavily prevalent among robots designed in the Five Cities. Some such examples will be the absence of contractions and instead the use of expansions or expanded forms.

e.g. – Cannot or will not instead of can't or won't.

Dedication Page

This book is dedicated to the Instagram followers who inspired me to write a Sci-fi series and to Klara. (Your enthusiasm and suggestions make me believe in my delulu. Thank you for being my supportive beta reader:)

Prologue

I remember…

I remember when my mother first took me to the Nobiles Academy for highly gifted children. I was only six years old, but my mind hasn't forgotten that moment. I've always had a good memory. I can even recall the first home we ever lived in. I was two years old, yet the image is still fresh. A small white house in the back corner of a streetway, private and secure. I always felt safe there.

The image of that first day of school at the Nobiles Academy is still so vivid. I'd been in awe of the magnificent height (it had four stories) and the large radius windows that lined the walls. I was fascinated by the width of the long halls. My curious nature wondered what my teacher would be like. As I walked into the new classroom behind my mother, I could still hear the voice of my old teacher ringing in my ears. *"She is too smart for us, Miss Elina. You need to send her elsewhere."*

Too smart. Was I too smart? I had never thought about it much. I just understood things quickly. I never really considered that I might be unusually intelligent. It was a strange thing to hear from someone else. I suppose it must have been true. My mother had always told me I was smart. I believed her, because she was very wise. Her employer would often call her a genius, and I agreed with that sentiment.

After my mother had talked to the new teacher, and I was introduced to everyone, I sat in my seat and glanced around at the other classmates. Once I'd taken everything in, I settled in my chair and minded my own business. I was so quiet that I even surprised the teacher. I wonder what she'd been expecting. As far as I could tell, I didn't need to talk to the other children. I was shy and preferred studying. I learned so fast that my teacher was astounded. If I had been more self-conscious, I might have noticed the other children were suspicious of me. I guess they thought I was odd. I didn't care. They left me alone, and I was quite fine with that.

After two weeks of school, I started to break out of my shell and began to look around more. I found it fascinating to watch others. Students whispered as they passed me. I heard gossip in the lunch hall: muttering and shared secrets in the stairways. I suppose I *was* terribly nosy, but I didn't realize it at the time. I just thought it was interesting to listen.

One day, as I was engaging in my professional eavesdropping in the stairwell, I heard a great shouting and scuffling outside. Obeying the curiosity that counterbalanced my timid nature, I followed a swarm of children to see what the noise was and came upon two tall boys beating up a slightly shorter one. He was thin and frail, his head was bald, and blood spurted from his nose. I watched in horror as the blood trickled down his face, splattering his white shirt. I wanted to help him, but I stood frozen in shock. I shuddered as his head hit the pavement - somewhere a girl screamed. As if frightened by the sound, the two boys dropped their victim and fled, but not without throwing out some insults as they ran off. The other children scurried away too, acting as if the boy were poison, and then it was only him and I...alone on the pavement.

Snapping to my senses, I rushed over to help him. He was moaning, and I could see the back of his head had been scraped by the concrete. Copious amounts of blood rushed from his nose, and it trickled all over my hands. I saw tears in his eyes and began to cry myself.

"Are you ok?"

"I...I think so." In a valiant effort to be brave, the boy struggled to sit up but fell back to the pavement.

"Here, let me help you!" I wrapped my arms around the boy's shoulder. He was taller than me but light as a feather. I could feel his bones through the white shirt he wore. We stumbled towards a nearby bench, and I made him sit down. Taking a handkerchief from my pocket, I pressed it against his nose. The boy held it firmly to his face; I could see his hands were trembling. I stared wide-eyed, for all the blue veins were visible in his thin hands. Then he turned his face towards mine, and I suddenly smiled. His eyes were a piercing blue: a crystal-clear color that was shockingly bright.

"Your eyes!" I exclaimed.

The boy looked confused through his tears. "What about my eyes?"

"They're as blue as the sky."

"Oh." A smile spread across the boy's face.

"Are you feeling better now?"

"Yes, a little." The boy sniffed, then coughed.

"Here." I handed him my water bottle and let him drink from it. After several swallows, he finally stopped coughing.

"Thank you!" he breathed.

"I'm Laeli." I held out my hand. The boy hesitated, but I grabbed his and shook it. "I'm six years old. How old are you?"

"I'm Kye. I am eight years old."

To me, eight years sounded very old and wise. I was impressed. "You must be very smart."

"Huh? Wouldn't you be too? After all, you are at this school."

"If you are older, you are smarter."

Kye made a funny noise. "I don't think that's how it works."

"Oh?" I paused, confused. "How does it work then?"

"Genetics." Kye coughed again.

"Oh." I sat and thought for a moment, contemplating what I knew about genetics. I decided I'd think more about it later.

"Yes," Kye continued. "Mine are bad."

"How?"

"I am sick."

"Oh. With what?"

"I don't know. They can't figure it out. But my mother will. She is a doctor." He coughed again, and I felt pity as I stared at his narrow frame. That was why he was thin.

"Why...why were they hitting you?" I finally asked. Kye sighed. His lips trembled.

"They always bully me."

"But why?" I placed my hand on his arm.

Kye took a deep breath. "They say I am a freak. They call me ghost and skeleton. It's cause I look awful." His voice wavered. "I'm in a class with older children. Some of them don't like that."

"If I were a boy, I'd protect you!" My voice rose angrily.

Kye laughed in between fresh tears that started to spill from his eyes. "No...you're too little to protect me."

"But I can always help." I spoke firmly.

Kye glanced at me hesitantly. "Can you help me now?"

"With what?"

Kye pointed his finger to a nearby tree. "There's a little bird nest up there." His eyes glowed. "I love birds! They're so pretty, and I like when they sing. I have birds in my room. Canaries."

"What are Canaries?"

"Colorful little birds that chirp all day. They look like mini parrots."

"Oh." I had no idea what parrots looked like but didn't say that.

"Yes," Kye continued. "I was going to climb that tree to see the nest. It has a little mother bluebird in it. I wanted to see it again. Bluebirds are the best." He gestured to the blue scarf wrapped around his neck. "Anything blue is beautiful. Blue and white are my favorite colors."

"I love those colors too," I wriggled with excitement, "and I can help you! But wait...should you climb?"

"I'm climbing." Kye spoke stubbornly. "They might be gone by tomorrow. The babies are getting big."

"Alright, then I'll help you." With much caution, I assisted him as we carefully scaled the tree. In the distance, the bell for class rang, but I didn't even notice. I watched intently as Kye shakily stretched across the branch opposite the bird's nest. We waited with bated breaths until the mother bird returned. As the babies chirped loudly, a huge smile stretched across Kye's face. I watched him, and my own heart warmed. More than anything, I liked seeing people happy.

That was how I first met Kye. For weeks afterwards, I stayed beside him. We did everything together and the bullies stopped bothering him. Kye had whispered something about his mother and father (who apparently were very important people) having come down upon the bullies' parents, but I did not pay much attention to that. I was just glad Kye was left in peace... somewhat at least. His breathing was often heavy, and at times his skin looked almost translucent. However, he would optimistically mention how his mother would heal him, and I always believed it.

Weeks passed to months. I studied at school, spent time with Kye, and went home to my mother. Those three months were bliss. I was happy and safe and everything was wonderful.

One morning, I woke up with a tummy ache. I bravely said nothing and went to school, but as the day went on, I realized I couldn't take it much more. I felt like I might throw up at any minute. How embarrassing it would be to throw up in front of everyone! Then and there, I decided I wanted to go back home. I could wait at home in comfort until Mommy got back from work.

The teacher left the room before I could ask to be excused and when she came back, her voice was spilling over with excitement and nervousness. Apparently, the newly elected President had just arrived in Nobiles, and he might possibly visit the school. My tummy hurt too much for me to care. I decided not to wait for the teacher's permission and crept out. I knew the way to our house. As I trotted down the hallway, I ran into Kye.

"What are you doing?" I asked.

"Going to the bathroom. What are *you* doing?"

"Going home. My tummy hurts."

"My mother is coming to the school. She is coming with the new President. She can help you!"

I hesitated then shook my head. That sounded like too much of a nuisance. "No, I'll just go home and wait for Mommy."

"Alright. I'll see you later, Laeli."

"Bye, Kye." I trotted down the hallway, feeling more and more nauseous. I started down the street. There were way more people out than normal, and I began to feel claustrophobic. I also felt cross. It was a bad day for the President to visit! I began to run. Home was calling to me.

Halfway home, I decided to take a backway. I had accidentally figured it out once when I was four and had gotten lost. It was pure luck that I had managed to get back to my house, but I'd always remembered that backway since. There were less people on it. I much preferred that.

I had barely walked two minutes of my new path home when a little toy car whipped out from behind a street corner towards me, an antenna dangling from its top. I halted and stared as it whizzed to a stop right in front of me. A little boy also appeared from behind the corner. He had dark coffee skin and tight dreadlocks pulled back in a ponytail. A mischievous smile with a dimple on the left side stretched across his freckled face, and his eyes were a sparkly green. I blinked in astonishment at the contrast of his features. Then I frowned. I could feel my stomach gurgling and this boy was slowing me down.

Hey!" the little boy called as he sauntered over. "Do you like my car?"

His bold greeting threw me off guard. "I...I don't know."

The little boy stepped closer and playfully flung a hand on my shoulder. He was taller than me, and his grasp was strong, but he looked close to my age. I said nothing, still entranced by his eyes. They were as green as Kye's were blue.

"I made it myself. My daddy taught me. My daddy builds motorcycles, cars...bikes. Someday, I'll make those things too!"

"Umm...*oh*."

"You're kinda shy, aren't you?" The boy grinned. "Here, watch this." Placing the remote control for his car down on the road, he flung himself on his hands and did a walking handstand. I watched in confused astonishment. I had forgotten all about my stomach at this point.

"Haha, see!" With a flushed face, the boy stood back on his feet. "What do you think? Here, wanna try my remote control car?" Without waiting for an answer, he thrust the controller in my hands. I stood there, holding it helplessly.

"No, no silly, like this." The little boy maneuvered my hand across the controller. "This makes it go forward, see! Press this to go backwards."

Without saying anything, I obeyed. I wasn't quite sure how I was supposed to talk to this boy.

"Yeah, see! You got it." The little boy laughed then looked at me, a slow smile spreading over his face. "You're kinda pretty. You got short hair, but I like it."

My mouth dropped, and I felt my face grow hot. The boy let out another laugh.

"You're quiet, but I don't mind. Want to play more with my car?"

"No." I spoke finally. "I need to go home."

"Oh, ok." The little boy shrugged. "I guess I'll find you later."

"You will?"

"Sure." With a casual wave, the boy strode off, following his car. "See ya!"

"Uh...bye." I finally smiled and watched as he backed away, turning around a few times to flash a last grin at me before disappearing from sight. Then I turned and went home. My tummy no longer hurt, and I began to feel guilty. Maybe I should have stayed at school. Suppose Mommy were to get mad with me?

Hours passed. The time when my mother would come home arrived, but Mommy had not gotten home yet. I began to wonder if her tummy had hurt too, and she'd take a while to get back. That thought made me feel better. If *her* tummy hurt, then she wouldn't be mad at me.

Suddenly, the door burst open, and my mother rushed inside. I jumped to my feet and stared at her, petrified. Mommy's face was a ghostly white. Her eyes were wide, and she was gasping for breath.

"*Laeli!*" She rushed over to me. "Where *were* you?"

"I came home early. My tummy hurt. Why, Mommy? What's wrong?"

"I went to the school looking for you! A little boy told me you had gone home, but I had to go a backway. The streets were crowded. Thank goodness you came home when you did."

"Kye told you?"

"I don't know what his name was. Laeli, we must go. *Now.*"

"What, why?"

"Don't worry why. Grab your clothes and help me pack them. We're leaving Nobiles."

My mouth dropped. I was in too much shock to argue. Blindly, I began rapidly packing my things. My mother's frenzied spirit had caught onto me, and I rushed as fast as I could.

"But Mommy, where will we go?"

A dark look settled over my mother's face. Her lips were pressed tightly together, but her voice was weak when she spoke.

"Far from here."

"When can we come back?"

"We're never coming back."

I shivered, and my mouth trembled. My mother dropped beside me, and her voice relaxed.

"It's all right, Laeli. I'm just tired of living here. I don't want to stay anymore."

I stared at her. "You're lying, Mommy."

My mother's lip quivered. "It's ok, darling, let's just go."

"Mommy, are we taking…"

"Yes." Rising to her feet, my mother walked towards a door to the side of the kitchen and entered the code into the digital lock on the wall. I had never seen a more grim expression on her face in all my life. I stood frozen as the door slid open, and my mother faced me. "Time to leave."

Chapter 1
Personal Schemes

F ourteen years later...

Javeer leaned over the cylinder head of the motorcycle he was fixing and with one arm, wiped away the sweat dripping from his forehead. A bright overhead light shone down from the shop's dark ceiling and several more lamps were lined up on the shelves, but the room still felt dim.

"Hey, Mimi!" Javeer waved his hand towards a little brown robot on wheels that obligingly rolled towards him. It had a petite, square face and two widely spaced eyes that gave it a constantly confused look. The robot's tiny rectangular mouth was unmoving as it skid to a halt in front of Javeer.

"Yes?"

"Shine some extra light on this cylinder, will you? I put new bulbs in the light fixtures, but I think imma have to install some extra lamps. Way too dark in here."

Mimi obediently activated her flashlight, but instead of working, the minuscule glow that erupted from her head flickered and died out.

"Uhhh, Mimi, not helpful."

"My light is...not...work...ing..." Mimi's voice rose two pitches higher, then glitched out and bouncily came back in as if skidding over pebbles. Javeer faced the robot and sighed.

"Don't tell me you need fixing too."

"Y...yes...uh n...no...uh, maybe? I do not KNOW." Mimi's *know* ended in a high-pitched squawk.

"For real?" Javeer frowned. "Of course this happens now." With a grimace, he squatted low and faced Mimi. "Yeah, you're definitely broken."

"Am...am...I?"

"Yes, you are, *dang it.* Now I gotta hire someone to fix you. I don't repair robots: only motorcycles."

"YOU can FIX me."

"Yeah, *no.*" Javeer rose to his feet and wiped his hands on a nearby cloth. "I don't have the time to try and figure out how to either. We're gonna have to take you somewhere."

"Far away?"

Javeer laughed. "Sure."

"But...but...I like it heraaaaa." Mimi's voice stretched out in another glitch.

"You can come back heraaaaa after you get fixed."

"Ok." Mimi docilely glanced up at Javeer and blinked.

"Javeer!"

Javeer quickly turned around as a young man entered the shop. The man was tall and well-built. A black leather suit covered his tattooed arms and more tattoos wrapped around his neck and behind his ears. Dark curly hair fell over his forehead and a smirk stretched across his brown face. "Whatcha doin'?"

"Not much. Mimi is broken, so now I gotta get her fixed. Why you here, Jace?"

"Oh, no real reason."

"Yes, there is."

"There is what?"

"A reason." Javeer leaned forward and crossed his arms. "What do you want?"

"Just to offer you again what I offered last time."

"Hah!" Javeer chuckled and flung the cloth on a nearby table. "No. Not happening."

"Why not?" Jace's voice rose coaxingly. "*Come on*. You ain't gotta stay cooped up in here."

"What are you saying? I like it here! Love it, actually."

Jace swat his hand in disbelief. "Nah, you could do a lot more. You're goin' about this the hard way."

"Says you." Javeer gave an amused snort. He stepped towards Jace. "I'm not interested in joining your gang. I already told you."

"Look, why not?" Jace flung up his hands. His voice lowered. "Malin runs this city. Cuniculum is the source of all the Black Market deals. Malin runs the Black Market. How? Cause he's got control of the Night Tunnel Gang. Now *how* he's got control of em, I don't know, but the only way to get any power in this city is buildin' it yourself! Now, if there were other sources that neighboring outlier cities...damn, even the five great *cities,* could turn to for black market activities, then we might be able to…"

"Hmph, good luck."

"Don't be such a downer," Jace complained gruffly. "You ain't got no right…"

"Look, if you think I plan on being a nobody, you're wrong." Javeer's mouth pinched determinedly. "But I'm not about to join some gang. Gangs are thievery and violence. If you want power, you'll have to fight the Night Tunnel Gang for it. If I want to get somewhere, imma do it differently. I'll play the system."

"Eh and how are you gonna do *that?"*

"You know as well as I do that gambling is rampant in Cuniculum." A slow grin spread across Javeer's face. "Malin owns the biggest casino in the whole city. If I had the money, think of the things *I* could own."

"And how would ya get the money, eh?"

"You know there's a motorcycle race every three years. Imma enter this year."

"What, with that measly thing?"

"No, you idiot, never mind with what. I've got schemes and plans of my own, and I'm not telling you all of them. But the winner of that race wins a boatload of money, so I will try to win."

"And then what?"

Javeer's eyebrows raised. "I'll guess we'll both find out won't we? Maybe I'll discover the cause of this city's problems without having to scrounge my way up from the roots."

An impressed smile spread across Jace's face. "You wanna do it the fancy way. I guess you could. But I got no fancy way. I got no family, and I got no money. Besides, someone's gotta stand up to that piece of shit. I ain't doin' it alone. I'll have my men with me, and we'll make our mark. We already are."

"Sure, but don't ask me to ever join your gang again, cause I never will. We've been friends for nine years, but I won't live life the way you do."

"Sure, sure." Jace sauntered backwards and turned to leave. "Have fun fixing your little crap-heap!"

"Hey, don't call Mimi that."

"Hah! Of all the names you had to pick."

"Why, what's wrong with Mimi?" Javeer grinned.

"Mimi? *Seriously?* You need to get yourself a woman." Jace turned around and walked back to Javeer. "I know some. Why don't you come to the bar with me soon? You haven't been in a while."

"To drink, sure. For women, no."

"*Pst.* I know you're lying when you say you don't want one."

"Never did say that now did I?"

"Well then, why not?"

"I'm not interested in any of the ones that go to the bar."

"Damn, you sure are picky. What could you possibly be waiting for? Sure, most of the girls are bitches, but they're pretty and..."

"They're not my type."

"Ah, yeah." Jace clicked his tongue in disapproval. "I forgot you was raised all *special.* You got standards." He laughed. "Ironic! You're damn handsome. You could have any girl you want, and you don't want any. They all love you, you know." His voice lowered again. "You better be careful! Bria is into you. Bria is Khar's girl. Now you wanna talk fine lookin..." Javeer made a face but Jace kept on. "I'm warnin' you, my friend. That girl is obsessed. I've heard things..."

"I want nothing to do with her."

"Good, good, cause if anythin' dirty were to go down, I'd have to back you up." Jace's voice became a whisper. "For you to become tangled up with Khar's girlfriend - that'd be dangerous."

"Didn't you just say you'd back me up?"

"Ah!" Jace swat his hand and turned away. "Well maybe I would and then again, maybe I wouldn't." He grinned naughtily. "What will ya give me if I do?"

Javeer shrugged. "Don't worry. You won't have to risk your mercenary neck for me. I'll stay away from Bria."

"Bria or no Bria, I'm findin' you a girl." Jace waved his finger and chuckled mischievously. "Unless you'd rather just stay with that Mimi bot."

"Get outta here!" Javeer tried to give Jace a push. Stifling a laugh, Jace ducked out of the way and with a final wave, raced out of the shop, disappearing into the dark street.

"Javeer," a deep voice from the back of the shop rang out. "You ready?"

"Yeah, Father. I'm closing up now."

"Hmph! Who was that you were talking to?" A tall man with a massive frame stepped from the back shadows into the light. His dark face was lined with a silver-streaked beard and thick black dreadlocks hung around his shoulders.

"Jace."

"*Hmph,*" Javeer's father snorted again. "Tell that boy to stay away from here. He's trouble. I don't want my business to become the center of a gang fight. We don't need any targets placed on us. There's no one to protect you in Cuniculum."

Javeer laughed sarcastically. "No one protected us in Nobiles."

"True enough, but I was a bodyguard there. It was *my* job to do the protecting. Here I am just a bike mechanic and a nobody. We might get murdered in the alleyway by a Night Tunnel rat, but ah well. Whether we're alive or dead, *here*...people will mind their business."

"So then..."

"So then stay *away* from the gangs and keep that fool friend of yours out of my shop. What's wrong with Mimi?" Lyon nodded to the little robot, whose head was bobbing up and down aggressively.

"She's broken. I gotta bring her to a mechanic tomorrow and get her fixed."

"Ah. Are all the lights off?"

"Yup." Javeer switched off the ceiling light and faced his father. "Let's go." The two men exited the shop through a back door, which led to an attached house. Down a small hallway was another door, which was tightly shut with an iron padlock. Taking a key from his pocket, Javeer's father unlocked the padlock and wrenched the heavy door open. The two walked down a winding staircase and once they reached the concrete bottom, Javeer pulled a light cord hanging from the ceiling that illuminated the room with a dim glow. It was a large wide room, divided two ways. One half was mostly empty; a boxing bag stood in the corner and lining the walls were rows of assorted weapons. The other half looked much like the motorcycle shop up above. Tool-filled shelves rested along the sides of the wall, as well as multiple narrow tables. In the center of it all was a large object draped in tarp, which Javeer glanced at fondly.

"Laser combat today, Father?"

"No. Hand-to-hand."

"Boxing?"

"No. You're a good boxer. Better than me. Your other martial arts need work." Lyon chuckled low in his throat. "Still waiting for the day you'll beat me, son."

Javeer said nothing. He gave a small smile and faced his father. Lyon raised one eyebrow, then swung an arm towards his son with accelerated speed. Javeer dodged the strike. The two remained locked in combat; the only sound in the room was that of their grunts and heavy breathing. For five minutes, neither man gave way. Then Lyon struck Javeer hard in the shoulder. Javeer stumbled back and almost fell but caught himself. Sweat dripped from his forehead, and his green eyes were narrow with determination. The two resumed the fight; for five more minutes they circled each other, delivering and dodging blows.

Suddenly, Javeer ducked under his father's arm, swung rapidly behind him, wrapped an arm around his neck, and flung his leg behind Lyon's. With one quick twist, he tripped his father, and Lyon landed heavily on the floor. In stunned shock, Lyon lay gasping for air as Javeer stepped backwards, his chest heaving. Then recovering himself, he leaned forward to help his father up.

"You ok, Father?"

Between pained gasps, a deep laugh erupted from Lyon. "You have learned the art of speed. I do believe you've gotten stronger." He grabbed his son's hand, his eyes gleaming. "I am proud of you."

"You are not hurt?" Javeer asked anxiously.

"Not much." Lyon stretched his shoulder and winced. "I'll be bruised, but it'll pass." He slapped his son on the back. "Haha! I see you have been practicing."

"Yes." Javeer grinned and glanced at his scraped and calloused hands. "Every night."

"Good, good." Lyon's voice grew stern, and he placed a hand on his son's shoulder. "You know I teach you skills unknown to most. Knowledge of self-defense is vital. Only *you* can protect yourself. Many die because they don't know how! I will *not* let happen to you what happened to..." Lyon's voice broke, and he stared heavily at the floor. Javeer bowed his head.

"You don't know if that would've changed anything."

"*No,*" Lyon muttered. "If she could have defended herself she might have..."

"Against a gun there is no chance! Mother could not have fought a gun."

Lyon bit his lip angrily and turned away. "Well, here in Cuniculum there are few who have guns. They..."

"You'd think the gangs would have them, considering they are minions of Malin and the Black Market."

"Be glad they don't!" With a snort, Lyon faced Javeer. "This is why I teach you; *here* you have a chance. There are no guns, so stay away from the gangs and let no one trample over you. Do that, and you are less likely to be overpowered."

"No!" Javeer stepped closer to his father, breathing hard. "The only way you can remain untouched is if you have power. And I plan to have power; you can trust me on that."

Lyon grabbed both of his son's arms. "Then by all means. Find your power and once you do, never let *anyone* take it from you."

Chapter 2
Fixing Mimi

Mid-afternoon the next day, Javeer strolled down one of the many marketplaces of Cuniculum. Close behind him was Mimi, her wheels bouncing over the cobblestones of the narrow street. Shouts and yells from store owners and salesmen rang through the air as they tried to lure guests over from under their store doors and tents. Robots of all different sizes followed their owners: robots much like Mimi: clumsy and clunky - built to serve. A tall thin robot with rusted joints and long arms walked past slowly, its metal feet clanging against the ground. Javeer glanced up in admiration.

"Hey, Mimi. We should get one of those, aye?"

Mimi didn't answer. She only blinked rapidly. Javeer shook his head and observed the massive city around him. It was a dusty, dirty city, full of smoke and strong pungent smells. Unwelcoming alleyways hid in the back of street corners and the city roads were winding and twisted. Three-story, dingy townhouses stretched as far as the eye could see and everywhere there was movement: people, robots, dogs, cats, and the rats.

Not like Nobiles. Nobiles was bright and clean. The streets were wide and the buildings were white, with tons of windows.

Here everything is just grey and black. There's not much space either. Yet... Javeer did some internal pondering. Did he like Cuniculum? Most of the time he felt disgust for the place. It was so crime-ridden and filthy. He paused for a moment, deep in thought, only for Mimi to crash into his leg.

"*Ow!* Mimi, what's wrong with you? That *hurt.* Why'd you do that? Oh, wait, yeah, you're broken. Come on, let's go. We're almost there." Javeer waved a hand and approached a frazzled-looking tent, its covering hanging haphazardly from the poles that held it up. Underneath sat an old woman, small and bent with age, her stiff gray hair tied back in a thick braid. She let out a chuckle at the sight of Javeer .

"*Javeer!* It's been two years, huh? Last time I saw you was with your father. My goodness, you're big. You still buildin' those bikes?"

"Yup. What else would I be doing, Heathel?"

"Young people are always doing somethin'." The old woman laughed again. "I was." Her eyes held a naughty glint. "I was partying! Now I repair robots; robots that help their owners clean houses and tackle mechanical malfunctions. I've been domesticated."

"You'll never be domesticated, Heathel."

"Hehe, but I won't! Never had a man, so never had to. Oh, but I liked lots of men. There was one..." Heathel paused and squinted up at Javeer. "Why are you so big? What are you eating? You're a damn, handsome boy. What made you come see an old woman like me? You need girl advice?"

"How'd you know?" With a flourish, Javeer pointed to Mimi. "*Tada!* She's broken."

"Eh." Heathel rolled her eyes. "You trickster! Here I was, all excited. What's wrong with it?"

"Not sure. She can't talk now, and her flashlight isn't working. Her arms are stiff, and she has poor motor control. Just about bruised my leg a moment ago running into me."

"Tsk, tsk." Heathel circled the robot. "A 3-10 model. Standard and dull but very loyal."

"Hey, don't say that about my Mimi!" Javeer joked. "You'll fix her then?"

"*I* won't. I've been workin' on stuff all morning. I'm getting too old. I'll have my new assistant take care of it. See..." Heathel wagged a finger at Javeer. "That's what happens when you age. You can't do so much, so you have young people do it for you. You'll find my assistant in the shop." Heathel laughed again. "I didn't have to teach that girl anything. She's the best assistant I've ever had. From day one, she knew every model that's ever existed and exactly how to patch them up. She's got the memory of an enhanced android. She'll help your Mimi. Go, go! Bring Mimi to her and take care of yourself, will you?"

"I'll try. Shall I go ahead and pay you now?"

"You can pay me once Mimi's fixed. Tell your father hello for me. Get along, now."

"Yes, *ma'am*." Grinning, Javeer ducked under the shop's open door, Mimi wobbling behind him. Squinting in the dark light, he glanced around looking for the assistant but no one was there. Frowning, he wandered towards the back door that led to an outside patio, covered with an orange-red canopy. An assortment of robots, most of them broken, sat against the door. Tables that were neatly organized showcased tools, oil, paint, and wiring. At one of the tables sat a girl, her head bent over a robot that looked similar to Mimi. At the sound of Javeer's footsteps, she glanced up, and Javeer froze. He knew that girl! Without a doubt, she looked older, but he could swear he knew her. Her face was small and oval, and her short brown hair fell in clean layers down her neck. Her stature was petite, and her movements cautious. She stared at Javeer, and his heart skipped as her large brown eyes met his. Everything about her looked familiar. He was almost certain she was the girl he had done a handstand for in Nobiles when he was seven years old.

The girl tilted her head, a puzzled expression on her face. Then her eyes widened in recognition. She froze in astonishment and in a small voice whispered, "Green eyes."

A huge smile spread across Javeer's face. It *was* her. "Hey, I remember you!" he exclaimed. "You're the girl I showed how to use my remote control car."

The girl smiled shyly but said nothing. She glanced at the ground, then back up at Javeer. Her eyes traveled over his face and shoulders, and her posture relaxed.

"You're the boy with the green eyes and the freckles. Yes, I remember you."

Dang, her voice is pretty. It's so soft and gentle. Everything about her seems gentle. Javeer's heart began to race, and he tried to ignore it. "Well, this time I need you to do something for me...for my robot I mean. She's kind of broken." He waved Mimi over as the girl knelt down to take a look. "She tried talking to me this morning, and it sounded as if there were rocks all in her mouth. She's real wobbly and glitches all the time. I guess she'll be an easy fix for you?"

The girl glanced at Javeer in quiet amusement. She placed a hand on Mimi's arm. "Hi, Mimi. How are you?"

Mimi blinked violently. "I am WELLLLLL!"

The girl laughed. "That is good!" She rose to her feet and faced Javeer. "She'll be all fixed in two weeks."

"That's great. I'll come for her then."

"Of course," the girl murmured.

Momentarily flustered, Javeer turned to go, then spun back around. "I'm Javeer. What's your name?"

The girl raised her eyebrows. "I'm Laeli."

Javeer grinned, as words he had spoken long ago danced in his head. "You're kinda pretty. You've got short hair, but I like it."

The girl's mouth fell open, and her face turned pink. A big smile stretched across her face as she stared at her feet. Laughing loudly, Javeer turned and walked back to the building's entrance.

"Hey, Heathel, I'm gonna leave. I think I'll be back tomorrow."

"Alright my boy, take care," Heathel replied then glanced at him suspiciously. "You look awfully happy! You're breathing pretty loud." With unnatural speed for an old woman, she flung a hand around his wrist. "Gracious, boy. Your pulse is racing!" Heathel chuckled sneakily. "I'm guessing you met Laeli?"

"Of course I did, and I'm coming back to see her again."

"*Hah*. Only because your bot is here."

Javeer's eyes twinkled. "We'll see."

***

Laeli walked swiftly through the shadowy street corner. She had turned away from the bright main road and veered off into a darker side road that was meagerly lit by a few flickering street lights. The walk home from Heathel's shop was long, but Laeli didn't care. Nighttime had never scared her and for some reason, the danger of the city didn't seem to make much of an impression. She was small but walked fast; she would get home soon enough.

A dog barked from a nearby alleyway, startling her. Taking a deep breath, Laeli shrugged her shoulders and kept on walking. Deep in thought, she didn't even notice the rat that scurried past her feet. All she could think of was Javeer.

What's he doing here? Cuniculum is a city of outcasts. Did he escape something too? How did he remember me? It's not hard to forget HIM, but it's odd that he'd remember me. He only met me once, and my eyes are not an interesting color. They are just brown. He's got such beautiful eyes. His face is strange - so dark but with freckles. His smile is pretty. He still has that dimple.

Laeli glanced upwards; she had reached her home. It was the final house at the end of a long row of attached homes: dingy buildings of black brick. Taking the card from her pocket, Laeli slid it through the lock on the door. The lock's light flashed green and pushing the creaky door open, Laeli stepped inside. Descending the two steps that led into the kitchen, she placed her backpack on the table and rinsed her hands. She filled a cup with water from the sink and fixed herself a plate of cold food from the fridge. Then she grabbed the plate and cup and walked to a back door at the end of the hallway. Balancing the cup in her arm and holding the plate with one hand, Laeli manually entered a complex code into the lock on the wall. The door slid open, and she walked into the little room.

This room was nothing like the rest of the house. It was small but brightly lit by blue LED lights that lined the ceiling and walls. Several lamps sat on the surrounding tables next to two computers and a steel lock box rested in the corner of the room. In a sliding chair next to the lock box sat a figure, facing one of the tables.

"You should not go out alone at night without a weapon. It is not safe."

Laeli rolled her eyes. "I'm fine."

"Tomorrow you will take a taser with you."

"What...are you my father?"

The chair wheeled around to face Laeli. In it sat a figure that appeared human but wasn't quite. The right side of the face was gentle, in spite of its sharp features. The mouth curved down slightly beneath a perfectly straight nose. Underneath the raised eyebrows were two hooded eyes of reddish-brown. Straight chestnut hair, as fine as thread, was pulled back into a high short ponytail, while delicate strands framed the face. Stretched across the face's skin were barely visible thin white marks, like little veins. Surrounding half of the left eye was a thin layer of titanium. It stretched to the ears and down part of the neck, all the way to the left shoulder and chest, giving the being its robotic features. The figure's muscular build was covered by a light brown shirt, hanging loosely around its form and tucked into baggy trousers. The figure leaned over to tighten the strings of the high-rise boots it was wearing, then rose to its feet and approached Laeli.

"I am your friend. I care for your safety."

Laeli smiled. "I know. You are my *only* friend."

"You should have more friends. *Real* friends."

Laeli shrugged as she began to eat the food on her plate. "I don't need real friends. I'm fine with just having you. You're all the friend I need."

"That is not healthy."

"Mommy thought it was."

"Your mother did not think it was. Your mother lived in fear. Her fear and grief killed her, but she did not want you to hide in here forever too."

Laeli's mouth quivered. "I miss Mommy. She was always hiding secrets. Can't you tell me what they were?"

"No."

"Ren, *please*. I know you know them!"

"Your mother did not want you to know. She wanted you to have a clear mind. A happy life."

Laeli sniffed. "You *definitely* think you are my father."

"No, I am just your friend."

"I know." Laeli sighed and finished the food on her plate. Then she walked over to a record player that stood in the corner of the wall and placing the stylus on the vinyl record, leaned over and listened to the song that began to play. Ren's eyes lit up.

"It's your favorite song," Laeli laughed. "I know you listen to it every day because this record is always on when I come home." She leaned back and stretched. "You have showed me every dance move to go with it and when I was a child, you always whispered the lyrics to me."

"Yes." Ren's eyes had a faraway look in them. In a quiet voice, he began to sing the lyrics, his rich tone piercing the silence of the little room.

"I sing a song to you across the sea,
A siren's call that rings clear and free.
I'll bend my love and will to yours,
Through sun and storms, we will endure."
Now I dance with you in marbled chambers,
You and I are no longer strangers.
Tattoo your love across my heart,
That we may never be far apart."

Leali's eyes glowed as she watched Ren. "You said it so beautifully. Why do you like it so much?"

Ren gazed at the wall as if seeing something far away. "It is part of me."

"I love it because you love it. *But*...I like the dance song Mommy always listened to more. I'll put that one on." Laeli changed the record to a smooth jazzy song and walked over to Ren. "Want to dance?"

With a smile, Ren placed a hand on Laeli's waist and held her other hand in his. As they rocked back and forth, Laeli hummed to the song's lyrics. Ren gave her a puzzled look.

"Your heart rate just rose. What are you thinking of?"

Laeli's face turned red. "Wh...what? It did?"

"Yes, your adrenaline levels have risen. Who did you meet today?"

"N...no one." Laeli protested, blushing furiously. "I mean...just a boy I met years ago."

"A boy?"

"A man! I mean a man."

"Mhm." Smiling, Ren twirled Laeli around.

"Anyway," Laeli continued, "it's nothing. I've only met him once."

"*Twice*."

"*Twice* then. I'll be fine."

"I am not worried. Not yet."

Laeli made a face. "You don't have to worry. I won't be seeing him again after his robot is fixed. I'll work and come back here like I always do."

Ren sighed. "You cannot hide in here forever."

"No," Laeli murmured. "But I will try to make it last."

Chapter 3
Reunion

With her typical fast walk, Laeli strolled down the street, her backpack bouncing on her back. She wanted to stop somewhere to get breakfast before work started. The two weeks had passed, and she was almost finished with fixing Mimi. The shouts of children playing rang in her ears, and she watched as two boys chased a dog that was running in circles. The air was filled with the sound of people's voices buying and selling. A skinny robot with the build of a tree branch approached her, its high-pitched voice grating in her ears.

"I am CJ. I can offer you the best food for the lowest price. Griddle cakes, steamed greens, flavored beans. Follow me, and I'll show you to our restaurant. My master's name is Guster. I..."

"Not now, thank you. I already know what I want."

Instead of turning away, the robot got annoyed. "What? You don't want to come? Why..."

"Why are you so annoying? Who programmed you?" Dodging sideways, Laeli left the robot standing in the middle of the street and quickened her pace. She needed to hurry. Not once had she ever been late to work. Her tummy rumbled. She began to sprint, weaving through the crowds of people. Subconsciously, she began to study the different faces walking past. Tired mothers, dirty mechanics, sharp-eyed tattoo artists, grimy children...the haggard face of a prostitute. Her eyes shifted to a large bearded man with bushy eyebrows and several piercings in his ears. *My goodness he's huge. Why does he look so angry? I wonder...*

Slam! An elbow bumped hard against Laeli's shoulder as she crashed into someone. The impact hurt and knocked the wind out of her. With a cry, she stumbled to her knees.

"Are you all right?" The figure turned around and seizing her arm, helped her to her feet.

"Yes, thank you," Laeli gasped. She took a deep breath and placed a hand on her throbbing shoulder. She glanced up into the face of the person who had knocked her over and cocked her head in mystified confusion. Staring back was a pair of blue eyes: thin blue eyes...the color of the sky. The man's face was a faint pale, the skin stretching firmly over the cheekbones. "You...you look awfully familiar." Laeli took a sharp intake of air. "Is...is there any chance that your name is Kye?"

For a minute, the man hesitated. Then a brilliant smile flashed across his face, his eyes crinkling into narrow slits. "*Laeli?* Is it really *you?*"

Laeli let out an exclamation of delight. "It IS you! Oh, Kye, I'm so glad. You look so *different*. I almost didn't recognize you."

"Then how did you?"

"No one has eyes as blue as yours." In her excitement, Laeli grabbed both his arms, practically jumping up and down. "You've gotten so tall and your arms feel so strong. Why, you don't seem sick anymore. Your mother must have found a cure!"

"Yes..." For a moment, Kye hesitated. "Yes...yes she did."

"I'm so *glad!*" Laeli gushed. "I see you still have no hair. I guess it rather suits you." She took a step backwards and made a mocking face. "*What.* No white? You're wearing all black."

"Black is my favorite color. Black and dark blue."

"Really?" Laeli cocked her head. "It used to be white and light blue."

"It is black now." Kye smiled again. His voice grew warm with affection. "It is so good to see you. I am so happy...you do not know how happy. Where were you going just now?"

"I'm going to get food. Want to come with me?"

"Of course."

"Come on then." Laeli grabbed Kye's hand and dragged him to a nearby food stand. "I come here all the time. They have good fried bread and bacon. You can get the bread savory or sweet."

"What are you getting?"

"Sweet. I feel like sweet today."

"Then I will get that too."

The two of them ordered their food and sat down at an outdoor table near the edge of the street.

"So," Laeli began, "why on earth are you in Cuniculum?"

"I wanted freedom. I had no freedom in Nobiles."

"Umm." Laeli's face crinkled in confusion. "Freedom from what? Cuniculum is a dangerous, ugly city. This place is no great escape."

"Why would you say that? *You* are here."

"My mother brought me here. I've no reason to leave, so here I stay. Anyway, I must stay."

"Why?"

Laeli's face suddenly darkened. "Don't worry about it." She shifted the topic back to Kye. "What do *you* plan to do?"

"My father left me quite a lot of money. I purchased a large house outside the city limits. It is very secure and on a high hill, so I am quite safe. I did not want to live in the city." A flash of disgust passed over Kye's face. "I will decide what to do next within the upcoming weeks. I will find some way to invest my money."

"It is very strange."

"What is?"

"You being here. You do not belong in Cuniculum. You are so brilliant. I always thought..." Suddenly, Laeli sprang to her feet. "*Work!* I'm going to be late for work."

"Work? Where do you work?"

"I am a robotics mechanic. I'm so late!" Seizing her food, Laeli stuffed the bread in her pockets, not bothering to fully answer the question. "I've got to go. When can I see you again?"

"I do not know. I will be busy but soon. I will find you."

"I don't know how. Cuniculum is crazy big." Laeli laughed. "Good luck finding me!"

"Didn't I already? Fate has its ways." Kye smiled and then grabbed her arm. "Laeli, I really missed you. You do not know how much I missed you." His face clouded. "I need to see more of you...so much has happened."

Laeli placed her hand on his arm. "I missed you too. It's been so long." She pursed her lips. "Tomorrow morning is my day off. I will meet you here, and we can find things to do."

"Not at your house?"

"No. Meeting here is better."

"Very well. We will meet here. I will wait for you."

"Bye." With a huge smile, Laeli sprinted as fast as she could to Heathel's shop. She was gasping for air by the time she arrived.

"Sorry, sorry!" she panted as Heathel raised an eyebrow at her. "I know I'm late. It won't happen again."

"Where were you, girl? I figured something awful must have happened. Do you have a taser on you? This city is mighty dangerous."

"Uh, no...I forgot it. Ugh! Yesterday night he...I mean, why does everyone keep telling me to bring one?"

"It's a sign you need to do it!" Heathel shook a wrench in Laeli's face. A mischievous smirk spread over her face. "Who's *he*? Is *he* the reason you were late?"

"Wh...what do you mean?"

"Javeer. That young man from last night."

Laeli felt her face growing hot. "Oh, no, not him. I was just referring to a friend of mine."

"Hmm." Heathel clicked her tongue in disappointment. Then she chuckled. "I never guessed you even knew one man. This is an improvement!"

"It doesn't matter." Embarrassed, Laeli scurried into the shop. *It was so good to see Kye. He was always so ill. It's amazing how well he looks. I wonder how he was able to find a cure? Oh well, I will find out the truth from him sooner or later. I will make sure of it.*

***

Laeli rose to her feet and stretched. Then she crouched down in front of Mimi and tilted her head. "Mimi. How are you feeling? Talk to me."

"I am fine." Mimi twittered. "Where is Javeer?"

"He'll be here soon, don't worry."

"He needs a light. I need to shine the light."

"You will." Giving the robot a pat, Laeli wiped a smudge off Mimi's face.

Mimi let out a cry. "There he is!" Laeli turned to see Javeer standing behind them, his tall frame casting a shadow across the ground.

"Oh, hello," she said hurriedly. *Ugh, why does my voice sound so shaky?*

"Hey."

"*Hey.*" Mimi mimicked Javeer's voice. "My light is ready."

"Haha." Javeer crouched down next to Laeli and gave Mimi a pat. "That's my girl." He faced Laeli. "Thank you."

Laeli stared at her shoes. "You're welcome." She looked up, startled, as Javeer's shoulder brushed against hers, but he was only leaning over to inspect Mimi.

"She looks good."

"Her sensory system was damaged. The algorithm was unable to transmit data through clearly, and that's why her speech and movements were jerky."

"Well, her voice is smooth. And she's shinier than before. I think she's gonna glow in that shop of mine. Ha, Mimi. Now maybe I won't trip over you in the dark. You're practically brand new."

"You tripped over her?"

"All the time. She kinda blended in, not gonna lie. I don't know...maybe I accidentally knocked something loose and that's why she became all glitchy. She got revenge on me though. Slammed right into me on my way to the shop. I still have the bruise."

Laeli laughed quietly. "Is the bruise better though?"

"I barely notice it. I get bruises all the time. This one's nothing."

"Why are you always bruised?"

"I am a mechanic too, my girl." Flashing a grin, Javeer rolled up his sleeve and stretched out his arm, revealing the veins that rippled underneath his skin. "I got this bruise when my dad knocked a hammer off a shelf. It fell right on me."

"Oh, I see." Laeli cautiously pointed her finger. "How'd you get the bruise on your hand?"

"That's from boxing."

"You box?"

"Yes. Want to see something else I can do?"

"I...I guess so. Sure."

"See this?" Javeer dangled a rubber band that he had pulled from his pocket. He stretched it around his hand and then held up his palm. "Place your hand on mine."

Holding her breath, Laeli gingerly touched her hand to Javeer's.

"Not like that, silly!" Javeer's deep laugh rang through the shop. "Touch it all the way."

Laeli flushed and pressed her hand firmly against his. Clasping his own around hers, Javeer flipped her hand over and released his grasp. Laeli's mouth dropped; the rubber band was wrapped around her palm instead. Seeing her speechless, Javeer laughed even harder.

"You can keep the rubber band. I don't need it."

"But I don't need it either."

"Ah, well then let's give it to Mimi." Gently sliding the band off Laeli's hand, Javeer slipped it around Mimi's arm. "There you go, Mimi. You've been decorated now!" Mimi blinked.

"Why?"

"Why not, you great silly?"

Laeli gave the robot a pat. "You look very nice with it, Mimi."

"I do?"

"Yes."

"Are you sure?"

"Yes."

"Why?"

"Oh my gosh!" Merriment danced all over Javeer's face. "You definitely fixed her. She's back to asking questions."

"She's a sweet little bot." Laeli glanced at Mimi affectionately. "Whoever programmed her did a good job. Many designers create their robots like themselves...rude and annoying."

"My father had her custom made for us. She's great at giving advice when it comes to different motorcycle models and how to fix them. She's good at fetching things for me too. She asks a ton of questions but that's what makes her funny. You like robots a lot?"

"I love them." Laeli's voice softened. "My mother was a robotics mechanic. She taught me how to fix them and how to build them too."

"You mean you can build your own robots?"

"Yes, but I don't have enough money for the parts I need to make the one I have in mind. I am saving for that."

"Impressive." Javeer's eyes twinkled. "Now I know I was right."

"Right about what?"

"That you were clever. You're quiet, but I figured it's only because you're always thinking. And..." Javeer's voice warmed, "I think you're also shy."

Laeli flushed. "You're not wrong."

"I'm guessing you also got that from your mother. Do you still live with her?"

Laeli's eyes dropped sadly. "My mother's dead."

"I'm sorry." Now it was Javeer's turn to look sad. "My mother is dead too."

"I am sorry." The two of them sat there silently, both sensing one another's sympathy. In an effort to make him feel better, Laeli tried to change the subject. "Why did you come to Cuniculum?"

A scowl settled across Javeer's face. "We escaped here, my father and I. My father had a bounty on his head."

"But why?"

"He was the personal bodyguard to someone very important in Nobiles. He will not tell me who. My father was guarding him at an event in his mansion when someone started shooting. They murdered the family and killed nearly all the security. They shot my father in the arm. Shot my mother too." A look of rage appeared in Javeer's eyes. "She flung herself in front of my father and was killed. I was with a friend at the time so I never saw it happen."

Laeli's eyes widened in horror. "How *awful*."

"My father was the only one who managed to escape that room. He immediately found me and left the city right away. He came here, as no one from Nobiles dares comes to Cuniculum. They are too afraid of the gangs." He gave a scornful laugh. "Why did *you* leave Nobiles?"

"I...I don't know."

"You don't know?"

"Mommy never told me why we left."

"Not at all?"

"No."

"So you'll never know then?"

Laeli's mouth set firmly. "Someday I will know."

"How...never mind. I'm sorry." Javeer ran a hand over his face and sighed. "That was none of my business. I guess you board with someone now?"

"No, I live by myself."

"By yourself? Aren't you lonely?"

"No, I'm used to it. I've been alone seven years now."

"*Seven years?*" Javeer leaned closer to Laeli. "My girl, that isn't healthy! Don't you have any friends?"

"Well, uh...no, not really." Laeli decided not to bring up Kye and mentioning Ren was out of the question.

"Then what do you do with your life?"

"Well, I work."

"Yes, but besides that."

"I take care of myself at home."

"That's it...you need some friends." Javeer held out his hand and grinned. "Can I be the first? Or second...I imagine you've had at least *one* friend in your life."

"Yes, I don't see why not." Smiling bashfully, Laeli shook his outstretched hand.

"Great!" Javeer laughed warmly. "Your hand is so tiny."

"Well, *I am* tiny."

"What are you...five-three?"

"I think so."

"I guessed right again." Javeer sprang to his feet and with a flourish, waved his hand dramatically. "As your first friend in Cuniculum, may I invite you to hang out tomorrow night? There's a place called the Iron Drift Club. It's close to where I live. I could pick you up here after work."

"Iron Drift Club?"

"Yeah. There's music, dancing, food. It's an underground bar."

Laeli hesitated. Her first instinct was to refuse, but she could hear Ren's voice echoing in her head. *You need to go out...make friends. Staying home is not healthy.*

"I'll come."

"Great! I will pick you up then. Let's go, Mimi." Javeer turned to leave then whirled back around. "You're not afraid to ride a motorcycle are you?"

"I don't think so."

"Good. Then I'll see you." Whistling loudly, Javeer sauntered out of the shop, Mimi rolling behind him. A shivery little chill of excitement shot up and down Laeli's spine. Tomorrow suddenly seemed very close and scary. Then she yawned. *I need sleep.*

***

Javeer raced down the stairs that dipped underground to the entrance of the Iron Drift. He had dropped Mimi off at his house and was now going to meet up with Jace. He shook his head as he opened the club's double doors. *I wonder why Jace wanted to meet me. He better not cause any trouble. It could get ugly if word gets out that he comes here.*

The club's low ceiling was illuminated by neon white and purple lights, splashed with blue. Heavy concrete pillars provided support, and benches attached to the stone wall lined the left side of the building. Further to the right, down a short flight of steps, was the bar, surrounded by lights of gold and green draped on the overhanging ledge. Booming music sent a steady vibration throughout the building. Javeer could feel the trembling underneath his feet. He pulled out a bar stool and nodded to the bartender.

"Hey, Trixi."

"Hey, Javeer!" The girl winked flirtatiously at him. "It's been a while since you've been here. Wanna see my new tattoo?"

"Why not?"

Grinning, the bartender pulled her sleeve below her shoulder. "Gotta bat. He's a cool one, huh?"

"For sure. What, is that like your thirtieth tattoo now?"

"I don't know; I've lost count." Trixi shrugged. She leaned over the counter. "Maybe thirty-first, who knows. Perhaps next week I'll get another one."

Javeer raised his eyebrows. "Did you get a new nose ring?"

"Wow, you noticed! Yes, yes I did." Trixi had to yell over the noise. Resting her face against her hand, she fluttered her lashes. "So darling, what is it you want today?"

"Just a burnt rum. The cheap kind."

"Cheap!" Rolling her eyes, Trixi grabbed a nearby glass. "Hey, help me decide my next tattoo."

"Uh...gee I don't know. Get one of something you love."

"That's what I've *been* doing. Hell, you're no help." With a snort, Trixi leaned over the counter, pushing a strand of red hair out of her face. "What about you, *mister?* You got any tattoos?"

"Only one."

"Where?"

"Back left shoulder." Javeer took a sip of the drink Trixi handed him.

"Back left shoulder?" Trixi leaned even farther over the counter, her eyes twinkling. "Think you could show me?"

"Not tonight, I'm afraid."

"You know, you got pretty eyes. Even in the dark I can see them. They're a cool green...kind of like cat eyes." Trixi tilted her head and grinned. "I like cats."

Javeer shook his head. "You're a weird girl."

"What do you mean?" Trixi stepped backwards, an exaggerated pout on her lips. "*You're* the weird one. Won't even let me see your tattoo."

"Why should you want to see it?"

"Why shouldn't I?" Trixi leaned forward again, her voice exasperated. "Honey, can't you tell when someone is tryin' to flirt with you?"

"Why would anyone be trying to flirt with me?"

"*Really?*" Trixi put a hand on her hip. "Don't be such a junk head!"

"I'm sure I don't know what you're talking about." Javeer's eyes gleamed mischievously as he took another sip of rum.

"You *brat.*"

"Mm...maybe."

"Mister, you're in an especially obnoxious mood tonight. Somethin's up." Trixi pointed her finger in his face. "Did you get somethin'? Drugs? A black market deal?" She lowered her voice. "A girlfriend?"

"No, no, and no. Sorry to disappoint."

Trixi's eyes wandered over Javeer's shoulders and a smug look appeared on her face. "There's your crooked friend. That's why you're here."

"Crooked? Everyone here's crooked, Trixi."

"*Uhuh.* Everyone except *you*, of course. You won't even flirt to pass the time! I don't know who you're being loyal to."

"Let me tell you a secret." Javeer leaned forward and whispered in Trixi's ear, "I'm not being loyal to anyone. I...simply...don't...*care.*"

Trixi stepped back and made a face. At that moment, two girls slid over to the empty seats next to Javeer.

"*Hey,*" one of them catcalled. The other giggled. Trixi scowled at them.

"I'll go to Jace." Javeer stood to his feet. He placed some coins in front of Trixi. "See ya, Trixi." He nodded briefly at the girls and walked away as they stared after him, wide-eyed.

Trixi began rubbing the counter with her cloth viciously as the two girls whispered to each other.

"See! That's the one I was telling you about."

"You weren't kidding. He's all muscle."

"*Ripped!*" The girls giggled again.

Trixie slapped her cloth on the counter. "I wouldn't waste your time, ladies. He's not gonna be interested in *either* of you."

"Oh, come now," one of the girls replied scathingly. "Just because he don't want you doesn't mean he won't want us. You needn't be all sore about it." She side-eyed her friend. "I think someone's *jealous.*"

Trixie glared at the girl. "And I think you're a bitch."

"*What'd you just call me?*"

"I said a *BITCH*. Need me to spell it out for you, honey?"

***

As the women's fight grew more heated, Javeer had already given Jace a handshake and sat with him at one of the wooden benches.

"Hey, Javeer! How long you been here?"

"Just a few minutes."

Jace's eyes held an amused glint. "Guess that was long enough."

Javeer made a puzzled face. "Huh?"

"Look behind you. You got the females all riled up."

Startled, Javeer turned to see Trixi waving her cleaning rag in one of the girl's faces. Both women were on their feet, pointing fingers in Trixi's face and yelling. Then one of them grabbed a glass and flung it at Trixi. Trixi ducked and the glass shattered against the wall behind her.

"*What the hell,*" Javeer swore under his breath. Springing to his feet, he sprinted to the bar and slammed his hand on the counter in front of the women, who were screaming insults in Trixi's face.

"That's *enough,*" he bellowed. "Cut that out and get out of here." Wide-eyed, the two women scurried away.

"Thanks, Javeer," Trixi gasped. She leaned backward against the wall, breathing hard, and fixed her hair. Her eyes sparkled. "You're a darling."

"I can't say the same about you." Giving her an amused grimace, Javeer walked back to Jace, who was laughing.

"Just pick one already will you? You're driving these bitches crazy. *Though,*" Jace smirked to himself, "if you picked one, it might drive em even *crazier.*"

Javeer made a face. "Why am I friends with you?"

"Cause you like me, that's why." Jace leaned back and crossed his arms smugly. "You know I'm right."

"Well they're just gonna have to calm down cause...I already found a girl."

"*What?*" Jace straightened rapidly. "*What'd you say?* Don't tell me you actually got a girl!"

"I did and now I'm going to ask you a favor. Don't bring any of your *men* here tomorrow night. I don't..."

"You don't want any shit to go down. I see where this is goin'." Jace fingered his chin. "You do know I never bring anyone here, right?" He lowered his voice. "My rank in the group is a secret to the public. I don't mix any of that stuff with this place. You should know that!" Jace stopped frowning and chuckled. "You know, *you're* the one who ain't being careful."

"How so?"

"You really wanna bring that girl here? Some of these women are gonna lose their shit!"

"Let them."

"Oh, I see." Jace squinted his eyes. "You plan to show her off. Let them all know it's time to back away. Does this girl know what she's getting herself into? What kind of woman is she anyway?"

Javeer crossed his arms. "Guess you'll find out, won't you."

"I'll be sufferin' all night from curiosity." Suddenly Jace's eyes widened. "Bria is here!"

"*What?*" Javeer half turned in his seat.

"Shit, I gotta go!" Cursing quietly, Jace sprang to his feet. "I'll see ya, Javeer." In a whisper, he added, "You know why I can't stay." With a quick turn, Jace dashed through the back of the club and vanished.

Flustered, Javeer also stood up. *I can't run, and I can't leave unless I walk past her, but I'm not staying*. Straightening, he turned and without glancing at the tall figure in front of him, walked past. A hand on his arm stopped him.

"Javeer," the voice murmured. "I need to talk to you."

A passive expression on his face, Javeer turned towards Bria. "What do you want?" he asked sharply.

"Not here." Bria glanced sideways, her amber eyes cat-like in their subtle movements. She turned to the front door, her hand still on Javeer's arm. As he followed her out of the club, his eyes swiftly glanced her over. Her thin curvy figure was sharply visible in her tight tank top and high-waisted pants. Gold bracelets lined her wrists and large gold earrings dangled from each ear. Her light brown skin was shiny from the perfume mist she had sprayed on and long dreadlocks swung back and forth from the ponytail that sat high on her head. Walking up the steps away from the club, Bria turned and then halted in a dark section of the street. She faced Javeer.

"I *had* to see you."

"Why?"

Bria stepped closer, her eyes tragic under her long lashes. "Can't you guess?"

"I can, and you can forget it." Javeer tried to step away, but Bria clutched his arm.

"Wait! I'm not finished..."

"I don't..."

"I've seen you before! It was a random passing on the streets, but I haven't forgotten." Bria sidled closer to him. "It's your lucky day! When I see a face I like, I don't forget it." She reached out and twirled the dreadlock dangling over his face. Javeer pushed her hand away.

"Forget it! What about Khar?"

Bria gave Javeer a surprised look. "What about him?"

"Won't he find out what you're doing?"

A small smile lifted up the corner of Bria's mouth. "He don't have to know."

"So you're telling me you're not in love with your boyfriend?"

"In *love?*" Bria's warm laugh was swallowed by the noise from the nearby club. "Oh...Khar's fun, but he's not someone you fall in love with. Of course, I can't leave him...you understand. Even so..."

"Save it. I don't want you."

"I promise!" Now Bria was gripping Javeer's arm. "He'll never find out. He doesn't even know I'm here."

"It's not about whether he finds out or not, Bria. I *don't want you.*"

"You're lying!" Bria's voice grew defiant. She lowered it to a whisper. "*Everyone* wants me. Why do you think Khar has me?"

"What do you mean?"

"Don't you understand?" Bria ran her finger down Javeer's arm. "Khar always has to have what everyone else wants. And I..." She flashed Javeer a seductive look. "I always get what no one else can."

Javeer jerked sideways, freeing himself from Bria's touch. "You're a fool! Stay away from me." Without another look, he quickly turned and disappeared into the dark, Bria staring angrily after him.

***

Laeli tossed fitfully in her bed. She couldn't fall asleep at all. The stories Javeer had told her about his past kept replaying in her head, and it made her restless. With a frustrated sigh, Laeli tossed her blanket off and tip-toed across the floor in her bare feet. She entered the locked side-room, and her eyes fell across the lock box. After a moment's hesitation, she knelt in front of the box and entered the digital code on its side. The steel door swung open as Laeli sat there, staring at the objects within the safe. She reached out and held one of them in her hands. It was a thin circlet of grey blue, with a wiry exterior and multiple tiny sensors on the interior. Voices of old memories began to ring in her head.

"What does this do, Mommy?"

"It's a device that was given to me long ago. It had been designed specifically to fit my brain. You place it on your head and the sensors provide a powerful signal to your frontal lobe. This signal then interacts through the brain waves' electrical current and connects to the artificial object you wish to control."

"Like a light bulb or a robot?"

"Yes, darling. You could compare it to a form of Wi-Fi. Whatever you command that object to do, it will obey. This device even

permits you to override the objects initial programming. Your thoughts and your will determine that object's actions."

Laeli's mind shifted to yet another memory. She could almost see her own tiny form sitting in a chair, resting in a corner of the old house she used to live in. The circlet was on her head, and a wire that attached from the back end was plugged into a strange device which almost looked like a computer. Her mother and Ren were bending over the device; she could hear her mother asking Ren a question…

"Why are you up?" Ren's voice from behind broke Laeli's train of thought.

Laeli took a deep breath. "I can't sleep. *Ren.*" Her voice cracked a little. "I need you to do something for me."

"What should I do?"

Laeli shifted and faced Ren. She rose to her feet. "Tell me why we escaped from Nobiles."

"I cannot."

"*Why* not?"

"Your mother did not want you to live in fear."

"Fear? Fear of *what?*"

"I cannot say."

"*Ren.*" Laeli squeezed his arm. "If I am in danger then I should know why."

"You are in Cuniculum. You are not in that kind of danger here."

"Then what fear are you talking about?"

"The fear that knowledge brings."

"You don't have to worry about that. I can handle it!"

"Laeli." A sad expression shadowed Ren's face. "If you were to know everything, you would be filled with bitterness and grief. Your mother wanted you to have a…"

"Do not say normal!" Laeli interrupted. She sharply turned her head away. "I always knew my life was never normal. First I was at that school in Nobiles, and then it was us running to hide here: to hide *you*. Yes, you have always been kept a secret. I remember when Mommy would work on you back in Nobiles. She would often stare at your face and start to cry. Why did you make her cry, Ren? What was she thinking of?"

"I cannot say. She forbade me to tell you."

Laeli shook her head. "I always knew Mommy was suffering. Whatever happened to her had made her ill. I know that illness is what ended up killing her." Tears spilled from Laeli's eyes, "And all that time, I was too afraid to ask her what happened! Too scared to find out why she was even sick in the first place. Why can't *you* tell me? I don't even know who my father was. I…I tried to ask Mommy once, but she cried so much I was scared to ask again. *Ren.*" Laeli shook his arm. "What happened to my father? Who was he?"

"Do not ask me to tell you."

"Ren, listen to me! You are a humanoid robot. My mother designed you to mimic a human in every way. She gave you your own personality; you practically have free will. There is nothing stopping you…you can *tell me.*"

"Yes, but your mother also programmed me to protect you. You are my primary concern. That instinct influences all my decisions. Even though I want to tell you, I *will not*. I promised your mother I would not. It is in your own best interests that I keep my promise."

Despairingly, Laeli released her hold on Ren's arm and stared at the circlet in her other hand. "You do not understand," she whispered. "I know I am different! I recall everything clearly. Every conversation, every face...every voice I have ever heard. All day, a thousand thoughts run through my mind: hundreds of ideas. The yearning to know more eats at me. I feel that if I do *not* know, I shall lose my sense of purpose." Laeli raised her eyes tragically. "In my free time, I used to make things. When Mommy died, I found this in the safe and tampered with it. I found a way to enhance its power. *You* remember that night when I put it on. The entire city lost power, and I was terrified. I realized then that I had done a dangerous thing. Yes, I was able to turn the city's lost power back on but *listen...*" Laeli's voice tightened. "I've been too scared to create anything since! I always feel hollow and empty now and if I do not know the truth, I shall feel even *more* so."

"Laeli," Ren murmured. "What your mother knew destroyed her life. Do you not think it would destroy yours too?"

"I'm not Mommy! You don't know that it would."

"Even so...unless it becomes necessary that you should know, I cannot tell you." Ren raised his bowed head and gazed sorrowfully at Laeli's tear-soaked face. "I am sorry."

Chapter 4
Outing with Kye

Laeli pressed her hand against her forehead as she walked through the city to meet Kye. Last night had left her with an awful headache. She sighed and wrapped her hand around the taser at her belt. Ren had sternly insisted she take it with her before she left. As she pressed through the bustling streets, someone rudely bumped into her and automatically Laeli's hand tightened against the taser. Frowning, she shook her head and then looked up and smiled. She could now see Kye, waiting for her by the food stand they had sat at before. He was dressed in a sleek black jacket with a high collar and high-laced boots over his black pants.

"Hello!" she greeted eagerly. "It's good to see you."

Kye returned the smile, his eyes crinkling in their typical way. "What would you like to do first?" His gaze fell to the taser at her side and a strange look passed over his face. Then it vanished. Laeli wondered why seeing the taser displeased him, but she pretended not to notice.

"I am guessing you are still new to the city?"

"Quite new."

"There are certain parts it would not be safe to go through. Follow me."

"Why is that?" asked Kye as he fell into step with her.

"Don't you know about the Night Tunnel Gang? They inhabit the outer ends of Cuniculum and use the tunnels that run underneath the city. Just last week someone was murdered by them in an underground club."

"I see. Do you fear them?"

"I have never seen one of them, so I guess not. Sometimes I wonder how I have not."

"Is that what the taser is for?"

"This? Uh, no, well...sort of. I just decided to bring it with me today. I usually forget."

"I suppose it is because of me you brought it." Kye smiled again, but his voice was tight.

"What? No!" Laeli protested. "Why on earth would you think that? You are my closest friend."

"It relieves me to hear you say so." The scowl vanished from Kye's face, and he gently placed a hand on Laeli's back. "Where are we going first?"

"There is an antique shop I've wanted to visit. My mother took me there when I was young, but I've not gone back yet."

"Your mother? Where is your mother now?"

"She's dead." Laeli's mouth tightened.

"Oh." Kye fell into a deep silence and then after a little while suddenly said, "I am sorry."

"Thank you." Laeli glanced up at him and saw his eyes had narrowed as if he were trying to solve the clue to a puzzle. "What are you thinking of?"

Instantly, Kye's face relaxed, and he laughed. "I think so much. I know you do too, so you understand."

"Yes," Laeli murmured. "I understand very well. Tell me. How did your mother cure you?"

A shadow passed over Kye's face. "I would rather not talk about that. I find it painful."

"Painful?" Laeli was confused. "I would think...very well. Did you stay at that school we went to together?"

"The Nobiles Academy for gifted students? No, I did not stay there for long. My father had me privately tutored until I was eighteen years old."

"Did you prefer that?"

"Very much so. I like to be alone. Do you?"

"I...I'm not sure. I mean...I never usually feel alone."

"Do you have many friends?"

"Not really. Do you?"

"No."

Laeli realized that the entire time they had been talking, Kye had never once looked at her. His eyes were constantly scanning his surroundings, like a hawk searching for prey. *Strange. He used to always be fixated on the person talking to him. Not once would he even look away.*

"There is the shop." Laeli pointed to a grey building with deep windows on either side, attached between two larger shops. The windows were full of tools, watches, toys, and furniture. Forgetting her thoughts, she eagerly separated from Kye and rushed inside. By the door, a rusted silver robot with an oblong face welcomed her in a monotone voice.

"Greetings. Please make yourself at home. Should you wish to purchase something, approach the desk in the back right, and you will be taken care of. Enjoy your visit."

"Thank you," Laeli murmured automatically. She immediately began to browse the shelves. Behind her, Kye stepped through the front entrance. His eyes fell over the robot as it gave him the same greeting. His eyes narrowed.

"*Inferior*," he muttered coldly. Brushing past the robot, he followed Laeli from a distance as she continued to look around. Her eyes fell upon an object on one of the shelves, and she gently picked it up to examine it. Her hands were holding a little brown music box, sparkly mist still clinging to its dented exterior. She opened the lid, and Ren's favorite song began to play. Within the box was a small girl-figurine in a delicate purple dress that matched the color of Laeli's shirt. The figurine's arms curved lightly above its head and the tilted face held an abstract expression. From behind, Kye approached silently. "I know that song. You used to hum it as a little girl."

"Yes." A swift flood of memories swept through Laeli's brain. She could see her and Kye sitting together under the tree with the bluebirds and on the bench in the school hall, holding their books and comparing sketches where their notes were supposed to be.

"It is one of my favorites." Kye smiled. "Let me buy you the music box."

"Oh no, you don't have to do that!"

"But I will."

"Maybe you won't. Maybe I won't let you." With a playful grin, Laeli turned away and continued walking around the store. Kye stared after her and kept following from a distance. As Laeli vanished through another door in the back of the shop, he halted by a dresser with a large mirror attached to it. As if in a trance, Kye continued to stare into the mirror at his reflection, a dark shadow flickering in his eyes. He did not turn his head as Laeli walked up behind him, still holding the music box. "Are you ok?"

"Do you ever feel…" Kye's words were heavy and detached, "like a part of you is missing? A piece of your soul is gone and left in a void?"

"No, I…"

"It is *gone*," Kye repeated, staring intensely into the mirror. His voice dropped, and a chill snuck up Laeli's spine, for it sounded hollow and tormented, like someone who was speaking in the midst of a haunted dream. "And no matter how you search, you cannot find it." As if suddenly released from a spell, Kye turned away from the mirror and smiled. "Have you found anything else you like?"

Laeli shifted anxiously. "Are you sure you're ok?"

"I am fine."

Laeli said nothing, only eyeing him worriedly.

"You are going to crush that music box." With a laugh, Kye pried loose Laeli's grip and gently took it from her. "What else do you want to get?"

"I...uh...nothing," Laeli faltered. Still smiling, Kye walked over to the back desk. On the top sat a bell and next to it was a note that said *Ring Bell for Assistance*. Kye rang the bell and a little old man with wiry, grey hair and a lopsided face came out from behind a back door.

"Hello, hello! What did you decide to buy?" he asked enthusiastically.

"Just this." Kye placed the music box on the desk.

"*Oh*...that thing."

"Yes...where did you get this? Who gave it to you?"

"How am I supposed to know *that?*" the old man snorted. "I can't keep track of where all the stuff in here comes from."

"It plays a song that originates from Votum." On hearing that, Laeli gave Kye a strange look.

"Hmph!" the old man grunted. "Isn't that the name of a city or somethin?"

"It is the capital of the Five Cities."

"Well aren't you learned?" The old man caught sight of Laeli and chuckled. "Did ya know that fun fact too, miss?"

"No, I did not."

"Welp, I didn't either. Makes me feel better about myself. Did you wanna get anything else, mister?"

"No, just the music box. It is for her." Kye placed the box into Laeli's hand.

"Hmm, ok." The old man squinted his eyes, focusing on Kye's clothing. "You got decent style, mister, if I do say so myself. Ain't it kinda hot out though to be wearin' black?"

"Does that matter?" His voice suddenly indifferent, Kye shrugged and turned away from the man without saying goodbye.

"Goodbye...thank you!" Laeli exclaimed hurriedly. She followed Kye out of the store. "Kye, what is wrong?"

"Nothing is wrong."

"Then why...why did you just talk like that?"

"Talk like what? What do you mean?" Kye tapped the music box in Laeli's hand. "Are you not happy to have found a music box with this song?"

"I...I guess so." Confused, Laeli stared hard at the box.

"I was happy to buy it for you."

"You should not buy me things, especially since you haven't found a job yet."

"Do not worry about that." Kye placed a hand on Laeli's shoulder. "It was nothing...nothing at all. I did not mind." His eyes swept over the city streets as if scouring them for something. His vision had become laser focused, and his face momentarily seemed to freeze into a state of sharp concentration. Then just as suddenly, he relaxed, and his countenance transformed into a wide smile. "I know something that we can do."

Still baffled, Laeli obediently followed as he strode away from the shop down the streets. The city was absolutely crowded now, but Laeli hardly noticed. She was walking swiftly, wondering how to ask Kye if something was bothering him.

Suddenly, Laeli noticed a dead cat lying in the middle of the road, its body crushed. Someone must have run it over with a motorbike. Three vultures surrounded the carcass, their beady eyes tilted in Laeli's direction. With a grimace of disgust, Laeli stepped far away from the birds. Then she realized Kye wasn't next to her. Turning around, she saw that he was standing beside the carcass, gazing directly at the blinding sun above. Squinting upwards, Laeli saw a fourth vulture circling the sky. Her eyes narrowed in bewilderment for Kye was watching it as one entranced, seemingly unaffected by the sun's brilliant rays.

"What are you doing?" she finally asked.

"They are *wonderful*," Kye exclaimed under his breath.

Laeli took a step closer. "What do you mean? You always hated vultures. Your favorite birds were bluebirds."

Kye did not answer. He continued to observe the vulture in a state of absorbed fascination. Then his eyes narrowed, and he lowered them to Laeli's height. "Bluebirds are nothing." Squatting down, he reached out to touch the vulture nearest to him on the ground. Hissing, it hopped sideways, dodging Kye's touch. "Vultures, crows, ravens," he whispered under his breath as if reciting a spell. A weird fluttering settled in Laeli's stomach.

"Since when do you like ravens? They scared you when you were little."

Kye raised his head slowly and directly stared at Laeli. "They are fascinating," he muttered.

Laeli took a step backward. "I...uh...did you still want to go somewhere?"

Without answering, Kye rose to his feet, stepped away from the vultures, and placing a hand on Laeli's back, continued down the packed street. Laeli stiffened, but Kye's hand remained where it was.

Something is not right, Laeli thought anxiously. *This does not feel right. Kye is acting strange. He was never like this as a child. I must find out what has made him change.*

Crash. Someone bumped into Laeli and the force sent her sprawling to the ground. With a cry, she dropped the music box and flung out her hands to break the fall. The music box hit the cobbled street with a thud, the lid snapping off. The song inside began to play and then glitched before cutting out completely.

"Oh no!" Laeli gasped. She lay where she had fallen, gaping at the music box. Then she turned to her side to see that Kye was gripping the shoulder of the person who had knocked her over. His voice rang out in hostile tones as he violently shook the man.

"You *imbecile,"* he hissed. "I'll..."

"Kye, stop!" In alarm, Laeli scrambled to her feet and grabbed Kye's arm. When that did not work, she sprang between him and the man, holding her hand out. "Kye, *stop."* Kye's eyes dropped to meet hers and the harsh anger slowly dissipated from his face. As if nothing had happened, he released the man's arm and leaned over to pick up the music box. Without moving, he stood there, staring at it in his hand. The man he had just grabbed loomed up beside him, planting his face next to Kye's.

"You wanna fight? I'll fight you!"

As if he didn't even hear the man, Kye spoke in a far-away voice. "Laeli, the box is broken."

"Kye, let's go." Laeli realized her hand was trembling and pressed her other hand on top of it in an effort to keep still. She began to walk away, disappearing into the crowd. Kye continued to stare un-movingly at the music box.

"*Well?*" the man growled. "You wanna fight??"

Kye turned and gripped the man's shoulder with a force that made the man yowl in pain and sink to his knees. Then with a blank face, he murmured calmly into the man's ear, "I will kill you next time." Releasing his grip, Kye strode off casually, leaving the man holding his shoulder in terrified shock. Within moments, he caught up to Laeli, who was still clutching her own hand. "Are you ok?"

"I...I don't know."

Kye reached out to touch her shoulder reassuringly, but Laeli shook him off. "*Don't,*" she muttered.

"Laeli, please." Pleadingly, Kye stepped in front of her. "I do not like seeing you look that way."

Laeli said nothing. She only walked faster. "What happened to the music box?"

"You do not want it. It is broken."

"What did you do with it?"

"I did nothing with it." Kye shrugged and then pointed his finger past Laeli's face. "This is what I wanted you to see."

In front of them stood two separate booths. One was full of shelves that held all sorts of paintings: paintings of rivers, smoky buildings, robots, random, colorful zigzags, and strange faces with bulging eyes. The other booth sheltered a long table covered with paint brushes, easels, and canvases of multiple sizes. Laeli glanced at the booths, then at Kye in bewilderment.

"What's this?"

"You paint your own picture."

With a sudden flashback, Laeli remembered little Kye talking about paintbrushes and sunsets. She gave a small smile. "Yes, you do like to paint."

"Do you? I cannot recall you ever mentioning it."

"I have never painted before." Laeli sat at the table as Kye paid the woman standing beside the booth. "But I shall try."

"Yes, try. You will enjoy it." Kye sat beside Laeli, his back facing away from her as he picked up one of the canvases. Laeli side-eyed him, a strange feeling in her stomach. Something was wrong; she could sense it. There seemed to be a hollowness to Kye that was never there as a child: a strange feeling of tension and coldness. But yet, there were moments like now, where he seemed so much like the little boy she had used to know: light-hearted and excited. Baffled, she bent over the square canvas of her choice and stared at it, thinking hard. Sketching, creating complex digital designs, robotic models; all of that she was familiar with, but never before had she painted anything.

Suddenly, an image formed in Laeli's mind. Her lips set in concentration, she reached for a paintbrush and easel and began to paint. Somehow it was easy for her; she was merely sketching something she had seen many times and adding color. As if guided by an invisible hand, she worked rapidly. The lady who owned the booth wandered over and peaked in curiosity over Laeli's shoulder. Her raspy voice let out an impressed grunt.

"You're fast. You paint much?"

"No," Laeli muttered. Caught in her own world, she barely heard the woman's compliment.

"What model is that? I know someone who's got one just like it."

"A 3-10 model."

"Ahh." The woman gave another grunt. "You're right good at it."

"Thank you." Laeli quickly added a splash of dark brown, blending it into a shadow. The woman nodded and stepped away, leaving Laeli to work in silence. She had forgotten about everything: Kye, her discomfort, Javeer, even Ren. All she saw was her painting.

After thirty minutes had passed, Laeli leaned forward and blew over the canvas. Then she carefully raised it and stretched out her arms to survey the finished product. A happy feeling surged inside of her and from behind, the booth lady give a cry of exclamation. "It's about perfect!"

"It *is* quite nice." Laughing happily, Laeli placed the painting back on the table. "Hello, Mimi," she murmured to it. "You've been immortalized." She turned to look at Kye, who all this time had been silently absorbed in his own work. "Can I see what you've done so far?"

Kye didn't answer. Curious now, Laeli leaned over his shoulder, and her mouth dropped. Kye's canvas showed a huge arched window lined in black trim. Grey, misted sky reflected through the window panes, which displayed multiple crows flying below the clouds. Standing in front of the window looking out was a figure dressed all in black, the face hidden. The walls of the building were a shadowy grey-blue, as were the floors. Standing beside Kye was a girl; a girl with a face that looked just like Laeli. Behind his black figure was the long shadow of another person stretching eerily across the glossy floor. Once again, a chill ran up and down Laeli's spine and a strange heaviness settled in her chest at the sight. "How did you paint that so fast? Why am I in the picture?"

Smiling to himself, Kye turned and looked at Laeli, but his eyes seemed to be seeing something else far away. "You have been immortalized," he whispered, the same words Laeli had just said to herself a moment ago.

Laeli's eyes widened? *"What?"* She leaned away, but her eyes fell again on Kye's picture. "What is that shadow?"

A dark look, followed by a flicker of hatred, settled into Kye's eyes. "Do not ask! It is merely the shadow that follows me."

Laeli swallowed hard. "Kye? Are you alright? Is there something you need to tell me?"

"Is there something *you* need to tell *me?"*

"What? No, of course not!" Laeli gripped the side of the table. "Kye, you're scaring me. You've been acting very strange."

"I am not strange. Do not say it! I am only..." His voice fading, Kye looked away. "*Lost.*"

"Why are you lost?" Torn between fear and sympathy, Laeli automatically placed a hand on Kye's shoulder. Swiftly, he turned around and seizing both of her hands, spoke pleadingly.

"Laeli, please. Come visit me...at my house. I want you there."

"What? No, I can't." Laeli quickly yanked her hands free. She was beginning to feel very frightened. The desperate look on Kye's face unnerved her. Snatching her painting, she quickly rose to her feet. "I need to go now."

"Laeli, *please.*" Kye reached out and grabbed her wrist. "I *must* see you."

"No...I mean no...I don't know."

"Laeli, you are my only friend. The only friend I ever had."

"That can't be true." A feeling of guilt washed over Laeli. Kye's voice sounded so sad, so tragic. "Surely you have other friends."

"No, only you."

"I...I'm too busy. I can't."

"Not even once? Just once?"

"I...I don't know. I'll have to wait and see."

"You do not understand..."

"Please, Kye!" Laeli's grip on her painting tightened as she once again pulled away. "Let me think about it."

"Very well." A look of severe pain on his face, Kye stood up and thrust his painting into Laeli's hand. "I will wait." He turned to walk away, but not before glancing back one last time. Laeli stood frozen, for though his face oozed misery, a strange glint had appeared in his icy blue eyes. Then he quickly whirled around and strode away, his black coat flapping behind him.

"He's a bit odd," the booth woman interjected suddenly. "He your lover?"

Laeli took a deep breath: a sharp breath that stung like a knife. "No. *Never.*"

Chapter 5
Laeli meets Jace

Laeli sighed as she opened the sliding door in her house that led to the secret room. Ren glanced up as she came in, his eyes wandering to the paintings she held under her arm.

"What do you have with you?"

"I made something." Laeli handed him the painting she had done of Mimi. Ren brought the image close to his face, eyes narrowed as he examined it.

"You did quite well," he murmured. "Your technique is tasteful for a beginner. Who is this you painted?"

"Her name is Mimi. She belongs to a man I met two days ago."

"Fascinating." Ren raised his eye from the picture. "Did you work on her at Heathel's?"

"Yes." Laeli took another deep breath. "Ren, I will be going out again...tonight."

"Ah, and so?" Ren lowered the painting and tilted his head. "Where will you be going?"

"To Heathel's shop. The man who owns that robot is going to pick me up. He is bringing me to a club." Taking the painting from Ren, Laeli placed it on the table against her computer and removing the taser from her belt, set it beside the painting. "I've never been to a club before."

"So that is the man you mentioned the other night." Making a low rumbling noise in his throat, Ren stood to his feet from the chair he was sitting in. "When you leave tonight, keep the sliding door unlocked."

"No, Ren. Mommy said..."

"Just in case. I will not leave unless I have to."

"I'm sorry, Ren, but I can't. Mommy said you were to never leave this room. No one is supposed to see you. That's why she designed the door to be unlocked from the outside only."

"But if..."

"No, Ren. I can't. I'm sorry."

Ren sighed deeply. He squinted his eyebrows as he noticed the second picture Laeli was holding. "What is that?" Without waiting for an answer, he slid it out from underneath her arm. His eyebrows went up. "Who painted this?" he asked in a strange voice.

"Kye," Laeli replied shortly.

"Kye? Is that not the little boy you always talk about so much? How did you get this?"

"He's in the city. I saw him for the first time two days ago."

"I wonder what he is doing here," Ren whispered under his breath. He maneuvered the canvas in his hands. "The painting is flawless. Almost as if it were created by AI and not a human."

"Well, Kye was always a genius. He painted a lot as a kid. That's not surprising." Laeli snatched the painting from Ren's hands. "I need to get ready before I go."

"Laeli." Ren's voice stopped her before she could leave the room. "Something is disturbing you. I can tell."

"Don't worry about it! I'll be fine." Blinking hard, Laeli shut the door behind her and went into the kitchen. Placing the painting on the table, she drank a large glass of water and nibbled on some food from the fridge. Then her eyes wandered again to the painting. The sight of all three figures looking away seemed eerie to her. She bent forward to observe it more closely. The shadow of the figure behind Kye was long and thin, but there was a definite shape to the shoulders. The figure of herself was fixated on Kye's back, staring at him with a strange intensity. Shuddering, Laeli flipped the painting over. Why ever would Kye portray her like that? Never *once* had she ever given him that kind of look. She drank another glass of water in an attempt to make herself feel better. Glancing out the narrow window above the kitchen, she realized she needed to get ready to leave. She still had to walk to Heathel's shop.

***

"Hey, girl!" Heathel waved enthusiastically when she saw Laeli approaching. "What are you doing here? It's your day off."

"I know. I'm just waiting for someone." Laeli seated herself on the ground, close to the shop's front entrance.

"*Someone?*" Heathel's eyes grew alight with mischief. "Who's this someone gonna be?"

"No one special." Flustered, Laeli tried to focus her view on a group of children playing across the street, but Heathel was not deterred. She hobbled over to Laeli, her voice high-pitched with excitement.

"Not special my ass. It's gotta be someone special if you consentin' to it."

"Heathel!"

"Is it Javeer?" For answer, Laeli frowned at her. Heathel cackled loudly and clapped her hands. "I figured it was. Haha! You goin out with him then, eh?"

"*Shhhh.* You're being too loud." Laeli glanced around anxiously.

"Loud? Pst girl, who's gonna care? You need to calm down. You're all pins and needles." Heathel slapped Laeli across the shoulder. "That's a fine boy, that is. Wild, but he's no scoundrel. Hehe, isn't this funny."

"I don't think so." Laeli was starting to feel annoyed.

"Eh, girl, relax. You'll be fine." Heathel gave her a friendly shove. Still chuckling, she tottered back to her seat behind the shop window.

Thoroughly embarrassed, Laeli concentrated on a tiny ant crawling past her shoe. She was staring at it with all her strength, trying to ignore the feeling of heat in her cheeks, when she heard the rumble of an approaching motorcycle. Tearing her eyes away from the ant, she watched as Javeer appeared, his motorcycle skidding to a stop. Even above the growl of the engine, she could still hear Heathel's witch-cackle from inside the shop. Laeli rose to her feet and immediately felt her heart flutter. Javeer looked even more imposing in his black leather suit. His shoulders appeared bulkier, and his tall frame swaggered forward confidently after he dismounted. In consternation, Laeli pressed her hand against her chest as if somehow that would slow her heart down.

Just breath. Just breathe. Why did I agree to this? What am I doing? I wish I were home. Why does that suit make him look so different? He's very tall. Taller than I remember. I wonder what Ren is doing. I hope Heathel stops laughing. Ugh, why am I so nervous? It's ok. Just breathe. Stay calm. Stay calm.

***

As Javeer rounded the corner and parked his motorcycle, he immediately caught sight of Laeli. She was sitting on the ground in front of Heathel's shop, watching something on the dirty road with great intensity. As she glanced up and rose to her feet, he could see the flush in her cheeks. Her brown eyes were especially large, and she kept diverting them in all different directions. She placed her hand across her heart briefly before moving it back to her side. Immediately, Javeer realized his own heart was beating fast. Jokingly, he mimicked Laeli by placing his hand over his chest. She noticed, and her eyebrows shot up, while the pink in her cheeks turned to a fiery red. Grinning, Javeer sauntered over and raised his eyebrows.

"Hey!" he exclaimed. To his embarrassment, his voice suddenly cracked, the word coming out one pitch higher in the middle. He could hear Heathel tittering from inside the shop. Pretending not to notice, he halted in front of Laeli. "How're you doing?"

"I'm not sure yet." Laeli rubbed her arm.

She's pretty nervous, Javeer thought. *I'M pretty nervous*. He could still hear Heathel's muffled snickers. He let out an annoyed grunt. "Heathel's being rather obnoxious, huh?"

"I suppose she is." Laeli gave a nervous giggle.

"Well, Heathel is just in bad need of some excitement. She's being dramatic."

"I heard that you scoundrel," Heathel's voice squawked from behind the window.

Shaking his head, Javeer motioned Laeli to follow him. "You ever ride before?"

"No, I haven't."

"My dad and I built this bike," Javeer said proudly. "It's one of my best friends. You ready?"

A sudden flashback of a little boy's voice echoed in Laeli's head. *"My daddy builds motorcycles, cars, bikes. Someday, I'll make those things too."*

"Yes, I am. Where do I sit?"

"Behind me." Javeer swung his leg over the bike and grinned at the startled look in Laeli's eyes. "Unless you want to drive."

"No." Blushing, Laeli stood frozen still.

With an amused sigh, Javeer swung out his arm to help her up. "Here." Laeli carefully took his arm and hoisted herself behind him. At that moment, Heathel emerged from the shop again.

"Boy, you better not take that girl on that thing without a helmet!"

"Don't worry Heathel, she'll be fine."

"Hah! Will she? I know you're a daredevil. You better not do anything crazy or..."

"Yes, Heathel, I know, I know. You'll come kill me for it."

Heathel's voice suddenly grew teasing again. "Where you plannin' to go?"

"The Drift."

"Hehe, well, have fun. Take good care of her, Javeer. If he doesn't, Laeli, you tell me!"

"I will."

"Good. Off with you then." With a final hoot and wave, Heathel retreated inside her shop.

"You ready?" Javeer asked Laeli.

"Yes."

"Are you sure? You're not holding on to anything."

"Oh." Laeli gingerly wrapped her arms around Javeer's torso.

"You're gonna have to hold on harder than that," Javeer joked. He felt Laeli's arms squeeze his waist and grinned to himself. Leaning forward, he tightened his grip on the handlebars. "Alright, let's go."

***

Javeer parked his motorcycle outside of The Iron Drift and waited as Laeli slid off the bike. The club was especially loud and crowded tonight; hordes of people were lingering outside the entrance and the sound of heavy bass vibrated through the ground. Laeli gave Javeer a puzzled look as he dismounted.

"Won't your bike get stolen?"

From his pocket, Javeer pulled out a small remote with a switch on it. "I installed a special device next to the engine. Should anyone try to steal it, I flip this and the engine is temporarily disabled. The motorcycle runs on an electrical battery and that's how I control it. I also added a tracker under the seat." Javeer then pulled a second object from another pocket and gestured to the bike's braking holes. "See right here? I have a disc brake lock that I put on through one of those tiny holes. If someone tries to remove the lock it'll set off an alarm."

"Where did you find a gadget like that?" Laeli pointed to the remote in his hand.

"I made it."

"Oh." Impressed, Laeli smiled. "You create things like that too?"

"Yeah! Do you?"

"Yes. I love creating technological devices."

"Ahh, I see. That's not surprising. After all, you do repair robots." Having secured the brake lock, Javeer stuffed the remote back in his pocket and walked inside the club. Laeli followed close behind. He placed a hand on her back as he guided her through the unmoving crowds of people, caught up in their own pleasure. He could feel Laeli's shoulders tighten, and her back grow stiff as she stepped into the main dance hall. The flashing purple lights contrasted sharply with the black walls and blue rays that shone from the ceiling bulbs. Everywhere there were people and serving robots who navigated their way through the crowd, handing out food and drinks. A stiff, blank expression washed over Laeli's face, and Javeer immediately began to second guess his decision to bring her here. Her entire body language screamed discomfort.

"Javeer!"

Partially startled, Javeer swung around as someone placed a hand on his shoulder. Then he relaxed and laughed. "Hey, Jace."

"Who's this?" Feigning surprise, Jace gestured to Laeli.

"Laeli, this is my friend, Jace." Javeer watched as Laeli cautiously shook Jace's hand. Her eyes looked him up and down and then focused sharply on his face. *She is studying him. Sizing him up.*

"Hello," she yelled, her voice barely audible above the din.

"Hey!" Almost uncomfortably, Jace pressed his hand to his side and covered up his discomfort with an aggressive smile. "You Javeer's girl then, huh?"

Laeli's eyebrows shot up and instantly Javeer panicked. Thoroughly annoyed at his friend's boldness, he reached out a hand to Laeli. "Let's dance shall we? I'll be back, Jace." Quickly,

Javeer led Laeli to the dance floor. He was afraid she might complain about Jace's manners, but she didn't. She only stood there rigidly.

"I...I'm sorry. I'm not used to this."

"WHAT?" Javeer leaned down close to her face.

"I'm not used to this!" Laeli repeated loudly.

"*Oh*. Uhh, I forgot to ask...do you want to dance?"

"I don't know how." The fib spilled out of Laeli's mouth without her thinking.

"I'm sorry. Maybe I shouldn't have brought you here." Inwardly beginning to panic, Javeer scanned his surroundings. His eyes met Jace's, and Jace took it as a sign to get up from his seat and walk over. Immediately, he began babbling to Laeli.

"So...what you think of my friend?" Jace slapped Javeer across the back.

"I'm not sure yet."

"Oh, uh, well, I think considerin' the kind of girl you are, you'll like him! I mean...if you agreed to come to a place like this then it means you already do."

Javeer was completely embarrassed at this point. He could see the shock on Laeli's face and inwardly cringed. He thought she would surely get mad, but instead she eyed Jace up and down again.

"How do you know Javeer?"

"Girl, I've known him for years. When we was little, we used to do everythin' together. I taught him the front and back of this city and all he needed to know about the people in it."

"But you don't do everything together now?"

Jace shifted his stance uncomfortably. "We do different things. Not much time to hang, you know what I'm sayin'?"

Laeli's eyes shifted to Jace's upper neck, behind his left ear. "You've got a cut."

Jace's face became a deep red. Javeer turned and looked to where Laeli was pointing. "Say, Jace, what happened to you?"

"It's nothin'! Anyways," Jace continued hurriedly, "that's how long I've known Javeer."

Laeli tilted her head and a mischievous curve appeared at the corner of her mouth. "I've known Javeer since I was six years old."

Jace's mouth dropped. "You lyin', girl." He turned to Javeer. "She lyin'!"

"No, she's not." Javeer grinned wickedly. He gave Laeli a quick wink as he teasingly pushed Jace sideways. An upbeat song with a deep bass and fast lyrics began to ripple across the club, and Javeer started to dance, his body swaying in rhythm with the beat. Jace followed suit, and soon multiple people caught notice and joined in, their cheers drowned out by the song. As he danced, Javeer noticed that Laeli's posture began to relax and the first genuine smile she had shown all evening lit up her face. Exuberantly, Javeer flung himself on his hands and did a walking handstand. As he leapt back to his feet, he saw that Laeli was laughing, her eyes alight with merriment. In a graceful fashion, completely unlike the wild swinging of the people around her, Laeli slid her way next to Javeer. Her dips and bows were poised and far more tasteful than what Javeer was used to seeing. It was a strange contrast against the music but somehow it worked, and he liked it. He swung her around, and she maintained hold of his hand while they spun back and forth. The club had become rowdy now and loud shouting and hoots began to fill the air. With a laughing gasp, Laeli nodded her head and taking the hint, Javeer guided her off the dance floor.

"Hey, girl." Jace rushed after them and skid to a halt beside Laeli. "You've got an interestin' way of movin'."

"Do I?" Laeli suddenly pressed her hand against her forehead. She laughed breathlessly. "I have a headache. It must be the noise."

"Do you want a drink?" Javeer bent over her anxiously.

"I'd like some water."

Ignoring the look of amusement on Jace's face, Javeer turned and strode towards the bar. "Hey, Trixie! I'd like a water."

"A *water?*" Trixie scrunched up her nose. "You can get that at home."

"It's not for me."

"Ohhhh, *right*, it's for that delicate schoolgirl you came in with. Where'd you find *her?*"

"By accident...at a robotics repair shop. Why do you sound so scornful, huh?"

"I don't know what you're talking about." Trixie rolled her eyes as she filled a cup with water. "Robotics shop? She's a mechanic? *Pft.*"

"You know, Trixie." Javeer leaned forward, grabbing the glass she slid towards him. "I think *you* need a drink."

"Huh?"

"So you can calm down a little. You seem a bit on edge."

"Don't poke fun at me," Trixie sniffed. "It's not like I ever thought there would be anything between us anyway. Just didn't expect you to like a girl like *that*."

"Like what?"

"*Hmph*...I don't know. She just doesn't fit. Doesn't seem like she'd be from a city like this."

"Even if that were true, why should it bother you? *I'm* not from here."

"Yeah, I know *you're* not."

"Well, what. Do you want me to like the kind of girl that you got in a fight with the other day?"

"I know you're not dumb enough to fall for those specimen of bitches!" Trixie suddenly laughed. "Even a shy awkward girl is better than them." Her voice lowered. "Have you heard?"

"Heard what?"

"There was a gang fight late last night, at the lower end of the city. Don't know who they were but two people were killed. No one knows what they were fighting over, but I say it's better they kill each other than civilians don't you? Not that the civilians in this place amount to much but ya know..." Trixie leaned forward on the bar, her hand pressed against her face, "we still all try to get somewhere, even in a trash-heap like this. That might just mean not getting mugged or killed but...well...you *know*..."

Trixie straightened, her voice half-serious, half sarcastic, "better than nothin'." She waved her hand. "Have fun with your little *date*."

***

Once Javeer had walked towards the bar, Laeli studied Jace again. His eyes, in spite of their lazy droop, were hyper aware - ever shifting and glancing in all directions, even between conversation. His movements were quick and jerky and a look of curiosity and vague suspicion constantly fluttered about his face. His long, lean body was restless and though his words were casual and callous, Laeli sensed in him a stubborn fierceness.

"What do you do?" she asked.

A startled expression briefly crossed Jace's face and just as quickly it was gone. "What you mean, girl?"

"Are you a mechanic too?"

"Hell, nah! I ain't no mechanic."

"Then what?" Laeli tilted her head. "Is whatever you do risky?"

Jace stiffened. "Why you ask?"

"Well it *seems* dangerous. After all, you have an injury, and you won't talk about your profession. My guess is that it's a secret – a dangerous secret."

"I see, I see," Jace muttered. "You wanna know everything about me, don't you? Should I tell you everything? I see no need to trust you! You surely got some secrets yourself. You gonna tell em to me?"

Laeli said nothing: only returned Jace's gaze unflinchingly.

"I thought not! We all got our secrets – let's not air them alright?" Jace's mouth curved ever so threateningly, then settled in a tight pinch.

Laeli only stared at him calmly. "Deal."

Jace suddenly relaxed. "Sorry. Just don't need you caught up in anythin'. I promised Javeer."

"Promised?"

"Yeah. *Promised*."

At that moment, Javeer returned to Laeli's side, handing her the glass of water. "Here."

"Thank you." Laeli took a sip and made a face. "Cuniculum's water tastes old."

Jace snickered. "Well, what other water is there?"

"Better water...in other places."

"You been to other places?"

Laeli paused, mid-sip. "We all have our secrets."

"What are you two talking about?" Javeer interjected. "What secrets?" He suddenly smiled. "I've got a secret myself." Javeer turned to Laeli, his face alight with pride and suspense. "Want to know what it is?"

"Sure, as long as it's a good secret."

"I think it is."

"Hey!" Jace complained. "You never told *me*."

"You'll survive." Slapping Jace across the back, Javeer nodded his head towards the door. "Let's get out of here shall we?"

As the three of them slid through the crowds of people, several girls smiled in Javeer's direction. "Hey, Javeer. Where you going?"

"Outside, ladies."

The girls' faces went from flirty to sour the instant they caught sight of Laeli. One of them sidled up to her, a scowl on her face. "Who are you?"

Laeli paused serenely, still holding her water. "I'm a mechanic."

The girl frowned. "You tryin' to be funny?"

"I am being completely serious."

"*Hmph.*" With a snort, the girl backed away, still giving Laeli the stink-eye. Jace slowed his pace and waited for Laeli to catch up to him. He leaned over close to her ear.

"You're not gonna be loved too much by these females. They all been wantin' Javeer for quite a while now."

"Do you mean they like him?"

"Like him? They're obsessed with him! Can you blame em? Look at the man."

Laeli glanced at Javeer's wide shoulders and tall frame as he walked ahead, and her face flushed slightly.

"Haha, you see what I mean! Ya know," Jace continued, "if I had his looks I'd be a dangerous man."

"What a pity."

"Pity what?"

"That you don't have his looks. I'm sure the whole world suffers for it."

"Hey! You pokin' fun?"

"Of course not." Laeli blinked innocently.

"And I thought you were the timid type." Jace rolled his eyes. "I been tricked. But no!" His voice lowered again. "Even Bria is after him. You know who Bria is?"

"No."

"Good. You don't want to."

"Who is she?"

"She's Khar's girl."

"Who's Khar?"

"Malin's son."

Laeli's eyes widened. "How does she know Javeer?"

"Guess she saw him once. That's all it took."

"What does Javeer think of her?"

"He hates her."

Laeli said nothing, only walking up the steps behind Javeer to his motorcycle. She stood ready to mount the bike when Javeer motioned to her.

"I need to talk to Jace for a moment. I'll be right back. Promise." With a reassuring wave, Javeer rushed over to Jace and led him to a dark corner of the street. "Come on, Jace. How'd you get the cut?"

Jace frowned. "It's nothing."

Javeer grabbed Jace's arm. "It's something, and you're gonna tell me! Trixie said there was a gang fight last night and two people got killed. Was it your men who died?"

Jace yanked his arm out of Javeer's grasp. "Not here!" he hissed. "Not now! You got your secrets. Lemme keep mine. Besides, you don't wanna be involved remember? And now you got the girl to think of."

Javeer's mouth set in a hard line. "Alright. I won't ask again. I just don't want to learn one morning that you're dead in a gutter, that's all. You're the leader. They're gonna try and take you out."

"*And?* You think I'm scared of that?" Jace glared at Javeer. "I need this. The city needs this. Don't interfere! Take care of Miss Mechanic and mind your own business. I wanted you in before but now I don't. You're not cut out for it."

Javeer's eyes hardened. "If you think I'm staying out cause I'm a coward, you're mistaken. I don't believe in your way. There're smarter methods to getting somewhere in Cuniculum than yours. What makes you think I'm going to fight and scrap in the streets and under tunnels when I can gamble freely above ground and...ah, what's the point. You can only see things your way."

"So what if I do? I ain't gamblin' any less than you are!"

"You're gambling with your *life*."

"And you think you're not?" Jace's voice tightened in a harsh whisper. "You think if you take your chances, if you gamble and *win*, Malin won't come for you? You're putting your life on the line as much as I am; you're just playing the long game. I ain't playin' any long game. I'm playin' *now*, and I aim to succeed." Jace bit his lip hard. "I'll stay away from you for a while. It'll keep your girl outta danger anyways. Go chase life the way you want! That's what I'm gonna do."

Javeer took a deep breath. "Alright. I'll let you be."

Jace shrugged and started to turn away, then paused with an exasperated groan. "Oh, Javeer. I don't expect it, but if you and the girl *should* get in any sort of scrap...tell me. I've a hunch Bria ain't gonna take too kindly to her."

"I'm staying far away from Bria," Javeer snapped.

"That's what you think! You're tryin' to get somewhere...remember?" With a final shrug, Jace turned and disappeared into the street.

With an angry grunt, Javeer walked back to his motorcycle. Laeli was watching him with inquisitive eyes.

"What's wrong?"

"It's nothing. Don't worry about it." Javeer's glower was replaced with his mischievous smile. "You want to see my secret?"

"Is it a big secret?"

"Pretty big. You've gotta swear silence." Javeer's eyebrows went up, and his voice lowered. "You'll be the first to learn of it."

"I will keep your secret. Show me. I want to see." Taking his held out hand, Laeli hoisted herself behind Javeer on the bike. Somehow, holding onto him no longer felt awkward. In fact, it was exhilarating. The bike's rumble as it maneuvered through the streets was strangely soothing and a cool night breeze whipped Laeli's hair. She smiled to herself, and her arms tightened around Javeer's waist. *He smells nice. I wonder what he'd do if I leaned my face against his jacket...but no, it's too soon for that. I shouldn't...*

After what felt like an incredibly short ride, Javeer halted in front of a large building with an iron gate covering the front door. In spite of the dark light, Laeli instantly realized they were at Javeer's motorcycle shop. Her curiosity piqued, she swung down from the bike without waiting for Javeer's help and watched as he dismounted and walked over to the iron gate. Taking a key from his pocket, he unlocked the gate and slid it aside to then unlock a second door. Beckoning to Laeli, he stepped inside, and bolted the doors behind her. Laeli wrinkled her nose at the heavy scent of oil and grease.

"Mimi," Javeer called softly. A little glow suddenly flashed from the corner of the room, and Mimi rolled forward, the light on her head illuminating the shop.

"Javeer!"

"Hey, Mimi."

"It is dark. I have my light! It is fixed!"

"Yes, haha, thanks to her." Javeer pointed to Laeli.

Mimi faced Laeli and blinked. "My light is fixed. Thank you."

Laeli laughed. "You're welcome! How are you doing, Mimi?"

"Very well. My light is fixed."

"She's got a one-track mind," Javeer joked. "Here, just follow me. Watch your step." He walked through the room, Mimi gliding in front of them. They reached the shop's back door, and Laeli stepped inside as Javeer held it open for her. Mimi halted as Javeer pulled a flashlight from a nearby shelf.

"Alright, Mimi, you're good."

"You don't want my light?"

"Nah, I'll use the flashlight. Besides, you can't go down stairs."

"I can shine the light from here."

"No, Mimi, it's alright," Javeer laughed. "You're good. Just stay here."

Mimi slid towards Laeli, her brown head tilted. "Do you want me to stay upstairs?"

Smiling, Laeli pat Mimi's head. "Yes, it'll be ok. Javeer doesn't want you to get hurt."

Mimi blinked, looked at Javeer, back at Laeli, and then at Javeer again. "Ok. I'll stay upstairs."

"That a girl." Giving Mimi a playful tap, Javeer unlocked the padlock across the door and beckoned to Laeli. The two of them walked down the spiral stairs to the bottom. Pitch black greeted them.

"It's so dark," Laeli exclaimed.

"Hang on." Using the flashlight, Javeer stepped forward and pulled the light chord hanging from the ceiling. Laeli winced at the sudden brightness, then glanced around as her eyes focused. Concrete walls, half of which were covered in shelves and tools, met her gaze.

"This is the basement of our house. My father built it. Our house is on an incline and unlike most homes in Cuniculum, our house is separated so my father was able to make the basement without much trouble."

Laeli caught sight of the boxing bag and the line of assorted weapons on the wall. Her eyes widened.

Javeer noticed Laeli's face. "My father was a security guard once. Those weapons are his."

"Oh yes, I remember you telling me that. Do you know how to use them? I thought you were only a boxer."

"My father taught me what he knows." Javeer stood beside Laeli and crossed his arms. "So yeah...I use them. For practice, anyways."

"Practice...for what?"

"In case, for some reason, I shall have a real need for them."

Laeli pursed her lips. "Why did you invite me down here? I'm assuming this is the secret that you mentioned. Won't your father be displeased?"

"He honestly might but don't worry about it. He's not home right now and this is my thing. I've got the right to show it to whoever I want."

Laeli gave a small smile. "I can hear it."

"Hear what?"

"Your Nobiles accent. Also, you phrase some sentences a certain way."

"Yeah, sometimes I slip back into it." Javeer laughed and scratched his head. "I guess I can blame Jace for my use of slang. However, my father's accent is still pretty strong."

"It's a noble sound."

"For sure! My father's voice is quite impressive when he talks." Javeer raised an eyebrow. "Your accent is just about as thick as his. You talk like him too…with your words. How have you not lost it after all these years?"

A rapid image of Ren appeared in Laeli's mind. "My mother spoke it," she answered quickly.

"But even so…well, you seem pretty smart. I guess you don't forget."

Laeli laughed. "No, I don't forget much. And I will keep your secret."

"Thank you, but the basement isn't what I was planning to show you." With a chuckle of anticipation, Javeer led Laeli to the tarp-covered object on the opposite side of the room. "This is!"

"What is it?"

"Imma show you. Here, let me get out an extra light. Too bad Mimi can't catapult herself down the steps. She'd be very helpful right now."

"Don't let her hear that. She might just try."

Javeer grinned. "She probably would, the little bugger. She's always trying to help." He grabbed another flashlight from one of the shelves. "*Whew*, it's hot down here. Are you sweating?"

"I…I don't think so."

"I am." Javeer slid his leather jacket off, leaving only the black tank top underneath on. He walked back to Laeli, his brown skin glistening against the glow of the flashlight, which he placed upright on the floor. Then he dragged the heavy tarp away, revealing a sleek motorcycle. Its black exterior, decorated with dark blue spirals, was smooth and shiny. Everything from the leather seat to the ridged handlebars screamed elegance. Laeli's eyes widened.

"Did you make this?"

"Yes! She is my baby. I've named her Black Swan."

"Black Swan?"

"Yeah. Growing up I was told a legend about a black swan. It was fast and smart and could fly long distances without tiring. The bird was thought by my family bloodline to be a symbol of good fortune and blessings. I thought it'd be a fitting name."

"It's gorgeous!" Laeli circled the bike, examining every section carefully. She straightened. "But why is it a secret?"

"It's an advanced turbo bike. I'm saving it for the upcoming race."

"You mean that gambling race? The motorbike race that Malin sponsors?"

"Yeah, that's the one. It's in a few weeks."

"How fast does the bike go?"

"It reaches up to about three hundred miles per hour."

"Three hundred! Have you tried going that fast?"

"Not yet. I haven't ridden it yet."

"Not ridden it?" Laeli placed a hand on her hip. "Why ever not? Won't you need to test it?"

"I can't until the day of the race."

"How come?"

Javeer's face grew serious. "I've been experimenting on motor bikes my whole life. The last time I was able to build a model similar to this one, I was fifteen years old. I took it out for a test ride. It needed a few adjustments so I went home, fixed what I had to, then took the bike back out for a second run. Someone must have seen me because that night, I was beaten by several men, left bleeding and unconscious on the ground, and my bike was stolen. That's when I developed the lock for my current bike, and I learned a very important lesson about Cuniculum. If you draw attention to yourself in any way, you'll be in danger. You'll be stolen from, injured, or killed." Javeer ran a hand along the bike's leather seat. "This bike is the key to my success. I won't let anyone steal it from me. No one can know about it."

"But if it shouldn't work?"

"That's a chance I'm gonna have to take."

"Why?" Laeli stepped closer to the bike across from Javeer. "What makes this bike so special? Why are you risking so much to enter that race?"

"I need money." Javeer's mouth set stubbornly. "Everyone gambles during the races. If I win, a huge chunk of that money goes to me."

"But what would you use it for?"

"I'll start a nightclub similar to the one my father used to work at. I'll invest my money. Meet people. Make more money. Learn...listen. Find out how Malin runs the gangs. Where he gets *his* money from."

Laeli's mouth dropped. "What will you do if you find out?"

"I'll decide that when it happens." With a shrug, Javeer leaned down, seized the tarp, and began to cover the motorcycle.

"But why?" Laeli circled round the motorcycle next to Javeer. "Why do all of that? What's the point?"

Javeer faced Laeli, clutching the tarp. "I hate this city!" he exclaimed sharply. "I hate the lack of order, and I hate its squalor and misery. I hate the corruption. And Malin encourages it! If Malin's power were weakened; if Malin had any sort of competition, then perhaps it would be just enough to change the stinking flow that this dump runs on."

"If you gain any power, Malin will go after you." Laeli shook her head anxiously. "He'll kill you or find someone else who will. What makes you think you'll survive to..."

"I'll manage." Javeer's voice calmed, and he covered the rest of the bike with the tarp. "I can be very charming when I want to. I have my ways. I will get what I want." His eyes narrowed and fierce determination settled in them.

"What made you decide to tell me all this?" Laeli asked curiously. "You hardly know me. You don't know me at all."

"Whatever are you talking about?" Mischief danced across Javeer's face. "I've known you since you were six years old."

Laeli turned pink then laughed. "I was only joking when I said that. But really, you don't actually know me. Why tell me so many deep things?"

"I don't know." Javeer glanced at his shoes then back up at Laeli. "In fact, that's a lie. I do know. When I met you at eight years old I had a funny feeling that I'd never gotten before. I liked you and couldn't explain why. When I saw you again for the first time years later, that feeling only got stronger. I somehow felt like a shadow that had been following me ever since I left Nobiles was suddenly filled. Oh, I don't know how to explain it! It doesn't make sense...not even to me. But it is what it is. I trust you, and I like you."

Laeli stood speechless, unsure of how to respond. The customary red flush was burning in her cheeks like a tiny hot fire. "I...I don't know what to say." She placed her hands behind her back and stared at the floor before peaking up timidly. "But I kind of like you too. So far."

Javeer threw back his head and laughed. "So far? Are you planning to not like me at some point?"

Laeli blushed even harder. "I don't know...it's too soon to say! People are strange. They can change a lot." Her mind flew back to Kye and an uneasy sensation fluttered in her stomach.

Javeer sobered. "That's true." He stepped closer to Laeli. "I'll try my best not to change too much."

"Yes, I suppose some change is inevitable."

"Life will always change you. It's just up to you to decide how. My father always told me that." Javeer raised his eyebrows.

"Let's go back upstairs. He'll be very angry if he sees you down here."

"Where is he now?"

"He went out to make a business deal. There was some bidding war on a bike he put up for sale. I imagine it went on longer than expected. I don't think he's back yet." Snatching the spare flashlight from the floor, Javeer grabbed his leather jacket and shone the light for Laeli up the steps. She waited for him at the top of the staircase while he turned off the ceiling light and followed suit, locking the basement door behind him.

"*Hello.*" Mimi's voice from the hallway broke the silence, startling them both.

"Agh, Mimi!" Javeer scolded. "Were you waiting there the whole time?"

"Yes."

"*Eesh*, what's wrong with you? You needn't have stayed."

"Why not?"

"Well, I guess it doesn't matter. You just scared us." Javeer ran a hand over his face and chuckled. "Gosh, dang it, Mimi! Where are you? I can barely see you."

"Right here. You need my light." With a tone of satisfied simplicity, Mimi's forehead light activated, blinding Laeli in the face.

"*Mimi.*" Laeli laughed, shielding her eyes.

"Can you see?" Mimi asked worriedly.

"Well she can't see if your light is in her face." Placing both hands on either side of Mimi's square torso, Javeer wheeled her away from Laeli's direction. "There! Shine your light right here."

"Here?"

"Yes, right there. Perfect! That a girl." Javeer straightened and grinned at Laeli. "Now you see why I am always tripping over her."

"I do. You you must walk more slowly from now on."

"I forget she's there. She's always underfoot." Javeer grimaced.

"Poor Mimi." Laeli sympathetically clicked her tongue. She glanced up at Javeer and saw he was watching her with an affectionate expression. Taken aback, she immediately felt her face warm and subconsciously began to admire him as well. A gentle smile played about his mouth, and his green eyes seemed to glow in the reflection of Mimi's light. A strand of his hair fell over his forehead, and Laeli felt a fluttery feeling suddenly whirl inside her stomach.

The two of them stood gazing at one another as if in a trance when a deep voice rang through the hallway. "Javeer! What is this? Who is with you?"

"Father!" Javeer snapped to attention, and Laeli stiffened, her body straight and alert. "This is Laeli. She's the girl from Heathel's shop who fixed Mimi."

Lyon stepped into the light's glare, his eyes holding both suspicion and welcome. "Greetings, Laeli. How long have you been working for Heathel?"

"A year, sir."

"How long have you known Javeer?"

Laeli's gaze met Lyon's. Though she did not break eye contact, her voice came out low and small. "A little over two weeks."

Lyon's eyebrows raised ever so slightly. He glanced at Javeer, then back again at Laeli. His features softened, and he held out his hand. "It is my pleasure to meet you."

Laeli slowly returned the handshake. "And meeting you is mine."

"A very formal response. One that is not used often in Cuniculum. Are you from here?"

"My mother was from Nobiles."

"Ah, I see." A strange look crossed Lyon's face then vanished. "Very well, then." He turned to Javeer. "It is quite late, son. Bring her home safely."

"Of course, Father." Javeer gently moved Mimi aside, and Laeli followed as he walked down the hallway to the shop.

Lyon watched as they stepped through the shop door. "Goodbye, Laeli."

"Goodbye, sir."

"Be careful, son." A secret look quickly passed between them before Javeer shut the door. Laeli waited as Javeer turned on his flashlight. She made for the shop's exit, then halted as Javeer veered sideways and walked over to the wall. From a hook, he grabbed a large taser, much bigger than the one she carried, and slung it to the belt on his side. Laeli realized she had forgotten hers at home...again. She followed him outside to the motorbike, and they were quiet on the ride to her house, except for the moments when Laeli had to direct Javeer where to turn.

Once they reached Laeli's home, Javeer turned off his bike as Laeli slid from the seat. "Laeli, I...uh...I hope you're not bothered."

"No. Why should I be bothered?"

Javeer grimaced. "I feel that was kind of an awkward way to meet my father."

"It didn't bother me." Laeli spoke reassuringly. "I had fun...thank you."

"Would you...uh...I mean...would you like to hang out again sometime? I'm afraid I work all day, but I have some free time at night...if you want to of course."

"I would not mind. Yes, I will do that. Tomorrow?"

"Sure!" A relieved grin lit up Javeer's face, and he laughed. "I'll pick you up from work?"

"Of course, but Heathel will tease you."

"Whatever, I can just ride away."

"That's true. Good night, Javeer."

"Bye. Oh...wait, Laeli." Javeer walked up to her before she could turn away. His face grew serious. "Are you sure you're safe living here? Does anyone else know you're alone?"

Laeli nodded solemnly. "Don't worry. Nobody knows but you."

"Alrighty, then." Javeer gave a big sigh. "Make sure you lock your door."

"You do know I've been here for thirteen years and everything's been fine." Amusement lined Laeli's voice.

"Ah, well." Javeer shrugged. "Anything could happen. You just never know. Night, Laeli."

"Good night." Laeli gave him a wave and walked back into the house. After securing the lock behind her, she made her way into the dark kitchen. She drank her customary glass of water and then filled it a second time. As she went to set the glass down so she could peak inside the fridge, some of the water sloshed out and spilled over Kye's painting that she had left on the table earlier. With a stifled gasp, Laeli quickly slid the glass away and flipped the painting over. The water had not penetrated the back but some had spilled on the table, soaked underneath, and wet the front. Laeli decided she'd check the damages in the morning. She didn't want to draw attention to her house by putting on a light this late at night. She would go into the locked room and enjoy her LED lights there. With a tired yawn, she slipped off her shoes and pulled her shirt out from her pants. Then she entered the locked room to see Ren standing there judgingly, his hand holding her taser. He blinked slowly and frowned.

"You forgot this." He held the taser out to Laeli.

"I'm sorry. I got distracted."

Ren shook his head. "It is the one thing you can never remember."

"It's alright though. I was safe! Javeer had a taser."

"Nothing is safe." Ren shrugged and placed the taser on the desk. "All of life is a danger."

"No," Laeli murmured. "Here, I am safe with you and with Javeer, I felt quite safe. He's not dangerous. I feel that I know that...though I don't know how."

Ren's red-brown eyes gazed into Laeli's. "Your pupils are large. You like him very much."

"Why I... I barely know him!" Laeli protested.

"Still..." Ren stepped back and cocked his head. His voice warmed. "You like him very much."

"Ren..."

"Yes?"

"Do you ever get bored sitting in here?"

"Not bored but lonely. I miss you."

"Thing is..." Laeli fiddled with her fingers and stared at the floor. "I will probably be out a lot more now. Will you mind?" She looked up anxiously.

"No," Ren spoke solemnly. "I will miss you, but I do not mind. I can wait until you get back. I did say you must make friends."

"It's only *a* friend."

Ren sat back down in his chair and a flick of mischief appeared on his face. "A friend you will fall in love with."

"Ugh, why are you always being such a romantic?" Laeli swat at him and rolled her eyes. "Dancing, music, poetry, romance...what was Mommy thinking when she programmed you? You're the strangest creature to ever exist!"

"A robot is but a reflection of its designer. If a robot displays certain characteristics it is because..."

"Because he cannot help but follow the protocol that was imbedded in his system. He is a creature of obedience, subject to the rules under which he was created...yes, yes! You say it a thousand times but even so... you're different. Mommy created you in an almost perfect imitation of a human. You make your own choices and think for yourself. It's not the same."

"But in spite of all of that, my protocol still influences all my decisions, and you already know that is impossible to disobey. And you know what the protocol is." Ren gazed at Laeli fondly.

Laeli sighed and smiled. "Yes. Yes, I do."

Chapter 6
Villian Schemes

C uniculum was built over a massive hill that sloped down at one end and snaked upwards on the other in a twisted fashion. The lower ends of the city were narrow and filthy, but as one worked their way up the roads became wider and slightly more clean. At the top of the city, resting on an overhanging stone wall, sat Malin's mansion. One street below his house was the Casino, an impressive two-story building made of black stone, brick, and marble. The first floor was filled with gamblers, some dressed in sleek apparel and decorated with shiny accessories: others, more grungy and rough-looking, but all of them willing to risk their money in hopes of earning more. They sat over round, dark mahogany slabs and iron-rimmed poker tables, their laughter and fighting rising loud above the music that played through the ceiling speakers. Dark blue lights glowed from the walls and tiny white lights rested inside small ceiling domes. A bar ran through the center of the room, surrounded with black chairs that were square and tall.

The second floor was much like the first, but slightly more luxurious. Instead of being centered in the middle of the room, a bar was tucked against the far left-side, and its counter tops were made of quartz-covered mahogany. From the ceiling hung stylishly fashioned chandeliers of thin black. Magnificent circular booths of polished wood and pine-green cushions were carved into the walls, providing a sense of privacy against passing eyes.

In one of the booths near the end of the bar sat a man alone, leaning forward and alert as if waiting for someone. The years had increased the lines around his bronzed mouth and forehead, and his silver hair was slicked back against his neck, but there was not a hint of age to his sharply inclined eyes. His movements were subtle yet quick and an expression of sardonic judgement rested on his face. He wore well his grey vest trimmed with olive green and fur that adorned his shoulders and torso. His ring-covered fingers impatiently tapped the table in front of him as he waited.

A waitress walked up and spoke in a low voice. "He's here, sir."

The man nodded and waved the girl away. She obediently scuttled off and the man straightened, but did not rise, as his guest approached and spoke.

"Greetings, Malin."

Malin's eyes swept up and down over the individual in front of him: an exceptionally tall figure, wearing a fitted black coat, pants, boots, and a deep blue scarf. His gaze met the icy blue eyes of his guest. Without waiting for further invitation, the guest sat opposite him.

"So," Malin leaned back carelessly in his seat. "What was your name again?"

With a pinched smile, the guest's piercing eyes rose and met Malin's. "Kye."

"Ah, *yes*. You can be sure that next time I won't forget!" Malin took a small gold box from his pocket and removed a cigarette from it. Taking a match, he lit the cigarette and exhaled, thin wisps of smoke curling upwards and melting into the glow of the light fixture above. Then he leaned forward and waved the box towards Kye.

"Thank you. I do not smoke."

"Very well." Returning the box to his pocket, Malin leaned back and inclined his head. "How do you like your house?"

"It is very satisfactory. I have made the changes I want and appreciate the privacy."

"Changes? What changes?"

A tiny curve tightened at the end of Kye's mouth. "Merely some decorative ones."

"I see. You know...that house is at a prime location. I would not have sold it to just anyone, but then again, you and I have a deal together, so I made an exception. Besides, it was a tremendous place to upkeep. I already have my own mansion: a second is, well...*such* a burden." Malin took another puff from his cigarette. "You come from Votum, right?"

"That is correct."

Malin chuckled low in his throat. "What's it like there, eh?"

"Strange."

"That the only word you have to describe it?"

"For the present." Kye stared unflinchingly, his voice monotone.

"I see. You're a cautious man. I can respect that." Malin lowered his cigarette and laughed softly. "I'm cautious, but I'm also a gambling man. I take risks where I think best." He lowered his voice. "The special models you promised; how soon can you get them to me?"

"Consider them yours within the next three weeks. They shall be here...ready and in perfect condition."

"Excellent." Malin pursed his lips in satisfaction. "I'll see that the right people come to you so that they will be delivered to me properly." As he was speaking, Malin waved the waitress back over. "Where's Khar? I ordered him to meet me here."

"He said he'd arrive in a moment."

Malin frowned. "Tell him to come now!" The waitress nodded, and Malin eyed her swinging figure as she walked away. "You know what the secret to a successful place such as this is my friend?" He turned his gaze back to Kye.

Kye shook his head. "Please... illuminate me."

"Beautiful women." Malin chuckled and exhaled, another stream of smoke snaking from his mouth. "Oh, of course, money is another enticement. The possibility of becoming rich always draws men in. Stimulating music, good food, quality alcohol: all of these things are crucial to tempting man and his senses. But women..." Malin smirked to himself. "Women are the key. They're both the pawns and the players of all things in this world. What are your thoughts on that?"

"I have none. I do not care for women."

Malin's eyebrows raised. "Then what entices you my friend, if not women?"

Kye's mouth turned slightly in a strange manner. "Personal ambition."

"Haha. So money?"

"No."

"Not money...not women. What then? Where does your ambition lie?"

Kye's voice shifted from monotone to intense. "In freedom."

"*Ah*. A difficult thing to attain in this life. But I will not begrudge you your longing for freedom, so long as it does not interfere with *mine*. You..."

The sudden motion of an approaching figure cut Malin short. A third man had arrived at the table. He had Malin's slanted eyes, but they were less devious and more malicious. His black hair was pulled back in a short ponytail, and his sharp mouth was etched in a demeaning line across his face. Strands of hair fell against his clear-cut jawline and down the left side of his neck below his ear was a line of inverted letters. He wore a dark red shirt, a color that contrasted strongly with his tan skin, and there were piercings in his ears and nose. Viper tattoos completely covered his left arm and on his belt was a long knife in a black leather sheath. He darted a suspicious glance at Kye, then slid into the seat next to Malin.

"Who's this?" he questioned, glaring at Kye.

"My new business partner."

With a scornful grunt, the young man took a cigarette from his pocket and lit the end. After the first smoke, he leaned forward on his elbow, his dark eyes glittering. "So you're the guy my father has been telling me about. You gotta have high connections if you've managed to sneak out of Nobiles...*what was it called?"* The young man leaned back and laughed. "Oh, yeah, *advanced technology*." He inclined forward again, his face threatening. "You better bring my father what you promised, or I'll find a way to make you regret comin' to Cuniculum! Just remember, I know where you live and how to get there."

Kye unshrinkingly returned the young man's gaze with a smile of vague amusement. "You are Khar."

Khar titled his head, his eyes narrowing. *"And?"*

"It is a pleasure to meet you."

A derisive snort sounded deep in Khar's throat. Malin chuckled. "He brought his city manners with him! I have respect for such refinement in speech. It's refreshing."

"I ain't got time for it." Khar shifted in his seat and smirked. "You don't need me here. Imma go now." He gracefully rose to his feet, and Kye also stood to say goodbye. The two men were similar in height and stood unmoving, sizing the other up. Kye bowed his head politely, and Khar took a deep breath. Then with a scowl, he sauntered away.

"You must excuse my son. He does not share the same love for etiquette that I do." Malin's voice was cynical. "His mother was never around to show him any, good riddance to her. Unlike him...I had my mother and learned there is a benefit to being polite...on the outside anyway. My mother was a devious woman. She got what she wanted in life and so will I."

At the word 'mother', Kye stiffened and a slight look of horror appeared in his eyes. His gaze froze ahead as if seeing a ghost, and his pale skin grew white.

"You look ill, my friend." Malin reached for a whiskey bottle seated next to him on the table. "Have a drink!"

Kye's eyes unfroze, and he spoke slowly. "No, thank you. I do not drink."

"You don't like women, you don't drink. If it weren't for the fact that you're sitting here with me, I would say you are a paragon of virtue. Extraordinarily glad you're not." Malin poured himself a shot and raised the glass to his lips. "I *despise* men of virtue. They are a walking plague to their own success... and mine."

Kye displayed a tense smile. "I share no love for virtue or vice. All is just a means to an end: neither matters."

"I see what you mean." Malin's eyes narrowed though his smirk remained. "I have a particular fondness for vice. I suppose it suits me well. Tell me. What code *do* you live by, if not virtue or vice?"

"I live for myself. There is no code." With a shrug, Kye rose to his feet and bowed. "It was a pleasure seeing you again. Goodbye."

"Goodbye." Malin watched Kye walk away, then with a grunt, placed his cigarette on the little plate beside him and left the table.

***

Bria leaned over the bar, a pout on her lips. Her countenance was one of scornful boredom as she observed the throng of people who were playing poker and drinking. The familiar sight felt especially tedious to watch today. She frowned in irritation as a young man, teetering from excess alcohol, separated himself from the crowd and approached her. She could see his blood-shot eyes shining with admiration and excitement.

"Why...hello! Can...can...can I get you a drink?" The man swayed sideways, one hand waving in the air. "*Whew.* Come on, little girl. Let me buy you one!"

"Buy me a drink?" Bria pressed her chin on top of her hand, a smug expression on her face. "Now why would you do that?"

"Cause you're pretty...*dang* pretty. Why..." the man hiccupped then continued, "why else?"

Bria raised an eyebrow. "You think that's wise? Don't you know who I am?"

"*Nope.* I'm about to find out though, baby."

Bria's glance shifted to over the man's shoulder and a look of sardonic amusement appeared in her eyes. "Yes...yes you are."

A violent hand fell upon the drunk man's shoulder and whirled him around. Khar had appeared silently from behind, his eyes alight with anger. With one swing, he struck the man in the face, knocking him to the ground. Hushed silence fell over the casino. Behind the bar, the bartender went on wiping dishes with an air of uninterested complacency. Khar leaned over and yanked the man to his feet. With a forceful shove, he slammed the young guy into the bar counter. The man let out a howl of pain. Blood dripped from his swollen nose and down his neck.

Khar shoved his face towards the young man's. "Don't ever go near my girl again, or you'll pay for it!" he hissed. He released his grasp, and the young man crumpled to the floor. With a sigh, Bria slid from her seat and walked out the casino's back door, letting it slam behind her. Khar quickly followed and found her lighting a cigarette. Bria gave him an unimpressed look. She brought the cigarette to her mouth and gave him a sulky face.

"Was that really necessary?"

"Was *what* necessary?"

Bria glared at him. "Your theatrics!"

"*Theatrics?*" Khar stepped closer. "Listen here. You know what I am and how I am. *No one* gets to look at you. Nobody but me!"

"You think that man could have taken me from you?"

"Course' not." Khar's mouth twisted into a spiteful grin. "It don't matter though. Nobody goes near my woman...cause you're *mine.*"

"Am I?" Bria studied her cigarette before taking another puff. "How many people do you gotta prove it to...or do you not trust me?"

With an angry swipe, Khar swat the cigarette from Bria's hand. Just as quickly, Bria stepped close to him, wrapping her arms around his neck.

"*Baby*," she murmured. "You don't gotta worry about me. I know I'm yours." She leaned forward and kissed him on the neck. "It's just it looks bad...you fighting anyone who glances at me. Looks as if you can't trust me to be your woman. Don't you trust me, baby?"

"I don't know," Khar muttered. "I don't think so. I know *better*...."

"*Mhm*." Bria buried her face in Khar's shoulder, then flung her head backwards, widening her alluring eyes. "Want to know what *I know?*" She traced her figure down the tattoo on his neck. "I think you worry too much. You ain't got nothin' to worry about, baby. *Nothin*..." She kissed him again, and Khar aggressively returned the kiss.

Bang. The back door swung open, and Malin stepped through. Khar turned to face him with Bria's arms still around his neck. Bria's cat-eyes watched Malin with narrowed focus as he walked up to her.

"Anyone ever tell you that you have a sphynx-look to you, girl?" Malin began sharply. "Remove that cool expression from your face! I'm not your average fool...you can't intimidate me."

Bria relaxed and detached her arms from Khar. Her voice rolled out smoothly. "Me...*intimidate?* Why sir, I don't know what you're talking about. How could I intimidate anyone?"

"I wouldn't know." Malin gave Khar a discreet look and nodded his head.

"Go on, Bria," Khar ordered. "I'll find you later." He shot her a warning glance. "Remember what I said."

"I know you won't forget what *I said*." With a sensual smirk, Bria tossed her head and disappeared into the casino. Malin's eyes followed her.

"Most beautiful girl in the city. Hang on to her...don't ever let anyone else take her from you."

"Who else could?"

"None...but there are many who *would*...if the opportunity arose. You know that."

Khar stared ahead of him into space, his eyes aggravated. "I don't trust her."

"Good...don't ever." Malin chuckled. "I kept a tight hold over your mother. No one dared go near her, and she grew to hate me for it. She killed herself because of me...but better to let a woman die than step outside of your control. Imagine the shame I would have felt had she gotten her way! Of course...I suppose she saw defiant suicide as a victory, but I could care less. A man never limits himself to one female. I had many to replace her with."

"I'll have no one replace Bria."

"Then you're a fool! All women are replaceable. If you think that way, then it'll be her who has all the power over you. Promise me...never limit yourself."

Khar snorted under his breath. "What *did* mother think of me? I don't remember her well - can barely even see her face anymore."

"That bitch had as little love for you as she did for me. Be glad you're rid of a woman who hated her son because she hated the father. Oh...also, what I was going to tell you when I came out here; you understood your assignment?"

"I got it." Khar eyed his father. "You think *he* got the message?"

"I'm sure he understood. My new business partner does not seem to be unintelligent."

Khar scowled. "You oughta stay away from him! He gives me the creeps."

"Suspect everyone, my boy, but don't let it paralyze you from taking risks. You know how valuable the product is that he's giving me?"

"And what are *you* givin' him in return, huh? What's he asking for?"

"I gave him that house...at a very low price."

"Don't it seem kinda odd?" Khar began to pace back and forth. "Why would that man want a *house?* A house *here* of all places? And what would you even give him that place for? It was in a prime location!"

"I'm not sure why he wanted it, but I have my ways of getting it back...when the time comes."

"That might be a little hard if this man has access to the same products you plan on buying. He could easily use them against you."

"I'll find a way to make it work." Malin shot Khar a side glance. "You think I'm being a fool, eh?"

"Never said that." Khar shrugged as he began to walk away. "Just sayin'...I don't trust him."

Chapter 7
Moonlight Moment

Day after day, Javeer came after work to pick up Laeli. Laeli was not fond of the club, so they would often hang out at Heathel's shop, or he would take her for rides through the street on his motorcycle. Soon, Laeli spent less and less time in her house, and Ren was left alone, waiting patiently until she would return home and finally have a chance to talk to him.

After three weeks of this regular routine, Laeli was sitting on a stool at work, repairing a robot for Heathel, when the old lady appeared in the back of the shop, a surprised expression on her face.

"You didn't tell me, girl, that you've been picking up male friends lately."

"Huh? What do you mean?"

"There's a young man here who says he knows you." Stepping aside, Heathel made way for a tall figure whose black outline blended in against the shadowy background. As he stepped into the light, Laeli froze. Her eyes widened.

"Kye, what are you doing here?"

"I came to see you."

Startled beyond words, Laeli sat there and said nothing. With a shrug and a wink, Heathel turned around and walked away. Finally finding her tongue, Laeli spoke. "How did you figure out where I work?"

"I was walking down this way and overheard the old lady mention your name."

"Why were you down this way though?"

Kye smiled. "Am I not allowed to walk where I want? I have been getting to know every corner of this city."

Laeli stiffened, and her eyes dropped to the frozen-still robot in front of her. "Well," she murmured. "You've found me. Was there something you wanted to say?"

Kye knelt down beside her. "I just wanted to see you. Have I hurt your feelings in any way? Are you angry with me? You never said anything after we last saw each other."

Laeli picked up one of the tools lying beside her. "I've been busy...with work."

"What about your day off. Is it not tomorrow?"

"I had other plans for tomorrow. I'm sorry."

"I thought you would say that. That is why I came here." Kye's gaze wandered to the robot in front of Laeli, and he stared at it strangely. "Where did you learn to do this?"

"Do what?"

"This kind of work. Who taught you?"

"My mother." Laeli side-eyed Kye. "What about you? Your mother was a doctor. Why didn't you become one? You often talked about it."

With one abrupt movement, Kye sprang to his feet and turned his back on Laeli. For a moment he was silent, saying nothing. Then he began to wander around the room, observing the shelves and picking up random tools, turning them about in his hands.

"To be a doctor is to play the part of a god."

"What do you mean?"

Kye turned to Laeli, a look of mixed amusement and scorn on his face. "Why should you save a life if it is doomed to die a natural death? You only expose them to more years of pain and suffering."

"But what if they don't see life as just pain and suffering? What about the people that love them? That want them to stay in their life? What if that person *wants* to continue living?"

Kye silently put down the tool he was holding. "They are a fool then."

"You make no sense." Harshness crept into Laeli's voice. "*You* were the one who wanted to keep on living. You talked about it all the time!"

A pained expression came over Kye's face. His mouth opened but no words came out and for a second, it seemed as if he were about to plead for help. Then his mouth shut tightly, and his eyes went blank. With a stiff motion, he turned his head away, his body still in the same position.

"I do not know what you are talking about."

Laeli gripped the tool in her hand so hard her knuckles went white. "I think you should..." Before she could finish the sentence, Heathel walked into the room, a customer behind her.

"Laeli-girl! This man has a 3-11 model with a broken arm. Can you fix it as soon as you're done with the one in front of you?"

Laeli nodded, still clutching the tool in her hand. She watched as Kye walked over to Heathel, his persona suddenly warm and respectful.

"I think I shall leave now. I do not want to distract Laeli from her work any longer. I hope, ma'am, that you have a wonderful day."

"Why, sure and thanks!" Astonished, Heathel turned to watch as Kye exited the shop. "Don't he have the manners. How'd you meet him, girl?"

"I knew him as a kid," Laeli muttered.

Heathel gave a low grunt. "I see. I ain't gonna lie; somethin' about him makes me feel strange. Maybe it's just the lack of hair. I think that must be what it is. He pretty though! A little too pretty for Cuniculum.

"Heathel," Laeli spoke as soon as the customer left. "Don't let Kye come back here."

"What, girl, so you don't like him?"

"I don't want people visiting me when I'm working."

"You got no problem with Javeer visiting," Heathel teased. "He coming again tonight to get you, right?"

Laeli rolled her eyes. "Yes, he is."

"Thought so. Alrighty, girl! I'll let you get back to work, and I won't let that Mister Whatever-His-Name-Was back in."

***

Later that evening, after he had picked Laeli up, Javeer brought her back to his house instead of going out on their usual motorcycle ride. Lyon was closing up the shop when they arrived.

"Hello, Laeli. You hanging out here tonight, son?"

"Yes, Father." Javeer replied as he helped Laeli from the motorcycle.

"Very well, then. Be on the look-out for thieves. There's been an increase of theft in this area. It is probably best that you're staying home."

Laeli shot Javeer a questioning look. "What about the registration form you were going to fill out tomorrow?"

"We can still go," he reassured her.

In a small voice, Laeli asked, "What was stolen?"

Lyon shrugged. "That I did not learn."

With a discreet nod of his head, Javeer urged Laeli to follow him. Silently, they left Lyon in the shop and slipped into the house. Motioning Laeli to wait, Javeer disappeared down the hallway and then returned, holding an oblong object in his hand. With a length slightly longer than a ruler, its pole-like shape had a clasp on one end that was meant as a belt attachment, while the other end was of a thicker size and covered with tiny ridges.

Laeli's mouth dropped. "A robot taser. You have one of these? How?"

"My father smuggled it out of Nobiles with him."

"This is a good one. High quality." Laeli gently took the taser from Javeer's hands and examined it. "It's heavy. *Very* heavy."

"Yes, they're always heavy."

With a funny look, Laeli returned the taser to him. "Not always. My mom and I figured out a way to make them more effectively without being heavy, so a woman could use them easily."

"Wait! You mean you know how to *make* these things?"

"Yes...my mother taught me."

"Damn, girl, don't tell anyone that! You'll have half of Cuniculum breathing down your back wanting one."

"I won't tell."

"Good. I'll bring this with me tomorrow...just in case." Placing it on a nearby table, Javeer reached over towards a shelf and from it grabbed two earbuds and a small radio. "Come with me!" Laeli followed as Javeer walked through the hallway to a door at the back of the house. The door opened to a tiny back patio and an iron staircase that scaled the side of the house's exterior, all the way up to the roof.

"Can you do heights?" Javeer asked.

"Yes, I'm not scared of them."

"Ok, good. I'll help you." Javeer swung Laeli up on the metal rungs and then climbed up after her. With steady swiftness, Laeli reached the top of the ladder and saw a section of the roof had a flat overhang. Javeer brushed past her to sit on it, his legs dangling over the edge. He plugged the earbud's chord into the little radio, then waved Laeli over.

"Hey, Laeli, you can sit here." He patted the area beside him.

Laeli walked over and settled next to Javeer, imitating him by letting her legs hang over the roof's rim. "What's up here?"

"Something I planned on showing you two weeks ago." His eyes alight with suspense, Javeer began fiddling with the setting on the radio. "A full moon is out tonight, and you've gotta see it!"

Laeli raised her eyes to the sky. It was speckled with stars and the clouds almost appeared transparent against the reflection of the moonlight. "But you can't see the moon right now. It's behind the clouds."

"Yeah, but it won't be for long. The clouds move fast. We'll wait for it." Javeer placed one of the earbuds in his ear and handed the other to her. "Wanna listen? It's one of my favorite songs."

"Sure." Laeli placed the bud to her ear and was met with the sound of a soothing lo-fi melody accompanied with a gentle drum beat. A slow smile spread across her face. "I like it."

"Do you? I used to do this in Nobiles. We had a big patio, and you could always see the moon so perfectly from there." Javeer's voice grew quiet. "My mother used to come out and watch with me."

Laeli glanced at him and saw Javeer's face was suddenly pierced by nostalgia and sadness. A little ache rose in her heart as she thought of the pain and love he must be feeling at the memory. Carefully, she scooted closer, her arm touching his.

***

Javeer's heart skipped as he felt Laeli's arm rest against his own. He glanced fondly at her, but she didn't notice. Her eyes were fixed on the sky above them and a small smile played about her mouth as she listened to the music. The song was reaching the part right before the climax – a tune that burst open like a breath of wind, carried by the invigorating beat in the background. Laeli's face suddenly transformed from calm to excited, and she pointed upwards.

"Look at the clouds!"

Javeer raised his eyes, and even his mouth dropped in awe. In perfect timing with the music, the clouds before them parted, revealing the moon, strong and splendid. Its brilliant glow illuminated the sky, sending streaks of blue and white against the ink-tinted indigo. A little gasp of pleasure escaped Laeli's lips.

"So beautiful," she breathed. With a happy sigh, she looked up towards Javeer, her eyes shining. Then she snuggled further against his arm and leaned her head on his shoulder. A deep warmth spread all over Javeer's body. Gently adjusting his arm, he placed it around Laeli's small form and hugged her close. For a long while, they both sat in silence. Then Javeer lowered his earbud and spoke quietly.

"What was it like for you...living in Nobiles. Do you miss it?"

Laeli lowered her earbud as well. "I miss how it felt living there. It was so quiet and peaceful and the city was so clean. It was the last bit of peace I ever had with my mother."

"Why'd you leave?"

Laeli sighed deeply. "I don't know. One day she came home, absolutely terrified. She packed up everything we had and traveled here. She had to pay someone to smuggle her out with a car; I don't know how she knew them exactly. She never told me what she was running from."

Javeer nodded. "I also loved Nobiles. I hate Cuniculum, but I'm the kind of person that's determined to conquer what I hate. It's a thing I feel deep inside." Now Javeer spoke passionately. "I *must* make myself love what I hate, and I will do whatever is necessary to get to that point. I like the challenge. I want to see if I can change it into something to be proud of."

"But...what if it was someone or something so *awful* that there was no chance of changing it? Then what would you do?"

"If it cannot be changed, it must be conquered."

"Conquered?"

"Destroyed, annihilated, *wiped out*." Javeer's voice roughened. "If it's too evil to be transformed then there's no point in letting it exist."

"And if it's a person? You can't just kill a person."

"There is more than one way to destroy someone. It doesn't have to be through death. They can be stripped of power, jailed, judged...sentenced. But sometimes, death *is* the only option."

"I have never thought about it."

Javeer glanced at her troubled face. "What do you think about?"

Laeli's voice dropped to a whisper. "Too many things. I feel a great weight is always following me, waiting to catch up: as if it wants to crush me to the ground. My mother died carrying a secret, but she never told me what it was. I feel that secret lurking in every corner. I know my mom wanted to protect me, but she's only ended up doing the opposite. It's so hard to feel peace."

"She left you with no clues? No way to figure it out?"

Laeli laughed strangely. "I feel as if she's left me with clues that stare at me every day, and I cannot read them. We did everything together. She was the only person I had. Now I don't have her *or* the answers. I won't lie, I'm angry at her. Sometimes, I lie awake at night and wonder how she could do this to me. I've become numb to recalling our good memories. It's all swallowed by this *shadow;* this *secret*...that I can't figure out. And yet...I miss her so badly." Laeli bowed her head. "I want her back."

Javeer gently squeezed her arm. "At least your mother was not killed like mine. It's good you didn't have to see that."

"No," Laeli protested in a tight voice. "She *was* killed. Whatever she was hiding from me was killing her...slowly. She was wasting away day after day and wouldn't tell me why. I just had to watch." Laeli shivered. "I should stop talking about it. I don't want to talk about it."

"I'm sorry. It's my fault this got brought up."

"No, no, it's ok. It's just life I suppose." Laeli rested her head against his arm again. "We all have some dark struggle don't we?"

"I guess we do. It's kinda funny though. You can find the most beautiful things in the dark." Javeer nodded towards the moon. "Look at it! It's so dull looking during daytime, but at night it's the most epic thing you'll ever see."

"No, not the most epic."

"*No*? What could possibly be better?"

"You," replied Laeli in a tiny voice.

"*Me?*" Javeer's voice erupted in laughter. "You're a silly girl!"

"*Hey...*"

"In the best possible way," Javeer finished. Laeli flung her head back and beamed at him. To Javeer, her large eyes seemed as bright as the stars: two pools of warm brown that gazed at him affectionately. His heart racing, he caught his breath. "I know I've said it before but...you're so pretty," he whispered.

A shy smile stretched across Laeli's face, and she let out a tiny laugh. "I know you have..." she tilted her head and smiled up at the moon before letting her gaze drift back to his, "but it's ok. I like hearing it again. It makes me happy." Closing her eyes, she let her herself melt more snugly against his arms as the two of them sat in content tranquility, the distant echo of a factory whistle being the only thing that dared to disturb the silence.

Chapter 8
Khar Causes Trouble

"Ren," Laeli murmured. She lay sprawled out on the floor, her eyes dreamy as she stared at the ceiling.

"Hmm?" Ren replied, glancing up from his view behind the computer. "I hope you do not mind; I am providing an update to your software."

"No, I don't mind. Ren, do you think I should be careful?"

"Of what. The young man?"

"Yes."

"Which one?"

"Javeer...*obviously.*" With a sniff, Laeli rolled onto her stomach and faced Ren.

"I am sorry. I was not sure which one you were referring too."

"I wasn't referring to Kye." A hard edge crept into Laeli's voice.

"About Kye..."

"I don't want to talk about Kye."

As if he hadn't heard her, Ren continued. "I have been contemplating him and based on how you described his body language, thcrc is certainly something wrong. I have thought and thought what it might be, and I have decided; Kye demonstrates symptoms of someone who has undergone a negative traumatic experience."

"He says nothing about it."

"That is precisely all the more reason to believe his past disturbs him. He shows signs of dissociation and isolation. His mood swings shift rapidly, and he is very secretive. His heightened mental awareness and sensitive personality, which once made him more susceptible to emotions, have been affected by this experience, and it has rendered him cold and emotionally numb."

"I know he is not the same. Kye scares me now. But Ren...I don't want to talk about Kye. What about Javeer? How would you describe *his* body language?"

"So far, from what you have told me, nothing seems dangerous or alarming. He appears to be attracted to you but is maintaining healthy boundaries. Though I do sense a rise in your oxytocin and dopamine levels - signs the boundaries have shifted slightly?"

"You're impossible! Why must you read my chemical levels?"

"Because I simply can."

"*Hmph.*" With a snort, Laeli rolled over to her back. "I am going out again tomorrow with Javeer. He is signing up for that motorcycle race. Oh, I almost forgot to tell you! A rumor has it that there have been multiple thefts lately. More so than usual."

Ren's head snapped to attention, his pupils shrinking as he squinted his eyes in suspicion. He turned to face Laeli. "You *must* bring the taser." Walking over to a box in the corner of the room, he opened the lid and pulled out a taser similar to the one Javeer had held earlier, only this one was smaller and a silver-grey instead of black.

"Don't worry…I'll bring it." Walking over to Ren, Laeli placed a hand on his arm. "And this time, I promise I *won't* forget."

***

Early the next morning, Javeer met Laeli at her house and together they drove further up into the city. As Laeli sat behind him on the bike, she pelted him with questions about their destination.

"How exactly does this work? Does it cost money to sign up? Do you know how many people are entering?"

"So we're going to this gambling house that registers the names of the people who enter the motorcycle race. The names get published and bets are placed all over the city on who people think will win. Some entries are previous winners, while others are newbies." Javeer shrugged. "I'm not sure how many people will be there to sign up. This race happens every three years, so there's lots of hype for it. The bikers pay a small fee to enter. Everyone who bets has to supply an added sum to the biker of their choice. If that biker wins, all the contributions towards that extra sum go to him. If he loses, all the money placed on him goes to the winner. A prize of ten thousand silver pieces is also given to the one who comes up first. If the crowd loves you, your chances of earning more through bets in the next three years goes up even more. You can see why this is such a big deal! If I were to win this year, I'd have even better wagers made on me in the future."

"Who won the last race?"

Javeer's mouth set in a tight line. "Khar did. I wasn't in the last race. This is my first time entering."

"It sounds awfully dangerous."

"It is kind of dangerous," Javeer admitted as his bike skid to a stop on the side of the street. They were in a section of the city filled with dingy restaurants, bars, and gaming houses. Laeli's nose wrinkled as she observed the surrounding people. Most of them were men, and they all had a thug-like appearance with their strange hairstyles, tattoos, and piercings.

"The gambling house is half a block away from here." Javeer slid off the bike. "I just realized; it's probably safer if you don't go in. Don't want people knowing you're with me before the race. They might put a target on your back. Just wait here. I feel like a fool for not thinking of this before. Sure you'll be ok?"

Laeli nodded. She placed a hand on the taser attached to her belt. "I'll be alright."

"Are you *sure?* Honestly, I should probably drive you back and just return on my own."

"No, I want to wait for you here." Laeli insisted stubbornly.

Javeer sighed. "Well, just be careful. I'll be back soon." He strode off, and clutching the taser on the side of her hip, Laeli watched until he was out of sight.

***

As Javeer swung open the door to the gambling house, a little bell rang and a line of men craned their necks to see who had entered. Javeer rapidly sized them up. Some of the men were tall and thin, others short and stout. A few were like him - decent height and muscular build, but all of them had one thing in common – the unnerving air of hostile competitors. They looked Javeer up and down, suspicion and scowls stretched across their faces. Javeer was new; they didn't recognize him. Slowly and steadily, with a passive expression on his face, Javeer took his place at the end of the line.

"Alright, alright!" a rough burly man behind the counter barked. "You all know how this works. You gotta pay an entrance fee. Only twenty-five men can enter the race. If there's more than twenty-five of you, then there'll be a bid. Whoever can rack up the higher price is in." The man stretched out his neck to eye the line and laughed roughly. "Looks like there's twenty-six of you. This must be a lucky year! Only two of you bastards will have to bid." The man narrowed his eyes and pointed his fingers at the two men ahead of Javeer. "You unlucky bums are up."

"That ain't fair!" one of the men growled. "Why pick us?"

"My gambling house, my rules. You don't like it...get out and there won't be a problem."

The man who had complained stepped back into line, muttering angrily. Javeer watched him shoot his competitor an evil glare. Then Javeer's attention shifted quickly, and his posture straightened. Up ahead, having just paid and turning around to leave, was Khar. Javeer glanced at him before discreetly looking away. He had seen Khar at the last race three years ago but there wasn't much of a difference to him now. The same mean look rested on his face, and his poised stride screamed arrogance.

As Khar drifted past the line, he caught sight of Javeer and a malevolent spark lit up his eyes. He tilted his head and stepped towards Javeer. "What have we got here? You new, huh?" He inspected Javeer and snickered. "What's your name?"

Javeer said nothing. With a sneer, Khar stepped even closer. "Didn't your mama bother to name you, boy? Or maybe you haven't got a mama."

Javeer's nostrils flared, but he still refused to look at Khar. At this point, the entire room had gone silent and everyone was watching to see what would happen.

Khar's eyes widened. He pushed his face towards Javeer. "Do you even *have* a name?" Javeer gave no answer. With an aggravated laugh, Khar stepped back. "We've got a quiet one over here!" He faced the man at the counter. "Make *him* bid. Let's see how lucky he is."

This time Javeer looked at Khar with an expression of silent rage. With a dramatic flick of his hand, Khar waved him forward. "Good luck, pretty boy! I guess I'll be seein' you." He walked towards the door then glanced back, a mocking grin stretching ear to ear. "Well...*maybe*."

***

Laeli leaned against Javeer's bike, fingering the top of her taser and observing her surroundings with laser focus. She wondered how long it would be before Javeer came back. A slight feeling of nervousness fluttered in her chest, and she hoped he wouldn't take too long.

As she continued to stand there, Laeli noticed a man approaching, his gaze fixed on the motorcycle. Immediately the hair on her neck stood up, and she straightened her stance. With bated breath, she watched as the man came closer, thoroughly surveying the motorcycle. Then his attention shifted to her, and their eyes locked. With rigid tension, Laeli maintained position, her heart racing. She did not like this man. His eyes displayed contempt, and his handsome features were lined with cruelty. He inclined his head and stepped closer.

"Not a bad bike. It yours?"

"No."

"No?" the man laughed. Suddenly his face lit up with realization. "Ahh! It's gotta be your boyfriend's. He must be entering the race. You're waitin' for him while he signs up, aren't you? Which one was he, eh?"

Laeli glared at him. "I don't have to tell you."

The man laughed tauntingly. "You don't, huh? You mean you don't *want* to tell me?" He placed a hand against his chest in fake surprise.

"No, and I'm not going to."

A tinge of angry red tainted the man's tanned cheeks. "You're a bold little wench," he sneered. "Don't you know who I am?"

A sudden flash of realization pierced Laeli's brain, as she recalled her brief, distant glimpse of this man. She had seen him walking beside Malin near the Casino once. *I remember thinking they looked so similar.* "You're Khar."

"So you do know. Still sure you're not gonna tell me?"

"Go away!" Laeli snapped.

With one swift motion, Khar seized Laeli's arm and dragged her into a nearby alleyway. She gasped as he pushed her hard against the brick wall, still holding onto her arm. "I can *make* you tell me."

In spite of her great fear, Laeli refused to break eye-contact. "No, you can't." As she spoke, her hand slowly inched towards her taser.

"How are you going to stop me?" With lightning speed, Khar grabbed her other arm and pinned it to her side. "You little *bitch.*" He laughed low in his throat. "Why don't I make you go out into the middle of the street and call for him?"

"I *won't.*"

"What if I make you scream? You think he'll come running? Think he'll hear you?"

Laeli said nothing. Fright and rage had rendered her speechless. She stood there trembling. Now it felt like she was *unable* to look away.

"What kind of girl doesn't call for her man? Are you afraid he'll get beat up? *Huh?* Are you protectin' his ass?" Khar placed a finger against Laeli's cheek. Laeli winced at the touch.

"You know…" Khar looked Laeli up and down and then pushed his face so close it was almost touching hers. "I was told to give other girls a chance, but after lookin' at you I've decided you're nothing compared to my girl." His lips twisted in a condescending sneer. "So let's make a little deal! We'll share a secret…you and I. You come to the race…bring your boyfriend…and then you'll get to see why I ain't interested in a tramp like you. I've got a girl worth looking at. But be sure not to tell your man about this. It might cause some trouble, and I wouldn't want anythin' to happen before the race. He might try and stand up for you and well…" Khar straightened and stepped away from Laeli, "let's just say that would spoil the surprise." With a sarcastic wave, he began to back out of the alleyway, still facing Laeli. "Remember…say nothing! I really want to meet your boyfriend…on the day of the race, of course. If I meet him before then there might end up being a little…*accident*. And I'm sure you don't want that." With a final laugh, Khar turned and sauntered away.

Shaking all over, Laeli leaned against the alley wall for support. A surge of anger and shame overcame her as she realized how helpless she had been. Choking back a sob, she stumbled out of the alleyway and leaned against Javeer's bike, her back to the street so that no one would notice how scared she was.

Suddenly, a hand touched Laeli's shoulder. With whirlwind speed, she seized her taser and swung around only to see Kye standing there. Laeli lowered the taser, her breath heavy.

"Why did you point that at me?" Kye asked in a pained tone.

"I...I'm sorry! I thought you were somebody else."

"Who did you think I was?"

"Don't worry about it." Rubbing her hand across her face, Laeli placed the taser back on her belt. She looked up in confusion. "Wait...what are *you* doing here?"

"I was walking up this way and happened to see you."

A worried feeling flapped in Laeli's chest. How was it that no matter where she went, Kye always seemed to show up? Closing her eyes, she pressed a finger against her forehead and tried to think. "I...uh...have you found a job yet?"

"I have found one of sorts."

"Wh...what is it?"

"Nothing worth mentioning."

Laeli made a face. "Why can't you tell me?"

"It would not interest you."

"I think you have forgotten what kind of things interest me!" Laeli spoke sharply. Sudden pain shot through her head, and she winced.

"Laeli, what is it?" Kye leaned forward worriedly. "What is wrong?"

"Nothing, nothing. I'm just stressed is all."

"You are stressed badly. Tell me...what has happened?"

Laeli cocked her head and frowned. "Why should I tell you when you won't tell *me* anything? You..."

"Laeli!" At the sound of Javeer's voice, both Laeli and Kye snapped to attention. Instantly, Kye straightened and the strangest expression Laeli had ever seen came over his face. Suddenly noticing Kye, Javeer's pace slowed. With narrowed eyes, he walked up to Laeli.

"Who's this?"

"He's a childhood friend of mine. He's recently come to live in Cuniculum." Accusingly, Laeli added, "He works here but won't tell me where."

In an almost commanding tone, Javeer asked Kye, "Where do you work?"

Kye's face went blank: so blank that it was almost robotic. "It does not matter."

"What are you doing here?"

"It does not matter."

"Kye, stop being ridiculous!" Laeli interjected sharply. She turned to Javeer. "Did you get in?"

"Yes...*barely.*" Javeer gave a snort, still side-eyeing Kye who was staring at him intensely. "I had some trouble...I'll explain later."

Laeli nodded. "Kye, we've got to go." Kye's gaze shifted as Laeli spoke, and his facial expression became slightly more alive. He smiled tightly.

"Goodbye, Laeli." Without a word to Javeer, he walked off into the street. Laeli watched him go, his black coat flapping behind him.

"How do you know *him?*" Javeer's suspicious voice distracted Laeli from Kye, and she looked away.

"I knew him as a kid but...but he's different now. I don't know what happened; he's not the same anymore." She glanced again at the street, but Kye had vanished. "What trouble did you have?" she asked as Javeer helped her onto the bike.

Javeer exhaled bitterly. "If there're too many entries, random guys are chosen to bid their way in. Whoever can pay the higher price lands a spot in the race. Khar, that son-of-a-*bitch*, convinced the operator to have *me* be the one to bid. I about lost all my extra money."

Laeli's face went white. "You saw Khar?"

"Yeah, that scheming bastard. I'm not gonna let him forget me!" Javeer's voice went sharp with anger. "Not after this."

A new wave of panic threatened to overwhelm Laeli. Closing her eyes, she tried hard to control her breathing. In her mind, she could hear her mother's voice: old instructions refreshing themselves in her memory.

"Breathe slowly; clear your thoughts. You have strong mental focus when you choose to, Laeli. Imagine the ocean. The waves are white; seagulls are calling. Calm yourself. Hear the waves as they crash against the rocks. You are floating now...deep, deep within yourself. Look for the thing you want to think about. Bring it to mind slowly...there it is...floating above the waves. Reach for it..."

Breathe. Laeli thought to herself. *Breathe slowly.* With a steady respire, she opened her eyes and situating herself on the motorcycle, placed her arms around Javeer's waist. *I will not say anything about Khar to Javeer. If I do, he will hunt Khar down and then he might not be able to enter the race...or worse. I can't let anything happen to Javeer!* Taking another deep breath, Laeli pressed her cheek against Javeer's shoulder.

"It'll be ok. You'll be ok! Just don't go after Khar."

"He's gonna be coming after me regardless," Javeer muttered.

Laeli lifted her cheek from his shoulder in alarm. "What do you mean??"

"I'm winning this race! And when I do, I'll make friends...and lots of enemies. Whatever safety I have left in my life will be gone. You might as well know that. Perhaps..." Javeer's voice grew quiet, "perhaps you should just leave me. Maybe it'd be better that way."

For a moment, Laeli felt like someone had knocked the air out of her lungs. Then a wave of stubbornness she'd never experienced before swept through her body. Once again, she rested her face against Javeer's shoulder.

"*No.* I don't care how dangerous it gets. I'm not leaving you."

"But Laeli..."

"I'm *not.*"

Now it was Javeer's turn to take a deep breath. He gave a pleased laugh. "I thought you were gonna agree with me."

Laeli cocked her head. "There are some things that I will never agree with." She gave a tiny smile. "This is one of them."

Javeer craned his neck to look at her, his green eyes shining. "You're more stubborn than I thought." He chuckled low in his throat. "And you know what? I don't think I mind."

Chapter 9
Old Man's Message

"Laeli-girl!" Heathel's lively voice punched the silence, startling Laeli from her corner where she sat lubricating a robot joint. The old woman hobbled over, her face alight with excitement. "Sorry for scaring you, Laeli-girl, but I need your help."

"What do I need to do?"

"I want you to take me uptown." Heathel's eyes were sparkling with anticipation. "I'm gonna go place a bet for Javeer."

Laeli's eyes widened. "You are?"

"Of course, girl, why not? Gotta show support. But I need a walking stick in case I lose balance and that walking stick will have to be you. My sight kinda bad now too so..."

"Of course I'll help you, Heathel." Laeli rose to her feet and wiped the oil stain from her hands on her apron. Untying the apron and placing it on the stool, she walked up to Heathel and took her arm.

"Pft, girl...not yet! We haven't even started walking. I'm not that crippled. Let me get some movement in first."

Laeli giggled. "Sorry."

"It's ok, girl. You ready?"

"Yes." Still smiling, Laeli walked beside Heathel as she limped out of the shop and locked the door behind her.

"Just walk straight, girl, until I tell you where to turn. I know where to go." Erupting with confidence, Heathel chatted endlessly, commenting on every passerby and telling stories about Cuniculum from her youth until they reached their destination.

As Laeli opened the building's gaudily lit door and helped Heathel down the entrance steps, her eyes immediately scanned the area. It was a dark room, illuminated with yellow hanging bulbs and a long bar nestled in the corner. Beside the bar was a table on which a hologram rested, displaying the facial profiles of the contestants. A funny feeling fluttered in Laeli's chest as Javeer's face appeared, his competitive eyes staring straight ahead into her own. There were people everywhere - packed so tightly that it was hard to breathe. Yells of laughter and verbal arguing vibrated in Laeli's ears and several elbows jostled her on their way in.

"Heathel, are you sure you want to be in here?"

Heathel swat her hand. "I didn't walk all this way for nothin'. You forget girl; I was born and bred in Cuniculum. This city don't scare me."

"So what are you going to do? How does this work?"

"I just go up to the counter, tell the guy behind the bar who I'm bettin' on, and how much money I'm gonna put down. My choice will be saved and publicized on a screen the day of the race. Here girl...go wait for me in a corner where it's less crowded. I'll be fine."

"You sure?"

"Yes, yes. Go on, go on." Heathel playfully pushed Laeli away and wobbled forward. Obediently, Laeli made her way to the corner. The guffaws of the gamblers were loud and aggressive but with her back to the wall, hidden away from the noise and the lights, she felt safer. The only person close by was a withered old man, his shoulders bent and left leg crooked. His left hand gripped a metal cane and his right hand restlessly tapped his other leg. A scraggly beard hung from his wrinkled, narrow chin, and he squinted while observing his surroundings.

"You know...this is all rigged." The man's raspy comment caught Laeli by surprise. As he turned his head towards her, she saw one of his eyes was grey and cloudy, thick scar tissue running over his eyebrow and eyelid. "None of this...none of it means *anythin'*."

"What...what do you mean? How do you know?"

"Cause I raced once." The man grunted and shook his head. "Thirty-two years ago, girl! I went up against Malin, and that's how *this* happened." He gestured to his eye, and his voice dropped to a whisper. "Malin has always had connections. It's how he controls the Black Market. I was a bouncer for his casino once: before it was his. I *knew* things...stuff no one else knew. Wanna know what they offer the Five Cities in exchange for money, eh? Know why the Night Tunnel Gang is so rich and powerful? Do ya?" For answer, Laeli shook her head, her eyes big.

"Oil! Not regular oil either; it's oil that's essential to the creation of their robotics. Somehow it works well for that stuff. Now, I dunno *exactly* where the oil well is, but I know for a fact it's a real place right outside the city. Met lots of folks who work there. Malin buys off people or blackmails them, has them dig up his oil, and ships off the stuff through his gangs under the tunnels. But ya see, Malin don't want guns cause then the gangs might get hold of em' and turn on him. So he accepts gold, technology...trinkets here and there, in return for oil. *Hmph.*" The old man rolled his one good eye. "Them Five Cities are way more advanced than us! They got robots they say that act and talk like humans...imagine! They sure must want that oil to run those things. And Malin wants his money: his *toys*." The old man leaned even closer and pointed to his eye. "That's how I got this. One of his toys did it. You ever see a bike race, girl?"

Laeli anxiously shook her head. "No."

"It's dangerous! The only rule is to win, and it don't matter *how*. I learned that real quick. I was under a tunnel..." The man's arms gestured wildly as he explained. "A big tunnel! It's a shortcut, but not everyone goes that way, cause to get there you gotta go over a lot of steps and alleyways; it can slow ya down if you're not skilled enough. But I made it...and Malin was there too." The man's one eye narrowed. "That bastard flung somethin' at me - this black *stick* – and it attached to my bike. Blew the front wheel off! I went flyin' and bust up my leg. A metal shard flew out and pierced my eye and the whole bike skid past me and exploded."

"That's *awful*. Then what'd you do?"

"What did *I* do?" The old man laughed bitterly. "*Nothin*. I got patched up and packed away to a hole like this where I do odd jobs and wander through the streets. And I said nothin'. Didn't fancy being murdered in an alleyway so I disappeared."

"Then why are you telling me all this?"

"Cause," The old man's face scrunched. "I gotta mighty good gut, and I get strong feels with people. It's what made me a good bouncer. And I get a strong feel around you: like you're gonna need to know this. There's somethin' different about you. Better watch out! I've got a hunch that there's gonna be more trouble. A man was killed in the last race. Bound to happen again."

"But what happens if you *do* win?"

"I wouldn't know. If anyone wins, they're either racin' for Malin, or they get..." The old man ran a finger across his neck. "Khar won last time; ya see what I mean? So yeah, I never had a chance to find out the answer to that one."

"But wouldn't everyone know the bikers are racing for Malin? That it's all a scam?"

"Nah...he makes secret deals with the bikers...buys em off. It's not like they'd dare do anythin' behind his back anyway: not when Malin has a whole gang he could send after them or their families. And even if that *weren't* the case...people in

Cuniculum are stupid. They're not gonna notice...or hear of it either."

An ugly feeling curled in the pit of Laeli's stomach. She glanced back at the hologram until Javeer's face re-appeared, then stared at the floor, clutching her arms together.

"I can see I scared ya, girl." With a pained grunt, the old man leaned closer. "You got someone you know in the race? Tell em to get out...it ain't worth it!"

"No...no, I'm thinking." Laeli closed her eyes. *Javeer will never back down. He's too proud - too determined. There has to be something else...some other way.* A sudden idea pierced Laeli's brain and immediately she turned to go. "I have to leave...but thank you...thank you for telling me!"

"Not at all, girl." As the old man watched her rush away, he muttered to himself, "I knew telling her would change some-thin'. Stuff's about to happen."

***

Laeli shoved her way through people until she caught sight of Heathel exiting her place in the line. With a wave of her hand, she hurried towards her. Heathel greeted her with a big grin.

"Ahh, girl! I just finished. You ready to go?"

"Yes. Heathel, let's go now."

"Sure. Ya know..." the old woman began blabbering, obliv-ious to the urgent alarm written all over Leali's face. "I placed a mighty good bet. Was probably the most I've ever spent on anythin' in years. Javeer will appreciate this. That boy better win or imma beat his ass. *Gracious* girl. The way you're grabbing my arm! I didn't know you had such a strong grip. You ok? You look kinda funny."

"I *have* to get home. I just realized there's something I need to do."

"Well ok, girl, no worries! I'm leavin' now. Good grief! You're a lot stronger than I thought you were. You and Javeer will have sturdy kids one day."

"*Heathel!*"

"What, girl? Did I say something wrong??"

"That's...I mean...you didn't have to say *that*."

"Pish, posh, girl. Nothin' wrong with what I said. And you know I always say what I want. Besides..." Heathel's eyes twinkled naughtily. "It's *true*."

***

Javeer and his father bent over the turbo bike, examining it for anything that might need last minute adjusting. It was two days before the race and for the past week, Javeer had been spending all his free time in the basement, checking and double checking the bike. He needed to be sure there was nothing he had missed.

"Have you inspected the brakes?" Lyon asked, breaking the silence. "Tires, coolant...the oil filter?"

"It's all been checked. Honestly, I think I've spent the last day just polishing and staring at her."

"And Laeli? What of Laeli? I haven't seen her at all this week."

Javeer grew quiet for a moment before speaking. "I did tell her she needn't stay. Told her this was all dangerous. Maybe she decided to listen to me."

"If a woman leaves you when things become dangerous, she's not worth having at your side, son."

With a shrug, Javeer got to his feet and dropped the microfiber cloth he was holding onto a nearby stool. "Maybe that's true in some situations, but you can't expect so much from someone you just met."

"You're wrong. Your mother..." Lyon paused mid-sentence and glanced up at the ceiling. A girl's voice could be heard talking upstairs. With wide eyes, Javeer gave his father a relieved look.

"It's Laeli!"

"And *how* is she in the shop??"

"I gave her a spare key last week." With one quick sprint, Javeer reached the staircase and raced up the steps.

"*What?* Son!" Lyon rose abruptly, frowning with disapproval, but Javeer was already gone.

***

"Where is Javeer, Mimi?" Laeli stood in the shop, holding in her hand a small object wrapped in a grey cloth.

"He is not in here."

"Is he in the house?"

"Yes!" Mimi gave Laeli her customary blink. "Should I go get him?"

"Yes, please."

Just then, the back door of the shop opened, and Javeer burst through the door. Startled by his sudden entrance, Laeli jumped, and Mimi whirled around wildly.

"There he is!" she cried, waving stiffly.

"Laeli, why are you here?" In three long strides, Javeer stood in front of her, his chest heaving. Laeli gave him an amused smile.

"Were you running?"

"I...um...I might have been, yeah." Javeer gave an embarrassed laugh. Then his face became more serious. "Is something wrong?"

"It's something important...very important. I *have* to tell you." Grabbing his arm, Laeli propelled him to the back door. Standing in the hallway waiting was Lyon, his arms crossed.

"Sir," Laeli walked up to him, too worried to care about the glare on his face. "I learned something last week: something about the race that you and Javeer need to know. It's vital information."

Lyon's stance relaxed, and he un-crossed his arms. "What is it, Laeli?"

In rapid sentences, Laeli reiterated everything the old man had told her. As she spoke, looks of alarm came over Lyon and Javeer. At the end of her explanation, an angry grunt exploded from Lyon's throat.

"*Bastard.* Vile bastard! His type is the slime of the earth." Lyon began to pace back and forth, clenching and un-clenching his fists. "So much makes sense now."

"I have a solution though. At least...I think I do." Laeli clutched Javeer's sleeve as he stared with furrowed brows at the ground. His face met Laeli's.

"My bike is a turbo. I can still outrun him."

"You were planning to use the tunnel weren't you?"

"It's the quickest way so long as you know what you're doing." Javeer bit his lip. "But I can go a different way. The turbo will still make me the fastest."

Laeli shook her head. "It doesn't matter. I researched this kind of device. It's utilized by police in the Five Cities to attach to vehicles; they use it to track down criminals. It's called a crī-men wand. There is an option on the device to scan the vehicle of your choosing. This ensures it will attach to that particular vehicle, even if you're surrounded by others. Don't you see? Khar can just scan your bike before the race starts. There are no rules; you can't stop him. The wand is magnetic and once it attaches, it initiates a shock wave that blows up or disables whatever part of the object it lands on. But look..." Laeli eagerly unwrapped the cloth from the object she was holding, revealing a black oval device, half the size of her palm. "I had my...I spent days learning how to perfect it. It activates a force field around whatever you attach it to. It should prevent the wand from connecting to the bike."

Javeer took the device from Laeli's hand. "How do you know it'll work?"

"I had it scanned for errors. It'll work."

Lyon's eyes narrowed at Laeli's answer. "You had it scanned? What is this, girl? How could you possibly have had it scanned? There's no machine or computer system in Cuniculum advanced enough to do something like that. And how would you be able to figure out how to make this so quickly? Where did you get the equipment?"

"My mother left behind many things for me." Laeli's voice dropped uncomfortably. "This was one of them. I...I learned how to create and design a lot before she died. She taught me, and I...I taught myself the rest."

Lyon stroked his chin, still staring at her. Then he reached out and took the device from Javeer's hand. "Hmm," he mumbled. "And you think this will work?"

"I *know* it will work."

Lyon shot a side glance at Javeer, who gave the slightest nod before taking back the device. He held it out to Laeli. "Where does it go on the bike?"

"It can be attached to any external section of the vehicle."

"Laeli," Lyon reached out and placed a hand on Javeer's shoulder. "Let me talk to my son for a minute." The two of them left Laeli in the hallway and went into the kitchen, shutting the door behind them. "Look, Javeer," Lyon whispered. "Even if the girl is honest, how would she know all of this? How well do you know her? How much has she told you?"

"Only that her mom was a robotics mechanic and died seven years ago."

"No mere robotics mechanic would know how to make that. It requires a lot of expertise, engineering skill, the right materials...and a *scanning device?* None of those things can be found here! I remember the girl mentioning her mother was from Nobiles." Lyon's eyebrows furrowed. "I wonder who her mother was and why she left."

"Her mother was running from something. Laeli said she doesn't know what from; her mother wouldn't tell her. It could be her mom was an important person. Perhaps that was why she kept it a secret from her daughter," Javeer turned the device around in his hand. "She must have wanted to protect Laeli."

"I don't like it." Lyon frowned. "It's too strange. I watch that girl when she's here. She's shy and quiet, but her eyes are intense, and she's extremely observant. She reacts to the slightest move or sound. I catch her examining my every action. She's studying us, but she does it so naturally; it's second nature to her."

"You don't trust her?"

"I don't sense anything evil in her, but I dislike what I don't know. And I don't know enough about her." Lyon's eyes locked with Javeer's, and he sighed. "All I know is that she likes you."

A strange warmth, mixed with a nervous twisting in his stomach swept over Javeer. He glanced again at the device in his hand. "I'm using it, Father. I've *got* to."

Lyon shook his head. "I can't stop you." He seized Javeer's shoulders and shook him. "You must...*you must* understand...there will be a death warrant on your head if you win. You will never again know safety or peace."

Javeer clutched the device harder. "I know, but it doesn't matter. I will...I *will do this*. Nothing shall stop me." He grabbed his father's arm and squeezed it. "As for Malin...I'll beat that son-of-a-bitch at his own game."

***

Laeli paced back and forth restlessly in the secret room, Ren watching her from his corner. With a groan, she halted and ran her hand through her hair.

"Ren, you are sure that device will work? Even if Mommy had used it once?"

"It will work. I scanned it...twice. Your mother used it, but it was never damaged. The blocker might as well be new."

"I don't know." Laeli hugged herself anxiously. "Ren, this is so bad. What if Javeer gets killed?"

"I hope that he does not."

"He *can't* die," Laeli exclaimed fiercely. She resumed her pacing. "He *mustn't*."

"You will still go to the race? You will watch?"

"Yes, I..." Laeli froze, and her eyes grew big. "Watch. *Watch*. Ren! That's what I can do. Watch!" Racing to the desk, she yanked open a drawer and pulled out a small camera. "Mommy also used this that night. The night we escaped Nobiles, remember? She put it on you so she'd be able to locate you if you became separated or stolen. The screen attachment should still be here." She began rummaging through the drawer. "I found it." Walking up to Ren, she held out a tablet, its green-blue screen so delicate it was see-through. Ren gently took it from her hands, and his pupils suddenly seemed to sink into themselves, merging into another layer.

"The device remains intact. Nothing is damaged. Let me see the camera. Yes...the camera is also functional. Both will work."

"I'll give it to Javeer! I'll tell him to put the camera on his bike. If something bad happens, there will be proof. He can use that as blackmail. And I can watch him through the screen during the race."

Ren put a hand on her shoulder. "Will you be able to watch that? What if you see something terrible."

Laeli bit her lip. "I *have* to watch," she whispered. "I *need* to know what is happening."

"If you do this, Laeli, you will become involved in the danger." Taking the devices from her and placing them on the desk, Ren clutched her hands. "Please, Laeli. Do not go! Stay home. It is not safe to go."

"You don't understand." Laeli shook her head. "I must be there for him. I *have* to be there for him."

"Why must you?"

Laeli's eyes met Ren's. "Because I *love* him."

Ren's chin drooped and sadness filled his eyes. He raised his head and a strange tone took over his voice, as if he were speaking words that were being uttered by another person far away.

"Love and bitterness go together. The price of happiness is *pain.*"

Chapter 10
Motorcycle Race

Laeli shoved her way through the crowd, her face furrowed in concentration as she tried to make room for Heathel, who followed close behind. It was the day of the great race, and Cuniculum's streets were packed to the brim. Someone collided into Laeli and almost knocked the screen she was carrying out from under her arm. With a rapid movement of her other hand, she managed to keep a grip on the object.

"It should be ok, girl," Heathel yelled at her above the din. "You've wrapped it well enough...whatever it is."

"I can't drop it!" Laeli gasped. She scowled at the passing people, as if that would somehow force them to make space for her.

"It's still a long walk to the top of the city, Laeli-girl. We left early; we should get to the starting point in time. Why didn't you just go with Javeer?"

"*Shh*, Heathel," Laeli shook her head. "Don't mention Javeer."

"What, why not?"

"Just don't. Not here."

"No one can hear us, girl. I can assure you of that!"

"You never know." The words Javeer had spoken to Laeli the day before rang in her head.

"*You shouldn't be seen with me tomorrow - not before the race, and probably not after. There'll be gang members scattered throughout the crowd. They're gonna be watching. Just don't come up to me, regardless of what happens. It's better if certain people don't know you're my girlfriend.*"

"I don't *know what?*" Heathel interrupted Laeli's thoughts. "Girl, you're on edge! Don't worry...it'll all be fine."

For answer, Laeli gave a thin smile. She and Heathel kept on, trudging through the restrictive crowds. After an hour walk, they began to near their destination. An explosion of firecrackers were set off on the corner of the road, and Laeli jumped. Hollers and shouts rang from the excited people and not far from the eruption, three men had gotten into a street fight. Angry cursing curled through the air and one of the men pulled out a knife. Laeli froze, her eyes huge.

"Agh, girl." Heathel gave her a nudge. "Don't watch; keep walking."

Quickly looking away, Laeli took a shivery breath and marched on. They had reached the hill not far from Malin's casino, and as she lifted her eyes upward, Laeli could see his magnificent house resting on top of its stone wall. A large flag flapped above the starting point of the race and makeshift railings on either end of the track separated the crowd. All across the city, holograms and billboards, surrounded by flashing lights, displayed the contestants' faces. Underneath their profiles, Laeli noticed large numbers presenting the amount of money that had been bet on each contender. Javeer's face appeared, and her mouth dropped open.

"Heathel, how on earth did Javeer get so many bets placed on him?"

"Seventy thousand silver *koin!*" Heathel's cackling laugh vibrated in Laeli's ears. "Sure wasn't me. Didn't know Javeer was so popular! The boy deserves it. He's gonna win. Ah well, it's not as many as that Khar fellow. He's got almost ninety thousand. His face kinda mean lookin' ain't it?"

Without answering, Laeli abruptly resumed walking. A chill twisted up and down her spine. Heathel was still babbling behind her, but she could no longer hear what the old woman was saying. The very sight of Khar's face filled her with a stifling dread.

***

Malin took a sip of rum and stared at the hologram in front of him. He was lingering on the balcony of his house and a slight breeze shifted the blue curtain across his open window. With an expression of amused perplexion, he drained the glass and slid an emerald ring sitting atop a nearby dresser over his finger. Then he glanced back at the hologram.

"Marten...two thousand bid. Lucian...one thousand bid. Khar...eighty-nine thousand bid. Javeer...*seventy thousand...*" Malin's voice trailed off, and his eyes narrowed. Rapidly, he turned and swept out of the room, his sage green cloak billowing behind him. Flying down the polished steps that led to the lower floor, he rushed past the massive double-decker doors and outside down the stone slope that led away from his house and in the direction of the casino. Waiting for him at the bottom was a shiny, silver four-wheeler, which he mounted and drove away on in the direction of the race's starting point. Behind him followed three body guards who had been waiting beside the wheeler.

Once Malin had reached his destination, he dismounted and rapidly walked among the crowd, followed closely by his guards. He ducked under a makeshift tent where Khar was pacing back and forth. In the corner of the tent stood Bria, her sharp gaze shifting from Khar to Malin. Malin greeted them with a sarcastic grimace.

"So! I suppose you saw the displays? Who is this *Javeer?*"

With a bitter sneer, Khar picked up a nearby glass and fingered it. "I only know his face. Other than that I don't know a single thing. Damn it! *Son-of-a-bitch.*" Furiously, he flung the glass against the floor, shattering it into many pieces. "That piece of shit passed the gambling entry!"

"That piece of shit has a bid of *seventy-thousand* put up on him. What I'd like to know is *who* is backing him up? This could be bad for us. I don't know anyone here with that kind of money...besides *me.*"

"You think *I know?*" Khar laughed and pushed his face near his father's. "I'll be damned if I do!" His voice turned into a hiss.

"It don't matter. I've got the turbo bike...and if I have to, I'll use the little contraption on him. He won't know what hit him. That seventy-thousand will go straight into our hands."

Malin's voice lowered to a whisper. "I've already bought off sixteen of the bikers: all the ones I thought might pose some threat. A couple weren't very cooperative so...you know...I sent them a warning. A few I left untouched. But now we *have* to keep an eye on those few. I underestimated the danger of ignoring even one." Malin took a deep breath. "I don't know this Javeer...but I won't be making *that* mistake again." He fingered the folds of his cloak. "I shall make sure I get to know him *very well*, whether he wins or not."

"And what if he dies in the race?" Khar tilted his head, his eyes becoming mere slits. "A crash might kill him."

"Better for me to suffer unanswered curiosity then lose thousands of silver *koin* to a brat whose name I don't even know. Make sure you win!" Malin leaned forward and whispered in Khar's ear, "Dead or alive, I'll learn who he is. Be sure of that."

"I leave the learning to you." With a final sneer, Khar whirled around and stomped out of the tent.

Malin side-eyed Bria, who had maintained her standing position in the corner. "Well, girl. What do *you* think of all this?"

"What do *I* think?" Bria fingered the whiskey glass she was holding. She took a sip, and her eyes rose above the glass rim to meet Malin's. "I think if Khar's not careful it will all go like this..." She tipped the glass and the whiskey sloshed out onto the ground.

Malin's mouth twisted in suspicious amusement. "Is that a warning or a threat?"

"I don't know what you mean." Bria's voice lowered innocently. "I'm just telling you what I think. You asked me."

Malin's eyes slowly traveled over her elegant figure. He reached out and fingered the tip of one of her long dreadlocks. "I don't know if I like your answer."

"I can't help that...can I?" Bria stepped closer, her face near Malin's. "I know what to say around Khar. I know how Khar's mind works...but I'm afraid I don't know *yours* all that well. It's not my fault if I offended you." She tilted her chin downward and smiled. "I'm just a simple girl."

Taking his finger and tipping her chin upwards, Malin leaned over and kissed her on the lips. Once he pulled away, Bria took a deep breath, the corner of her mouth curving upward. "You better not ever let Khar hear of this. I'm afraid he wouldn't like it."

"Don't worry; he'll never know. *You* aren't going to tell him."

Bria laughed - a tinkling laugh that held a note of mockery. "Well...it's clear you know me *very well*." She walked towards the tent flap and halted before exiting. "I won't say anything...*of course.*"

***

Shouts and cries erupted while Javeer and his father made way through the packed crowd. As people scrambled aside to leave room for their motorcycles to pass, hoots of excitement began to ripple through the onlookers.

"You see his bike? It's a stunner!"

"I bet on the wrong man, *damn it*."

"Imma kill myself. No way my man's gonna win."

"You think *that* bastard has a chance? *Ha*."

"Look at him! The man on the black motorcycle with the blue spirals. He's so *hot*."

"*Mhm*, that's why I bet on him."

"I know that guy! He fixed a bike of mine a year ago. Didn't know he was entering."

"You idiot, how could you not? His face has been plastered all over the streets for days."

As the crowd went on commenting, Javeer and Lyon continued to make their way to the starting line. As they got closer, Lyon signaled to Javeer and slid to a stop beside him. "We separate here. You ready son?"

Javeer's gaze fell upon the camera and blocking device that Laeli had given him, situated securely in their spots on the bike. "Yes, father." Scouring his surroundings, Javeer squinted upward, and his eyes widened as he noticed the nearby hologram. "What the *hell*," he muttered. "How did the bids for me reach *seventy-thousand?*"

"I don't know, son." Lyon's face scrunched in confusion. "It's almost as if someone is secretly supporting you."

"Who on earth...?" Javeer's voice trailed off. "I gotta go! The bikers are lining up. See ya, Father."

"Remember…" Lyon's voice hardened, and his tone lowered as he gave Javeer's arm a firm shake. "*Don't* let those bastards beat you. *Win*, my son."

***

Laeli separated herself from Heathel and shoved her way through the packed crowd. She needed someplace to hide in order to watch the camera footage without anyone noticing, but that was starting to seem like an impossibility.

Suddenly, her eyes fell upon a section tucked behind the race's starting point: a raised platform that rose beside a four-story building undergoing construction. The top of the platform was wrapped in heavy tarp. Trying to appear casual, Laeli slowed her pace and braved her way through shoulders and elbows until she reached the platform's ladder. Carefully scaling the wooden rungs, she slipped under the tarp and settled against the corner of the platform rails. Unwrapping the cloth from the device, Laeli activated the screen and took a shuddery breath.

Javeer said that the bikers will ride to the end of the city, turn around, and make it back to the finish line in whatever way they choose. So if Javeer wants to win, he must not only avoid crashing but also find the quickest route on the way back. Come on, Javeer! You can't lose this. You've GOT to win.

***

The roar of surrounding motorcycle engines vibrated through Javeer's ears as he placed himself within the horizontal line among his twenty-four fellow competitors. Clouds of dust and gravel shot up from the ground and the riders leaned over the handlebars, glaring down one another. Then, without any warning, a motorcycle separated from the line and skid to a stop next to Javeer, sending a shower of dirt spraying in all directions. It was Khar, and he laughed mockingly as his voice rose above the din.

"So it's *you*, pretty boy. I see you made it. Must be your lucky day! Or maybe *not*."

Javeer didn't answer. His stunned eyes were fixed on Khar's bike. It was almost identical to his in both shape and size. Even the swirled edges on the saddlebag were of a similar design, but instead of blue they were a deep glowing purple. The motorcycle was newer, shinier, but Javeer knew right away that it was his model. "Where did you get that bike?" he growled.

"*What?*" For a moment, Khar looked taken aback and then his eyes wandered to Javeer's motorcycle. An expression of realization took over and a hostile look settled across his face. "What's it to *you*, pretty boy?"

"That bike is my design, you bastard!"

"What a coincidence. May the better rider win." With a sneer, Khar turned his head away.

Javeer gave his handlebar a furious thump. *The wretch! He stole my bike design. Now I know who those men were that took my bike years ago. They were Tunnel Gang members. They gave it to him, the ass!* A violent wave of rage surged over Javeer, and it took all his self-control not to throw himself upon Khar and pummel him. The noise of the crowd seemed to fade away and everything in front of him blurred into a mass of melted colors. Javeer's gloved hands tightened over the handlebars. *I will win...I will win. I will not let this villain beat me. I will destroy him. I... will...win.*

Now the announcer was shouting something; Javeer could hear his enthusiastic yells sweeping over the mass of spectators. Pulling the helmet visor down he leaned forward, placing one boot on the foot peg. A horn sounded, accompanied by the erupting roar of the crowd. With a rumbling vroom that exploded in a variety of frequencies, the motorcycles shot forward, sending billowing clouds of gravel and dust into the air. The blue spirals on Javeer's bike flashed brilliantly as he sped away, their neon glow leaving behind a blurred trail of light that vanished in the distance.

*****

As the bikes zipped through the city, people scattered into corners while those inside their houses leaned out of the windows to watch. Cuniculum's narrow roads served as a difficult challenge, for they were full of sudden corners, steep steps, and the occasional robot lingering on the street. As the contestants drew closer to the city's end, one of the riders accidentally swerved and crashed into a pile of crates. Screams from onlookers erupted as his motorcycle veered out of control and wooden splinters went flying in all directions. A nearby robot flattened itself against a wall, a string of terrified exclamations gushing from its mouth as the bike whizzed past its legs, almost crushing them.

Further up ahead, Javeer took a sharp turn, separating from the other riders. Deviating to the left, he made his way down a winding alleyway. Downshifting the gear, he began to weave through the twisted passages. This alleyway he knew well; it was where he used to practice riding before his previous bike had been stolen. The engine on his motorcycle was running smoothly, all the gears were working, and a slight thrill of exhilaration shot up Javeer's spine. He was nearing the infamous tunnel now. He tightened his grip on the handlebars.

The sound of an approaching motorcycle immediately caught Javeer's ear. *Khar...Khar is going the same way I am.* Exiting the alleyway, Javeer upshifted the gear and the bike shot forward. From another nearby alleyway, Khar's bike emerged, its advancing bulk not far behind. Peering ahead, Javeer could now see the tunnel: the arched interior lit by dim lights that barely pierced the shadowy blackness. He quickly began to accelerate; he *had* to get through the tunnel before Khar, but he couldn't go too fast. If he did, he would crash on the upcoming curve waiting at the tunnel's end.

The two bikes were now close: Khar's a few feet behind Javeer's. The purple and blue glint of the motorcycles illuminated the tunnel, casting flashing reflections across the brick wall. A red light suddenly joined them; another rider had braved the alley route and now all three bikes were together in the passageway. Javeer glanced behind briefly and in that split second, he saw Khar's arm fling itself outward.

Instinctively, Javeer's hand dropped from the handlebar to below his seat and with one quick flick, he switched on the device Laeli had given him. A blurry film wrapped around his motorcycle just as the wand struck it. Repelled backwards by the shield, the wand whipped through the air and attached to the wheel of the third biker next to Khar. A powerful shock wave vibrated through the tunnel, the ear-splitting noise causing both Khar and Javeer to wince. Behind Javeer, the third bike tipped forward and exploded into a shower of orange flames, the blast shooting smoke and fire across the tunnel. The wand was more powerful than Khar had anticipated. Both Javeer and Khar's bikes were pushed forward by the force of the eruption. Losing his balance, Javeer made it out of the tunnel only to slip off the road into the deep aqueduct pool resting beside it. Flying forward, Javeer crashed into the water beside his bike.

As he rose to the surface, rage filled Javeer, and he flung his helmet into the water with a yell. Overcome with dread, he tread through the murky water towards his bike to see that the protective shield had prevented it from sinking to the bottom and was guarding the exterior from the water. A stab of hope struck Javeer in the chest. He peered over the bike's handlebars and noticed a row of steps that started just outside the tunnel and made their way down under the water.

A splintered cry rang through the air, distracting Javeer. He turned to see that Khar had dismounted and was struggling to rip off his jacket, which was covered in flames that curled past the shoulders and down the sleeves. With a muttered curse, Khar flung the jacket to the ground and staggered forward, holding his ears. Grunting low in his throat, Javeer quickly began to push his bike towards the steps. As he did so, a strange hissing noise, followed by a snap, made him halt. His eyes widened. The water was leaking through the protective shield: the top part of it was already disintegrating. Clenching his jaw, Javeer renewed his pace towards the steps; he *had* to reach them before the rest of the shield was gone.

As he caught sight of Javeer making his way out of the aqueduct, Khar turned and stumbled back to his bike, leaving his helmet behind. With a muffled shout, Javeer pushed faster. The added adrenaline rush was just what he needed to get his bike out of the water before the rest of the shield vanished. Now back on firm ground, Javeer swiped away the wet dreadlocks dangling over his eyes and re-mounted the motorcycle. Then he pressed the throttle control and zoomed off after Khar. Within seconds, he had re-gained sight of his opponent. They were now on a back road, far away from the main streets, and the slope upward was wide and flat.

"Come on, baby," Javeer muttered to his motorcycle. "You can do this." He accelerated his pace and with a whirring rumble, the motorcycle picked up speed, effortlessly gliding across the level ground. Like a blue bullet, it soared forward, catching up to Khar with ease. Khar shot Javeer a look of wild hate and fear. With a shout, he deliberately swerved sideways, almost crashing into Javeer's back wheel. With one quick thrust, Javeer managed to dodge the collision and then blew past Khar's bike with a velocity that Khar's bike could never hope to reach. A string of curses flew from Khar's mouth as he tried to gain momentum, but Javeer was already out of sight.

***

Laeli gripped the screen so hard her knuckles were white. She had heard the crash, seen the collision, and a terrible fear settled in her chest. The tablet sliding from her hand, she put a palm to her eye, trying to push back the hot tears that were threatening to overflow. Then a muffled shout from Javeer made her grab the screen again. He was back on the bike and picking up speed. A wild flutter of hope pushed away the fear in Laeli's chest. She shook the screen as if that would somehow make Javeer go faster.

"Come on! *Come on,*" she gasped. She watched as Javeer passed Khar and sped up through the city, back towards the starting line. Leaving the tablet on the wooden surface, Laeli sprang to her feet and pushing the tarp out of the way, leaned over the platform's balcony. A slight breeze whipped her hair as she scanned the area. Her heart was pounding, its impatient thud striking against her chest. A raggedy breath escaped her lips.

Just then, a flash of blue caught Laeli's attention. A huge smile brimmed over her face. It was Javeer, and he was coming...alone and fast. Hopping up and down on her feet, Laeli shrieked with delight, but her cry was drowned out by the roar of the crowd. As Javeer crossed the finish line, the horn sounded loudly, declaring the winner.

Banging pans, blowing whistles, clapping and screaming – the crowd surged forward like a title wave, pressing so close together the guardrails were almost overwhelmed. As Khar's bike appeared, no one noticed; everyone's attention was fixed on Javeer as his motorcycle skid to a stop. A haze from the returning bikers settled across the horde of people, mixing with the smoke of random firecrackers being set off.

I don't care if I'm supposed to stay hidden. I'm too excited. I've got to go see Javeer. Racing down the platform rungs, Laeli jostled her way through the crowd. A random hand jabbed her neck and someone's leg bumped her own, almost sending her sprawling, but she pushed on. By some random miracle, she managed to claw her way through the mob and catching sight of Javeer, she sprinted towards him. The expression on his dirt-streaked face was one of pride and when he noticed Laeli, his eyes lit up. With a squeal, she flung herself on him and with one arm he picked her up and gave her a warm squeeze.

"You did it, you *did it.*" she exclaimed. "You made it, and I'm so proud!" She wrapped her arms more tightly around his neck. With a half-hug, Javeer buried his face in her neck.

"And you helped me! Do you know..." Javeer leaned back slightly, "that without your help I would have been *ruined?* That wretched trickster almost got me."

"It doesn't matter." Laeli's eyes shone as she looked at him. "*You* won, and that's all I care about."

"You know," Javeer whispered. "I think I remember telling you that you're not supposed to be here."

Laeli leaned back and pursed her lips. "I don't care! I couldn't stay away a minute longer, so don't even bother scolding me." Javeer laughed as she hugged him again.

As Javeer continued to hold her, Laeli's eyes drifted over his shoulder, and she noticed a beautiful woman standing a few feet away. The woman was clothed in a tight purple dress that hugged her figure, splitting open by the side of her left knee. Her long dreadlocks swung over one side of her shoulder and silver bracelets lined her wrists. The woman stared back at Laeli, her nostrils flared and an expression of wild envy in her eyes. She refused to break eye contact, and it was only until Javeer gently set Laeli down that she lost sight of the woman.

***

From the raised dais he was standing on, Malin's face contorted, and he twisted the ends of his cloak violently. From his view point, he had been able to see Javeer cross the finish line with perfect clarity.

"My *worthless son*," he seethed. "That dingus just lost me everything! Where did that Javeer-fool get that kind of turbo bike? *DAMN HIM."* Giving a furious shout, he dismounted the dais, followed by the ever-present bodyguards and Bria, who had been standing behind him. Together, they made their way down to the contestants. Khar was among them, his eyes bloodshot with envy and dust as he watched the crowd scream their compliments to Javeer. He noticed the scowl his father gave him and for answer turned his glance accusingly on Javeer. Narrowing his eyes, Malin slightly shook his head and beckoned Khar to come closer. Khar obeyed and dismounted from his bike.

"What happened?" Malin's eyes scoured Khar and took notice of the blood on his cheek and missing jacket. "*Why* didn't you use the *wand??"*

"I did, but the bastard had some device that repelled it! It blew up on someone else, and we both lost balance and fell. *Damn it*, why didn't you tell me that thing would be so powerful? My jacket caught fire and..." Khar bent over in a coughing fit before continuing, "we were able to get back on the bikes, but he caught up to me, and I couldn't pass that stupid turbo of his."

"Something isn't right. How'd he know about the wand! Where'd he get the device?"

"I dunno!" Khar began hacking again. "All I know is that shit bike is his."

"You mean he designed his own bike?"

"Yeah." Khar's voice lowered. "Get a load of *this*. He said *my* bike was his; that *I stole* it from him!" He laughed bitterly. "An arrogant dog, ain't he?"

Malin's eyes thinned until they were mere slits. "Riots will start soon," he muttered. "People who lost money will start fights."

"Let em!" Khar snarled. "Maybe one of them will go after him. He can see what it's like to get pummeled by a mob or have his throat slit in an alleyway. Unless you want me to..."

"No!" Malin replied sharply. He shot his son a sly smile. "Don't touch him! I will uphold his position as the winner. I'll befriend him, invite him to my house...I'll get to know this Javeer. Then I'll find out just who he knows and how he won."

"Let me..."

"*No.*" Now Malin glared at Khar with hostility. "I will do this *my* way. Don't even *think* about interfering." He glanced past Khar's shoulder. "Who's that girl with him?"

Khar looked where Malin nodded, and his mouth dropped. "The little *wench*. It's the girl I saw near the gambling house."

"You've seen her before?"

"Yeah, I..." A new wave of humiliation swept over Khar, and he cursed wildly. The remembrance of his conversation with Laeli now stung sharply.

"So he has a girlfriend. *Hmm.*" Malin studied Laeli with a smirk. "*Very* interesting. I shall get to know her too. Both of them will be invited to my casino." Her face paling, Bria tore her gaze away from Javeer and Laeli and shot Malin a resentful look. Malin didn't notice. "I am in a tight spot, so it's time to play a little game. I'll have to play it well."

Chapter 11
Jace's Warning

Javeer scanned the crowd, squinting his eyes against the glare of the evening sun. He pressed a hand over his forehead. "Laeli, have you seen my father at all?"

"No...but oh. Heathel! I forgot about Heathel. And the tablet! I've got to get it. I'll be back." Letting go of Javeer's arm, Laeli pushed her way through the crowd and rushed back to the construction platform. *I hope no one sees me,* she thought as she scaled the ladder. *I hope they are too distracted.*

After wrapping the tablet in its grey cloth, Laeli carefully descended back into the crowd, searching for Heathel. Unfortunately, everyone was taller, and it was impossible to see much.

"*Heathel!*" she yelled. There was no response. She continued to make her way through the onlookers, scanning every direction possible. Then an aggressive shoulder push sent her tumbling. Her shoulder blade hit the ground with a thud and in the towel, she could hear the sound of the glass shattering.

"*Nooo,*" Laeli moaned. "Why does this always happen to me?" Seizing the towel, she bunched it up tightly and rose to her feet.

"Laeli-girl!" Startled, Laeli jumped and whirled about to see Heathel standing behind her.

"*Heathel*. Javeer won. Did you see? He won!"

"I didn't see, but I heard. People have been chanting his name. Take me to the boy. Imma see him!"

"Alright." Linking an arm through Heathel's, Laeli guided her back to Javeer. As they got closer, she saw Lyon was standing beside him, his hand on his son's shoulder. He was whispering something in Javeer's ear and for answer, Javeer thumped him on the back affectionately.

"Javeer, my boy." With out-stretched arms, Heathel hobbled over and grabbed both his arms, shaking them. "You won, you bold, stubborn fool-of-a-man!"

Javeer leaned over and hugged her. "I accept your insults, Heathel."

"I feel right proud to know you! It was a dang-lucky day when I met you and an even luckier one when I met Laeli."

"What, why me?" Laeli asked in astonishment.

"Cause, without you, Javeer never would have kept coming back to my shop, and I wouldn't be at this race."

Javeer laughed, and Laeli blushed. "Yes," Javeer agreed. "That *was* a lucky day." He gave Laeli a warm smile, his green eyes glowing.

As Heathel pulled Lyon aside and began to chat excitedly with him, Laeli inched closer to Javeer. "You've got a smudge." She reached out and rubbed her thumb against his cheek.

"It's ok. I'm going to go wash up in a minute." Javeer gently pushed her hand away. "Maybe it's a bit late to be telling you this, but you probably shouldn't touch me. I fell in dirty water. I'm absolutely gross."

"It's ok. I saw it on the recording. I don't mind."

"I'm all sweaty."

"I don't care. So what if you are?"

"I probably smell."

"*And?*"

"And now you probably do too cause you hugged me."

Laeli casually shrugged then tilted her head. "I can hug you again," she suggested playfully.

"Hey now, girl! Without my permission?"

"Sure."

"Are you *sure?*"

"Yes."

"Then here...I'll do it for you!" Javeer lunged forward. With a squeal, Laeli tried to rush away, but he grabbed her and pulled her towards him. "You silly," he chuckled. "You thought you could escape."

"I don't want to escape. *See.*" Placing her hands on his jacket, Laeli pulled him towards her and gave him a quick kiss on the cheek. Laughing at the astonished look he gave her, she gently rubbed away another smudge on his face. "There, it's almost gone. I can see your freckles now...like your own little constellation." Laeli cocked her head anxiously. "What is it?" A glassy look had appeared in Javeer's eyes.

"My mother once said that to me," he murmured. "Just the way you did."

"Oh." Laeli froze for a moment. A flashback of her own mother wiping away her tears after they fled Nobiles overwhelmed her, and she immediately had to fight the urge to cry. Noticing her changed demeanor, Javeer reached out and brushed away a single tear drop that had started to slide down her face.

"Hey now, stop that," he ordered gently. "You are not allowed to cry today." Then he winced. "*Oops.* Uhhh, I might have just gotten dirt on you. I forgot to take my glove off."

Laeli laughed and wiped off the remainder of her tears. "It's ok. I can wash my face later."

"Speaking of washing...imma go do that now." Javeer yanked off his glove and placed his hand on top of Laeli's head. "You silly girl...go back home with my father and Heathel. I'll meet you there."

***

Javeer gave a small groan once he reached the public showers. It wasn't until now that he realized just how sore he was. His back and shoulders ached and a throbbing pain pulsed in his neck. Inwardly cringing, he peeled off his jacket and pulled his shirt over his head. He gave a sigh as the cold water rushed over his shoulders. The icy sensation felt good against his skin.

As Javeer washed, a few of the other contestants who were also rinsing themselves kept side-eyeing him. Some did so with curiosity, while others with scowls on their faces. Then one of them stepped forward, his hand outheld.

"Congrats!" he exclaimed. Somewhat suspiciously, Javeer paused and glanced at his outstretched hand. "I mean it," the man continued. "Congrats." Javeer took the man's hand and shook it firmly.

"Thank you."

"Yes, congratulations," a smooth voice interjected. Startled, the man slid aside, and Malin stepped forward, accompanied by his three bodyguards. Many of the contestants quickly turned away, guilty expressions on their faces, while the rest watched wide-eyed. Javeer stiffened; his face shifting from friendly to passive.

"I'm afraid we've never met before," Malin continued. "It's good to meet your acquaintance. How does it feel to be a rich man?"

Javeer slowly pushed the wet hair away from his forehead. "Not sure yet. I haven't thought about it much."

Malin smiled. "You will once you have the money in your possession. The feel of *koin* in your hand is such...such a *soothing* one. You beat my son in the race. I must extend my compliments! I did not think that was possible."

Javeer smirked. "Neither did I." By now, the tension in the room had grown exponentially. Everyone was watching with bated breath to see what would happen next.

Malin's smile only grew wider. "An honest man. I admire that! You know...you are one of the richest men in this city now. If I'm not mistaken, a young smart man like you wants to make good use of that prize money. I imagine you have a head for business. I would love to be able to partner with you. You see...I like anything related to business, and I think you and I could work very well together. What do *you* think?"

Now it was Javeer's turn to smile. "If I should find that to be profitable to me then I might be open to it."

"I'll be sure to see that you do."

"I hope so." With another grin, Javeer turned his back away and continued washing. "Was a pleasure meeting you."

Malin took a tight breath, the smile still firmly imprinted on his face. "We can meet again soon. I always host a celebration at my casino after the race. Usually a small fee is required for entry, but I think I can waive that for you. In two days: nine at night. Invite anyone you like. Shall we talk more then?"

"Sure." Javeer faced Malin and held out his hand. "Till then."

Exhaling through his nose, Malin slowly extended his arm. A sparkle that was both wary and dangerous twinkled in his eyes. "It will be my pleasure! I'll be waiting." He brushed past Javeer and strode out of the washroom, followed by his bodyguards. Javeer watched him go, his heart thumping loudly. Malin had acted as if he had no idea he'd just attempted to sabotage him completely. Yet...he had also just offered him the chance he'd been waiting for. *Malin is going to try and play me. If I want to be successful, I'll need to play the game too...and play it better.*

If I get close to Malin...pretend friendship...maybe I'll learn some things.

Realizing that he'd better control his emotions around the other men, Javeer relaxed his posture and finished his wash. He dried his hair and face with a towel and reached for the spare jacket his father had handed him a few moments ago. He had it half way on when suddenly all the men in the room began fidgeting nervously. Javeer stiffened, for standing in the middle of the washroom was Bria.

"You're not supposed to be in here," he declared harshly.

"What are you going to do...kick me out?" Bria took a step closer, tilting her head and placing a hand on her hip. "I don't know if that would be wise."

"It was unwise for you to come here."

"I don't understand you." With a sad droop to her mouth, Bria got even closer. "What is it you want?"

"Nothing."

"Liar! Every man wants something." Bria's eyes drifted over Javeer's chest and shoulders and then back to his face. "I know what *I* want."

Glaring at her, Javeer buttoned up his jacket and picked up the dirty clothes hanging nearby. He turned to go, but Bria seized his arm.

"Javeer!" She quickly blocked his way, both hands clutching his arms. "Whatever you want; I'd give it to you! Why do you refuse me? *Why?"*

"I don't want you."

Bria let go of him, her nostrils flaring. "Oh, yes! I suppose you want that little girl who clung to you after the race. Her and her admiration. *Ha*. Why, she's simply using you. All your success, all your aspirations: how soon did she know about them? I'm sure she found them *very* inspiring. But I...*I* wanted you long before you were anyone! I humiliate myself in front of everyone here to prove it. What more do I have to do?" She pressed her face close to his. "What more shall I say to convince you of...of what I *feel?*"

Javeer gave her look of disdain. "You'll never convince me." He brushed past her and started to walk out of the washroom. Bria whirled about, her bracelets trembling, and her face livid.

"Answer me! What has she got that I haven't??"

Without looking back, Javeer replied, "A heart."

A breathy hiss escaped Bria's mouth. "I have a heart too, and I can show you just what kind! I can make her life a living hell. I can have Malin..."

Bria didn't get any further because dropping his clothes to the floor, Javeer lunged around and grabbing her by the neck, shoved her into the damp wall. Bria let out a terrified gasp. The watching men advanced in a half circle, their bodies poised to spring.

"You stay away from her," Javeer seethed in low tones, "or I'll tell Khar what I've heard today!"

For a minute terror flickered in Bria's eyes, but then she laughed. "He would never believe you."

"Oh, I think he would."

Bria scowled and then smiled sneakily. "Go ahead…take that chance." She giggled. "Now I know what it takes for you to touch me. I've got to get you angry, eh? You do it *very* well."

Disgusted, Javeer released his hand from her throat and grabbing his clothes, strode out of the washroom. Removing herself from the wall, Bria watched him go, rubbing her hand against her neck. Then with a furious exclamation, she rushed away in the opposite direction.

***

Laeli rested her head on her arms, her elbows stretched across the table. Heathel was still chatting away to nobody in particular in the corner of Javeer's kitchen, and Lyon had left with Javeer, who had gone to lock the prize money in the basement. A yawn overtook Laeli, just in time for Heathel to notice.

"What? Are you tired, girl? You're not the one who did the racing!"

"I might has well have," Laeli joked.

"What do you mean?"

Laeli shook her head. "Never mind." She yawned again.

"Go step outside. The cool air will wake you up."

"Alright, Heathel." Laeli flung back her head playfully. "I *will*." Rising from her chair, she walked down the hallway and opened the door that lead to the back patio. She closed her eyes and sighed as the night breeze fanned her hair. Throwing back her head, she gazed at the sky but there were no stars out tonight. The moon too was hidden and only thick clouds could be seen.

Suddenly, a rustling sound distracted Laeli from her thoughts. Her fists clenching, she faced the direction the noise was coming from. The silhouette of a person became visible; it was getting closer. Laeli hesitated, her heart racing. Should she confront the figure or fetch Javeer? Before she could decide, the figure emerged from the shadows. Laeli breathed a sigh of relief. It was only Jace, his hand outstretched.

"It's just me, girl! Didn't mean to scare ya."

"What are you doing here?"

"I gotta speak to Javeer. Where is he?"

"He's inside. Want me to go get him?"

"Yup...I mean please."

"Ok." Making her way back into the house, Laeli peeked into the kitchen. "Heathel, is Javeer back yet?" From behind, she felt a hand touch her shoulder.

"Right here."

"Oh." Laughing, Laeli whirled around. "Can you come outside with me? Someone wants to see you."

"You're so popular!" Heathel interjected merrily from her corner in the kitchen.

"Who is it?" Javeer asked.

"It's Ja..."

Javeer shook his head, and Laeli paused in confusion. With a slight head gesture, he nodded towards Lyon, who was starting to come up from the basement steps. Realizing what he meant,

Laeli nodded and stealthily, the two of them snuck down the hallway and outside.

"My father doesn't like him," Javeer whispered as he shut the door behind him.

"Why?"

"I'm afraid I can't tell you why."

"Javeer!" Jace interrupted the conversation, his arms outstretched. Flinging himself on Javeer, he roughly pushed him and immediately they were locked together in a playful tussle.

"Stop!" Javeer ordered between chuckles. "My dad will hear and then he'll come out and see you."

"What is this? You two or somethin'? Scared of daddy?" Jace placed him in a chokehold. "I don't give a damn what your dad thinks. I had to see you. Somethin' important you gotta know."

"Really, huh?" With one rapid twist, Javeer broke free and knocked Jace to the ground. Jace winced and groaned.

"Ow, *son-of-a-bitch*. What'd you do that for?"

"Sorry, are you hurt?" Javeer held out his hand. Jace reached out, but Javeer quickly pulled it back. "*Sike.*"

"Ass! You gotta teach me. I can fight but not like that." Jace rose to his feet. "You'd be so great as..." His voice trailed off, and he glanced at Laeli.

She smiled politely. "I'll go inside."

"Hey, girl, don't take offense. It's just somethin' I gotta tell him alone."

"Don't worry, I'm not offended." As she walked back towards the door, Laeli gave Javeer's dreadlocks a gentle tug. Then she dashed inside with a stifled giggle before he had time to react.

Jace squinted his eyes. "What's it like...having her?"

"It's amazing. She's the best girl ever."

"*Huh.*" Jace shook his head and rubbed a hand through his curls. "She is kinda cute and all. Wouldn't know what that kind of girl is like. I only...well...*you* know."

"Yes, *I do.*" Javeer gave him a shove forward. "What was it you were gonna tell me?"

"I been sneakin' around the city. You got popular real quick! Everyone be talkin' about you. Your little place here is gonna get flooded with business."

"It'll be good for my dad." Javeer lowered his voice. "What have you heard?"

"People all over the city are wantin' to work with you. Help you *invest*...all that shit. Everybody is wonderin' who bet so much on you."

"So am I."

"You mean you haven't guessed?"

"Guessed what?"

"Damn, you didn't even suspect?"

Javeer frowned. "What are you talking about?"

Jace smirked. "Consider sixty-eight thousand of that prize money as a little gift from me."

Javeer took a step back in stunned disbelief. "*What?*"

"You heard me."

"You're lying."

"I ain't lyin'!"

"How the hell did you get sixty-eight thousand *koin??*"

"I have my ways." Jace gave a proud sniff.

Shaking his head, Javeer backed away. "I don't want any of your dirty money. Who knows how you got it."

Jace scowled. "What do ya mean? You think I'm foolin'? That money's yours now! I can't take it back. And what's wrong with it anyways?"

"I don't want anything that you got illegally from one of your crime schemes. I won't..."

"See here!" Angrily, Jace thumped Javeer's shoulder. "You think I *stole* that kind of money? The hell I didn't! I made a deal...and a good deal it was too."

"What deal? With *who?*"

"I can't tell you yet."

"Why not?"

"You'd gotta do somethin' for me before I'd tell you."

Javeer glared at Jace. "What does that mean? Do *what?*"

"*Look.*" Jace flung both his palms up. "You're in a lot of danger! Sure, majority of the city might love you right now, but love ain't gonna protect you. Malin runs the gangs, and Malin..."

"You don't need to tell me about Malin. I've already..."

"Yeah, yeah, I know. You got your own plans, your own ways. But Malin has a gang workin' for him. You need somebody workin' for you."

"Meaning??"

"Meanin'…accept my help…join my gang! No one else needs to know, but my men will help you if you join. You'll be gettin' power and protection. *I* can give that to you."

"I'm not joining your gang!" Javeer snapped. "This stinkin' city is ruined cause of gangs. It'll…"

"Get a damn grip and face reality!" Jace snarled. "This ain't Nobiles. This is Cuniculum. Your high and mighty ideals don't work here! You think that race was legal? It was full of cheatin', through and through. Everyone here's a criminal at some point. You better work with what you've got, or you'll be kicked aside so fast you won't know what's happened. Think about your girl! How you gonna protect her, huh? Everybody saw her at the race. Yeah, *I* was there…I saw her. Ya think the Night Tunnel Gang didn't see her too? It's just your damn pride, nothin' else. You're no better than anybody else in this shit-hole. Stop pretendin' like you can afford to be."

"I'm not listening to you." Javeer swat Jace away and turned his back on him.

"Yes…you are gonna listen. You be listenin' right now! Deep down you know I'm right. You just afraid what you're old man gonna think if you do as I say…if you do what you *should!*"

"You still haven't told me who gave you the sixty-eight thousand *koin*."

"And I ain't gonna…until you let me know if you'll accept my offer. I'll let you sleep on it. You oughta know my gang's not the average kind. There's no shame in joinin' it." Jace began to back away. "Just remember…you're a rich man now cause of me! You can't do this alone. I hate Malin and the Night Tunnel Gang too. They killed my mom and dad. They killed my sis. Better watch out, or they'll kill Laeli."

Javeer said nothing as Jace rounded the corner and disappeared. He could feel his heart pounding violently in his chest. Letting out an angry shout, he kicked a nearby bush, sending its leaves spraying in all directions. Then he crouched to his feet, his hand over his face. With a muffled groan, he stayed there, Jace's words repeating in his head.

Jace is right. I know Jace is right, but I hate that he is! If something happens to Laeli, it will be my fault. Bria has already threatened her. With another groan, Javeer rubbed his forehead and rose to his feet. *I'll say nothing to Father…or Laeli. I'll meet Malin at the casino and see what happens. He wouldn't try anything yet…it's too soon. I'll wait…I MUST wait…before I decide.*

Chapter 12
Party Planning

Khar slammed his glass down on the table, his bloodshot eyes staring heavily ahead at nothing. He moodily fingered the rim of the knife in his hand. It was a knife with an elongated silver blade, a black snake curling around the hilt. Picking up the glass, Khar raised it to his lips and took another drink. At that moment, Malin swiftly approached.

"Well? What have you heard?"

Khar set the glass on the table and gave an acidic laugh. "One day later and the whole damn city is *enthralled* with him. Yes, Father, can you believe it? I used the word *enthralled*. You should be so proud. I'm using fancy words like that icy-eyed business partner of yours."

"Don't mess with me!" Malin snapped. "I don't have time for your jokes. They stink - almost as much as you do right now. How much have you drank?"

"Not enough." Khar pushed the glass away and gripped his knife. "Why not, Father?" he grunted. "Why not let me..."

"You *fool*. If you go after him now everyone will know who did it. He's not like any other contestant. No biker ever had seventy thousand *koin* bet on them! I need to know who put up that bet."

"It doesn't matter, Father. If I get..."

"*No.* They'll know it was us." Malin began to pace back and forth. "It's too soon. Too soon for us to do anything."

"So what then? You gonna become friends with the stinkin' rat?"

"There is more than one way to destroy a man." Malin opened his arms wide as if he were releasing a wave of wisdom. "You just have to be patient."

"Ha! *Patient.* And before you know it, he'll have you in a jam - the whole city on his side...*forever.*"

"I didn't realize you were so dramatic." Malin chuckled condescendingly. "You forget; people have short memories."

"Well I don't." Khar drained the rest of his drink and waved the knife in his hand. "Oh look, here comes your pretty business partner. The devil himself couldn't have better timing. Imma leave him to you. Can't stand the sight of him." Letting the glass drop to the table with a thud, Khar shoved past his father and glowered at Kye before leaving the room.

"He's drunk...don't mind him." Malin gestured to a chair. "Please, sit down."

Kye seated himself at the table, his shoulders thrown back and head held high and stiff. "I trust all is well?"

"I'm having a bit of trouble, but I'll find a way to handle it." Malin grinned slyly. "I suppose I should let you know; I'm hosting an event tomorrow here at the casino. That's why it's empty right now. Preparations are being made. I extend an invitation to you. Hope to see you then."

Kye nodded. "Very well. I shall come."

"Good, good."

"And how are you enjoying our trade deal so far?"

"It's working beautifully for me. The specimen you gave me is very...*efficient*."

"And the others?"

"I'll have them on full display tomorrow."

"Wonderful. I am glad I came to confirm." Kye rose to his feet. "I shall be at your event tomorrow. Until then." With a slight bow, he turned and walked away.

***

"I'm telling you, Bria." Khar had his arms around his girlfriend's waist but now he loosened them, twirling his knife between his fingers. Both of them were standing near the entrance of the main room in the Casino, which had been emptied for a thorough cleaning. "My father plans to associate with that wretch. The *humiliation*...that I should have to bear with the likes of him! What does my father think I am?"

Bria placed a hand against his arm. "He knows what you are...but he doesn't care. He would rather play it safe and..."

"You don't understand my father. He's not playing it safe. He's playing a game. He's *always* loved to play games. I don't have patience for games. I like to fight."

"Will *you* fight him?"

"My father? No. I see no profit in that...*yet*." Khar ran a finger along the flat part of his blade. "But there're others I'd fight...if he'd let me." He laughed cynically and wrapped his arm around Bria, his chest against her back. With his other hand, he brought the knife close to her throat, the blade gleaming in the reflection of the overhanging light fixture. "Look...look how it shines. Beautiful ain't it?"

Taking hold of Khar's wrist, Bria stretched the knife away from her neck and turned to face him, throwing one arm around his shoulder and the other around his waist. "Don't worry," she whispered. "I know you...you'll have revenge. Let me help you plan it!"

Khar chuckled low in his throat. "You're a snake, just like me. That must be why I love you."

"Because you love yourself? How disappointing."

"Disappointing? I don't think so." Khar leaned in to kiss her, then paused to stare past her face with a disgusted expression. His voice dropped. "Here comes my father's business partner. White-faced fool! I *hate* him." Khar released his hold on Bria. "I can see him judging us from here."

"So? Let him judge. Who cares what he thinks?"

"What do I think?" Kye halted in front of them, a small smile on his lips.

"I don't know!" Khar stepped towards him, the knife pointed to his chest. "Why don't you tell us? Why are you *really* in Cuniculum?"

"I am here to conduct business. Why do you find that so distasteful?"

"I find the way you *talk* distasteful," Khar jeered. "Your accent almost sounds familiar. I'm trying to think where I've heard it before." He pointed the knife even closer to Kye's chest. "Perhaps you can tell me."

"I do not see how you would expect me to know."

"Oh...my apologies." With a dramatic wave of his hand, Khar bowed low. "I should've known better than to ask you any questions. Please...*forgive me*." With a final sneer, he turned and stomped away.

Kye turned his head towards Bria, who raised one eyebrow at him. Without speaking, his eyes bore into her own as if searching for something.

Bria frowned. "Why do you look at me like that?"

"I find it humorous."

"You're making fun of me. Find *what* humorous?"

"What do you think it is?"

"I'm telling you, you ass...I don't know!"

Kye gave her a patronizing smile. "That is what is humorous. Good day."

With perplexed irritation, Bria watched as he casually strode out of sight. "*Prick*."

***

Laeli burst into Heathel's shop, panting from excitement and exhaustion. "Heathel, *Heathel*. I need your help!"

Heathel emerged from behind the counter, clutching an iron wrench in her hand. "Goodness, girl. What's wrong?"

"I'm going...to the casino tomorrow," Laeli gulped. "Javeer didn't want me to come, but I insisted. I told him it would look like we were scared if I didn't show up. You can't be scared in front of these people."

"My, my! You are learning the ways of this place very quickly now." Heathel waved the wrench in Laeli's face. "Though I still don't know if goin' with him is a good idea. I think you know it ain't too safe...but I guess there's no changin' a girl's mind when she's got a crush. Besides, who knows...maybe it'll be real interestin'"

"Yes, but you see...I don't know what to wear. I got a dress of my mother's, but I don't want to wear that to an event like this. I want to save it."

"No problem girl. *I've* got just the thing. You forget, I was quite the partier back in the day! Ahh, the stories I could tell." Chuckling, Heathel hobbled over to a closet covered with a makeshift drape and pulled out an old chest. "Granted, it's a little flamboyant, but that's just what you want for this kind of event. I was the same size as you when I was your age so this should work." Undoing the lock, she opened the chest door and pulled off a layer of thin cloth, revealing a dress underneath.

"It's neon green?"

"I wouldn't say neon. More like a very bright green leaf."

"Will I look all right in that?" Laeli asked anxiously.

"If you let me fix you up you will. I know just how to do it." Heathel rose to her feet, unfolding the dress and letting it dangle to the ground. "I think it'll fit nicely, but you better try it on." She shoved the dress into Laeli's arms. "Go, go; put it on and see how it fits. If nothing needs alterin', you can take it home and come back to me tomorrow before the event. I'll fix you up all proper." Seeing Laeli's perplexed expression, Heathel gave her a playful push. "Go on! Try it on. Get going, girl."

***

"I do not like this."

"It doesn't matter, Ren. I'm going." Setting her mouth stubbornly, Laeli ran the brush through her hair.

"It is not safe! You will be surrounded by criminals. Many of these people are going to hate you."

"If I don't go, these people will think I'm afraid. And I have to be there for Javeer."

"If you go you will only refresh these peoples' memory of you. Avoid them! If Javeer was any good he would not tell you to go."

Laeli slammed the brush on the table and whirled around to face Ren. "He didn't tell me to go! He told me *not* to. *I* insisted on going."

"You should listen to him."

Laeli's shoulders drooped. "I...I *can't*. I can't stand not being around him. If something were to happen...I *need* to be there. When he crashed during the race I..." Laeli took a shuddery breath. "Maybe being present is painful but not knowing what is happening is even worse."

Ren bowed his head. Then he placed a hand on Laeli's shoulder. "You are like your mother."

Laeli looked up quickly. "What do you mean?"

Ren slowly shook his head and walked away. "I cannot tell you."

Laeli sighed. "I should have known that would be your answer." She smoothed the hair from her face and walked towards the door.

"Wait." Ren picked up the taser lying on the table beside him and held it out to her. "Bring this."

Laeli took a deep breath. "Ren, if something happens I don't think that'll help much. I..."

Seizing her hand, Ren pulled it towards him and placed the taser in her palm. "*Take it.*"

Laeli took a deep breath. "All right."

***

"Heathel?" Laeli poked her head through the shop door. It creaked loudly as she pushed it open. Shutting the door behind her and locking it with her spare key, Laeli carefully stepped through the dark room. From the bottom of a side door in the very back of the shop, she could see a light glowing. As she made her way to the door, something metal poked her arm and with a gasp Laeli sprung back, grabbing the taser from her waist. Then she breathed a sigh of relief. It was only a deactivated robot, its limp form leaning against the wall.

"Laeli-girl?" The side door swung open, and Heathel stepped out. "I just heard you. You ok?"

"I, uh...yeah. I just got startled is all." Shakily, Laeli placed the taser back against her belt.

"Goodness, girl, you've got the jitters. No worries! I'll make sure to get them out of you. Let's start, eh? Javeer should be here in a few hours." Guiding Laeli into her living quarters, Heathel gently pushed her into a chair and turned on a nearby lamp. "I've got everything right here. Eyeliner, blush, hair accessories...You ever wear makeup before, girl?"

"Uh...no."

"Pft! Have you been living under a rock? What kind of girl are you? Here, go put the dress on." Heathel dumped the outfit into Laeli's lap. "Go...come on, *come on*. I want to see you in it." She propelled Laeli towards a nearby closet and shut the door. "Haha, I'll be waiting."

In the dark closet, Laeli clutched the dress towards her chest. She could feel her heart thumping. She stared at the sea of green in her hands and then nervously unwound her belt. *I've never worn a dress before. I wonder if that's why I'm nervous. Or maybe I'm just scared. Perhaps Ren was right...I should have stayed home. I don't know what I'm doing. Ugh, stop thinking! Just put the dress on.*

Once Laeli was finally in the dress and stepped out of the closet, Heathel squealed and clapped her hands like a little child. "Laeli-girl! It looks so *good* on you. Gracious, you're tiny. You've got less waist than I do. Do you eat enough?"

Laeli laughed anxiously. "Yes. I...uh...I don't know how to do the back."

"Here, turn around." Spinning Laeli in the opposite direction, Heathel tied the ribbon that dangled from the silk collar around Laeli's neck and then straightened out the folds that cut open to a small V-shape over Laeli's upper back. "There. Look in the mirror." Laeli obeyed, and her mouth dropped. The silk dress hugged her slim hour-glass figure, its bottom loosening in a flowy manner around her lower legs. Laeli stood speechless as she gazed at herself until Heathel gently tapped her bare shoulder. "See how good you look? Sit down, girl. Imma do your makeup, but first we gotta do somethin' about that hair. It can't stay like that. *Ooh.* How about I do dreadlocks?"

"I mean...would that look good?"

"Of course girl, of course! I'll do the braided ones. It'll look good, don't worry."

"Ok, Heathel. I trust you." Laeli obediently seated herself in front of the mirror and for the next hour, Heathel meticulously twisted her hair into petite braids that ran down her head and against her neck. Then she applied eye-liner and mascara to

Laeli's eyes and a light touch of blush to her cheeks. She slid a silver bracelet over Laeli's wrist and stepped back.

"*Ahh*," Heathel gushed. "You look stunnin'! Don't you think so?"

Laeli giggled shyly. "Yes." She leaned in more closely towards the mirror. "It doesn't even look like me."

"Oh...I forgot lip rouge."

"No, I don't like lip rouge."

"Ah, well, suit yourself." Heathel walked off and returned holding Laeli's taser in her hand. "Don't forget to bring this with you."

"But where will I put it?"

"Strapped around your leg under your dress of course! I did that once. I have the straps still...let me see where I put them. Hmm...I know they're here somewhere. Ah, found it."

Laeli took the taser from Heathel's hand and hastily set it down. "Are you sure this is a good idea?"

"Absolutely." Heathel straightened, and her eyes lit up. "I hear a motorcycle. You better hurry."

***

Javeer slid off his bike, a strange sensation churning in the pit of his stomach. As he walked up to Heathel's shop, his hands automatically shifted to the tasers at either side of his belt. All day he had felt more and more on edge. Jace's words would not leave his mind. Like a swarm of bats, they swirled around in his head, confusing him. Javeer took a deep breath and closed his eyes. He would make up his mind soon. He just had to get through the casino event first.

Heathel's bubbly voice distracted Javeer momentarily as she swung open the shop door. "Javeer, my boy. Hello! I'm so glad you're here. Why do you look so dark? Are you wearing *all black?* Good grief, I can barely see you. Get inside." Clutching his arm, she yanked him through the door. "There, that's a bit better. *OH.* You look *very* dashing. The black works after all."

Javeer laughed. "Glad to hear it meets with your approval."

"*Mhm.* You came at the perfect time. Laeli is all ready." At that moment, Laeli walked out of the back door and stepped forward shyly. Javeer's mouth dropped open, and he stood there speechless. Heathel chuckled naughtily. "Hehe, cat got your tongue?" She winked at Laeli. "The cat *definitely* got his tongue."

"Good evening," Laeli greeted him in a tiny voice. "How are you?"

"I...I'm well. And you?"

"Pft! What is this nonsense! Why are you getting all formal?" Heathel rolled her eyes. "Stop being ninnies and say something normal." She gave Javeer a shove.

"I...uh...you look so different," he stammered.

Heathel flung up her hands. "What an idiot. You look *different.* How do you like that, eh? Not...*you look beautiful*...or *I'm so impressed.* Different! That's all he could think of to say. *Men.*" She pushed Laeli towards Javeer and placed her hand into his.

"There! Both of you get out of here. *Different.* All the men I knew when I was young were much bolder."

"Sometimes I question the kind of men you must have known, Heathel," exclaimed Javeer sarcastically.

"Oh, so now he can speak. Get out of here you *punk.* And take good care of her!"

"Always." Smirking, Javeer opened the door for Laeli. "Night, Heathel."

"Yes, good night, Heathel," Laeli chimed in. "Thank you so much."

"Not at all, girl, not at all. Be careful now." With a final wave, Heathel shut the door behind them.

"She's so sweet." Laeli glanced back at the shop fondly. "She gave me this dress."

"It's very beautiful." Javeer took a step back. "You look stunning," he murmured. "It almost doesn't look like you."

"Is...is that bad?"

"No...I love it. It's an amazing look." Javeer ran a finger lightly over her hair. "The braids are *perfect.*"

Laeli laughed in happy relief. "I'm glad you like them. They took Heathel a long time to fix." Her eyes wandered over his midnight black shirt, gold neck chain, and neatly, pushed-back dreadlocks. "You look very nice too! I like this." She fingered the open collar of his shirt.

"Thank you." Guiding Laeli to the motorcycle, Javeer slipped his jacket over her shoulder, mounted, and held out his hand.

"Umm, I think I'll have to sit sideways."

"I'll drive as fast as possible!" Javeer joked. "Haha, just kidding. No, worries, I'll go slow." Meticulously helping her behind him, Javeer started the motorcycle. His voice became more serious. "Did you bring anything to protect yourself with? Just in case?"

"Yes, I have a taser with me."

"You do? Where is it?"

"Under my dress," Laeli blurted out. Then she blushed.

Javeer grinned. "*Ah*, I see." He revved the motorcycle engine and together they rode off down the street towards their destination.

Chapter 13
Casino Drama

Malin's casino was brilliantly lit, floods of yellow light spilling out of its many windows. The music's bass could be heard over a mile down Cuniculum's streets, and people's laughter rang out into the air as they chatted on the multiple overhanging balconies. As Javeer's motorcycle pulled up close, Laeli flung her head back to stare at the building's height. She let out a shaky breath.

"It's so *big*."

"Yeah, it is. Malin wouldn't accept less." Turning off his bike, Javeer bolted it with his key and disc lock. Then he removed the jacket from Laeli's shoulders, slung it over the bike's seat, and placing a hand behind her waist, walked with her up the steep hill to the casino's entrance. By the front door stood a bouncer, a slick smile on his face. He inclined his head politely as they approached.

"Greetings! It's an honor to have you here. I understand that you're permitted free entry tonight."

"Yes, thanks." Javeer took a step forward. The bouncer held out his hand.

"I'm afraid *she* has to pay though."

Javeer's expression darkened. "I was told to invite whoever I wanted. No charge was mentioned."

"Sorry for the misunderstanding, but I'm afraid it's still required for her. Just cause she's with you doesn't give her a free pass." The bouncer smirked. "She's not the type who could get in for free anyway."

"*You little...*" Bristling with rage, Javeer took a threatening step towards the bouncer, but Laeli quickly shook her head at him. Javeer scowled and took a step back. "Where's Malin?"

"You'll find him on the second floor."

Without answering, Javeer pushed past him into the casino. The bouncer gave Laeli a condescending grin. "Your boyfriend has a temper."

Laeli eyed him stonily but said nothing. With a little shrug of his shoulders, the bouncer turned to the next wave of people. Stepping sideways, Laeli tried peering through a nearby window, but Javeer was nowhere to be seen.

***

As Javeer angrily weaved his way through the crowds of people in the casino, exclamations and whispers began to ripple through the building like a momentous shockwave. People lowered their drinks and others their cigarettes, as they observed up close, the celebrated winner of the motorcycle race. People began to talk among one another, their heads bent close together in fascinated suspense.

"That's definitely him! He's got the green eyes and freckles."

"An odd look ain't it?"

"So is Malin friends with him now?"

"I bet Malin hates his guts."

"I hate Malin's guts too but *shhh*. Don't repeat that! Where else in town can I have so much fun as here?"

"No, you're wrong; him and Malin are partners. Malin personally invited him to the casino."

"So we'll have two scumbags running the city instead of one."

"Not that I care but this will be *interestin'*."

"They say he's the second richest man in the city."

"Why does he look so mad?"

"What a fine lookin' specimen! Does he need a girlfriend?"

"*I'd* be his girlfriend."

Oblivious to all the comments, Javeer marched on, his mouth set and brows furrowed. Just before reaching the staircase to the second floor, a young woman stepped in front of him.

"Hello, *handsome*. What's your name?"

"Not now." Javeer tried to dodge her, but she blocked his way.

"Come on, *tell me*. I want to know."

"Haven't you heard?" A second woman sidled over. She took a puff from her cigarette and blew the smoke in Javeer's face. "He's the young man who won the motorcycle race. The city's new champion."

A third woman suddenly joined in. "I didn't know you were so pretty." She placed a hand on his chest. "*Very* pretty."

"Careful, girlie," The woman with the cigarette raised an eyebrow. "He's already taken. Where's your little girlfriend, love? You didn't leave her behind did you?"

With an agitated breath, Javeer removed the woman's hand from his chest and physically pushed past the three of them. They all watched as he raced up the stairs. One of them sniffed. "Where's he goin' in such a hurry?"

The woman with the cigarette snickered. "Getting away from you, my dear."

***

Laeli clutched the side of her arm with her hand; the night air had become very chilly. She shifted from one foot to the other, wondering if Javeer was alright. The thought of possibly having to use the taser ran through her head, and it made her anxious. She let out a shaky sigh.

"Hello, my dear," exclaimed a voice, startling her. Turning quickly, she saw a middle-aged man approaching, wearing a pine-green suit thinly lined with mink fur and glossy brown boots. Rings of gold bearing emeralds and rubies rested on his fingers and a large silver band sat on his left thumb. As Laeli's eyes scoured him rapidly, she noticed behind him two tall robots. Her eyes widened, for these robots were not like any of the kind seen in Cuniculum. Their opaque forms were female, and their outer layer was smooth and creamy-white. Their blank eyes lacked pupils and both of them had perfectly identical noses and mouths. At their waists hung two shotguns. Seeing the perplexed hostility on her face, the man laughed.

"Don't worry, they're just my bodyguards. I'm sure they'll have no reason to bother you. What are you doing out here?"

"You're Malin, aren't you?"

"So you know my name. What's yours?"

Laeli didn't reply. Malin chuckled.

"I don't know your name, but your face looks very familiar. I think I must have seen you at the races...but where? Ah, yes! You're Javeer's girl; now I remember. Where is he? Surely he hasn't deserted you in this cold night air?"

"He's inside...looking for you. We were told you were on the second floor."

"Eh! I was not. Who told you that?"

"Him." Laeli pointed towards the bouncer.

"My deepest apologies. The man is a dunce. I'll set this straight." Malin placed a hand on Laeli's back and led her to the entrance. Her entire form grew rigid, but he did not let go as he turned to the bouncer. "What's this, man? Why did you inform the young lady that I was on the second floor?"

"Just obeying your orders, sir. The lady needed to pay in order to get in. Her boyfriend made a big stink about it so I told him..."

"I never gave you those instructions. I told you my guest was free to bring as many friends as he liked, without charge. You're a damn fool!"

"Very sorry. My..."

"Shut up." Turning to Laeli, Malin seized her hand and brought it to his lips. "So sorry this happened. I hope to make it up to you."

"You don't have to…"

"Of course I do." Winking at the bouncer when Laeli's back was turned, Malin took her arm and linked his own through it. Laeli's face paled slightly, but she made no resistance as he led her through the doors, followed by his robotic guards. "I have *every* intention of making it up to you in any way possible," he whispered in her ear. A ripple of astonishment ran through the casino at the sight of Malin's robots, but he pretended not to notice. "Please permit me to show you how."

Inwardly panicking, Laeli scoured the room to see if there was a way out of the situation and then her eyes grew large. "Kye!" she blurted out. Sure enough, Kye stood there a couple feet away in his customary black. With a few quick strides, he stood in front of her and then looked at Malin, a harsh glint in his eyes.

His demeanor shifting from one of charming confidence to perplexed disbelief, Malin loosened his hold on Laeli's arm. "You know each other?"

"Yes. Hello, Laeli." Kye offered her his arm. Grateful to see a familiar face, Laeli took it and let Kye lead her away from Malin, who remained rooted to the spot with an expression of almost comical consternation.

"Thank you," she whispered.

"Of course."

"Kye, how on earth did Malin get hold of those robots? They don't manufacture that model here in Cuniculum. Those are seven-99 models. They're used as guards for nobility in the Five Cities."

"I cannot say. I must assume they are a product of his black market deals."

"But the Five Cities don't trade seven-99 models. My mother told me so." Laeli frowned. "Wait, why are *you* here? You don't gamble do you?"

"No. I merely wanted to observe the celebration."

Laeli gave a snort. "This is no proper celebration. It's a set up!" Suddenly her eyes brightened. "Javeer!" Hearing her voice, Javeer scanned the room until he caught sight of her. Immediately, he walked in their direction.

A wary glower came over Kye's face. "What is he to you?"

"Why he..." Laeli paused mid-sentence. Something in Kye's tone made her unwilling to tell him the full truth. She slowly replied, "He's someone I admire."

Seemingly dissatisfied with the answer, Kye opened his mouth then clamped it shut once Javeer reached them. "Laeli," Javeer exclaimed, reaching for her hand. "How did you get in?"

"Malin let me in. He said there had been a mistake."

"Malin?" Javeer scowled. "I searched everywhere for him upstairs. No one had seen him." He turned to Kye suspiciously. "I recognize you. Pretty sure you said your name was Kye the last time we met. You come here often?"

"Yes."

"You don't strike me as the gambling type."

"Oh? What then, pray?"

"You kinda seem like someone who plans rather than gambles."

Kye's blue eyes held a glint of condescending surprise. "An interesting observation."

"Remind me; how do you two know each other?"

Laeli squeezed Javeer's hand. "We went to school together. We were little then."

"Ah, I see." Javeer spoke again to Kye sarcastically. "And now you're here, at a casino, but you don't like to gamble. So why show up then, huh? You came to see, Laeli?"

"Am I not allowed to be here?"

"Never said you weren't."

"Javeer, I need to talk to you." Laeli clutched his hand tightly. "Please, excuse us Kye." Kye nodded stiffly. Laeli pulled Javeer into a corner, the farthest place from listening ears that she could get, and lowered her voice.

"Don't let Kye get under your skin. I don't know why he's been acting like this. He used to be very happy...bubbly..."

"He's strange. I don't trust him, Laeli."

"He wasn't always that way." Laeli's face grew sad. "At times, when we're not together, I wish so badly I could help him, but whenever he's close by I almost lose all desire to. He makes me uncomfortable for some reason. I wish I could know what was wrong. He used to be so different!"

"That was a long time ago. Let him be. Trust your gut. People change, and not always for the better. He's a grown man; he's got to find his own way. I don't think he'd listen to what you'd say anyway."

Laeli bit her lip. "Probably not."

"Keep your distance. I don't know why he's here, but it's definitely not to gamble."

"I don't know why he's here either."

Javeer frowned. "I can guess one reason."

"What do you mean?"

"Think! I'm pretty sure it's already crossed your mind."

The sudden dulling of the lights distracted Laeli from answering. The deep boom of the song changed to a soft lull and several couples began to swing across the large space in the center of the casino. Gently putting a hand against Laeli's back, Javeer propelled her to the dance floor. Slipping his hand around her waist, they began to sway back and forth.

"Everyone's staring at us," Laeli murmured.

"Let them."

"What do you plan to do while you're here?"

Javeer laughed under his breath. "Get through this night! One thing I've learned already is every shallow person here is fascinated by me. In that sense, I guess I got an advantage. I feel Malin wants to ruin me, but he can't do it while I'm so popular."

"Then go...let people talk to you. Feed their interest."

"I'm not leaving you."

"It's all right. I'll wait here. I don't want to go up to all those people anyway."

"No, you're coming with me. I'm not leaving you alone again."

"You don't have to." Kye's voice emerged from behind, startling both of them. "I will watch her for you."

Javeer glowered at Kye. "There's no need."

"It would be no problem."

"I'm gonna disagree…"

"*Stop.*" Laeli stepped between them. "I will dance with you, Kye."

"*Laeli…*"

"It's fine, Javeer." Laeli gave him a pleading look. "Just for a little while." Javeer gave Kye one more glare and then slowly walked away. Laeli watched him as Kye lead her back to the dance floor. In the shadowy room, his blue eyes seemed translucent. Laeli gazed at them as if hypnotized. *How do his eyes look like that?*

"What is it?"

"Nothing. It's nothing." Laeli looked away and let Kye slowly weave her through the other couples.

"You used to share what you were thinking with me. Why do you not now?"

"That was a long time ago, and I never shared that much with you. I was little then."

"You are no longer the same."

Laeli's head shot up. "What do you mean?"

"I sense an apprehensiveness in you that was not present before."

Laeli frowned but in the center of her stomach, a tight knot twisted. "No, it's you who's not the same."

"How am I different from what I was before?"

"You...well...I don't know." Laeli looked at him helplessly, unwilling to say what she really thought. "You're moody...easily upset. You don't like the same things anymore."

A disturbed look crossed over Kye's face. "I have been living in my house alone. It is depressing. I have no friends here." His voice lowering, he spoke rapidly. "Laeli, come visit me! Then we could talk...away from people and distractions."

For one moment, Laeli was tempted to say yes. *I could help him maybe.* Then she remembered what Javeer had told her. "I...I'm sorry, Kye. I can't."

"Why not?"

"I'm too busy."

Kye's eyes seemed to penetrate hers. "You are lying."

Laeli took a sharp intake of breath. "Why would you say that?"

Kye paused, his eyes closing halfway as he stared her down. "You stutter when you are nervous. I have observed it. When you speak about something you are certain of, you do not stutter. I have concluded that you are not certain about me. Hence the stutter. Hence..." Kye's voice lowered to a whisper as he leaned towards her, "the *lie*."

Laeli turned her head away, her lips tightening. A cold weight seemed to sink in her chest. "Just keep dancing."

***

In a private corner of the casino's second floor, Bria sat across the table from Khar, glaring at him. He had already drained two glasses and was on his third, his shoulders slumped forward: eyes bloodshot. With an aggravated grunt, he sloshed the whiskey around in his glass before taking another sip.

"Are you going to come down with me or aren't you?" Bria finally exclaimed crossly.

Khar set the glass down with a thud. "I told you, I ain't goin' down there. My father can play his games, but I'm not gonna simp and smile for that *wretch*."

"You're a coward! You're just hiding because he beat you in the race, and I hate you for it." Bria slumped crossly in her seat. "I'm dying of boredom. I'm not waiting for you." She got up to leave, but springing to his feet, Khar reached over and pushed her back onto the cushion.

"You're stayin' right here!" he snarled.

"I am not!"

"You *are*."

"*I will NOT*." With a quick flip of her hand, Bria reached out and slapped his face. Then she froze, breathing hard. Instead of striking back, Khar only laughed and sat back down.

"That stung...a *little*."

Bria clenched her fist. Then she leaned forward pleadingly. "*Please*, baby. Come downstairs with me."

"No. I'm stayin' here and so are you. I don't care where you go so long as it's not downstairs."

"You're a bastard! I can't stand the sight of you." Bria slammed her hand on the table and rose to her feet. With an angry toss of her head, she walked over to the bar. "Give me a drink."

"Which one?" the bartender asked.

"Whiskey...*any* whiskey!" Bria snapped.

At that moment, Malin stormed in. Catching sight of Bria first, he rushed towards her. "Where's Khar?"

"In his corner...*sulking.*"

Malin grabbed her arm roughly. "*Why* have you not convinced him to come downstairs?"

Bria's eyes flashed. "There are a great many things I can convince your son to do *with* me, but I *can't* convince him to do anything *for* me."

Malin released his hold on her arm. "So...he won't come down?"

"No, and I'm stuck up here...looking at his drunken face. Well...it will be a drunken face...*soon.*"

"I won't let my own boy disobey me." A spark lit Malin's eyes. "I have an idea. For now, go downstairs."

With raised eyebrows, Bria obeyed. Malin walked over to Khar and sat across from him. "I'm screwed," he began fitfully. "A complication has come up."

Khar snorted into his drink. "What a shock! Did it make your heart skip?"

"This ain't funny," Malin's face reddened. "My *business partner* knows the little wench downstairs."

"Which one?"

"Javeer's *girlfriend*. You idiot, who else would I be referring to?"

"Don't know," was the sarcastic response. "With you it could be anyone."

"Shut up! It's no joking matter. Don't you see? If I do anything to her it could jeopardize my whole deal with *him*."

"I already told you how I would handle it if I were you." Khar tilted his head. "Let *me* take care of it...*my way*."

"*NO!*" Malin slammed both hands violently against the table. "You *will not* destroy everything I have put into place! I'll find another way."

"And..." Khar leaned back against his seat, "*what way* would that be again?"

"You're vexing me, boy," Malin seethed. "Don't test me!"

"Wouldn't dream of it."

"You remind me a great deal of your mother right now." Malin's tone became venomous. "She would give me the exact same insolent look and tone."

"So? What does it matter? You kept her in her place, just like you're keeping me in mine."

"And I'll continue to do so. You'd not be who you are without me."

"I think you forget...I could easily turn against you if I want-ed. I..."

Khar got no further. With a yell, Malin grabbed him by the collar and slammed him up against the wall.

"You'd not be where you are today were it not for me...*boy.*"

Khar's hand drifted towards the knife at his waist. "And you *forget*...how *I came* to be where I am today."

Malin dropped his hands from Khar and laughed raggedly.

"So what...are we going to keep this up then?"

"I mean... we *could* end it."

"I *will* end it. Come downstairs with me. Stop hiding up here like a skulking rat."

"I ain't hidin'. I'm just not goin' down. You can take care of this shit on your own. The only games I play are mine...*Father.*"

As if he weren't listening, Malin scanned the room. "Why, where did Bria go?"

Khar jumped to attention, his eyes searching for her. Then he scowled. "That bitch. I told her to stay up here!"

Malin chuckled. "You want to run more than you can chew, but you can't even keep hold of your own woman."

"Shut up." Shoving his father out of the way, Khar quickly made for the stairs.

***

Javeer shifted restlessly. In his ears, multiple voices pummeled him with eager questions but all he could think of was Laeli dancing with Kye. *I don't like it. Something about that man makes me uncomfortable. He's up to something. Laeli should stay far away from him. I shouldn't have let her dance with him. Ugh, I can't force her though. That wouldn't be right. Why does she put up with him anyway?*

"What do you think?" A woman's squeaky voice distracted Javeer from his thoughts.

"Uh...sorry. What were you asking?"

"I've heard you own your own business here in Cuniculum. They say you designed the motorcycle that *you rode* in the race. That true?"

"Uh, yeah...yeah."

"Ah, well I'd *love* you to work on something of mine! I've got the funds and been wantin' my bike fixed. It's got *three wheels* stead of two. I'd pay well. What do ya think? That something you could do?"

"Sure. Send the bike to my shop. We'll discuss the price after I take a look at it."

"Ahh, wonderful," the woman gurgled. She whipped out a piece of paper and a pen. "Write the address here." Javeer complied, then handed the paper back to her.

"Please, excuse me." Removing himself from the group, he walked close to the dance floor, his head spinning. He glanced again at Kye and Laeli. *I can't stare. Don't want to look weird. I need to find some sort of distraction.*

As Javeer stood there moodily, he suddenly felt a hand seize his arm and pull him onto the dance floor. It was Bria, and she smiled sneakily as he tried to tug free.

"You really want to cause a scene here and now? Dance with me, or I'll tell Malin to keep an eye on your little girlfriend. Just in case you didn't know, Malin listens to *me*." Sucking in his breath angrily, Javeer let his hands remain in hers. "That's better," she murmured.

"You *snake*."

"I know." Bria giggled quietly. "But I always get what I want, *remember?*" She smirked at the lethal glare Javeer gave her. "Is it really so bad...dancing with me? You should be pleased. You know how many men would want this?"

"Then give them what they want. You seem to have no problem doing it."

"You misunderstand me. *They* might want it, but I don't. I only wanted you...*of course*. You know, I could have given you *so* much."

"Oh, and I'm sure Khar would be ok with that."

"Khar, *hmm*. He has killed a man over me before. It was the man I was with before Khar. And you know what? I *let* Khar kill him."

Javeer dropped his hold on Bria's hands. "Get away from me."

Bria continued, "Because you see...I *always* get what I want. I wanted Khar. I got him. Then I wanted you, but you didn't want me back. And that's too bad...cause now I want *revenge*."

So quickly that Javeer didn't even have time to step away, Bria seized his hands and leaning forward, kissed him on the mouth. She abruptly pulled away, grinning smugly. "Have fun explaining that to your little girlfriend," she whispered. "I know she saw it." Without giving Javeer another glance, she swept past him and exited the room. Too stunned to react, Javeer stood rooted to the ground. Then he glanced up to see Laeli across the room, clinging to Kye's hands, her eyes wide. Yanking her hands from Kye's, she turned and walked off the dance floor. Kye's gaze traveled from Javeer, to Laeli, and then back to Javeer.

Javeer regained control of himself and hurried over to Laeli. "Laeli," he murmured miserably. "I did not do it! She..."

Laeli stared at the floor, clutching the side of her dress. "I...I don't know. I only saw the end..."

"Laeli, I *would not* do that to you. *Please* believe me! That hateful woman threatened you so I danced with her...she kissed me when I wasn't expecting it."

"Who saw?"

Javeer closed his eyes, his fists clenched. "I'm not sure."

Laeli took a deep breath. She recalled the wild look of hate Bria had given her at the race. She had seen the jealousy in her eyes, just as she saw now the distraught look in Javeer's. After a moment's hesitation, Laeli reached out and took Javeer's hand. "I believe you," she murmured. A poignant look of relief became visible on Javeer's face.

"Thank you," he whispered. His eyes darted sideways, and he straightened his posture. "Here comes Khar."

Barreling down the stairs, Khar stomped into the main room. His eyes scoured the area and with an angry grunt, he raced out the back exit, slamming the door behind him.

"Do you really think anyone else saw what Bria did?" Laeli asked again, nervously squeezing Javeer's hand.

"I don't think so. The room is very dark, and she came quietly."

Laeli tore her eyes away from the door Khar had just gone through. "I hope you're right."

At that moment, the room's atmosphere changed. The lights began to flash and a deep boom burst out, vibrating the floor beneath them. Cheers and yells erupted and soon the room was filled with drunken people, waving their drinks and laughing hysterically. As the music got louder and louder, the dancing became more and more wild.

"We need to go," Javeer muttered.

"Wait, where did Kye go?"

"Don't know, but it doesn't matter. Let's go." Javeer began to walk towards the entrance. Laeli turned to follow him when a rough hand grasped her shoulder.

"Hey, girlie, come dance with me!" a voice drawled. A tall lanky man with a scraggly beard and alcohol-glazed eyes yanked Laeli towards him. "Come on, girl, let's go!" The man flung both hands around her waist and lifted her off the ground. She could feel his hot breath all over her face.

"*Let her GO,*" Javeer roared. With a flying swing, his fist struck the man in the jaw. The man's head propelled backwards and blood spouted out of his mouth. He dropped Laeli and with one quick scoop of his arm, Javeer pulled her to safety. He landed another blow to the man's face. The man immediately catapulted backwards with a thud to the floor. Cries and shrieks erupted throughout the room as people desperately scurried out of the way.

"*Hey!*" The bouncer's voice emerged from behind, his fists raised.

"Javeer, look out!" Laeli cried. The bouncer lunged for Javeer but dodging sideways, Javeer grabbed his arm and with one twist, flipped the bouncer on his back onto the floor. A second bouncer snuck behind Javeer, his posture poised to spring. Laeli began to fumble under her dress, trying to reach the taser.

"*Curse this dress.*" Finally getting a grip on it, she aimed the taser and pulled the trigger. With a ragged yell, the second man collapsed to the ground, writhing wildly. Laeli then aimed the weapon towards the first bouncer still sprawled out across the floor.

"Don't move!" she gasped. Javeer slid a hand through her arm and guided her away as she continued to point the taser at the bouncer. They had almost reached the entrance when a familiar voice stopped them.

"You're not leaving already?"

Javeer whirled around and faced Malin. "The hell we are!"

Malin's robotic bodyguards strode forward threateningly. Malin held out a hand, and they halted. He stepped forward and laughed.

"I see you beat up my bouncers! Quite impressive. Would you like to take their place? How about working here, eh? For me."

Javeer shoved his face towards Malin. "What kind of fool are you? You think I want to work for you? You think I *need* to work for you?"

Even though he kept the smile, the corner of Malin's mouth twitched furiously. "Now, isn't that just what I'm trying to figure out?"

"Let me spare you the trouble. I'll *never* work for you."

"I wouldn't talk to me like that if I were you, *boy.*"

"*Don't* threaten me."

"Cocky, aren't you? It would be wise for you to remember what I'm capable of. I'll threaten as much as I like. *I* can afford to."

A surge of bravery, fueled by rage, prompted Laeli to interject. "Are you sure?"

A look of trepidation crept into Malin's eyes as if he suddenly recalled something. With flaring nostrils and a withering glare, he quickly turned and stomped away.

***

It was late night, and Khar had made his way back up to the casino's second floor, unable to find Bria. He downed his fifth glass and stumbled over to the bar, slamming his hand on the counter.

"Get out!" he snarled to the bartender. "Get out...*get OUT.*"

"Yes, sir!" Hurriedly, the bartender scurried away. Mumbling under his breath, Kye made his way behind the counter and seized a bottle of rum off the shelf. Walking over to the closest bar stool, he seated himself and poured another glass.

"She *disobeyed* me," he muttered to himself. "That woman disobeyed me! The little *bitch.*" He flung back his head and took a long sip.

"May I join you?" Kye's dark silhouette emerged from the dimly-lit room. Khar shot him a venomous glare.

"How'd you get up here? Get away from me."

"There is something I need to tell you. Something you would want to know."

"Nothin' you say interests me. Now get out!"

"You are wrong."

Khar sprang to his feet and brandishing his knife, pressed it against Kye's chest. "I ain't in the mood! You're irritating me, and I'm not about to let you do it again. *Get...out*, before I kill you."

Un-fazed, Kye held his stance. "It is about your girlfriend."

Khar took a step forward. "What do you mean??" he breathed, pressing his knife harder against Kye's chest. "What about my girlfriend?"

"I saw her at the party. She kissed Javeer."

Shock caused Khar to loosen his grip on the knife. His blood shot eyes bulged. "*What did you say??*"

"Yes. It is true." Kye lowered his voice. "She does not love you. She never loved you. It was always *him* she wanted." Khar took a step back, his arm trembling. Kye continued. "Javeer is ambitious; the race has proven that. He believes he can have whatever he wants. However, I will be truthful with you. He does not want Bria. It is Laeli he cares about."

Khar clutched his head with both hands. "*No, no,*" he muttered. "This ain't true! *You're lyin'.*" With a gasp, he pointed his knife at Kye's face. "This is a trick! You know Laeli! My father said..."

"Forget what your father said. I have met Laeli in passing. Believe me, I only know her by name." Kye bent close to Khar. "Your father wants to keep you under his control. I know that you hate Javeer, so...I will offer some advice. Do what your father does; play a little game, but play it *better*. You want to get revenge on Javeer? Kidnap Laeli. Let Javeer know she is in your possession, and demand a ransom of all the *koin* he won in exchange for her return. Not only will he be fear-stricken and comply, but you will drain him of all his wealth. Javeer will be nothing again. And once you have publicly humiliated him...over time, he will be forgotten. *Then,* you can do to him *whatever...you...wish.*"

A ragged laugh erupted from Khar's throat. "What...why are you helping me, *huh?* What's in it for you?"

Kye titled his head sideways, a creepy smile stretching over his face. "I hate Javeer too."

Khar clutched his knife. "You do, eh? What's *your* reason?"

Kye's eyes flashed. "That is my own business!" He began to walk away, then paused, looking over his shoulder. "Laeli works at the robotic repair shop on the lower section of the city: street 18. Her shift ends at eight p.m." With a final grin, he walked away, his dark figure vanishing within the room's shadows. Khar watched him go, still clutching the knife. Then he tottered back to the bar and poured himself a sixth drink. Breathing heavily, he sat down and swallowed, clutching the glass in his shaky hand.

Betrayed me. She betrayed me! Bria's mine; she was always mine. I gave her everything, and still...she betrayed me. For Javeer. JAVEER! Wench. Bitch. Who does she think she is? Who does she think I am? If I can't have her loyalty, no one will. She'll pay for this. Reaching back his arm, Khar flung his glass over the counter. It crashed into several other glasses lined on the shelves, causing all of them to shatter with an ear-splitting crack.

"Are you *still* in here?" a sharp voice interjected suddenly. Bria's figure stepped forward judgingly from behind, her bracelets tinkling. "How many drinks have you had by now?"

"*Traitor*," Khar rasped, turning to face her with bloodshot eyes.

Bria froze. Her eyes wandered to the knife in his hands. "What do you mean?"

Khar snickered bitterly. "As if you didn't know. What'd Javeer think of your kiss, *huh?*"

Bria's face paled. "Are you crazy? You think I'd do that?" She rolled her eyes in disgust. "Where'd you hear *that* from?"

"I find out everything...sooner or later." Khar turned his back on her, his shoulders heaving with silent laughter. "What...did you think I wouldn't?"

Slowly, Bria reached down and picked up a piece of shattered glass. Then she straightened. "It's a lie! Whoever told you that lied."

"Did they?" Khar faced her, clutching his knife. "I don't *think so*."

"I don't know what you're talking about. I hate Javeer, so I wanted to..."

"To kiss him?" Khar gave a choked laugh. "Well, how'd it feel? Did you like it?" Trembling, Bria didn't answer. Rising to his feet, Khar strode towards her threateningly. "You forget! You're mine and nobody touches what's mine. If you won't be mine any more than you shan't be anyone else's neither!"

As he spoke, Khar noticed the hand behind her back. "What have you got there?" he hissed. For answer, Bria reached out and viciously swiped the broken glass against his face. With a strangled yell, Khar leapt backwards, flinging his hand against his face. Blood trickled through his fingers and down his arm – a red stain smearing across the viper tattoos on his arm. Trembling violently, he lowered his hand, his eyes glazed with rage. "*Die*," he hissed.

"Don't touch me!" Bria gasped, flinging out her arm as she backed away.

Khar took a step towards her, spinning the spiral-snake knife in his hand. With rapid speed, he raised his arm and slashed.

Bria's scream tore through the room. Her face paling, she clutched her throat, blood spilling from her neck. Then, with a gurgling choke, she collapsed to the ground, her panicked eyes frozen open as she stared emptily at the ceiling.

Chapter 14
Kidnap Rescue

"Laeli...Laeli-girl!" Heathel came rushing through the shop door.

"What's wrong?"

"Was just talking to a customer. They said Khar's girl is dead."

"Bria?" Laeli's face turned white.

"Yeah! Apparently someone found her on the casino's second floor, her throat slit. I wonder who killed her."

Trembling, Laeli sat down on a stool. "It was Khar," she whispered. "It had to be him."

"Huh? Why would he kill his own girlfriend?" Without waiting for an answer, Heathel kept on talking. "Never saw the girl, but I heard she was the prettiest woman in Cuniculum. They say there was a fight two years ago over her; a man ended up gettin' killed. Thank goodness I was never that beautiful. Sounds like a real risky thing. I mean, of course, I had a good body and great hair, but you know...I was never a stunner."

"*Heathel.*" In exasperated amusement, Laeli pressed a hand against her forehead, not sure whether to laugh or cry. Her entire body was trembling.

"What, girl? What's wrong? You don't need to cry now. Ain't nothin' to worry about. You're a right-pretty girl, but you're no drop-dead stunner either. You don't got to worry."

Laeli flung back her head and sighed, her eyes wet. "That's *not* what I'm worried about, Heathel. Sometimes you say the silliest things."

"If I do I can't help it. Besides, what was so silly about sayin' *that?* Don't worry, girl. There's *nothin'* to fret over. It'll be fine."

I hope she's right. Laeli returned to work, but a nauseous pit kept weighing in her stomach. She had the dreadful feeling that something terrible was about to happen. She closed her eyes. *Breathe. Just breathe. Work will be over soon. Then you can go home.*

After four hours passed, the streets grew dark. Laeli began to tidy up her work station and turn off the shop lights. While doing so, she bumped into Heathel, who rounded a corner the same time she did.

"Ow, girl! I think you just stepped on my toe."

"I'm sorry, Heathel."

"It's alright. I'll finish turning off all the lights. You don't have to stay."

"Are you sure?"

"Yes, girlie, yes. Go on, shoo! Go home now."

"Alright. Thanks, Heathel. Night."

"Night, Laeli. I'll see you tomorrow."

Laeli smiled. "Tomorrow's my day off."

"Woops, oh yeah. I forgot. See, my age is catching up to my brain. At first it was just my body. Now it's both. Really stinks. Well...I'll be seein' you."

"Bye." Laeli grabbed her belt with the taser and walked out of the shop, closing the door behind her.

As Laeli slung her belt around her waist, she inhaled a deep breath. The night air seemed cleaner tonight somehow. The streets were not as busy, and she could hear a cat meow from a nearby alley. Laeli pressed her arms together. *I feel chilly. I wonder if I'm just nervous. I have the strangest feeling that someone is following me.*

Laeli halted and looked behind her. She could see no one, but that was possibly because this part of the street wasn't well lit. Swallowing hard, Laeli resumed her walk. Then she spun around again. This time she was certain she heard footsteps. She squinted her eyes and noticed the silhouette of a person some feet away. She accelerated her pace, a hot shaky feeling curling through her body. *Someone IS following me. I got to get home! I need to reach the part of the street with lights. It'll be safer.*

As Laeli walked, she could hear the footsteps behind her quicken. They were coming closer. Up ahead, a second figure appeared, emerging from the alleyway like a dark wraith. Sudden realization hit Laeli like a slap to the face. *Gang members. They're gang members. It's the Night Tunnel Gang.*

The wraith-figure suddenly raced towards her. From behind she could hear the first person running too. With a panicked gasp, Laeli veered sideways and began to sprint down a long alleyway. Rats scurried out of the way, and a cat rushed past, jumping on a nearby ledge with a tiny hiss. From behind, she could hear the footsteps catching up. Laeli doubled her speed and turned down a second alleyway. At this point, she had no idea where she was. The ground was sloping downwards; she had never been this way before.

The alleyway opened into what looked like a four-way intersection, surrounded by dilapidated buildings and old abandoned robots, their broken pieces haphazardly scattered against the graffiti-streaked brick walls. Laeli skid to a halt, for a few feet in front of her was a third person blocking her way. From all four alleyways, multiple, black-clothed figures emerged. Sweat dripped down Laeli's face as she gasped for air. With shaking hands, she reached down and seized the taser from her waist, slowly removing it from her belt as the figures came closer.

Just then, one of the figures behind her sprang forward. With a cry, Laeli dodged sideways just in time and shot him with the taser. Letting out a muffled yell, the man collapsed to the ground, writhing back and forth. Two more men rushed forward, knocking her to the ground. Laeli was able to tase one of them before the other grabbed her arm and yanked her to her feet, causing her to drop the weapon.

"Let go!" she screamed and clamped her teeth on the man's arm. With an angry shout, he flung her violently to the ground. The impact knocked her breathless and another pair of hands seized her before she had time to recover. Laeli began to flail about wildly, shrieking at the top of her lungs. The man holding

her clasped a hand over her mouth while roughly pinning her under his arm. Then he dragged her forward towards the figure waiting up ahead. Tears in her eyes, Laeli moaned helplessly, her feet skidding as she tried to apply deadweight. Another one of the men stepped forward and handed Laeli's taser to the figure, who was waiting ominously.

"I see my men found you real quick." The figure spoke mockingly through his mask. "How lucky for me. This was too easy." He pulled off the mask, and Laeli's eyes widened, for in spite of the darkness, she could see it was Khar. He nodded and the man holding Laeli let go. Seizing her hair, Khar pushed the taser against Laeli's tear-stained face. She let out a cry and winced at the pain.

"You like usin' this thing don't you? Think I should try it?" He pressed it harder against her cheek. "Well, *huh?* Aren't you goin' to say somethin'?" When Laeli didn't answer, he let out a grating laugh. "You really are a quiet one aren't you? Quiet...and *loyal*. Let's test how loyal your boyfriend is! I think I'll believe in his faithfulness once he hands over his prize money for your return. Does that seem fair to you? Or..." Khar straightened, a malicious grin on his face. "I could just find him and kill him. I don't really like him you know. But *nah*...I think I want the *koin* he won first." Laeli's response was a muffled sob, helpless rage and despair written all over her face as he yanked her head back by the hair. "You know," Khar whispered. "I've heard my girl had a little thing for your man. Did you know that? She kissed him, they say. Maybe I should settle the score." He leaned closer.

Suddenly Khar paused, his eyes wandering over Laeli's head. A new figure loomed out of the alleyway dressed in a black cloak, the face completely covered past the eyes with a black cloth. All of Khar's men stiffened. Some displayed knives, while others clenched their fists.

The figure spoke in a muffled voice. "Let her go."

"*What?*" Khar bust out laughing. Several of his men joined in. "You think you can make me?"

"Just let her go." With an outstretched hand, the figure stepped forward.

Khar motioned with his eyes to his men. They slowly advanced towards the stranger. Then Khar whirled Laeli around and pressed her to his chest. "Not a chance!"

For a minute the figure stood motionless. Then with a quick movement, he lunged toward the closest man and struck him with a blow that sent the man flying into the air against the brick wall. The rest of the gang members rushed at the figure, but one by one they were all knocked to the ground. With a terrified yell, Khar brandished his knife and pressed the blade against Laeli's throat.

"If you come near me I'll kill her!" he rasped. The advancing figure paused. Teary-eyed, Laeli slightly shook her head. With a face scrunched in fear, Khar began to back away, pulling Laeli with him. "Don't come near me!" he repeated desperately "*Don't.*"

The figure shrugged and then vanished into one of the alleyways. Khar continued to clutch Laeli, turning every which way frantically. "*Scum!*" he screeched. "If you come back I'll kill her! I swear I'll kill her!"

There was no answer. Springing from behind, the figure suddenly re-appeared, wrapping one arm around Khar's neck, while another hand pushed his knife-hand away from Laeli. The figure knocked Khar off his feet with a punch that sent him rolling. As Khar's knife dropped from his hand and clattered across the ground, the figure grabbed Laeli's wrist and leaned towards her.

"*Run,*" it whispered. Together, the two of them raced back the way Laeli had come until they reached the part where the alleyway opened back up to the main street. With a gasping sob, Laeli sank to the ground, crouching over her knees with shaking shoulders. The figure squatted beside her, tugging off his mask. Laeli looked up and gasped.

"*Kye?* What...how...I'm so glad..." She pressed a hand against her eyes and tried to stop crying. "*Thank you.*"

"It is fine...it is fine. Are you all right?"

Laeli closed her eyes and took a raggedy breath. "I will...I will be in a minute. I'm so, so *grateful*. How can I ever repay you?"

Kye reached for her hand. "If you wish to show your gratitude, please...*please* come and visit me at my house. I have not been able to see you much and there is so much I want to tell you...to *show you*. Please come."

Laeli nodded between sniffs. "Yes...I'll come. Of course I'll come. You saved my life. It's the least I can do."

"I will have you picked up in my car. Let me know where your house is."

"Just...just meet me at Heathel's. It'll be easier."

For a moment, Kye didn't answer. Then he nodded slowly. "Very well. Let me walk you home."

Laeli shook her head. "No, thank you. I want go home alone."

"I cannot let you..."

"I don't think anyone will come after me now," Laeli gave a wry half-smile through her tears, "after what just happened. I'll be fine."

Kye placed a hand around her shoulder and helped her to her feet. "Are you sure? Laeli..."

"Yes, yes...I'm sure. Goodbye, Kye. And thank you...thank you so much." Laeli began to walk away, then halted. "Kye, how did you know..." She turned around, but Kye was gone. With wide eyes, Laeli stood there frozen.

What...where did he go? How did he vanish so quickly? Shivering to herself, she clutched her sore arms and began to walk home. *So Khar is the leader of the Night Tunnel Gang. He's one of them. That's how Malin has control of them. But how did Khar become the leader? I'll have to tell Javeer. But wait...then he'll know what Khar did. He'll try to kill Khar. He can't fight Khar and his gang; he'll be murdered. I can't tell Javeer! But Javeer needs to know.* Stressed out of her mind, Laeli clutched her hair. "I don't know what to do!" she whispered. "*Wait*...I will ask

Ren." In spite of her aching body, she ran the rest of the way home.

When she finally was in the house and had locked the door behind her, Laeli leaned against it and breathed a sigh of relief. Then she made for the locked room. As she stepped inside, Ren immediately rushed towards her.

"What has happened? You are disturbed. Your adrenaline and cortisol levels are very high."

Laeli sank to the ground, her trembling legs no longer able to hold her up. "It was Khar!" she gasped. "*He's* the leader of the Night Tunnel Gang. I don't know how I never guessed it before. He tried kidnapping me.

Ren slid his finger over a purple bruise on Laeli's chin. His pupils flickered in and out, a violent rage setting over his face. He made to exit the room, but Laeli quickly blocked the way.

"You *can't* go out! Mommy made me promise not to let you. It would endanger us both."

"It is too late now. You are already in danger! What does it matter? *Let... me...out.*"

Laeli's face tightened. "Will you tell me Mommy's secret?" Ren didn't answer. "I thought not! If you have to obey her than so do I. I promised her when she was dying. She..." Breaking down into tears, Laeli collapsed on the floor, her shoulders heaving. "I don't know what to do," she sobbed. "I can't tell Javeer, but I *need* to tell Javeer. And now Kye..."

Ren crouched beside her, placing a hand on her shoulder. "What has Kye got to do with this?"

Laeli raised her head. "He rescued me from Khar," she choked, "and then he asked me to visit him. I said yes...I was so emotional...so grateful to see him...I didn't even think twice. But maybe I shouldn't have...oh, I don't know what to do! Javeer told me to leave him alone, but I want to *help* Kye. To do that, I need to know what's happened to him. If I visit him, maybe he'll tell me."

Ren shook his head. "Your heart gets in the way of your head. That is dangerous." His eyes narrowed. "How did Kye know where you were?"

"I...I don't know." Confusion flickered in Laeli's eyes but then her mouth set stubbornly. "I'm going to find out."

"No...you should stay here. I do not like this Kye."

"You did not know him when he was little." Laeli's voice softened. "He was so gentle and sweet. There are moments when he does scare me, but he was the only friend I ever had. I want to help him but to do so, I must find out what has hurt him. Something *has* hurt him. I can feel it..."

Ren slid his hands over hers. "Do not be so kind-hearted that you lose sight of reason. If something were to happen to you it would cause me great pain. I would..."

"Dear Ren." Laeli placed her hand on his cheek and smiled through her tears. "You are a good friend, and I love you. Just let me try this one time. If it doesn't work, I'll let it go. I promise."

Ren gently pressed a hand against her face. "I just want you to be safe," he murmured.

"I know, I know. Please don't worry." Laeli smiled as her eyes began to water. "I will go and then I'll come back to you. I promise. Just wait for me."

Chapter 15
Kye's Mansion

Laeli stood in front of Heathel's shop, her hands fingering the vibrant red of her dress. She had planned to wear a normal outfit and then decided last minute she couldn't show up in her old clothes to Kye's fancy house. Heathel's green dress was too much for a visit like this, so as a substitute, she pulled out the red dress her mother used to wear. A twinge of guilt had run through her earlier when she put it on. Its frilled top fell delicately over her shoulders and the flowing skirt was elegant, but it still felt wrong to wear her mother's dress for something like this. Sighing, she watched as a mosquito fluttered towards her, landing on her arm. She smacked it and its form crumpled, a thin line of blood squirting out. Wiping off both the blood and the mosquito, Laeli continued to wait for the car Kye had promised. *Heathel is visiting a friend, and Javeer went out today. He wouldn't tell me where to, but I wonder if he is going to meet Jace. He didn't say, but I have a feeling.*

Just then a silver car approached, its shiny exterior reflecting the strips of sun penetrating Cuniculum's compact streets. Onlookers paused and gawked as the car did a U-turn and halted beside Laeli. The windows were tinted so that she couldn't see who was driving. With a suspicious frown, she reached for the door handle, but the back door swung open automatically. Startled, Laeli paused and hesitated, then realized that everyone in the street was stopping to watch. Biting her lip, she ducked under the car and sat in the back seat, shutting the door behind her. Looking up, she realized that nobody was driving.

"Hello," a voice greeted her. "Please make yourself comfortable as we travel to our destination."

Laeli's eyes widened. "Are *you* the one driving the car?"

"Yes. This is car is powered by artificial intelligence. Your safety is my prime concern. Please relax."

Laeli glanced out of the shaded windows. Cuniculum's streets passed by in a steady blur as the car made its way through the city. She turned and studied the car's dashboard. "What model are you? Who designed you?"

"I am a 3056 SM model. I was designed by Arlin Chear, and I am one of the eight prototypes to ever be released. My owner is Kyber Karlin."

"*Kyber?*" Laeli's eyes narrowed. "You mean Kye?"

"I am registered under the ownership of Kyber Karlin. The name Kye is not in my database."

It must be Kye. I never knew his full name was Kyber. Laeli raised her eyebrows. "How long have you been in Kyber's possession?"

"Two years."

"What is your particular design capable of?"

"My design is meant to provide secure passenger transportation and ensures complete protection in any circumstance. I am bullet-proof and fire resistant. A protective shield prevents me from the effects of exterior combustion. If necessary, I am capable of reaching speeds of up to two hundred miles per hour."

"Where is you designer, Arlin Chear, from?"

"Arlin Chear was from Votum City."

"*Was?*"

"He died in the year 3034."

"From what?"

"Heart failure."

Laeli frowned. "Under what company were you sold?"

"I was not sold under any company name. I found myself in the possession of Kyber Karlin on May fifth, 3035. I was sold through a private buyer."

"What was his name?"

"I do not know. I only know that I am the property of Kyber Karlin."

Laeli took a deep breath. "What do you know about Kyber Karlin?"

"I am afraid I do not possess that information."

Laeli sank back into her seat. The car had veered off the main streets and away from the city's limits. They were now on a winding dirt road that curled through a hilly terrain covered with brush. The sun had disappeared and the sky was filled with dull grey clouds.

"How much further is our destination?" Laeli asked.

"We will arrive there precisely at four-thirty p.m. The time now is four twenty-five."

Laeli's eyes scoured the bending hills. She had only once been outside Cuniculum and that had been thirteen years ago with her mother. She could remember seeing Cuniculum's black walls for the first time and thinking how ugly they were. With another sigh, she leaned over the seat, peering at the landscape ahead. Her mouth dropped in astonishment.

The ground had flattened, revealing a ravine splitting between a huge stone mountain. Within the right side of the ravine, resting partially against the mountain on a rising slope, was a massive mansion of dark grey. Its roof and windows had thick black trim and the front door was encased in a tall triangular design whose tip protruded past the roof and up towards the sky. The building was a perfect blend of a Cuniculum structure and that of architecture found only in the Five Cities. Laeli gripped the headrest of the seat in front of her. "Do you know how Kyber got this house?"

"Yes. Because I have access to the building's security system, I am able to see its ownership record. It has not yet been erased. This house was sold to Kyber Karlin on March fifteenth by a man named Malin."

"*Malin?*" Laeli gripped the headrest even harder. Her heartbeat quickened, and she began to think hard. *Was that why Kye was at Malin's casino? Is Malin the one he is doing business with? Why would he not have told me? He lied! He had said he was looking for a way to invest his money. If he's been working with Malin then that means he's already found one. But how...why...why would he work with Malin?*

Caught up in this disturbing revelation, Laeli was silent as the car smoothly scaled the paved driveway and stopped in front of the house's entrance. An uneasy feeling gnawed at her insides as her eyes wandered over the house's exterior. Up close, it looked less formidable but felt more disturbing.

"You may exit the vehicle." As the car spoke, Laeli's door swung open. "I will wait here. When you are ready to depart, I will return you to your original location."

"Thank you," Laeli murmured automatically. Stepping out of the car, she stood there for a moment, wondering what to do next. *Do I wait for someone or do I go knock on the door? I don't want to knock on the door. I don't even want to be here now.* The thought of Kye working with Malin left an acidic taste on her tongue. *Alright, I won't stand here any longer. I am knocking on the door.*

Summoning her courage, Laeli walked across the pavement to the double doors. Their rectangular shape was notably tall and the handlebars were fashioned like a blade but with a rounder edge and delicate ridges covering the entire surface. Holding her breath, Laeli knocked on the door. There was no answer. Exhaling, she tried again. Still...nothing. A sudden wave of frustration replaced Laeli's nerves. *He has no right to invite me here and not answer. What is wrong with him??* Seizing the door handle, she thrust down and pushed open the door.

As it slowly opened, Laeli took a step forward and caught her breath. Ahead of her was an extended hallway with vaulted ceilings. A mix of greys, blacks, and blues shaded the sterile walls and a spiked chandelier hung above her head. Cautiously, Laeli took a few steps forward into the hallway. Her red dress contrasted sharply against the hue of the mansion, its reflection stretching across the shiny silver floor.

"Laeli!" Kye appeared at the end of the hallway, a wide smile on his face. He strode towards her enthusiastically. "I am very glad to see you."

"I'm glad to see you too." Laeli watched as he walked past and shut the door behind her. "I...I'm sorry," she stammered. "I forgot to shut it..."

"Do not worry. It is quite alright." Kye extended his arm in a sweeping motion. "What do you think of my house?"

"I...uh, it's not what I expected. I do not have the words."

"Nonsense. If I recall correctly, you always knew what to say when necessary."

"That was a long time ago."

"But I have not forgotten it." Kye stepped closer to her, his arms behind his back. "I have forgotten nothing about you."

Unsure of how to respond, Laeli gave a small laugh. "Really?"

"Of course."

It was on the tip of Laeli's tongue to demand Kye explain why he had bought the house from Malin, but she restrained herself. "I see."

"Please, come with me." Kye strode down the hallway, his voice echoing through the room. Laeli followed, her eyes fixated on the impressive distance from the floor to the roof.

"Kye, this house's design is very different from anything I've seen in Cuniculum. Who built the house?"

"I purchased it and made some changes."

"How many changes did you make?"

Kye paused, his eyes traveling over the elegant molding that lined the many doorways. "Many."

"But you've only been here for about a month. How could you have made so many changes in such a short time?"

Kye turned his head away. "I made many changes. It was accomplished just the way I wanted it to be."

Laeli's eyes narrowed. *He must have been in Cuniculum longer than he said. He lied to me again...but why?* "Who did you purchase the house from?" Before he could answer, Laeli added sharply, "Don't lie to me." Kye made a noise like a stifled half-laugh.

"I had to buy it from Malin. Can you be mad at me for that?"

So he decided to tell me part of the truth. "I could, but never mind. Forget what I said. Show me the rest of your house."

"I will show you the drawing room." Kye walked through one of the doors on the left side of the hallway, and Laeli followed. Then she halted suddenly as if she had been splashed with cold water. Her eyes widened and a little chill curled up her spine. Bookshelves lined the ends of each wall: hundreds of books encased in mahogany shelves with spiral designs running over the top and sides. Two plush couches were spaced in a half-square around an ashen coffee table. This room also had a high ceiling, but what was more noticeable was its magnificently arched window that stretched across the wall looking out over the hills below. Kye took a few steps forward, his black figure pausing before the center of the window and an icy sensation spread through Laeli's body. Kye had just re-created the scene he had painted for her some weeks ago, and it was this exact room that he had portrayed on the canvas. The only thing missing was the shadowy entity behind Kye's form.

"Do you not like the way the clouds cover the sky, blocking out any unnecessary light?" he asked Laeli, his back still turned to her.

"I prefer the sun. You used to as well...if you can remember *that*."

Kye turned his head half-way, his voice stiffening. "I am afraid I do not recall it well."

"But you can remember everything *I* ever said? That makes no sense!"

"With you it is easy."

"But why?" Both disturbed and irritated, Laeli added sarcastically, "It's too bad there are no crows flying in the air. It would be a nice touch to the window scene."

Kye faced the window again, seemingly oblivious to her cynicism. "Yes," he murmured, "it would be."

Laeli bit her lip. She strode towards the bookcase, her eyes wandering over the collection of books. "May I look?"

"But of course."

Laeli pulled out a heavy volume, its title reading, *The History of Votum.* "You seem to know a great deal about Votum don't you. What's it like?"

"What do you mean: what is it like?"

"Well…I assumed you had been there, since you seem to be so interested in it."

Kye's face darkened, and he responded without directly answering the question. "I have no love for that city."

"Oh." Confused, Laeli placed the book back on its shelf, and her eyes fell upon a second book a few spaces away. She tugged it free and frowned, for the front was titled, *Neuroscience - The Essence of Memory and Perception.* As she thumbed through the pages, a new thought crossed her mind. *Did Kye lose a part of his memory? Is that why he can only remember things about me? If so, I need to find out what could have happened to cause such a thing. Sarcasm and silence do not work on him. I need to treat him like I used to. I must be kind.* "Kye," she began gently. "Do you recall the first time we met? How we climbed the tree to see the little bird's nest?"

Kye slid his left hand into the side pocket of his black vest. "Yes. You were very good to me that day. You came to me when no one else would." Taking his right hand, he reached for her own and guided her to the nearby couch. Seating himself next to her, he pulled from his pocket a small brown box. "I fixed it for you."

"The music box?" Astonished, Laeli opened the lid and the room filled with the sound of the tinkling tune. "You knew how to fix it?"

"I know how to do many things. Are you happy?"

"Yes...thank you." Slowly shutting the box's lid, Laeli pressed it tightly against her lap. "Kye..."

"Come." Rising to his feet, Kye held out his hand. "Follow me."

"Wait...where are we going?"

"I must show you the rest of the house."

For a moment, Laeli hesitated. Then she took the outstretched hand he offered her. *Just go along with it. If he becomes more comfortable, he will surely open up.*

Together, the two of them made their way out of the room, but this time through a different door that led to a second hallway. The walls were dimly lit by lamps that attached to intricate mahogany sconces lining the walls. The molding against the ceiling was dark and heavy and the walls were a rich red-brown. "I did not yet renovate this section of the house," Kye explained.

"So you plan to?"

"Yes. I hate this hallway. It feels like a museum."

Once they reached the end of the hallway, Kye veered right into a third smaller one. Laeli saw that they were making their way to an open door-frame at the very end. "What was on the other side of that hallway?" she asked. "I saw there was a fourth one to the left of us."

"Bedrooms. Nothing important."

"How many rooms are in this house?"

"One-hundred."

"*One-hundred?* Your family must have left you a lot of money! How rich is your father?"

Kye stiffened. "Father?"

"Yes, your father. What does he do? You never told me."

"You don't know?"

"*No.*" Laeli halted in disturbed exasperation. "You never told me!"

Kye slowly shook his head and resumed his pace. More confused than ever, Laeli followed as he walked through the door frame into an enormous dining room with one extended table. Twelve chairs lined either side but everything about the table was bare except for one single plate at the very end. Laeli scrunched up her nose. "How do you maintain this place?"

"I am the owner. It is my responsibility."

"But who cleans it?" Laeli's eyes wandered across the floor. This part of the house was just as immaculate as the front entrance had been. So far, not a single section of the mansion could be considered anything other than spotless. "Surely, you cannot clean the whole thing yourself?"

"I have servants who do it for me."

"You do? Where are they?"

"I did not need them for today. They have been ordered to leave." Kye's eyes narrowed slightly. "I do not recall you being this inquisitive in the past."

"I do not recall you being so secretive."

Kye gave her a hurt expression. "Am I offending you?"

"I...what...*no*, I..." Laeli pressed a finger against her temple. "I am just very confused."

"About what?"

"About so much!" Laeli turned her gaze away from the barren table beside her.

"I will show you more of the house." Still seemingly clueless to all of her hints, Kye gestured to yet another hallway. "I will show you the ballroom."

"This house has a ballroom?"

"Yes."

They walked down the hallway together, and Laeli halted. She shuddered as another chill crept up her spine. Full-length mirrors hung on either side of the wall, stretching all the way to the very end. Mounted between them were stuffed ravens, their open beaks and beady eyes staring ahead vacantly.

"Kye...*what is this?*"

As if he hadn't heard her, Kye didn't answer. Instead, he lingered by one of the mirrors, his eyes glued to the glass as if he were in a trance. Then his gaze dropped to the floor. "They help me focus, yet they also cause me pain."

"Who does?"

"The mirrors."

Holding her breath, Laeli went and stood beside him. "When you look in them, what do you see?"

Kye closed his eyes. "I see fragments of myself." His voice hardened. "But I cannot see *enough!*" Just as swiftly, his tone shifted from angry to sad. "There is only pain."

Laeli reached out and placed a hand on his arm. "Can I help you? What is it you are trying to see? What can you not remember?"

Immediately, Kye's tragic look was replaced with warm affection. "There are moments when I think perhaps I do not have to remember."

"Why? Don't you want to?"

"No. Not when you are here."

"I don't understand. Let me help you try."

"No. For right now, I want you to help me forget."

"Forget? Forget what?"

Kye quickly shook his head. "No, help me forget. Come!" Seizing Laeli's hand, he began to speed-walk down the rest of the hallway. Holding her skirt, Laeli tried to keep up. Kye's grip on her hand was so strong it was starting to hurt.

"Kye!" she gasped. "Slow down. Where are we going?"

Kye didn't respond, nor did he slow down. They had reached the end of the hallway and thick double doors with the outline of Cuniculum carved across the wood stood shut in front of them. With a single push, Kye opened one of the heavy doors and pulled Laeli in after him.

"*Kye...*" Laeli's protest was cut short, and her mouth dropped at the stunning sight that met her eyes. The ballroom had a glistening black floor and intricate molding curling up the sides of the walls. Against the walls, between the rows of arched windows, were round lamps that hung from gold arms that dipped in a half-U, almost like wilted flower stems. The trey ceiling was an indigo blue and a spiked crystal chandelier hung from its center.

"What a beautiful room!" Laeli breathed.

"Come." Stepping towards her, Kye removed the music box from her other hand.

"Wait, what? I'm confused..."

Kye stepped back in a half bow. "May I dance with you?"

"I...uh, it depends. What kind of dance?"

"We can dance to *this* song."

"The music box song?"

"Yes." Walking over to the edge of the room, Kye placed the music box on the floor and then pressed a button on the wall. The exact same tune began to play, penetrating every corner of the room.

"You know the dance that goes with this song?"

"But of course." Kye took her hand and led her to the center of the ballroom.

"Did you learn it in Votum?"

"Please, do not speak of Votum. It only pains me."

Laeli opened her mouth to do just that, then clamped it shut. *Kye still won't tell me anything. Why won't he tell me anything? Everything about this evening is starting to feel more and more odd. He looks at me so strangely at times! I don't understand what's going on. I don't know how to handle this situation. I should tell him I don't want to dance.*

However, instead of saying anything, Laeli took the hand Kye offered her. Her stance tightened as he placed his other hand on her waist. *Just do this one dance with him. Then it will be over, and you won't have to do any more.*

Within seconds, Laeli realized that Kye was a very good dancer. All of his movements were graceful, and he knew the steps perfectly. "Kye, who taught you the steps to this song? You do them so well."

"I taught them to myself."

"You didn't practice with anyone?"

"Yes...with *you*."

"*What?*"

"I imagined I was dancing with you. That made it easy." Kye leaned closer to her. "When I think of you *everything* becomes easy." Ignoring her perplexed look, Kye dropped Laeli's hands and walked backwards to the wall, his eyes fixated on her unmovingly. This time he pressed a second button and all the lamps against the wall went out. The chandelier lights dimmed and the indigo ceiling suddenly became flecked with hundreds of tiny blue stars, casting a brilliant glow over the room. A sigh of amazement escaped Laeli, but her astonishment was overshadowed by Kye's presence as he returned to her side and resumed the dance. The music had become faster, and as it increased in intensity, so did Kye. He swayed with an elegant speed that was hard for Laeli to match, but a nervous sensation gave her an adrenaline rush, and she managed to keep up. A spinning feeling began to whirl inside her head. The lighting of the room, the rapidity of their movements, Kye's peculiar behavior - all of it was becoming overwhelming.

Then, immediately following a particularly complex spin, Kye pulled Laeli close to him. Laeli suddenly realized he wasn't even breathing hard. As his blue eyes glowed in the shadowy room, she almost found herself unable to keep eye contact with him. There was a wild spark within his pupils that scared her. Once the music faded, she tried to pull away, but Kye did not loosen his grip.

"*Kye*," she whispered anxiously. "What are you doing?"

"I need you," he murmured feverishly. "I *want* you."

Fear struck Laeli's chest. "What are you saying?"

"I want you to..."

"Kye, stop acting strange." Laeli flung a hand against his chest, trying to push him away. "You're scaring me!"

"No, no, do you not see? Everything, this room, this dance, *you*...it is perfect! I will be yours...you are mine..."

"Are you *crazy?"*

As if he didn't hear, Kye repeated passionately, "You are *mine*." He ran a finger through her hair and leaned over to kiss her.

"*STOP!"* With a yell of anger and dread, Laeli flung up her arm between them. "*Don't touch me.*"

Kye paused, and his voice swiftly changed to a tragic tone. "Laeli...you do not understand...I need you."

"*Need...want.* What is this? What game are you playing?"

"Laeli." Now Kye's voice sounded as if he were about to cry. A glassy film spread across his eyes. "I am telling you...I *need* you...you are all I have left..."

"You lie! You have your father...your mother..."

"No, no, you are wrong!" Kye's voice rose frenziedly. "Do you not *see?* All they ever left me was *pain.* Their memory only causes me pain."

"Pain? Memory? *Kye...*"

"Yes, *memories.* They are *gone.* I do not know where they have gone! I cannot remember. I can only see fragments, and what I see *hurts.* You are the only memory: the only thing...that does not hurt."

"Memory, memory," Laeli repeated, her heart racing. "Why...*why* did you not tell me? What has happened to you? To *them?*"

"I do not know! I only know you are my last good memory."

"*Memory?* You speak as if I'm not even here! Like I'm some phantom from the past you're trying to re-live."

"I *will* re-live it. If I do not have you, I cannot have peace. I *must* have you."

Tears welled in Laeli's eyes. "I don't know what's happened to you," she began brokenly, "but I know you are not yourself. I have felt it for a while now. You must tell me what occurred after that day at school when I last saw you..."

"*No!*" Kye shut his eyes. "I will not. I *cannot.* I am not sure..."

"I will help you. We will figure it out..."

Kye's eyes opened. Like a switch had been turned off, the sorrow vanished and the impassioned expression returned to his face. "You *do* care for me," he breathed. He leaned forward again to kiss her, but Laeli turned her head away.

"*No,*" she muttered. "Not...*that*...way."

A glint of burning rage instantly replaced the ardent look in Kye's eyes. He loosened his grip on her. "I am certain now," he hissed. "You are in love with *him.*"

Saying nothing, Laeli took a step back. The wild fury with which Kye looked at her filled her with horror. She continued to back away and then rushed from the room. As she glanced back one last time, she saw Kye still stood where she had left him, his legs stiffly spaced apart. His arms hung limp, and he stared her down, his eyes like crystal sapphires glowing eerily in the dark. Without glancing back again, Laeli turned and fled.

Down the mirrored hallway she ran, her red dress flapping against her legs. She raced through the barren dining room and into the second hallway, past the yellow lamps and mahogany walls. Her footsteps echoed as they rushed through the gloomy drawing room and out into the main hallway. Then she lurched to a halt, her heavy breathing vibrating against the vaulted ceiling.

A few feet ahead, blocking her entrance to the front door, stood a robot identical to the ones she had seen with Malin. Its towering white form was unmoving, and at the sound of Laeli's footsteps it turned its head, staring at her with vacant, pupilless eyes. Laeli clenched and un-clenched her fists. She slowly walked towards the front door, never taking her eyes off the robot. The robot remained stagnant, only its head turning to follow her as she inched closer to the exit. Within seconds, Laeli stood right in front of the android. She paused, and they both stared each other down, neither one moving. Then Laeli inched past the android and carefully opened the front door. The robot tilted its head downwards then sideways, observing her with an intensity that sent a cold sweat over Laeli's body. She stepped over the threshold and the last thing she saw was the android's face still watching her through the door crack.

Once the door clicked shut, Laeli didn't waste any time. She turned and sped towards the car that was still waiting for her on the pavement. To her relief, its back door opened, waiting until she was seated to close behind her.

Clutching the headrest while still watching the front door, terrified that either Kye or the robot might come barreling through, Laeli spoke to the car. "Take me back. *Now.*"

"Leaving now." The car reversed itself and began to descend the driveway. Laeli did not take her gaze away from the house until it was out of sight. With a shaky gasp, she leaned back against the car seat and covered her face. *I can't...I can't go near him...not ever again. Not ever...EVER.* With a moan, she sank further into the seat. *Stop thinking. Breathe. Clear your mind like Mommy taught you too.* She took several deep breaths, pressing her hand against her diaphragm. *It's not working. I can't focus. I can't do this! I'm sorry, Mommy, but I can't do this. I need Javeer.* Stifling a moan, Laeli bent over, still clutching her face with her hands. *As soon as I get back, I'm finding Javeer. I HAVE to find him and this time...this time, I will tell him everything.*

Chapter 16
Ren To The Rescue

A clap of thunder hit Laeli's ears as she shut the door of her house. Going into her room, she yanked off the red dress and tugged on her shirt and trousers. Then she pulled a green jacket off the wall and slung it over her shoulders. She went towards Ren's room and unlocked the door.

"I'll be back soon, Ren." Walking towards the corner of the room, she seized the remaining taser left: a robot taser, thin and light, with a silver coil wrapped around the end. *This will have to do.*

"Tell me where you are going, Laeli."

"I'm going to find Javeer."

Ren glanced up at the ceiling. "A storm is coming."

"I know. I don't care." Biting her lip, Laeli locked the secret room's door and the front door of her house before making her way through the streets. Streaks of lightning cleaved the sky, and the air had grown humid. Sweat dripped down Laeli's face and wisps of hair began to cling to her forehead as she weaved in and out of robots and people. *I have to find Javeer! I think I'll go crazy if I don't.*

Laeli pressed on until she had reached Javeer's shop. It was getting late, but she could see Lyon was starting to close up. She quickly rushed to him, hiding the taser within the fold of her jacket.

"Hello, Laeli. You met me at just the right time. I was about to lock everything up. What can I do for you? Javeer is not here."

"He's not?" Laeli gripped the taser so hard that it hurt her fingers. "Where did he go?"

"I'm not sure. He didn't tell me, and he's old enough for me to leave him to his own business." Lyon gave a low grunt and peered outside. "It looks like it is about to storm. You should go home, Laeli, before you get wet. Come back tomorrow. Javeer should be back by then."

Another flash of lightning lit up the sky and a heavy shower of rain began to pour, its thunderous sound drowning out the squeals of scattering people. Lyon raised his eyebrows. "Well, never mind. You shouldn't go out in this. Come inside. You can wait there until the storm stops."

Too stressed to argue, Laeli went into the house and crouched down on the kitchen floor. Closing her eyes, she tried to calm herself, but her anxiety was only growing, and she began to feel as if she were hyperventilating. Gasping for air, Laeli clutched her chest and opened her eyes. She jumped. Mimi was sitting right in front of her, her square head unmoving as she blinked.

"Hello. Do you need help?"

"Mimi!" Laeli placed a hand on the robot's brown arm. She lowered her voice. "Do you know where Javeer went?"

"No. He left."

"When did he leave?"

"Six-thirty p.m. Do you need help?"

"Yes, Mimi. I need to find Javeer."

"I can't help." Mimi let out a tragic sigh. "He didn't tell me where he went."

"Not at all?"

"No. He is keeping a secret. I can't keep secrets."

Moaning, Laeli ran a hand over her face. *I have to...I have to find him. I feel like I'll go crazy if I don't.* She straightened. "Mimi, I know how you can help."

"Yes?"

"Stay here and wait for Javeer. If he gets back, tell him that I'm out looking for him. If Lyon asks where I went, don't tell him I've gone to find Javeer. Can you do that?"

"Yes."

"Thank you!" Giving the robot a little pat, Laeli tip-toed across the kitchen and carefully opened the back door. Throwing the hood of her jacket over her head, she then rushed out into the storm, shutting the door behind her.

Just at that moment, Lyon stepped into the kitchen. "Laeli, you..." He paused and glanced around the kitchen in confusion. "Mimi, where did she go?"

Mimi rolled backwards and spun around, her eyes stretching wide open. "Yes! How can I help?"

"Tell me where Laeli went."

Mimi blinked. "She is not here."

"I know *that*. Where did she go?"

Mimi blinked again rapidly. A strange gurgling noise arose from her insides.

"*Mimi*. Answer me."

Mimi turned her head and glanced at the door. Lyon frowned. "She left?" Mimi nodded slowly. With a sigh, Lyon opened the door part-way, staring at the heavy downpour. "Do you know why?"

"She said I can't tell."

"*Mimi...*"

"She is looking for Javeer."

"*Foolish girl*," Lyon muttered. He slammed the door shut. "Did she just leave?"

"Yes."

Lyon reached out and grabbed a cloak hanging from a nearby hook. "I am going to bring her back. Wait right here."

***

Laeli trotted through the rain, fat drops rolling off the sides of her hood and into her face. Blinking hard, she pressed on, trying to think where Javeer might have gone. *You're crazy! Cuniculum is huge, and it's dark out. You'll never find him.*

"*Laeli!*" A familiar voice suddenly pierced through the rain.

Mimi, no. Laeli groaned to herself. *You told Lyon. You really CAN'T keep a secret.* She began to run, splashing through muddy puddles and dodging stragglers bent over within the slight shelter of their hoods and cloaks. Glancing back, she saw Lyon was not following. *I've lost him. I better keep running though...just in case.*

As Laeli continued to push on, the rain began falling more heavily. Sudden despair rushed through her, and she slowed her pace. *What are you doing? Are you insane? You'll never be able to find him like this. Just turn around and go home. But then I'll have to explain to Ren...I don't want to explain to Ren. He warned me about Kye. Ren will get angry...he'll try to get out...I don't have the energy to argue with him.* Choking back tears, Laeli began to walk, her face miserable beneath her hoodie. Then she stiffened.

A cloaked figure was approaching up ahead, and unlike everyone else, his nose and mouth were covered with a mask. Laeli gripped the robot taser. It would still be an effective weapon against a human. Removing the taser from her jacket, Laeli held it out, her entire body poised and ready to fight. A sudden wave of anger replaced the fear in her bones. With a shout, she activated the taser, lunged towards the figure, and pressed it against his chest. With a muffled cry, the figure stumbled backwards and collapsed onto the street. Passing people turned and fled and soon it was only Laeli and the figure, alone together. The figure rolled on his side and groaned. He flung up his hands as Laeli stepped towards him threateningly.

"Woah, girl, hey now! What you think you doin? It's me...*Jace.*"

"Wh...what?"

"Yeah, it's me...*Jace*." The figure yanked off his mask. Laeli's grip on the taser loosened, and she took a step back at the sight of his confused face, half covered by his disheveled curls.

"I...I'm sorry," she faltered. "I...I thought you were..."

"Nah, girl...it's alright." Jace tried to rise, then winced. "*Damn*, that hurt. What *is* that thing?"

"It's a...I mean...it doesn't matter...I'm sorry."

"Whew!" Jace rose to his feet, clutching his chest. "Another hit from that and I'da been knocked senseless. Whatcha doin' out here in weather like this? You be all on edge."

"I need to find Javeer. Do you know where he is?"

"I...*uh*." Jace scratched his chin. "How about some other time?"

"No." Laeli shook her head forcefully. "I have to see him *now*."

"Yeah, but..."

"Jace, *please.*" Laeli clutched his arm. Seeing the desperation on her face, Jace faltered.

"Wellll..."

"*Please.*"

"I want to girl, but really I can't."

"Jace, you don't understand. I *need* to see him. Please, *please*, you've got to let me see him!"

"What for?"

Laeli's head dropped. "There's something he has to know."

"What about?"

"It...it's about the Night Tunnel Gang."

Jace's eyes widened. "I was gonna go fetch somethin', but it can wait. Follow me." Glancing around quickly, he turned back the way he had come, and Laeli followed. The rain had finally slowed, and their footsteps sank into deep puddles as they walked.

Veering onto a smaller side street, Jace skipped down a flight of stairs that dipped beneath the main street's level and strolled up to a rickety door frame that appeared to lead to a sort of basement. He motioned for Laeli to wait before slipping inside.

After a few minutes, he reappeared and beckoned for her to enter. Ducking under his arm, Laeli entered a dank, musty room, warmed by a fire lit in the back against the wall. Lanterns were placed about haphazardly and a blanket acted as a barrier to a back door. Laeli didn't even notice it. All she saw was Javeer, who rose in astonishment from his stool at the sight of her. With a sob, Laeli dropped the taser and flung herself into his arms. Her tears began to fall freely.

"Hey, my girl." Javeer hugged her close then held her back, pushing the wet hair out of her face. "What's going on? Laeli, what's wrong?" His eyes darkened on seeing her bruised chin. "What happened?"

"I *had* to see you!" Laeli choked. "I..." She broke down again and pressed herself against Javeer's chest. "I *found* you."

Javeer shot Jace a baffled look. Jace scratched his neck in embarrassment and shrugged. "I don't know what's goin' on. She tased me out there though! Thought I was someone else. Got me real good. I can still feel the sting."

"Hey, Laeli." Speaking in soothing tones, Javeer placed a hand against her cheek. "What's going on, girl?"

Taking a deep breath, Laeli stopped crying and tried to regain composure. "It...it happened yesterday," she choked between sobs. "I should have told you! Khar and his men tried to take me. Khar is the leader of the Night Tunnel Gang." Javeer and Jace gaped at her wide-eyed as she continued. "They were going to make you pay the entire sum of the prize money as ransom for me. Then..." Laeli paused and hesitated. *If I tell Javeer about Kye he might hurt him. For the sake of what Kye used to mean to me, I won't say anything.* "Then...then Kye came and...and rescued me."

"It makes sense!" Jace gasped behind her. "That's how Malin gotta hold of the NTG. He got his son to kill the leader. It's a rule of the underground gangs. You kill the leader...you take his place. Two-faced, stinky bastard! That son-of-a-bitch wanted to wipe you clean out Javeer, the slim-ridden..."

"*Laeli,*" Javeer clutched her arms. "Why did you wait to tell me this?"

"I...I felt like I couldn't. I didn't want you hunting down Khar. He would have killed you. He...he killed Bria. He's got a whole gang! You...you don't have anyone."

Jace shot Javeer a strange look. He walked up to Laeli and awkwardly put a hand on her shoulder. "Naw, girl. Javeer'll be fine. Imma be lookin' out for him. Trust me."

"Laeli, is there anything else I should know? How was Kye able to rescue you?"

"I..." A sudden thought almost made Laeli lose her breath, and she turned her head away. *What...what if Kye knew what was going to happen...before it happened? After all, he did buy that house from Malin. What if he has connections to Khar too? And he was so desperate for me to visit him. Maybe he set it up. Sent Khar after me and then saved me...so I'd visit him out of gratitude. No...no...no. That can't be true. Is Kye really that bad? Oh, I don't know...I'm not sure! If I tell Javeer, he might kill Kye. Could I live with that? I don't know...I don't know. No...I'll wait. I'll think about it...then decide tomorrow.*

Javeer frowned. "Laeli?"

"No," she breathed. "Nothing else."

Javeer eyed her suspiciously. "Are you sure?"

Laeli swallowed and nodded. "I'm sure."

Javeer rose to his feet, still clutching her shoulders. He let go and began to pace the room. "It doesn't make sense!" he muttered. "Something doesn't make sense. *Kye* doesn't make sense."

"Forget Kye," Jace interjected. "What *you* plannin' to do?"

Javeer straightened. "I'll let you know soon. Give me a little more time to think about it."

"You haven't got much time."

"Yeah, I know."

"Alrighty then." Jace flung his cloak back over his head. "I already told ya everythin'. What Laeli said just makes it all make sense even more! You know how to find me. I'll be seein' ya. Bye,

Laeli." Jace turned and disappeared from the room, and Javeer began to blow out the flames inside the lanterns.

"Laeli, how did you find us?"

"By accident." Laeli clutched her wet arms together and shivered.

"You have crazy good luck."

"No, I don't. I have the worst luck."

"And you tased Jace? No wonder!" Grabbing his own jacket from the corner, Javeer walked up to her. "Take off that wet thing. You're gonna get sick. Here." He helped Laeli slide into his, its huge sleeves and length swallowing her up. "Did you come straight from your house?"

"No, I went to your dad's shop first. He told me you weren't there."

"I see. Here, I'll walk you back to your house."

"Javeer!" Laeli gripped his sleeve. "Please...please don't leave me. Stay with me."

"You mean...at your house?"

"Yes...*please*. I don't want to be alone. I *can't* be alone. Not tonight."

For a moment, Javeer hesitated. Then he wrapped an arm around her shoulder. "Alright. Come on, let's go."

***

It was midnight by the time Javeer and Laeli reached the house. Javeer watched in surprise as Laeli swiped her card to unlock the door. "Where'd you get a key like that?"

"I made it." Laeli stepped over the threshold, and Javeer followed.

"You *made* it?" he whispered as the door shut behind them. "What *can't* you make?"

"Motorcycles," Laeli whispered back. Stifling a laugh, Javeer surveyed her tiny kitchen as best as he could through the dark. Laeli gave an exhausted yawn.

"You need sleep," Javeer announced. "But first, you need to dry off more. You're gonna get sick if you stay wet like this."

"There's a heater in my bedroom." Tightly holding onto his hand, Laeli led Javeer into the back room and plugged the cord into the wall. "It's the only room with an outlet I can use," she explained. Removing Javeer's heavy jacket, she curled up against the wall across from the heater. Javeer sat down beside her and flung an arm around her shoulders. Snuggling closer, Laeli leaned her head against his chest.

"You're shaking," he whispered.

"I'm cold."

"You're not *just* cold." Javeer tipped her chin upward. "Is there something else you want to tell me?"

Laeli shook her head.

"Laeli!" Javeer's voice hardened. "I know there's something you're not saying. You can't keep a secret like the last one from me again. It's too dangerous."

"It's...it's not something I can tell you yet. Give me until tomorrow. Then I'll decide."

"*Laeli...*"

"I promise."

Javeer took a deep breath. "Ok." His eyes surveyed her tiny bedroom. "Laeli, you shouldn't live alone here. It's no longer safe."

"No, it's all right."

"No, *it's not...*"

"Javeer, you have to believe me. There's a reason I stay here. I promised my mother..."

"That promise no longer stands..."

"No, you don't understand. It *does*. And I can't leave because of it. I..."

"Not tonight," Javeer interrupted. "You're tired and can't think straight. We'll talk about it tomorrow."

Laeli opened her mouth to argue and then realized she didn't have the energy. Still shivering, she snuggled closer to Javeer and let out a tiny sigh. Against her face, she could feel the steady thump of Javeer's heartbeat. A tear slid down her cheek.

"I haven't ever been able to be close this way with someone before," she whispered. "I've been by myself for so long. I didn't realize what something like this felt like. *Thank you.*"

Javeer kissed the top of her head and laughed softly through his nose. "No, *thank you.* Meeting you has made my life ten times better. You've added a whole new meaning to it. My father once said that when you fall in love that person becomes your entire life. You'd do anything for them. Now I know what he meant. I'd do anything for you, Laeli. *Anything.*" He pressed his lips gently against her forehead.

"And I'd do anything for you," Laeli murmured. "I love you more than anyone." Her words were followed by a long yawn.

"Yes...and now you need to get some sleep. You're tired."

"I'm not moving!" Laeli protested.

"You don't have to move, but you still need to sleep."

"But what about you?"

"I'll stay right here. I'll probably fall asleep too. I'm a heavy sleeper... like a *real heavy sleeper*...so you don't need to worry about waking me up."

"But...but I want to know what you and Jace..."

"Uh...no." Javeer pressed a finger against her lips. "*Shh.* No more talking."

Shaking her head, Laeli reached out and kissed Javeer on the cheek. Then she snuggled back into his arm and within moments, all he could hear was the tiny sound of her breathing. Pushing a strand of wet hair away from her face, he leaned his head against hers. *She feels so little in my arms. I wonder what she's afraid to tell me. I will make sure though, no matter what, that she doesn't stay in this house. Whatever she thinks is keeping her here will not convince me. She's coming back home with me tomorrow.* A wave of drowsiness swept over Javeer, and his eyelids lowered. His thoughts began to mix in his head and though he tried fighting it, it wasn't long before he too was asleep.

***

"Laeli, you must be careful. Stay here and don't tell anyone any-thing."

"What do you mean, Mommy?"

"You mustn't let anyone find out about Ren."

"But Mommy, why not. No one here could hurt him."

"I know but word might travel. Word always does. People will talk. The Five Cities might find out about him."

"Is that why you hid here, Mommy?"

"No, but it's why we must stay hidden now."

"There are no other reasons?"

"There are so MANY reasons."

"Please...tell me what they are."

"Someday Laeli, if you ever need to know. Then I will tell you."

"I need to know now."

"No...I can't tell you."

"Please. You have to tell me now!"

With a small gasp, Laeli's eyes flew open. *I was dreaming.* Taking a deep breath, she glanced up and saw Javeer was asleep, his head bent forward against his chest. Smiling gently, Laeli reached out and fingered the dreadlock that dangled over his forehead. Glancing around the room, she saw it was still dark out. Then she swallowed, realizing that it had been almost twelve hours since she had any water.

I'll get a drink and then come back. I hope I don't wake Javeer. Moving forward slightly, she paused, but Javeer did not even react. Slowly rising to her feet, Laeli tip-toed out of the room, down the hallway, and into the kitchen. Turning on the ceiling light, she poured herself a glass of water and gulped it down, the wet liquid sliding down her dry throat. With a sigh of relief, she set the glass down beside a kitchen knife she had used earlier and turned to go back to the room. Then she jumped and froze in alarm. Kye stood across from her at the end of the kitchen.

"What are you doing here?" Laeli asked in a whispered gasp. "How'd you get in?"

"I know your lock code."

Laeli's mouth dropped in shock. "How would you know *that?* How do you even know where I live??"

"I have known for a while. I have always known."

"*What??*"

"Yes!" Kye spoke in a hushed, aggressive voice. "*Everywhere* I followed you: for months and months! I did not expect to find you, but I did...and I will not let you leave me again. You are coming with me."

"No, Kye!" Laeli glanced towards the hallway, a terrible fear rising in her throat. *If Javeer hears and comes out they will both get hurt, maybe even killed.* "Kye, *please.* For old time's sake, I'm warning you...leave now and don't come back!"

"*Don't come back?*" Kye hissed. He stepped towards her threateningly, seizing her by the shirt.

"Yes, don't come back! You're all corrupt and twisted. I don't want you near me. You won't let me help you. You lied about everything...even your name." In spite of the dreadful burn within Kye's eyes, Laeli continued. "Your full name is Kyber Karlin. Even that you couldn't tell me."

Kye yanked Laeli even closer to him. "How do you know that?"

"It doesn't matter how I know. You're a liar! You're on Malin's side and I..."

Kye pushed his face close to hers. "I am not on his side you little fool!"

"How can you *say that...*"

"I am only on *my* side. Mine and mine alone! All my plans have changed. I *will have* what I want, and I want *you*. Nothing will stop me!" Kye leaned over into Laeli's ear. "Not even the man you love. You are coming back with me...and I will not let him get in the way! I will *kill...him.*"

A wild surge of rage and fear that she had never experienced before pounded through Laeli's blood. Impulsively reaching out her hand, she snatched the knife from the nearby counter and plunged it into Kye's arm with all her strength. To her horror, the blade snapped and clattered to the floor, barely penetrating Kye's skin.

"You're not Kye!!" she gasped "*What are you??*"

"I...AM...KYE!" Seizing Laeli by the neck, Kye swung her backwards and pinned her to the floor with a speed that knocked her breathless. He extended his left hand over her, a needle held within his grasp. Tears sprang from Laeli's eyes.

"Please, *don't*," she cried. "Kye, *NO!"* She tried to break free from his grip, but Kye's hand only tightened around her neck.

"You are going to come with me," he muttered. He pushed his mouth next to her ear. "I will take you away from here and then...we can *both* be free."

Before Kye could plunge the needle into Laeli's arm, Javeer sprang from behind, throwing one arm around Kye's neck and grabbing Kye's wrist with his hand. He jerked backwards, pulling Kye with him, and together they crashed onto the floor. The needle fell from Kye's hand and rolled under the counter while Laeli leaned over, gasping for air. Springing to his feet, Javeer drew a heavy knife from his belt. He ducked and slashed at Kye's neck, but with un-human speed, Kye dodged the knife, spun around, and violently shoved Javeer against the wall. Then he slammed Javeer on his back against the kitchen table. The table collapsed from the impact next to Laeli. The legs shattered in all directions, one of them striking her in the face. With a cry, Laeli doubled over, covering her head with her arms. As the knife slipped from Javeer's hand, Kye seized it and struck a blow towards Javeer's throat. With a quick jerk of his head, Javeer dodged the blow by half an inch and the knife embedded itself into the kitchen floor by his neck. While Javeer struggled to break free from Kye's iron grip, Laeli crawled past them and stumbled to her feet, staggering towards the hallway.

Dragging Javeer from the floor, Kye raised him from the ground and flung him across the room. With a vicious thud, Javeer's entire body hit the opposite wall, and he fell unconscious to the ground. Wrenching the knife from the floor, Kye strode towards him, letting the blade drag slowly against the floorboards. Then a sudden movement from the hallway made him halt. As he turned his head, an expression of confusion and terror settled in his eyes.

Standing in the hallway, fists clenched and shoulders back, stood Ren. He was motionless for a minute, his eyes locked with Kye's, while Laeli ducked under his arm and rushed towards Javeer's limp body. Ren let out an enraged yell, the white veins in his neck and face darkening. His eyes becoming engulfed by a blinding, red glow. He catapulted towards Kye, slamming him against the kitchen counter. The knife was knocked from Kye's hand, flying across the room with a clang. Behind Kye, the counter and cupboards crushed inwards from the force of Kye's body. Wrenching himself free, Kye yanked Ren's arm, twisted it, and struck Ren in the neck. Unaffected, Ren spun around, broke away from Kye's hold on him, and punched him in the stomach. Stumbling backwards, a strangled shout tore from Kye's throat, and he lunged forward. Within moments, both of them were grappling together at incredible speed, twisting and turning out of each other's grip.

Suddenly, Ren plunged low underneath Kye's torso, and with a deep-throated roar, lifted Kye off his feet and flung him into the ceiling. Laeli screamed as pieces of cement and plaster crumbled to the floor and glass fragments from the ceiling light shattered in all directions. She stretched herself over Javeer, shielding his face with her body as Kye landed on the already broken table with a crash. Scrambling to his feet, Kye reached out, snatched the knife lying on the floor, and with deadly accuracy, flung it at Javeer's torso. Ren leaped forward, seizing the flying knife mid-air, and with one complex spin of his body that propelled him off the ground, flew forward and thrust the knife into Kye's right eye. Letting out a strangled wail that ripped chillingly through the house, Kye stumbled backwards as grey liquid spilled from his eyes and down his face. A cry erupted from Laeli's throat as Ren dragged Kye towards him, then flung him back so violently that Kye's body entered the air and crashed through the kitchen wall. After rolling a few times, Kye's crumpled form collapsed in the street, the knife still halfway embedded in his eye.

With great effort, Kye staggered to his feet. Nosy onlookers who had heard the commotion and were stepping out of their homes to peak, gasped in fear. Alarmed shrieks split the air as Kye reeled backwards and then fled down the street, vanishing from sight. His eyes still glowing a brilliant red, Ren stepped forward to follow him.

"*Ren*," Laeli exclaimed from her corner. "You mustn't. People will see!" Halting in his tracks, the red in Ren's eyes dissipated, and he stepped backwards into the remains of the house, his form blending into the surrounding darkness.

"We have to hide!" Laeli exclaimed. Without saying anything, Ren lifted Javeer from the ground and hastily carried him into the secret room. Locking the door behind them, Laeli collapsed by Javeer's side as Ren gently placed him back on the ground.

"He's bleeding," she choked. She ran her finger over the side of Javeer's head, where a trickle of blood ran all the way down to his neck. Ren's eyes scanned Javeer's body.

"He's suffering a slight concussion. He is unconscious more from the shock of the throw's impact than the hit to his head. I predict a week's rest before he is able to function normally."

"You mean he'll be all right?" Laeli ran a shaky hand through Javeer's hair.

"Yes. Let me look at you." Ren lifted Laeli to her feet and surveyed her forehead. His calm voice shifted to one of deep concern. "Are you all right?"

Laeli took a shuddery breath. "Yes, I...I think so."

"You have a bruise on the right side of your head. Your throat and vocal chords appear to be unharmed." Ren squeezed her hands. "Thank goodness."

Her shoulders heaving, Laeli collapsed against Ren's chest, sobbing openly. "*Thank you.*"

Ren wrapped her in a deep hug. "You are welcome."

"This is all *my* fault. I should have never brought Javeer here! I should have told him about Kye...but I didn't know...I thought...I thought this whole time that it...he... Ren, *what was that?* I'm so confused and scared."

Ren frowned. "I did not get a chance to fully scan his body. The parts that I did scan told me Kye is robotic, but he is not like any robot in my database. Something about his internal structure is strange to me. On the exterior, he appears fully human; more so even than I. I do not know how that is possible. The interior...I am not sure."

"But Ren, it had Kye's face, his voice, even some of his mannerisms! He *knew me*. Ren, how...how do you explain that? If that isn't him, then what happened to the *real Kye?*"

"I do not know. It..."

At that moment, Javeer shifted and groaned. Rushing to his side, Laeli reached for one of his hands. "Javeer," she whispered. "Don't worry! It's *me*...Laeli. Do you hurt very badly?"

Javeer squinted his eyes and winced. "Laeli?" he groaned. "Where am I? What happened?" His eyes suddenly widening, he clutched her arm. "Are you ok? That *thing*..."

"It's ok, it's gone now. Ren saved us."

Javeer's face scrunched up. "Ren?" He tried to sit up but dropped his head back with a grunt. "*Ugh*. I'm all dizzy. It feels like a drum's going off in my skull. Laeli, you sure you're safe?"

"Yes, Javeer. I promise. Please stay down. Don't move yet."

"No." Stubbornly, Javeer used his arms to push himself up, cringing as a wave of dizziness struck him. "I gotta get you out of here. It ain't safe."

"Javeer, it's safe! Ren's with me. He's the one who protected us."

Ren stepped forward, holding out his hand. "Greetings, Javeer. It is a pleasure to meet you."

Javeer's mouth fell open in astonishment. He blinked and scrunched up his face, blood from his wound dripping over his eyes. "*Wh...What are you?*" he asked in disbelief. "Are you an android or human?"

"I am an advanced humanoid model: model R-17. It is my job to protect Laeli. Any friends of hers are friends of mine. I am happy we can finally meet."

"I..." Completely flabbergasted, Javeer glanced at Laeli in perplexed amazement. "Am I seeing stuff? There's two of you. The room's spinning..." With another groan, he lay his head back on the floor.

"He's real, Javeer. He's been with me as long as I can remember."

"Gee!" Javeer gave a dry laugh. "It's kinda alarming how human he looks. So...you protect Laeli?"

"Yes."

"I gotta thank you for saving me." Javeer grimaced, his eyes narrowing. "I'd be dead without your help." He reached out again for Laeli's hand. "Still Laeli, you can't stay here. You gotta come stay with me."

"Javeer, I can't. *Ren...*"

Javeer closed his eyes and chuckled. "Ren can come too. He looks pretty dang human! We'll cloak him up and get him to my house...hide him there. My dad will take you both. I know he will."

"But Javeer you can't move right now. Your head…"

"Heck, move me! Your android friend can help. We're going back to my place, and that's final."

Laeli glanced anxiously at Ren who nodded slowly. "If we move him carefully, he should be able to make it back without suffering further injury."

"But we don't have a stretcher."

"*Stretcher?*" Javeer chuckled again. "I don't need a stretcher. I just need support. I can walk."

"Then let us move now while it is still dark," Ren decided.

"Laeli, help me take off my jacket and give it to android Ren," Javeer suggested in groggy tones. "If…if he pulls the hoodie over his head, he should be good."

"Ok." With trembling hands, Laeli helped slide the jacket off Javeer's shoulders and handed it to Ren. "Are you sure you can do this?"

"Yup. Let's go." Javeer let Ren help him to his feet and then gave a low gasp under his breath. "Whew, the room's spinning. *Ow.*"

Laeli flung an arm around his waist to add extra support. "What is it? What hurts most?"

"My head." Javeer winced again. "Come on, let's hurry."

"Be prepared," Ren advised Laeli. "He is likely to lose consciousness again."

Javeer gave a sniff. "I ain't passing out! I'll be fine." Under his breath, he muttered, "I'm so confused. Laeli, I'm so confused...what's happening right now? You sure this android's real? Am I dreaming?"

"Shall I pinch you so you believe?" Ren jested as they opened the sliding door.

"*Damn*, he...he even *j...jokes* too." Javeer's words slurred over one another. "*Go figure.*"

As they had reached the house's crumbled front entrance, Laeli let out a gasp. "*Wait.*" Leaving Ren and Javeer, she dashed back inside and returned, clutching the circlet and taser in her hands. "This *has* to come with me. We can go back later for everything else." She returned her arm to its place against Javeer's waist and looked up at Ren. "I'm ready now. Let's go."

Together, the group of three hobbled through the streets until they reached Lyon's shop. Laeli glanced up through the darkness at Javeer's face, and her eyes widened in alarm. "Ren, he's bleeding again."

Javeer let out a groan that was meant to be reassuring. "It's *n...nothing*. Tell my father we're here."

Dropping her arm from his waist, Laeli trotted towards the house behind the shop and banged on the kitchen door. The door swung open almost instantly, and Lyon stepped out, taser in hand.

"Lyon, it's *me*, Laeli. Javeer's with me. He's been injured."

"*What?*" Stepping out the door, Lyon rushed over to Javeer, who was still being supported by Ren. "Son!"

"It's nothing, Father. I'm fine. I..." Javeer's head slumped forward, and his body went limp, throwing deadweight against Ren.

"He is still experiencing the effects of the concussion," Ren announced. "He needs to lie down on an even surface until his brain steadies and the injury heals. We also need to clean the wound on his head."

"Get him inside. Hurry!" Placing an arm around Javeer's other side, both Lyon and Ren helped Javeer through the kitchen door that Laeli held open for them. Bringing Javeer into his bedroom, Laeli removed the pillow from the bed while Lyon and Ren carefully laid Javeer out on the mattress.

"Laeli, turn on the light for me," Lyon ordered. Once Laeli did so, he leaned over and examined Javeer's head wound. "I need soap and warm water." Glancing up, he narrowed his eyes at Ren. "Who are you?"

"I am Ren, R-17." Calmly removing his hood, Ren inclined his head. "I am pleased to meet you."

Lyon's eyes bulged in shock. "Do my eyes play tricks?" he gasped. "What *are you?*"

"I am a humanoid android, and Laeli's protector. I am sorry we are meeting in such a circumstance as this."

"It's not possible!" Lyon shook his head in disbelief. "*Not possible.*" Under his breath he muttered, "It's unnatural for an android to appear so human." He turned to Laeli. "What is this thing you brought with you?"

"It's true what he said; Ren's a humanoid android. My mother made him. He's protected me ever since she died. He saved both of our lives today." She nodded towards Javeer.

Lyon scowled. "What happened?"

"A being similar to me attacked them," Ren began. "I was unable to scan him thoroughly so I do not know for certain what he was. He…"

Laeli sighed and closed her eyes, tears welling up inside. "This is all my fault, sir. If anyone is to explain, it'll be me." She took a shuddery breath. "It all started back in Nobiles, when I met this little boy…"

***

For a long while, Laeli sat beside Javeer, refusing to leave his side. After an hour passed, her legs began to cramp so she stood up and paced the room. Then she made her way down to the basement where Ren was. She found him sitting on a stool, his eyes narrowed as he stared at the wall.

"Ren, what are you thinking of?"

"Of Kye. He could have easily injured you when he had you by the throat, but he didn't. That was deliberate on his part."

Laeli pulled up a chair and sat across from Ren. Her legs were still shaking too much for her to stand long. "But Ren…that *wasn't Kye.*"

"But he believes he is Kye, based on what you told me. I have been thinking about what you said," Ren gave Laeli a perplexed look, "and I am deeply troubled. You even said it looks like him…"

"It does…at least I thought it did…I don't know anymore!" Laeli ran a hand over her face. "When I last saw him he was eight years old and dying. When I saw him…*it*…whatever that was…I assumed it *must* be him. It looked *so* like him…and he *knew me*. Why would I think anything else?"

"You would not." Ren bowed his head. "I am sorry I cannot help…but I do not understand."

"Me neither. Ren, before he tried to drug me, Kye said…he said…once he took me away, we could both be free."

Ren tilted his head and frowned. "What did he say?"

"He said we could both be free, but I don't know what that means. Free from *what*? What would I need to be free from? And back at his house he told me he can't remember the past well…the only thing he recalls clearly is *me*. And he had books: so many books at his mansion about the brain and Votum. If it *is* Kye…oh…I don't know. I'm so confused. It's *not* Kye, but why does he know who I am? Why? How could he possibly have any memories of me at *all?*"

"*Wait*," Ren murmured. He leaned forward, pressing his face against his hand, his eyes narrowing. "It is what you just said…the books, Votum, '*we could both be free*'. Whatever that being believes is haunting him also believes you are being haunted by it too. And if that is true then it means…" Ren rose to his feet, "it means there is a high probability you both have the same enemy." His eyes widened as he rose to his feet, his voice dropping to a whispered gasp. "*Votum, Votum. He is trying to find you. He knows about you.*"

"Same enemy? Trying to find me? Who's trying to find me? Ren, what are you talking about? I don't have an enemy...unless you count Khar, but..."

"This Kye knows something about you...something you do not. At this point, you can no longer afford to be ignorant. Ignorance would be a liability." Ren bowed his head. "I cannot keep the secret any longer. The danger is already upon you. It is too late to hide the truth now. You must know."

Laeli sprang to her feet. "You mean...you mean the thing Mommy would never tell me? You'll tell me now?"

Ren shook his head. "It is not something that can be told. It must be shown."

"Shown? I don't understand..."

"Before you were born, your mother discovered a way to imprint her most important memories and place them within a separate device. She chose that device to be me. Her intent was for you to understand who you were and where you came from, but only if absolutely necessary. She hid this from you and ordered me to hide it as well, in hopes that you would never need to know."

"Do...do you mean I'll see *everything?*" Laeli touched Ren's arm, tears springing from her eyes. "I'll see her? I'll see *my father?*"

"Yes, but it will cause you unspeakable pain. Your mother was like you. She had a photographic memory, so everything she transferred is incredibly vivid. Most of it will not be happy. The things she hid from you will haunt you for the rest of your life. The knowledge you shall acquire after this is not something you will ever be able to throw away. Yet..." Ren raised his eyes to meet Laeli's. "I will have peace knowing I waited to show you. I only show you now because I must."

"How do you show me?"

"You will have to connect to me in order to see inside."

Laeli's face paled. "You mean I have to..."

"Yes." Ren spoke gently. "You have more mental strength than you know, Laeli. You choose not to exercise it, but deep inside of you, it is there. Do not be afraid."

"But what if I connect to something other than you?"

"Whatever you focus on most, you will see. I do not think you shall have to worry about your focus drifting elsewhere." Ren gave an amused smile. "If you feel weak, it is because you are afraid...so do not be afraid."

Laeli's face set firmly. "I'm not afraid." She walked over to the corner of the basement and from one of the shelves, picked up the wired circlet. Going back to her chair, she sat down and placed the circlet on her head. Closing her eyes, she took a concentrated breath as the blue circlet began to glow. *Breathe. Breathe deeply. Do not be afraid. Calm yourself. Remember the ocean and let your heart rate slow. Focus on what you want to think about.*

A powerful surge of voices that were not her own began to echo unceasingly. The voices of every robot in Cuniculum swirled about in Laeli's head. Re-directing her will, Laeli pushed them out. She needed to link to Ren: only to Ren. She could feel him now: hear his thoughts; the connection set a deep tremor throughout her body. Ren's brown irises engulfed his pupils. He slowly raised his head and sat silently, saying nothing. Laeli opened her eyes.

Show me.

Chapter 17
Elina Taren

Twenty-one years earlier...

Elina clutched her wool jacket tightly against her chest as she quickly made her way up Votum's massive streets. Eight lanes of smoothly paved concrete were divided in half by a solid median and a spacious sidewalk ran alongside either end of the city's main road. Long buses and sleek cars drove up and down the different lanes, and people strode by foot on the sidewalks or over the glass-covered bridges that crossed high above the streets and freeways. Towering gray skyscrapers and elegantly-designed buildings made up the bulk of Nriv's capital city. It was indeed true that out of all Five Cities, Votum was the largest and most impressive. Its modernity was undeniable and the technological advances of the metropolis were great.

Elina pressed onward until she reached Votum's enormous hospital. Stepping through the rotating glass doors, she walked across the marbled floor and up the white steps to the second floor. From there, she entered the elevator and made her way to the fourth floor. Walking down a grey corridor to a door that was marked room number twenty-eight, Elina took a card from her pocket and pressed it against the padlock beneath the door handle. She quietly pushed the door open and stepped inside, loosening her hold on her jacket.

"Hello, Aunt Risa," she greeted quietly. "I'm here. How are you feeling today?"

"I'm dying. How'd you expect I'd feel?" a defeated voice replied from the white bed in the center of the small room. A frail woman with white hair and sunken eyes lay covered with a white blanket. A tall silver android sat by the side of the bed, its expressionless eyes and elongated face turning towards Elina as she stepped closer. It rose to its feet respectfully, clasping its narrow fingers together.

"Your aunt's condition is worsening," it began, its metallic voice pronouncing each word carefully. "Her bones are very weak, and her hyperalgesia has become more pronounced. The heart rate is slowing, and she is having trouble digesting food. The doctor wishes to inform you that the prognosis remains the same."

Elina pulled the seat the android had been sitting in closer to the bed and sitting down, leaned towards her aunt. "Aunt Risa, is there anything more I can do to help?"

Aunt Risa closed her eyes, her face pinched in pain and agitation. "You can have that soulless creature removed from this room. I can't stand its presence any longer!"

Elina turned towards the android. "You are excused." With a nod of its head, the android turned and walked out of the room, shutting the door behind it. "It's gone, Aunt Risa."

"Good riddance," the woman muttered. She gave Elina a tragic look. "Why must those machines spend all their time near me? Why can't they have human nurses and caregivers at this place? I cannot talk to that thing...it unnerves me. I can't rest."

Elina sighed and ran a hand through her short hair. "Because, Aunt Risa, the hospitals are all funded by the same companies that produce commercial androids. Those companies have lobbied the city councilors saying they needed to make it a regulation that androids take the place of humans in regard to medical staffing. They insisted it would be more efficient and sanitary."

"Could they have thought about the patients at all?" Aunt Risa moaned. "Curse those selfish companies and their thoughtless lobbyists. They could have at least made the robots a little more human. If only I could see a kind smile and pleasant eyes...it would make dying a little more bearable."

For a few moments, Elina sat in silent dejection, unsure of what to say. Then suddenly, an idea pierced her brain, making her eyes widen in excitement. "You mean...you wish the androids looked more human?"

"*Hmph*. Not *more* human. Exactly human. Even the illusion of humanity would be a relief at this point..."

Now Elina's eyes began to sparkle. "I've read about this sort of thing in the academic papers and research studies I did back when I was a student at the University. My lab partner Dreadon...he's also researched this a great deal. I have secretly been experimenting and doing my own research at the lab in my spare time and now I think it's possible.

"I...I don't understand. What's possible?"

"To make a robot that is human-like in structure and appearance! Like *completely* human-like. I just didn't know for what purpose I should make such a thing, so I never started the project. Now I know. I will create a specific design for patients at the hospitals, and I'll dedicate the venture to you, Aunt Risa. I'll do it for *you*."

Aunt Risa sighed and closed her eyes. "I won't be alive to see it, but I'm sure you'll find a way. When I adopted you after your parents died, I never imagined you'd be so incredibly brilliant. I'm afraid I never understood much of what you're talking about. I'm sorry to say I no longer care." A tear slipped from the old woman's eyes. "I just want to die." She squeezed Elina's hand. "*Please* stay with me."

Elina bowed her head sadly. "I can't, Aunt Risa. I've signed a contract with VTech. I can't afford to miss work."

"Wretched company," the old woman grunted. "This city is sucking all the life out of everything."

"Oh, don't say that!" Elina shook her head. "I love Votum. I could never have created so many amazing things if I didn't live in this city."

"Inventors and engineers...I don't understand them." Aunt Risa sank her head further into her pillow. "So what...now you're going to leave me again?"

"I'm sorry, Aunt Risa. I have to."

"I suppose it's because of the great money you make that I'm able to stay in what they call the best hospital in the world. Just find a way someday to make sickness and death less of a burden. It's a great loneliness for a dying woman not to see her niece often. It's worse when all I get to see instead is that horrid silver machine."

"I will...I will," Leaning over to kiss her forehead, Elina rose to her feet. "Goodbye, Aunt Risa. I'll visit you again tonight."

"Mhm."

Giving her aunt's hand a final squeeze, Elina walked out of the room and began to shut the door behind her. She was stopped by the android, who was waiting in the hallway.

"I am not permitted to leave her unattended. All her needs must be addressed by me."

"She *needs* to be alone. You don't have to go in right now."

"That is against hospital protocol. I must go in."

Elina frowned. "Well, just stay out of her sight then as much as possible." She turned and made her way down the hallway, back towards the elevator.

***

Elina skipped down the bus steps and half-trotted towards the entrance of the looming skyscraper in front of her. Its fifty floors were encased in a heavy layer of black opaque glass and the top spiraled into a slanted V. In the center of the skyscraper, the words *VTech* stretched from one end to the other. As Elina entered the lower level doors, she was halted by two security androids.

"Identification," they ordered simultaneously. Elina removed a card from her pocket and held it out.

"You are cleared to enter." The androids stepped sideways, and Elina made her way past the pristinely clean lobby towards the hallway behind it.

The hall was filled with people: most of them engineers, business owners, and government officials. Mixed in were security androids and guards who had tasers in their hands and guns slung at their belts. Elina's boots clapped against the smooth floor as she attempted to tread faster without running. She did not want to be late for work.

Glancing up, she could see a cluster of people walking in her direction, their clothing revealing that they belonged within the political sector. The group was comprised of seven men dressed in brown vests, but Elina's eyes noticed only one of them: a tall, well-built man with an affable, handsome face, whimsical smile, and soft brown eyes hidden by a pair of plain, rectangular glasses. For a brief moment, Elina forgot to breathe. Her pace slackened as the group of men seemed to pass by in slow motion. A spacey feeling filled her brain and a ringing sensation vibrated through her ears. She kept walking towards the elevators but turned her head to watch as the men exited the hallway and entered the lobby.

Bump. Elina accidentally collided into the corner of the elevator door which had just opened. Four people standing inside eyed her strangely and the two security androids that stood beside them slowly turned their heads to look at her. Flushing hard, Elina turned her back to them and took a deep breath. She began to nervously twist the hem of her coat as sweat broke out on her forehead and underarms. How embarrassing that everyone in the elevator had seen that!

It was a great relief to leave the elevator once they reached the fiftieth floor. Separating herself from the judging eyes, Elina walked down the corridor, the two security androids flanking either side of her. Together, they approached a heavy glass door at the end of the room, which required Elina's ID card to open. The two androids turned and left while Elina shut the door behind her.

"Almost late?" a cool voice asked from the corner of the black room. Squinting, Elina flipped on the nearest light switch, activating multiple fluorescent lights hanging from the lab ceiling.

"Dreadon, why do you keep the room so dark?"

"I dislike artificial light. You know that."

"It's better than no light at all. You'll ruin your eyes."

"I don't worry about that."

"Hmm." Elina took off her coat and walked towards the man speaking. He was a tall man with wide shoulders and a rectangular face. His pale skin contrasted sharply against his jet-black hair that was pulled back in a short, tight braid. His eyes were a chilly gray, set underneath a pair of arched eyebrows that raised slightly as Elina continued to speak. "How many more tests should we run?"

"Many more. The military division will be visiting us soon. If we are not prepared for their arrival that would be a great failure on our part."

"We'll be all right." Elina approached the object of their conversation: a black android of impressive proportions. There was still some exposure of the inner wiring under its muscled shoulders and torso, but the majority of the body was coated in glossy sheets of black tungsten. The head lay limp against the chest as the android stood unmoving on its stand.

"When should we activate it again?" Elina asked.

"Tomorrow. I will do some scans to make sure all the inner wiring is correct."

"Very well, then. I'll leave that to you." Suddenly Elina stiffened. "The military division is here. Did you know they were coming *today?"*

Without answering, Dreadon stepped forward as the lab's doors swung open and nine men entered the room, their faces somber like the dull grey of their suits. One of them stepped forward, his bushy mustache twitching as he spoke in stern tones. "Hello. How is the project going?"

Dreadon bowed politely. "Very well."

"As you already know, this model will be displayed by the company before the President in about a month's time." The official's eyebrows arched as he spoke. "Many advisors, governors, and military personnel will be there, as well as the private donors and investors who provide funding and hold stock within the VTech company. If we are to persuade the government to mass produce this product, we will have to convince them that it is worth their time and money." The man lowered his voice, but Elina's sharp ears were able to catch bits of the words he spoke to Dreadon. "Your mother has encouraged many of our investors to pour their money into this. She expects everything to go well so…"

"I want what my mother wants." Dreadon straightened, his smooth voice interrupting the official. "I would not undertake a project and leave room for any failure. You can be sure of the product's success." He gestured to Elina. "My partner's insight has proved invaluable. I have learned much from her innovations during this process."

"We are well aware of Miss Taren's contributions." The official faced Elina and nodded politely. "It is why we have chosen her to be part of this."

Elina returned the nod. "Thank you."

The official scanned the room, his gaze focusing on the immobile android. "Well, we shall take our leave. It appears you have made a great deal of progress since out last visit. We only hope that the testing process is successful."

Dreadon smirked. "I have never tested anything of mine and found it to be a failure."

"Of yours?" The official frowned. "This android is the property of V Tech. *You* do not own anything."

"That will change one day."

The official gave an annoyed grunt. "Just like your mother," he muttered. With one last nod, he turned and left the lab, the eight men following.

Elina relaxed her stance as the door shut behind them. "What did you mean just then? What do you hope to own? I've been working with you for four years. You never mentioned wanting to leave VTech."

"You're right. I never did." Dreadon gave her a half smile. "I do not plan on staying here forever."

"You mean you'll leave once your contract is up? Where will you go? Will you start your own company?" She let out a small sigh. "Maybe someday I will."

"Start your own company?"

"Yes." Elina walked in front of the android, studying it. "I might be good at designing weapons, but I don't prefer it."

"What would you do instead?"

Elina hesitated, then shrugged her shoulders. Something inside of her didn't trust Dreadon enough to tell him her plans. "I'm still thinking about it."

***

Diary Entry: 3/16/3016

Today, I have finally figured out what my purpose is in life. After visiting Aunt Risa in the hospital earlier, I realized so many sick people must feel the way she does, and I want to help them. I'll make an android that brings them comfort in their illnesses. My project with Dreadon and all my years working for VTech has prepared me for something like this. Having studied the aesthetics and internal structure of the human face for many years now, I know I can make a robot that mimics it. I have the money saved for all the necessary parts. I'll probably not have much money left after this. That'll be almost a tragedy, but it'll be a worthwhile tragedy.

I saw Renon Coren today at VTech. He's just so beautiful...and he has the most wonderful voice. The way he talks...it's so soothing and gentle. I remember when he came to my university to do a discussion on neuroscience. I was sixteen then...sigh. I was so little. A baby. I remember he called me Miss Elina...it sounded so nice. He must be close to thirty now...is that too old? I don't know. Dreadon's mother married a man twenty years older, so I guess I'm fine. I wish I could get Mr. Coren to notice me.

I've heard that Mr. Coren is one of the most influential men in the city. He's not only a neuroscientist, but he also inherited his father's chemical manufacturing business at the age of twenty-three. That's so young. All the men in his family were neuroscientists, and they're all brilliant. He's also a member of the President's advisory board. I guess the President really respects him.

I would love to be an advisor to the President. There're so many things I could suggest to him that would be good for Votum. I must work hard on this project so I can present it to him before his term is over, BUT...I mustn't share this with anyone yet. It will be my own independent project, outside of VTech. I want to have complete ownership of the model.

There are some parts that will be rather difficult for me to figure out. I want the robot's brain to mimic a human's as much as possible. I am quite comfortable with doing the exterior, but the interior worries me a little. I might need some help...

Chapter 18
Renon Coren

*D*iary Entry 3/20/3016

I have begun working on my project. I don't know what I shall call him yet, so his nickname will be R-17. 17 is the date of my birthday and R is for Renon. I wish I could tell Renon that. He'd probably just laugh. On second thought, maybe I wouldn't want to tell him.

It's very exhausting going to the hospital, work, and then spending late nights on this robot, but it'll be worth it. I won't have time to write much...

***

Diary Entry 3/21/3016

Aunt Risa is getting worse. She didn't talk a lot. I think she only likes me being there so the assistant android can leave. I feel so bad for her. I wish I could spend more time at the hospital, but work takes up the entire day.

Dreadon is obsessed with our military project. He has a great knack for designing weapons. His intelligence astounds even me.

We are opposites, I believe. I like creating things that protect people more...but I suppose a military robot fits under that category. It is meant to protect Votum's citizens after all. If our project is a success, all Five Cities will probably purchase it.

***

Diary Entry 3/29/3016

Aunt Risa died today. When I saw her face it rather frightened me. Her skin was so pinched, and it seemed like she was shriveling away before my eyes. I cried a lot. She was never the same after she got sick. I know that horrid android scared her to the very end. I tried convincing the hospital staff to remove it many times, but they always refused.

My heart hurts. I hate death! It scares me so badly. I don't understand how anyone could want to die. Living is so much better. I plan on living a VERY long time.

***

Diary Entry 4/25/3016

Hello, it's been awhile. I'm so, so busy at work. Our military project is nearly completed. The presentation is in two weeks.

I'm making good progress on R-17. I spend all my spare time on him now. I've got his core nearly completed and have begun building the physical structure. I've purchased tungsten for his interior skeletal form, but it's silver instead of black. He is to look as human as possible, so I don't think I'll be using much tungsten on the exterior.

I'm still undecided about how I'm going to create R-17's mind. The wiring of his brain determines how accurate his facial expressions will be. I need help. I've thought and I've thought, and I've decided to visit Mr. Coren tomorrow. I'm absolutely terrified, but he's a neuroscientist. If he would agree to assist me, I'd be so grateful.

I also just want a chance to see him. I wish so badly he could like me. He smiled at me when I was sixteen but that doesn't mean anything. I want his smile to mean something. I just need him to see me...

***

Elina stood on the front steps of Renon Coren's magnificent house, an uncomfortable bubble rising in her throat. It was very early morning, and she had boldly marched up the front steps, not even sure if he was home or not. Now she no longer felt bold. As she stood quivering under her coat, her eyes wandered over the sweeping porch she was standing on. Unlike most houses belonging to Votum's wealthiest, there were no androids standing guard. In fact, there was no obvious security anywhere other than the camera hanging over the front door. The iron gate in front of the house was unlocked, and Elina wondered why such an important man seemed so unconcerned with his safety.

Just then, the front door opened and a small older woman stood in front of Elina. Without the slightest show of astonishment, she asked, "How did you get through the gate?"

"Uh...what?" Elina stammered, her face growing hot. "It was unlocked. I...I didn't know..."

"Why are you here?"

"I came to see Mr. Coren...if he's home that is. If he's busy then it's not important. I didn't mean to be a bother...it's just so important...I probably shouldn't have come...I'm sorry..."

The woman blinked slowly, the corner of her mouth twitching slightly. "Please wait here. May I have your name?"

"Elina...Elina Taren."

"One moment, please." The woman shut the door, leaving Elina on the porch. She began to panic as sweat broke out over her body in all the worst places. She should never have come here; apparently the gate *was* supposed to be locked. She decided to turn around and race home as quickly as possible, but before she could, the front door re-opened and the old woman nodded.

"You may come in."

"What? I can?"

"Yes." The woman stepped aside, holding open the door.

"Th...thank you." Elina hastily stepped over the threshold, tightly gripping the folder she had brought with her. "Should...should I wait here?"

"No. Come with me, please." The old woman plodded down the hallway, and Elina timidly followed, hoping with all her heart that her sweat wouldn't release an odor. Already she felt wet around her neck and under her armpits.

The old woman entered a room to the right side of the hallway and as Elina walked inside, her mouth dropped open. The interior was nothing like the modern style of Votum's average house. The walls and the ceiling were covered in square-shaped, wooden paneling and the curtains hanging over the tall arched windows were a thick, luxurious velvet, tinted a rich red hue. At the end of the room was a magnificent stone fireplace, not tall in stature but beautifully designed, with its carved, wooden mantle. A large desk stretched to the right of the fireplace across from a leather couch and leaning over the desk was Renon Coren. Elina's heart skipped a beat, sending another bubble to her throat. Frowning, she swallowed hard and straightened. To be this nervous was absolutely ridiculous. She *had* to make a good impression.

As Renon turned and faced her, Elina caught her breath. He was wearing a brown dressing gown that split open at the chest, and his chestnut hair was pulled back in a short ponytail. It was not the most magnificent attire, but Elina thought he looked absolutely gorgeous. Renon's eyes squinted slightly behind his glasses as he looked up at her and then he held out his hand with a friendly smile.

"Hello, Miss Taren. I remember you. You were a student at the University. You were part of a group that listened to a talk I gave many years ago. Welcome to my house."

"Thank you." Overwhelmed by his polite greeting, Elina struggled to think of a response as she returned his handshake. "I...I'm so sorry. If I had known I wasn't supposed to come in..."

"My gate malfunctioned last night. I am home today because I wish to be here when it gets fixed later. You have impeccable timing." Renon smiled, the corners of his eyes crinkling.

"You mean you don't mind that I'm here?"

"If I had minded, I never would have let you in." Renon nodded to the folder in her hand. "I presume there is something you wish to show me? Aren't you a lead robotics engineer for VTech?"

"Yes, sir."

"You are very clever I hear. You graduated from the University at sixteen with degrees in Robotics Engineering, Biochemistry, Mechanical, and Electrical Engineering. Rather the patterns of a prodigy. I doubt you need to see me for anything."

"Oh, but I do!" Elina clutched the folder to her chest. "It has to do with a project I'm working on. I'm having complications with the internal structure of the brain."

"Brain?"

"Yes, sir. I know you're a neuroscientist, so I thought maybe you could help me. You...you are something of a prodigy yourself. Don't you have many degrees too?"

Renon gave a tiny laugh. "I have a few."

"Yes, so you see..." Elina struggled to speak clearly without her words falling over one another. "I need someone who understands the inner workings of the brain. You have advanced knowledge on the subject and I..."

"What exactly is it you are working on?"

"Oh...I am working on making an advanced humanoid android that can provide assistance to the sick and injured."

"Is this affiliated with VTech?"

"No sir...it's my own private project."

"Hmm." Stroking his chin, Renon began to pace the room. "Why make such a thing?"

"Because sir, the way the hospital systems are set up in this city do not allow for human nurses to take care of the patients. It has come to my attention that this causes discomfort for many sick people. If the Board of Directors will not budge on allowing human nurses to take the place of androids, they might at least permit a more advanced prototype to take their place." Forgetting her anxiety, Elina stepped forward, her words tumbling out eagerly. "That is why I wish to make a humanoid android, sir! I believe I can create a design that is more efficient and durable than any ever made before, with an exterior that accurately mimics a human. In order to do that, I need the brain to be extremely advanced so that the outer sensory and facial movements will be hyper-realistic."

Renon halted in his pacing. "You know...I am not an admirer of robotics nor anything related to their advancement."

Elina flushed. "What, sir? What do you mean?"

"I believe they are a hindrance to our empathy and emotional health. However, my biggest problem with them is that they are replacing every sector of life that was previously occupied by humans. Instead of soldiers we now have advanced androids. Instead of human nurses, as you pointed out...androids. Enforcers of the law, security, the defense system; all of it is being overrun by robotics. The tech companies fund many of the cities' projects, schools, hospitals: that gives them power over so much. They are even beginning to overtake the governing body of this city. Their lobbyists work tirelessly to ensure they have a stronger hold over the political sector. The advancement in robotics is just a shield for a group of people that are trying to gain political power. This disease is being pushed not just on Votum but on all Five Cities. I do not know how the opposing political parties will be able to stop it. However..." Renon stepped closer to Elina. "I do find your project fascinating, and I sympathize with its goal." He took a deep breath. "I will help you...and if I should find the results satisfactory, I will personally present the finished product to the President. You needn't look so discouraged, Miss Taren. I *will* help you."

Elina's face shifted from tragic to ecstatic instantaneously. "Oh, yes, sir. Thank you, sir! When would you like to start, sir?"

Renon laughed. "You can show me your design now. Then we will run some tests. Oh...and you needn't call me sir. You may call me Renon."

Chapter 19
Elina's Resolve

Diary Entry 5/2/3016

Renon Coren is an impressive man. In spite of his professed dislike for androids, he seems to have taken a great interest in mine. It's my opinion that he does not hate androids themselves but rather what people are using them for. I think he finds my motives noble, so that's why he's helping me.

The first day I visited him, he scanned his brain instead of mine. He decided last minute that if I'm going to construct a male model, his brain structure and functions would be better suited for the task. (Again, not the action of a man who has a deep loathing for androids.) He's discovered a way to examine the neurons in the brain with incredible accuracy. I shan't say more because I won't give away his work here, but I know for certain now that the man is a genius.

I'm so pleased he remembered me from the University. However, he might just remember everyone. I didn't get the impression he's interested in me THAT way. I'm very frustrated. I don't like this feeling. I need to find a way to get him to like me. I'm going back one more time tomorrow. Maybe something will be different...

***

Diary Entry 5/3/3016

What I write now will stay within these pages - no one else shall read this. It is a great secret. Renon has given me something that I never knew existed, and he calls it khilange. It's a rare metal from his hometown; his family has protected its existence for many years. Few know of it or where to find it. Apparently, Renon's family is very old and powerful, and they come from the city of Phylidrum, which is the great city beside the western ocean. I do not know much, (he would not tell me) but it seems to me there is a secret behind his family history.

This khilange is abnormally strong: even stronger than tungsten and diamonds. Renon says I could use it as a protective shield for R-17's core and for the internal frame of his skeletal structure. It occurred to me that this metal will permit R-17 to be capable of rescuing people from burning buildings or locked doors. He will be powerful enough to move cars and heavy objects without suffering internal damage. I am beyond thrilled!

I am also very disappointed. Mr. Coren has been unusually generous to me in every way, but I'm now certain he does not like me. I think he just sees me as a fascinating and brilliant woman – who is also much younger. I wish I were older. Maybe I just need more time with him? I don't know...I don't believe that's possible. I no longer need his help. I feel like a rock is sinking in my middle. It's a dreadful sensation.

I think I shall have to find a safe place to put this diary. I really can't afford to have anyone reading it...

***

Elina turned away from her reflection in the accordion crystal wall of the banquet room and took her place beside Dreadon. They were in a hotel not far from the President's palace and for the past hour, high-ranking guests had been pouring into the building. At the end of the room was a raised dais, entirely enclosed in a partition wall of see-through, bullet-proof glass. Resting in the middle of the glass partition was the android she and Dreadon had been working on, its body still and stationary, the head tilted downwards against its chest. Beside it stood a robot of smaller stature but also tall and sturdy. It too, was frozen still.

Across the dais were multiple tables covered with crisp linen table cloths and dainty vases filled with yellow and white flowers. The ashen walls were dimly lit by thick rectangular lamps wrapped in gold trim, and small ceiling lights provided the remainder of the room with the necessary illumination. Elina ran a finger over the crepe material of the evening gown she was wearing. Both she and Dreadon were dressed in black: the color representing VTech, who was funding the current event. Elina straightened her shoulders and took a deep breath, her eyes shifting towards the room's main door.

"The President has arrived," she whispered. Dreadon did not reply. His piercing grey eyes followed the President, who was responding to the guests that rose to greet him. Elina made a mental note of all the different people in the room. The President of Votum was present, surrounded by guards and advisors and the CEO of VTech was standing not far away from him. Men from the military board lingered close by and wealthy investors and families were also scattered at the various tables. There was an intense severity in the air that was palpable. Elina could feel the tension in her very nerves.

"I will take my place now," she mouthed to Dreadon. Nodding slightly, he turned and walked to the left side of the dais, while Elina went to stand at its right. Watching as the President seated himself at the designated chair before the platform, her attention shifted to a woman sitting a few feet behind him. Anyone could have seen, by the tightly clenched jaw and pale skin, that this woman was Dreadon's mother. Dressed in a black dress with a collar similar to the one Dreadon was wearing, the woman had hard lines running along the sides of her down-turned mouth and there was a deep furrow to her brow. Her silver hair, streaked with black, was pulled back fashionably. She kept glancing at Dreadon, their eyes speaking words that no one else would understand.

As Elina watched them both, an uncanny sensation prickled over her skin. Then her attention was suddenly diverted by the movement of a new person entering the room. Seeing it was Renon, Elina caught her breath and straightened her posture.

He looked extremely debonair tonight, wearing a golden-brown vest with a white collar underneath. His thick hair was slicked up front and waved back against his neck. Elina quickly averted her gaze, but she could feel her cheeks warming, and her arms beginning to sweat as he seated himself behind the President. *I wonder what his face looks like without glasses.*

Elina was momentarily distracted from her thoughts as the sound of a graceful tune wafted into the room. The orchestra in the adjoining lobby had begun to play and as if it were some sort of cue, the President rose to his feet, everyone following suit. Stepping ahead of the President and making his way to the front of the dais, VTech's CEO cleared his throat and raised a hand.

"I first of all want to thank President Cair for being present for this special moment. His attendance means a great deal to this company, and we hope that he finds the endeavors we have made for the military satisfactory. This project was presented to him many years ago and so it is with great pride that I stand here now to present the finished product. I also wish to thank the members of our board, our many generous investors, as well as the hundreds of employees who make what we do possible." The CEO gestured to Dreadon and Elina. "This particular project only exists because of the incredible genius of our top engineers: Dreadon Durus and Elina Taren." The crowd clapped as Dreadon and Elina bowed.

The CEO cleared his throat and continued. "Before you stands model K6-12. Each letter and number is a reference to the purpose and history of this model. K stands for *kill*, as this weapon is designed for military combat. Six stands for the number of years it took before this project was generously approved by our governing body. Finally, twelve is a nod of respect to the span of the Presidential term. The Five Cities are pleased and honored to have President Cair represent us as a people, and I look forward to a closer relationship with him and the ruling administration in the future. But now, I will pause my speech and let you all see what you came to see. Let us demonstrate how this model stands up to the one that is currently being used by our military." Nodding towards both Elina and Dreadon, the CEO went and sat back in his chair, eyes narrowed and arms crossed.

Stepping forward, Elina entered the glass enclosure and flipped a small switch on the android's neck. Instantly, the android's head straightened, and its pupils became visible: black eyes surrounded by a thin, yellow ring. Elina then activated the second robot and exited the enclosure, securing the door behind her.

Returning to her place by the dais, Elina held her breath as the K6-12 android rotated its head and eyed Dreadon. For a moment, Dreadon stood motionless. Then he gave it a barely perceptible nod. The yellow ring within the android's eyes glowed brightly and with one rapid motion, it charged for the second robot. With a complicated flip, the K6-12 flung itself over the robot and knocked it to the ground. Rising to its feet, the robot removed a gun at its side and fired at the K6-12. Raising its arm, the K6-12 activated a blue shield, using it to block the barrage of bullets. Swinging out its arm, the K6-12 then knocked the gun from the robot's hand and struck it in the chest. Before the stumbling robot could recover, the android swung around again and seized the robot's neck. Yanking a knife with a glowing grey blade from its belt, the robot slashed at the K6-12's arm, temporarily breaking free. In response, the K6-12 grabbed both of the robot's arms, pinned them together, and kicked out its leg, sending the robot to its knees. Yanking the knife from the robot's hand, the K6-12 lurched forward, plunging the knife into the robot's neck. The robot's head severed and slid to the floor, the rest of the body crashing beside it. Straightening, the K6-12 android raised its arm, and the entire room burst out into an eruption of cheers and clapping.

Elina gave a little gasp, realizing she had been holding her breath the entire time. She observed the excited fire burning in Dreadon's pupils and shifting her attention, she saw his mother had a strange smirk across her face as she applauded. The CEO rose to his feet, beaming with satisfaction, and the rest of the guests were nodding in admiration and approval.

As the android lowered his weapon at Dreadon's command, another misgiving rushed through Elina's mind. The invention that she had helped design and build for months on end suddenly seemed ominous to her. *Something doesn't feel right. I don't know what, but something is wrong. Perhaps I should have never agreed to make this thing. What if Renon was right about androids consuming our society? What if I just made a mistake?*

Trying to ignore her thoughts, Elina bowed low to the animated crowd. Then she raised her head just in time to see Renon get up from his seat and leave the room. A strong desire to follow him took over her, but she knew she couldn't leave. The CEO was saying something to her...now the President was stepping forward. Dreadon was also approaching...

***

A melodic waltz filled Elina's ears as she quietly walked passed the orchestra. She had finally been able to sneak out of the banquet hall and was making her way down the hallway towards the hotel's lobby. Her shoes clicked across the copper sheen of the marbled floor, and her eyes traveled over the murals stretching across the hotel's hallway. The skyscrapers of Votum, the oceans of Phylidrum, mountains behind Nobiles...all of the murals were stunning and rich with color.

Once she reached the lobby, Elina could see that no one was there other than the receptionist. Tip-toeing away, Elina veered down another hallway, passed a flight of stairs, and peaked through a massive open doorway to her left. The interior appeared to be a sort of gallery. Paintings of all shapes and sizes, rimmed in gold and copper trim, hung from the walls. A cuprum chandelier was suspended from the ceiling's center, its light casting reflections against the maroon hue of the room. Close to the ceiling was an overhanging balcony, providing a view to the room from above.

As Elina took in the space's beauty, she noticed Renon standing a few feet away, observing one of the paintings. Silently, she stepped through the doorframe and walked towards him, her hands pressed tightly to her sides. He turned his head towards her in surprise as she came closer.

"You like paintings?" she ventured. Her voice sounded obnoxiously loud against the deep silence of the room.

"Yes, I find them quite mesmerizing. There is such depth to a well-executed portrait." Renon gave her a searching look. "What are you doing here, Miss Elina?"

"I wanted to get away," Elina took a step closer, "And I also like to look at paintings."

"Get away from what?"

"The very thing I just helped create." Elina's eyes met Renon's. "Much of it is Dreadon's design, though most of the enhanced features and outer layer have my touch. Somehow though, I feel like it's all Dreadon's. It doesn't seem anymore like something I constructed. I feel empty and lonely after it all. I don't know what to think." She looked back at the painting; a woman in a long robe smiling at a man who lingered behind a nearby balcony beside a lush garden. "Who made it?"

"A woman named Chryllis. She was from the city of Phylidrum. Many of her paintings are viewed as masterpieces. They focus heavily on living and love."

"You like those topics?"

"They have more beauty than robots. They are about life...people."

Elina took a deep breath. "You hate robots very much, don't you?"

Renon shook his head. "I hate how they are being used. If a robot could contribute to the beauty of this world, then I would surely love it."

Elina's heart skipped a beat, but she maintained her calm exterior. "What else do you love?"

"Poetry, laughter, sunsets...the ocean. Have you ever been to the ocean, Miss Elina?"

"No, never. But I'd want to...someday. What else do you like?"

"Breathtaking architecture, mountainous landscapes, dancing, songs...music...." Renon inclined his head. "I can hear the orchestra from here."

"They're playing the national anthem." The epic sound of singing and violins surged through the hallway, wafting into the gallery.

"So they are." Renon bowed slightly before Elina. "Shall we dance?"

"Yes." Astonished, Elina took the hand Renon offered her and let him lead as he began to sway back and forth across the room.

"My deepest apologies, Miss Elina. I never asked you what *you* like."

"You can call me Elina. I don't mind."

"Very well, then. What do you like, Elina?"

"I like creating things. I enjoy beautiful moments and memories. Memories are everything to me! I can see all of them in my mind so clearly…as if they were yesterday. Everything anyone has ever done or said; once it happens, it never leaves my mind."

Renon smiled. "Then I will make sure to leave a good impression." He continued to guide Elina across the room, his movements matching the rhythm of the music. In a confused sort of ecstasy, Elina followed along, her mind whirling. She still felt he wasn't interested in her, yet he was acting as if he might be.

A sensation that someone was watching them suddenly distracted Elina from her thoughts. Her eyes darted towards the balcony, but she saw no one standing there. Then the music slowed, and Renon halted with a final bow and smile.

"Thank you, Elina. I wish you a good evening and sincerely hope that I have left you with a nice memory."

A panicked feeling rose in Elina's chest. *No, no. This isn't how it's supposed to end. I didn't even get a chance to talk to him more. I can't let him go like this. I must do something!* Stepping close to him, she quickly leaned forward and gave Renon a long kiss. He did not pull away and as she slowly let go, she could see the brown eyes behind his glasses round with astonishment. He gave her a questioning look.

"Goodnight," she whispered softly. Swiftly, she turned and rushed out of the gallery, leaving Renon staring after her wide-eyed. Making her way down the hallway, she pressed a hand against her chest, her heart beating wildly. Taking a deep breath, she slowed her pace and a shivery thrill shot through her body. Throwing back her head, she laughed with silent elation.

Suddenly, the sound of voices drifting from a nearby room caught her attention. Discreetly, Elina pressed herself against the wall, craning her neck forward to listen.

"You must keep her by your side!" a woman's voice muttered. "I know she doesn't come from a wealthy family, but she could very well be the most brilliant woman in all of the Five Cities. If you don't have her then someone else will and think what a danger that could prove to be. A woman like that would quickly become your adversary were she to become entangled with the wrong man. We cannot afford to have her become close to someone from an opposing political party."

Elina's face paled as Dreadon's voice responded, "I know what to do. You do not need to worry, Mother."

Tearing her ear from the wall, Elina turned and rushed back the way she had come, her heart pounding in her chest. *They're insane! Both of them are insane. They're more power-hungry than I thought. I will stay far away from Dreadon. I'm glad my contract is nearly over. Once it's completed, I will never work with him again. Never, never, NEVER.*

Chapter 20
Renon's Offer

D*iary Entry 5/27/3016*

I have two more months before my contract ends. I will be glad to get away from VTech. I have gained a great dislike for the company, and I refuse to contribute to any of their future endeavors. Somehow, I think they won't be glad to see me go, but I don't care. I've been here for four years. I'm leaving.

My work on R-17 is going very well. I'm happy with his success.

I'm also very happy because Renon came to see me last week! He says he wishes to view R-17's progress, but he was very comfortable and close with me. We ended up talking for a very long time. My kiss must have worked. I'm a little surprised at how easy this is all becoming. Is that really all it takes to win a man?

***

Diary Entry 5/28/3016

Dreadon is making me uncomfortable. He watches me with great intensity whenever we are together. I'm not sure what else his hateful mother told him, but he never takes his eyes off me, and I don't like it.

***

Diary Entry 5/29/3016

President Cair vetoed the bill that would have permitted K6-12 to become the standard model used by the military. VTech and much of the military board are outraged. I know many of President Cair's political advisors aren't pleased either. They all expected him to go along with it.

Renon visited me today, and he all but admitted he was never in favor of K6-12. I don't doubt that he has great influence over President Cair and convinced him to change his mind. I am inclined to agree with Renon. These tech companies are gaining too much political influence. I'm glad President Cair sees it.

I am worried for Renon. He has gained many powerful enemies.

***

Diary Entry 6/7/3016

Renon has been seeing me every day now. I'm so happy about it! He's such a beautiful man. The way he talks, his ideas, dreams, ideals...the smile he gives me and the way his eyes crinkle behind his glasses. I want him. No...I NEED him. I don't know how

I lived away from him all this time. If something were to ever happen to him, it would break my heart in two.

I still wonder what he looks like without his glasses. He never takes them off. I should ask him to tomorrow…

***

Diary Entry 6/10/3016

I forgot to ask Renon to take off his glasses. I only saw him briefly today. He had to attend a board meeting at his chemical company and stopped by on the way to say hello. CrC is his company's name. Renon explained that it's just an abbreviation for Coren Renon Company. Renon Coren is apparently a family name. His family is very old and rich. I feel like that's something I should've known, but I do tend to get wrapped up in my work, so that is the excuse I'll be using for my ignorance.

***

Diary Entry 6/11/3016

I'm exhausted. I've spent nearly all my nights developing R-17. A feverish feeling that I MUST finish him soon keeps nagging at my soul. His core and body are completed but much of him still looks like wires. I'm not sure what I want his face to look like.

***

Diary Entry 6/13/3016

Renon tells me the political tension is getting worse. The majority of President Cair's advisors heavily invest in VTech, and they are furious with the President for refusing to work with them. Renon tells me they are doing their best to convince the population to vote for a candidate of THEIR choosing once President Cair's term is up. I do not like this anymore than Renon does. These men just want power...they don't care about the Five Cities' citizens.

***

Diary Entry 6/14/3016

R-17 spoke for the first time today. His voice is very metallic, but I shall fix that soon. The more I enhance his mental function and decide how to program his personality, the more his voice will alter. Maybe then I can figure out how to do his face. I'm still undecided on that part...

***

Elina felt a hand on her shoulder gently shaking her. With a low grunt, she shifted her head against her arm and murmured, *"Hmm?"*

"Elina, you fell asleep. How long have you been here?"

"What?" Blinking, Elina raised her head and looked up to see Renon standing next to her. "What do you mean? Did I?" She gave a deep sigh. "I was so tired. I didn't mean to."

"Your eyes are bloodshot. Have you been sleeping enough? R-17 is still active. He said hello to me when I entered the room."

"Wait, you mean he's been standing next to me the whole time? I left him on?" Elina turned to R-17, who nodded his head.

"Hello, Miss Elina. I did not wish to wake you. Your brain showed a great decrease in mental activity, indicating that you were experiencing mental and physical fatigue. I decided to let you sleep."

"Thank you, R-17." Rising to her feet, Elina placed a hand on his shoulder. "That was very thoughtful of you. If you don't mind, I shall now deactivate you for a little while."

"Of course." R-17 stood still and his head drooped as Elina flipped the switch between his shoulder blades. Then she turned to Renon, who was watching her with a concerned face.

"Elina, you need to sleep more. It's unhealthy to stay awake so much."

"I know, I know, but I feel like I *must* work on him as much as possible."

"Why?"

"I'm not sure. I just have this sensation that I'm under a deadline, and I need to meet it. It's a strange feeling I can't shake." Elina's eyes fell to a package Renon was carrying under his arm. "What's that?"

"I have something for you. I recall you telling me last week during conversation that your favorite color was red, and you were tired of all your black clothes, so…" Renon handed Elina the package he was holding. "I got you this. It's a gift. Please do not be afraid to accept." There was an eager nervousness to his voice that Elina had never heard before. With a smile, she took the package from his hands and began to open it. Her mouth dropped as the brown folds of paper revealed a dress of bright red with delicate ruffles.

"Thank you…thank you, Renon!" she breathed. "It's so *red*. I'm sorry…my brain's super fuzzy…I can't think of much else to say, but I love it…*I love it.*"

"You can try it on tomorrow and…"

"No, no. I want to try it on now. Give me one second!" Before Renon could protest, Elina dashed out of the room. When she returned, the soft fabric flowing around her thin form with elegant grace, his eyes widened and a dazzled smile spread over his face.

"Well?" Elina murmured. "Do you like it?"

Renon chuckled. "Aren't I the one who's supposed to ask that question?"

"I asked first." Elina stepped closer and glanced up at him through lowered eyelashes. "Do you?"

Renon's eyes traveled across her shoulders, past her mouth, and up to her eyes. The warmth in his own eyes seemed to penetrate deep inside of Elina's soul, and she caught her breath.

"Yes," he murmured. Wrapping both arms around her waist, he gently pulled her towards him and kissed her on the lips. Elina closed her eyes. A feeling of heated exuberance coursed through her body. At long last, all her dreams were coming true. Before he could kiss her again, Elina placed a hand on his chest.

"Wait!" Carefully, she removed the glasses from his face and placed them on the table. "I've wanted to know for years what you looked like without them."

"For *years?"* Renon laughed. "How long has this obsession to know lasted, eh? Well, are you satisfied now?"

Elina caressed his face. "Your eyes are so beautiful," she whispered. "Without glasses your face is even more lovely."

"I never thought of glasses as an ornamental accent, so that's to be expected," Renon joked.

"With or without glasses; it doesn't matter to me. Even if your face *were* to change and shift, it still wouldn't matter. It'd be part of you, and I love *you*, Renon Coren."

"Elina," Renon began breathlessly. "Would you do me a favor?"

"Of course. Anything."

"Say those words to me tomorrow, the day after, *every day*...for the rest of my life." Renon brushed his forehead against hers and ran his hand through her hair. *"Marry me."*

Tears glistened in Elina's eyes. She laughed aloud in joyful disbelief. "*Really?"*

"Yes, really. Will...will you?"

Without answering, Elina flung her arms around Renon's neck and kissed him: a long kiss that melted into a tight embrace as he held her close.

Chapter 21
Gentle Love

D iary Entry 7/4/3016

Renon and I were secretly married yesterday. We leave on our honeymoon in four weeks once my contract with VTech ends. Renon will be taking me to Phylidrum. He wants to show me the ocean. I'll also get to meet his family.

I will resume work on R-17 as soon as I return...

***

Elina wrote out her name and the date on a paper slip and attached it to the folder next to her. Opening a file drawer, she placed the folder inside and secured the drawer shut with a key. Then she walked over to a man with a dark suit and scowling eyes who was standing next to Dreadon and handed him the key.

"Everything is secure, sir."

"Miss Taren, I do not understand. Why don't you wish to renew your contract? You have spent four years working for this company. We have benefited a great deal from your innovations.

Are you certain you don't wish to sign on for another four years? We'll increase your pay, and you'll gain a high position both in this company and in the city. You'd be a wealthy woman! Shall I have the contract brought in? You can still sign it."

Elina shook her head. "No, sir. Thank you for the generous offer, but it's not an offer I can currently accept."

With a stifled complaint, the man clutched the key Elina had given him and stormed out of the room. Swallowing hard, Elina turned and began to walk away, but Dreadon's voice stopped her.

"You turned down a very advantageous proposal. Money and status..."

"Those things don't matter to me..."

"But the ability to afford your own projects does." Dreadon stepped closer as Elina whirled about to face him.

"What makes you say that?"

"I've worked beside you for four years. I know you well. You've mentioned wanting to have innovative freedom outside of VTech. You can't do that without money or status...nor can you get far without the support of patrons and the government. Not in this city. You don't come from a prestigious family, Miss Taren. You have only your mind...and a very gifted one at that. I'm sure the inability to use it would drive you, well...*mad*."

Elina pinched her mouth together. "What you say might be true. However, I'm not presently concerned with such things."

"You aren't? How do you expect to make a living? Of course, you could you go to another city, but they haven't the resources that Votum has. You're ambitious, Miss Taren – just like me. I don't think that solution would satisfy you. However...there is another one."

"I don't know what you mean."

Dreadon inclined his head and stepped even closer. "Marry me."

Elina's eyes widened. "*What?*"

"Marry me, and your position will be secured. I come from a wealthy family and have a high standing with the majority of the governing body in this city. I am also a top engineer for VTech. Marry me, and you will not even have to be part of VTech in order to reach the heights you wish to attain. You'd have all the experimental freedom you could want beside me, and it will be under *our* ownership...not some corporation's."

A cold chill trickled down Elina's spine as she backed away. Dreadon's eyes were like grey ice as they bore into her own, waiting for her response. She shook her head.

"I can't marry you."

"And why not?"

"I'm already married." Without saying anything more, Elina turned and quickly left the room.

***

Diary Entry 7/6/3016

I've been unable to stop thinking of Dreadon's offer of marriage, and it enrages me. I can't believe he had the nerve to suggest such a thing. He would only want to use me! I'll NEVER let him do that. I'd rather die.

I won't say anything to Renon. I don't want to worry him...

***

Diary Entry 7/21/3016

We are leaving for Phylidrum tomorrow morning. I'm very excited! Renon keeps talking about how beautiful the ocean is and now I really want to see it.

I love Renon so much. I don't know how I could live without him. I hope I die before he does because I don't think I'd be able to stand him being gone.

I've been feeling oddly nauseous lately. I hope I feel better soon.

***

Diary Entry 7/22/3016

I am pregnant...

I'm so confused. How on earth did that happen so quickly?? I feel absolutely ecstatic...and terrified. I won't tell Renon just yet. I need to process this, and I want to wait for the right moment before I do. I'm scared. I don't know how he'll take it.

I have locked up R-17 in Renon's house and will be bringing the diary with me. I don't dare leave something like it behind. It's too personal. I wish I could bring R-17. I feel sick when I think of leaving him.

***

Diary Entry 7/23/3016

We entered Phylidrum at 7 p.m....

This city is absolutely dazzling. It's far less modern and elegant in a very different sort of way from Votum. The architecture is older and many of the houses belonging to the wealthy have arches and beautifully sculpted pillars. Even the robots are more beautiful here. Their voices are soothing and many are white. I've noticed there aren't a lot of them.

I met Renon's family: his mother and sister, who is close to his age. Renon is much like his mother, who is very sweet and good-natured. Renon's sister is nothing like him, even though they look very similar. She seems restless and always looks stressed. I can tell she is constantly thinking, and she often mutters to herself. She's a strange creature. I wasn't exactly sure what she thought of me. She has been treating me very aloofly.

***

"Hurry, Elina!"

"I *am*." Elina gasped laughingly as Renon pulled her along, both of them making their way towards the beach. Elina let out an ecstatic exclamation at the sight in front of her: an endless stretch of blue water against the golden orange of the setting sun. The salty breeze whipped Elina's hair, and she inhaled the clean air that swept through her nose. The brown sand crumbled beneath her toes as she ran and the cry of seagulls blended with the strong wind.

"Renon! It's...I..." Elina flung back her head and stretched out her arms. "I *love it.*"

"I told you." Eagerly, Renon continued to pull her towards the waves. "You've got to get in the water."

"What...all the way?"

"No, not unless you want to. Just step in it. See?" Still holding onto her hands, Renon stood opposite to Elina as the frothy waves lapped over her ankles.

"It's not that cold," Elina exclaimed.

"No, it's not. The western ocean is known for being warm."

"I *love it!*" Elina repeated enthusiastically. She leaned over and cupped her hands in the ocean, letting the water trickle through her fingers.

"This place was where I loved to come as a child." Renon shielded his eyes as he gazed out towards the sun's rays. "It reminds me of a song I read on the walls in Votum's museum; a song whose origin comes from this city. I found the melody and have loved it ever since. I can sing it for you."

"You can sing?" Elina leaned forward and laughed. "What other secrets are you hiding from me? You know, I can't sing to save my life."

"I don't believe you."

"No, I really can't. It sounds just awful: like a goose squawking."

Renon chuckled. "If you say so."

"I do. Now sing me *your* song."

Lowering his eyes, Renon took a deep breath and began, his voice blending against the rush of the waves.

"I sing a song to you across the sea,
A siren's call that rings clear and free.
I'll bend my love and will to yours,
Through sun and storms, we will endure.
Now I dance with you in marbled chambers,
You and I are no longer strangers.
Tattoo your love across my heart,
That we may never be far apart."

"I didn't know you could sing so well," Elina breathed. "How do you do it?"

"Sing? It's not hard..."

"Liar!"

"Now you try..."

"*No.* It'll sound terrible." Elina shook her head vigorously. "I refuse."

"I'll show you how..."

"Show me later." Elina grasped both of his hands in hers. "I have something to tell you."

Renon gently stroked her tangled hair. "All right then. Tell me."

"I've been keeping a secret...*secret.*"

"Huh?"

Elina flushed. "I don't know how to say it...I don't have the words...I sound so clumsy. No words seem good enough. I'm sorry, I'm not good at this." She took a deep breath and cleared her throat. "I'm...um...we...we're going to have a baby."

"*What?*" With a stunned expression, Renon stepped back, running his hands through his hair. "You...we are?" An emotional crack crept into his voice, and his eyes misted over. "*We are?*"

Seeing Renon's reaction, tears sprang into Elina's own eyes. "*Yes,*" she whispered.

"My girl...my love..." Pulling her towards him, Renon kissed her long and slow on the mouth. Then he embraced her tightly before tenderly pressing his lips to her forehead. "My dear girl..."

At his words, Elina burst into tears. "I...I wasn't sure how you would take it. I didn't know how to explain...I'm just so relieved now..."

Renon pressed his hands against her face. "*Woman...*you have just made me happier than you could possibly imagine! We are going to have a child...and I love you for it."

With a muffled sob, Elina flung herself against him, burying her face against his chest. "I love you *too.*"

***

Elina placed her book on her lap and smiled as Renon removed the hairband from his ponytail, his hair falling loose around his neck. Sliding his shirt over his head, he placed it on the bed post and slid under the blanket beside Elina. With a sigh, Elina rested her head against his shoulder.

"It doesn't seem like it's been two weeks," she began quietly. "I don't want to go back to Votum. I like it here."

"When President Cair's term is completed, let's come back," Renon suggested. "I have lived in Votum for twelve years. I was there to study at the University and after my father died, I inherited his business. It was then that President Cair offered me a position on his advisory board. I accepted, but I've never been able to forget this place. Phylidrum will always be home to me."

"Yes! I want it to be home for me too. I always considered Votum my home, but now when I think of it I get a feeling of great unrest. I feel our child isn't meant to grow up there. I'm certain of it."

Renon kissed Elina on the forehead. "Yes, we shall raise our girl here."

"Our *girl?*" Elina gave him a surprised look. "How would you know if it's going to be a girl?"

"I can feel it."

Elina laughed. "What, are you psychic?"

"Right now I am, and I know it will be a girl."

Elina smiled and snuggled closer to him. "I wouldn't mind. I think a little girl would be fun. Maybe she'll look like you."

"No," Renon replied dreamily. "She'll look like you. She'll have your eyes and your face. And she'll have your intelligence."

"Not just mine." Elina gazed up at Renon with glowing eyes. "She'll have yours too."

Chapter 22
R-17 Taken

Elina's eyes narrowed as the car halted outside Renon's house. They had left Phylidrum with the house's gates locked but now they were flung open and two black vehicles sat in the driveway. At the sight, Renon's mouth tightened into a scowl.

"What is this?" he muttered. "How did they get through the gate?"

Pushing open the car door, Elina quickly got out, a sharp fear clutching her throat. Rushing through the gate, she raced up the house's front steps and burst through the front door. In the hallway stood two security guards and several men in black. Between the two security guards on a stretcher lay R-17's limp form.

Rage immediately replaced the fear in Elina's chest. "What are you doing?" she yelled. "How dare you enter this house? Put him back. Don't touch him!"

"Elina Coren?" One of the men in black stepped forward and opened up his wallet, revealing the badge of a Votum Special Detective. "We have been authorized by the government to remove this object from your house. An unnamed source informed us that you were designing a robot that violates the safety protocols the President has been upholding in regard to androids. You have been constructing a weapon without authorized permission in this residence. The android will remain in our custody until further notice."

"You *bastards!"* Elina snapped. "That isn't a weapon. He's mine...all mine, and he violates no protocol! You can't steal my personal property under such nameless grounds. Did President Cair authorize this intrusion? Prove to me that he did! Show me a signed document. If you can't, then leave the android." Behind her, Renon approached, his eyes flashing.

"Get out of my house!" he snapped. "Get out and leave the android here."

The detective's face stiffened. "I'm afraid that will not be possible. My orders state that this android must be removed from the property. Step aside." He flung out a paper from his pocket, the President's handwriting signed on the bottom right.

Renon stepped forward threateningly. "Give me your name, *detective.*"

"I will do no such thing."

"Give it to me...now." Renon positioned himself right in front of the detective. "I think you're forgetting that I'm a member of the President's advisory board. If you fail this much to cooperate, I will make sure you are punished for it."

Nostrils flaring, the detective answered with a scowl, "Jerson Par."

"Year of initiation?"

"3016"

"A *newbie*," Renon snorted under his breath. "It explains your incompetence! Now get off my property. This isn't over."

Stuffing the document back in his coat pocket, the detective shot both Renon and Elina a withering look and motioned to the security guards behind him. Rolling the stretcher down the hallway, they followed the men in black out of the house. White-faced, Elina watched through the doorway as they loaded R-17 into one of the vehicles and then drove away through the gate. Her fists clenched.

"Liars! They're lying. I know they're lying! And I know who's behind it."

"If it's VTech..."

"No." Elina shook her head. "It's not VTech. It's Dreadon!" Her voice dropped feverishly. "Dreadon's behind this."

"Dreadon works for VTech..."

"I know but his contract ended when my did, and I've no way of knowing if he renewed it. That man never told anyone anything." Elina closed her eyes. "I still don't understand. I don't *understand* how he knew about R-17! But I know how he figured out we're married." She pressed a hand to her forehead.

"You told him??"

"No, not exactly, but...but he asked me before we went to Phylidrum to marry him."

Now it was Renon's turn to go white. "*What?* What did you say? Why didn't you tell me this?"

"I only said that I was already married. I didn't say to whom! I never trusted him. He must have checked the city's records." Elina ran a hand over her face and groaned. "I didn't mention it to you because I didn't want to worry you. I thought he would leave me alone."

Renon grabbed her shoulders. "Did he say *why* he wanted to marry you?"

"He wanted to marry me because I'm smart, and he knows it! He learned as much from me as I did from him over the years. He said I would have his name, and we would share joint ownership over our projects outside of VTech."

Renon dropped his hands from Elina's shoulders, his face ashen. "No, no, no..." he muttered.

Hot tears spilled from Elina's eyes. "But I still don't understand how he knew about R-17. I never told anyone. R-17's mine...he's *mine*. They *stole him*..." She let out an angry shriek that echoed through the hallway. "How did he get the authorization to do something like this? President Cair would never..."

"This isn't President Cair's doing." Renon's face hardened. "I know him well. He never would have signed a document like that. That had to have been a forged signature. Dreadon has more political power than I suspected. He has people deep within the government supporting him."

"How do you know?"

"I've always suspected. I just never had any proof." Renon faced Elina, and she recoiled at the sight of the wild fear in his eyes.

"You're not telling me something," she whispered. "What is it?"

"Follow me." Without further explanation, Renon rushed into his office and pushed his finger against the side of the wall. One of the stones in the fireplace loosened. Yanking it out, Renon grabbed a key from inside before pushing the stone back in place. As the stone locked shut with a click, he then grabbed Elina's hand and the two of them hurried outside to his car in the driveway. Elina said nothing as he drove swiftly through the city. She darted him a confused look when they approached a massive five-story building, the letters CrC stretched out over the front entrance.

"Why are we at your company building?"

"Don't ask. Just follow." Parking the car, Renon got out and made for the front entry, Elina right behind him. The automatic front doors slid open as they walked through the pristine, crème-colored lobby, filled with employees walking to and fro. Entering one of the elevators, Renon then made for the floor below. Once the elevator doors opened, Renon stepped out into another hallway, but unlike the upper level, it was dark grey and dimly lit.

Making his way to the very end, Renon halted before the wall and removed his glasses. There was a little buzzing noise, followed by a flash of green light that scanned his left eye, and suddenly the wall opened up, disclosing a room behind the camouflaged door. With a hissing snap, the door locked behind them as they stepped over the threshold. Elina gave Renon a bewildered look.

"Renon, what is this room? Why is it hidden?"

"I have to show you something," Renon replied as he entered an intricate number combination into a safe built into the wall. The safe's door swung open and from it, Renon pulled out a small, steel box. He then entered a second numeral combination into the box and opened the unlocked lid. From the box, he removed a thin circlet of grey blue, the interior filled with tiny sensors. With a grim expression, he placed the circlet on his head and nodded towards a silver robot, its limp figure leaning against a corner of the wall.

"Watch the robot," Renon ordered Elina. He faced it once again, the circlet on his head emitting an intermediate flash. Elina gasped as the robot suddenly activated, the hum of its voice vibrating within its metal insides.

"Greetings. I am at your service. How may I be of assistance?"

"Hand the woman the pen on my desk," Renon ordered. Obediently, the robot reached out and picking up the pen, gave it to Elina. Elina gaped at it wide-eyed.

"How...how are you *doing that?"*

Renon removed the circlet from his head and the robot's form dropped back still and stiff against the wall. "It's a device my grandfather created. I have been perfecting it over the years. It has the ability to control any object of artificial intelligence by emitting an electrical signal from your brain. Your will and thoughts dictate the object's actions, which are transferred through this device. If your focus is strong enough, you will be able to override the subject's standard programming. You gain total control over it so long as you maintain your mental focus."

"How was your grandfather able..."

"He was abnormally clever." Renon placed the device on the table, his face bitter. "This creation of his is something he worked long and hard on. It was my father's. I have altered the circlet so that it will connect with the neurons in my brain but now I wish to change the design so that it will connect to yours instead. We will have to do some scans..."

"Wait, wait...I'm so confused!" Elina ran her hand through her hair. "Do you know how dangerous it would be if anyone were to discover this? I don't understand...why are you doing this? Why are you giving this to me?"

"Elina..." Renon reached for her hands. "My family has been powerful for a long time, but in some way or another, our women have always seemed... *cursed*. My grandmother was almost assassinated by my grandfather's political enemies. He was able to stop the assassination with this device. My father's first wife died within two weeks of their marriage. Someone killed her out of spite towards my father, who was gaining much economic wealth and power. He kept the circlet close with him after he married my mother and fortunately nothing has happened to her. But now..." Renon cupped his hand against Elina's cheek. "Now...we have both made ourselves a powerful enemy, and it is the same enemy that has clashed with my family for decades. I can't bear the thought of you being a victim. I will alter this and give it to you so..."

"Wait...no! No, *no*." Elina shook her head. "Why do *I* need it? Why can't you..."

"It's better if you learn how to use it." Renon gazed at her tragically. "I cannot always be next to you. And you have the baby. You must keep this with you as protection. It will help."

"I can't use this!" Elina gasped. "Do you realize what would happen should anyone find out about it? They would be down upon our heads! They would try to take it from us...use it for themselves. Are you *crazy?* If Dreadon wants R-17, think how much more he'll want this!"

"I'm not crazy. You will only use this should you have no other choice. It will be your last resort. *Please*, Elina..." Renon pressed her closer to him. "I'm scared! Very scared. Last night, I had a dream..."

"Dream? Of what?"

"A dream that you were in an elevator...*dead*."

"No, no, it was just a dream!" Elina frantically shook her head. "That's not going to happen...it wasn't real. You can't believe something like that."

"I've had dreams come true before. I can't risk this one coming true! Obey me, Elina. *Please*. I will alter this for you and then I'll go to President Cair and let him know what happened with R-17. We will get him back! Just let me do this first: before I expose anymore corruption."

With a defeated sigh, Elina bowed her head. "All right, I'll let you do it. *But...*" She clutched his hand. "Don't you need it more? After all, you're an advisor for the President, and you own a large company. You're also the city's greatest neuroscientist! If anything, surely you'll be the one they go after first."

"Either way, I don't care. I want you and the baby to be safe. You'll take this. That's the end of the discussion. *Please*, Elina. Trust me."

Elina closed her eyes and took a deep breath, placing her hand over his. "I will." Her face darkened. "Please hurry. I want R-17 back. He's mine! I *must* get him back."

*****

Elina rose to her feet as Renon entered the house and shut the front door behind him. Walking up towards her, he pressed a wrapped object in her hand and gave her arm a squeeze.

"Here's the circlet. Take it and put it in a safe place," he whispered.

Elina nodded, clutching the object to her chest. "Were you successful?"

"I have a private meeting with the President tomorrow. We will get R-17 back soon. I promise you." Renon lowered his voice, almost as if someone would hear the words he was speaking. "I've discovered where they're keeping R-17."

"How'd you figure that out?"

For answer, Renon's eyes shifted to the package Elina held. She took a deep breath. "Where is he?"

"He's being held on the forty-eighth floor of the VTech sky-scraper."

Elina bit her lip, her words coming out in a hiss. "Those wretches! I still want to know how Dreadon found out. There's no one else I can think of who'd be responsible. He *has* to be the one behind this."

Renon frowned, his eyebrows furrowing. "I will find out for certain soon." His face relaxing, he leaned over and gave Elina a kiss. "Hide that somewhere safe. I'll be back later tonight."

"What? Where are you going?"

"I have a board meeting to attend. We'll be discussing new marketing strategies that I've wanted implemented for a long time now. I re-scheduled the meeting late; don't expect me back until 10 p.m."

For answer, Elina gave Renon a tight hug. "Please be careful!" she begged.

"Yes, my love." Renon pushed a strand of hair out of her eyes and smiled. "Don't worry, all right? We'll get R-17 back." He gave her nose a light flick. "Rest if you can. Stress isn't good for you."

Elina laughed, in spite of the unpleasant shakiness that suddenly rattled her insides. "You talk as if you're my father."

"No, my dear." Renon grabbed his jacket from the nearby hook and winked at her. "Just your husband."

***

A pounding noise in the distance woke Elina. Groggily, she opened her eyes, the room blurry. In her hands was the circlet Renon had given her, still in its wrapping. She must have sat down and fallen asleep. Leaving the circlet on the table, she rose to her feet and walked towards the front door. Someone was still knocking, their loud banging growing more and more urgent.

As Elina swung open the door, the face of a female officer greeted her. Immediately, Elina felt her former shakiness return, sending a tremor through her body. "Yes?"

"Mrs. Coren, I'm here to inform you that there's been an accident at your husband's company site. A chemical explosion occurred on the fourth floor of the building. While many have been evacuated, some have been found dead. We have not searched the whole building because of the contamination risk. We don't know if your husband is alive or not. Please remain here, for your own safety, until we are able to learn more."

Elina frantically clutched her head. "No, no, no," she choked to herself. "This can't be. This *can't* be true."

"I'm afraid it is, ma'am."

"I have to go find him..."

"No, ma'am, you cannot! The site is dangerous and has been taped off. You're not allowed on the premises. I am giving you orders to *stay here*. The government is afraid that further contamination will happen and have currently dispatched a special team of androids who should be scouring the building as we speak. They will be able to find your husband."

"The *government?*" A deadly calm took over Elina, and she lowered her arms. Her voice dropped to a monotone. "Of course, officer. I understand. I will wait here."

The police officer gave her a baffled look at the sudden change in her demeanor. Then she nodded. "Thank you, Mrs. Coren. I am glad to hear it. You have my sympathies. We will bring you news of any updates."

Saying nothing, Elina shut the door, her heart pounding violently. A cold and deadly rage, mixed with unexplainable fear, filled her insides. Thoughts began to swarm wildly in her head. With a stifled gasp, she tried to sort through them. Then her mouth set stubbornly. She stepped towards the door and paused, glancing back at the circlet on the table. Letting go of the door handle, she ran over and tugged the wrapping from the circlet.

As Elina put the circlet on, a sudden, strange clicking noise caught her attention. She could feel the circlet connecting to something: something foreign somewhere in the room. Straightening, she tried to focus on the object. The connection was growing stronger; whatever she felt was behind her. She remembered Renon telling her how a single command of the will and mind was all she needed to connect to an object. She turned around. *Come towards me.*

In answer, a round object emerged from the corner of the hallway ceiling, so tiny that it was barely visible to the naked eye.

It floated towards Elina, hovering in the air. In horrified silence, Elina stared at it. The little object was a drone about the size of her finger tip. A *drone*. That was how Dreadon had found out about R-17! He had been spying on them. At some point, the drone must have followed her home.

An angry shout erupting from her throat, Elina seized the drone and flung it to the ground. With her foot, she smashed it against the floor. Then she sank to her knees with a muffled sob. Taking a few gasps, she rose back to her feet and tried to regain focus. Grabbing her coat from its hook, she pulled the hood over her head. Without any more hesitation, she yanked open the door. It slammed shut behind her as she raced out into the dark streets, her breath a thin cloud against the chilly air.

***

Leaning over, Elina clutched her chest, her breathing coming in ragged gulps. For the past hour, she had run...sprinting through Votum's streets. Now she was close to the CrC building. She could hear the wails of people in the distance and straight ahead, a cloud of smoke and dust curled upward into the sky. Pulling her hood more tightly around her face, Elina continued forward. Her entire body was shaking so badly that her teeth clicked against one another as she walked.

Nearing the area, Elina saw the entire building was surrounded with yellow tape. A security guard stood watch every twelve feet, heavy guns slung over their shoulders, and their faces hidden behind thick black face masks.

Backing away out of sight, Elina scoured the area, looking for any spot that might have an opening. She slipped away to another section of the building and noticed at the very end by a single side door, a lone android, its legs firmly set apart. Elina shut her eyes and winced. The noise coming from the circlet was a chaotic blur, but as she neared the robot it began to clear. She could now hear the android's programming inside her head: a steady repetition of one sentence...*No one enters building CrC without government clearance. The code is Order G67. Suppress any resistance. Halt all obtrusions.*

Elina stepped closer, her fists clenched. She remembered how Renon had activated the robot in his secret room without even speaking. He only had to think the command...

At the sight of Elina, the android immediately straightened, raising the gun in its hands. "No one...

Order G67.

Lowering the gun, the robot stepped aside. "Clearance granted."

Stepping past the android, Elina entered the side door of the building. As it shut behind her, she held her breath, waiting. The air was thick with smoke and there was a pungent burning smell, but no scent of chemicals was in the air. Elina walked towards one of the robots pacing the floor. It turned to face her, the neon light in the corner of its face blinking as it tilted its head.

"We are finding traces of carbon dioxide, nitrogen, and lead in the air," it began. "Some parts of the building have less of these elements than others. The explosion took place on the upper left of the fifth floor. That floor was filled with offices. The laboratory floors were mostly untouched. We are trying to determine what caused the explosion. There appear to be no traces of deadly chemicals."

"There was no chemical explosion," Elina whispered to herself. Her heart began to thud so violently that she thought it might fly out of her chest. Sinking to her knees, she pressed her hand against her bosom. "It was just a regular explosion. Someone did this. All of this was deliberate." With a stifled cry, she sprang to her feet and fled past the robot into the nearby hallway. Then she halted in dismay.

At the end of the hall was a pile of debris. Part of the above floor had collapsed from the explosion's impact. Beneath the rubble lay a body, its form crushed. Glancing up, Elina could see a bloody hand dangling through a crack in the ceiling and immediately powerful nausea overwhelmed her. Stumbling backwards, she staggered towards the elevator, using the circlet to open the door. Fighting the urge to vomit, she leaned against the wall for support. Cold terror gripped her insides. She had to find Renon! What if he was injured? *Dead?* No, no...perhaps he would be all right. If he had been at a meeting, then there was a chance he hadn't been harmed. The fifth floor was below ground. That was the furthest distance from the explosion.

The little ring of the elevator doors as they opened sounded deafening against the surrounding silence. Trembling violently, Elina stepped into the hallway: the same hallway that led to Renon's secret room. Instantly her face paled, and her eyes grew round with horror at the sight that met her eyes. A cry escaped her lips.

Mangled bodies were scattered haphazardly across the floor. The ground was covered with blood and more blood was streaked across the walls, as if someone had splattered it with a paintbrush. In too much shock to even move, Elina's eyes dropped to the corpse closest to her. An expression of anguish was imbedded into its face and across the body were deep slash-es. Elina shook her head and moaned. These bodies had not been damaged by an explosion. They bore the marks of a sword.

Regaining use of her legs, Elina began to make her way around the corpses, feverishly looking for any signs of her hus-band. A wild hope that she wouldn't find him here danced in the back of her mind. Then glancing forward, she saw a form up ahead at the end of the hall, lying on its stomach. The form was wearing a familiar brown jacket. Her heart dropped.

"Renon!" she gasped. No longer caring, she leaped over the dispersed corpses and flung herself to her knees by his side, removing the hood from her head. "Renon?" There was no response. Elina grabbed his shoulder and flipped him towards her. A piercing scream ripped from her throat and filled the hall.

Renon's entire stomach and shoulders were drenched in blood, while his right eye stared vacantly ahead into nothingness. His left eye was completely gone. In its place was a deep hole from which copious amounts of blood had poured out, spilling down his face and neck. Another and yet another scream tore out of Elina's mouth at the horrendous sight. Unshed tears burned in her eyes and ragged gulps shook her body, almost choking her. Then the room began to blacken. Her eyes rolled upwards, and she fell unconscious to the floor with a thud, her limp body lying beside Renon's.

***

Elina's eyes opened halfway, everything in front of her a blur. Her blank mind did not register at first where she was and what had happened. Then her vision cleared, and she could see the outline of Renon beside her, his disfigured profile staring vacantly at the ceiling. A flash of realization hit her like a knife, and she let out a heartbroken moan. Tears rolled down her cheeks and dripped on the floor.

"*Why?*" she moaned aloud. "Why did you have to *leave me?* You're...you're not supposed to be dead!" With great effort, she pushed herself off the floor and crawled beside him, her shoulders heaving. Deep, racking sobs shook her frame. "*Renon.* You *can't* leave me! I can't live without you. I can't. I *can't...*"

Hunching over, Elina continued to cry until it was almost impossible to breath. With a gasp, she rubbed tears from her eyes. Renon's blood smeared across her skin as her hand touched her face. The sudden memory that she was pregnant hit like a tidal wave, and she burst into a second round of sobs. Renon would never see his baby. Her trembling hands clutched his cold stiff one as she sat there helplessly, unable to move or think.

Suddenly, all the hair on the back of her neck stood up. As if released from a spell, Elina regained control of her limbs and slowly turned around. Her heart all but stopped and an icy chill settled over her chest.

Amongst the flickering light of the hallway, a black silhouette against the shadowy room, stood Dreadon. He stepped forward silently, his boots making no sound as they crossed over the slippery floor. Then he halted, his pale skin almost white in contrast to the shadowy lighting.

"What are you doing here?" Elina hissed. She stretched out her arms, shielding her husband's body with her own. "How'd you get in?"

"I could ask you the same thing." Dreadon's eyes dropped to Renon's corpse and then slowly shifted back to Elina's face. "I came to offer you..."

"I'm not listening. Get out! You stole R-17! I found your drone in my house. There's nothing you can offer me..."

Dreadon released a sort of twisted laugh under his breath. His mouth curled in scornful amusement. "I agree! There's nothing I can offer you anymore. You already took a side. All that I will offer you now are some parting words."

A metallic taste settled on Elina's tongue. The stench of all the blood was starting to make her feel sick, and her stomach lurched. A trapped sensation began to close around her, causing her to shake uncontrollably. Behind Dreadon, an eerie clicking noise emanated from the elevator, vibrating through the hallway. "I don't want your words..."

"You don't have a choice. My voice is the last one you'll ever hear." Now Dreadon laughed mockingly. "You don't think I'll let you live do you? You have seen too much!"

Elina's eyes widened, and her hands began to tremble violently. "*You...*" she choked. "You did this. How...*why?"*

"You made your decision. If I couldn't have you by my side I'd make sure nobody else could either. You became a liability, *Mrs. Coren*. You and your husband..."

Fresh tears filled Elina's eyes. "You *killed Renon...*" She paused mid-sentence, and her eyes shifted to new shadows emerging from the hallway taking shape behind Dreadon. Four pairs of green eyes glowed out of the dark, their clicking noise twisting into what almost sounded like jagged laughter, high-pitched and piercing. Elina backed into Renon's body, her mouth dropping in terror.

Four androids appeared, their black-streaked forms tall and threatening. They were like no androids she had ever seen before. The mouths hung open on their skeletal faces, contorting in freakish hate, and in their hands they brandished long swords with serrated blades covered with blood. As their heads lurched downwards and sideways, they halted beside Dreadon, their burning eyes bearing down on Elina's inert body.

"You see," Dreadon began, still smiling as he spoke, "For someone as ambitious as me, there can be no sharing of power. For a hundred years now, my family has worked secretly to secure a position that we will never allow to be taken from us. My existence shall be a culmination of all the accomplishments my bloodline has produced. You could have been part of that! You refused. Instead you married a man I viewed as my mortal enemy." Dreadon stepped closer, followed by his wraith-like androids. "Renon Coren would have never sat still and let me seize power without retaliation. I now know you wouldn't either." Dreadon chuckled. "I have many secret talents, Elina Taren! I have created things you never dreamed were possible." He gestured towards his androids. "These are just a taste of what I am capable of. It is quite beautiful, is it not? Do they not strike fear into you? Think of what I can accomplish with them! See...that is the glorious irony of it all. When one creates death itself, they have complete mastery over...*life*."

A strange sensation stirred inside Elina: a feeling of adrenaline mixed with wild hate and determined desperation. She remembered the baby dwelling in her womb and a new energy brought life back to her limbs. Rising slowly, she stood to her feet and tightened her fists. Her gaze did not waver as she stared Dreadon down.

"The explosion was just a decoy: a *distraction*, so that you could come in here and murder your political opponents. You must have bought off a great many people to accomplish such a feat. How many people have sold their soul to you?"

"Nearly all of them. I'll grant you that one last bit of information." Dreadon stretched out his arms. "You *have* been helpful to me, Elina Coren. I learned a great deal from you. In truth though, you will never possess the intellectual genius that I do. Very few are gifted and even fewer have the capacity to properly use their gifts. Only one of us can have the final say." Behind him, the androids tensed, ready to spring. "Fate has proven which of us that will be."

"You evil bastard," Elina seethed through clenched teeth. "You're a *demon*. You deserve death a thousand times over! You killed my husband. You *won't* kill me."

"You're right," Dreadon agreed conceitedly. Laughing low in his throat, he began to back away behind his androids, making a signal with his hand. "*They* will."

Horrific screams of varying pitches rippled from the androids' mouths, and they lunged forward, their swords brandished high. A scream of equal strength ripped from Elina's throat and the blue lights on her circlet flashed wildly. She gained control of the android nearest to her and mentally commanded it to attack the other robots by its side. Spinning about wildly, the android turned sideways and lashed at the nearest robot, plunging the sword into its chest. With its other arm, it whirled about and struck the third robot, its blade scraping across the android's face. Baffled terror settled over Dreadon as his confused robots turned on the one android, whose movements obeyed Elina's every thought.

Another wave of focused rage swept over Elina. *STRIKE YOUR MASTER!* Dodging the blows of its fellow robots, the android turned and with lightning speed slashed at Dreadon's face. The blade ripped open Dreadon's cheek and with a strangled cry he crumpled to the ground. Using all her mental strength, Elina kept control over her android while simultaneously backing towards the elevator. The other three robots had gained the upper hand and were slamming Elina's android against the wall, thrusting their swords into its torso. Their horrible shrieks drowned out the wails of the mangled android, who collapsed against the wall, disfigured and destroyed.

Elina staggered towards the elevator as fast as she could. As the elevator doors started to shut, she saw the remaining androids flying towards her, their mouths hanging open, and their swords pointed. She yelled in panic as they drew nearer. The door closed just in time before the androids flung themselves against it. A large dent appeared in the center of the door from the impact.

Her body pushed against a corner of the elevator, Elina sank to her knees. Her ears were ringing from the androids screams, and her vision was blurring. Sobs of anger and sorrow wrenched from her chest and throat, convulsing her entire body. Then, making an extreme effort, Elina rose to her feet. The elevator's doors opened, and she raced out, past the lobby and through the side door. The robot who was standing guard outside whirled around and aimed its gun at her.

"*Shoot yourself!*" Elina shrieked. Pointing the rifle at its neck, the robot fired the gun. A sizzling noise, followed by a cloud of smoke, exploded around its head. It dropped to the ground, its black body folding over itself as Elina ran past into the dark street. She yanked her hood over her blood-stained face and doubled her speed in the direction of VTech.

***

Elina clutched the sides of her stomach, breathing heavily as she leaned against the elevator wall. She had been able to enter the VTech skyscraper with the help of the circlet and had reached the elevator before the security androids could stop her. She feverishly clutched her trembling palms together, keeping her back to the security camera. It would not be long before they sent someone to detain her.

Once the elevator stopped, Elina stepped out onto the forty-eighth floor and scanned the area in search of R-17. It was incredibly dark, making it almost impossible to see anything. "*Where are you?*" she muttered.

Suddenly, she noticed a large steel container in the corner of the room. Stepping forward, Elina saw it was locked by a digital code. With one simple command she was able to undo the lock, flinging the door open with a bang.

"*R-17,*" she whispered. Reaching out her arm, she activated the switch between his shoulder blades. His entire body stirring, R-17 straightened and raised his head.

"Greetings, Miss Elina. How may I be of assistance?"

"You have to come with me! I need to get you out of here. We're going to escape the city. There's a car back at my house. *Hurry.*"

"Your adrenaline and cortisol levels are abnormally high, Miss Elina. Are you in danger?"

Before Elina could answer, the elevator door opened and two security androids stepped into the room. They approached Elina, their rifles pointed towards her.

"Halt! You have violated the security of this sector and are under arrest. Put your hands above your head and step forward."

R-17 cocked his head. "Are they a threat to you, Miss Elina?"

"*Yes,*" she muttered. "Don't do anything yet."

The android stepped closer. "Put your hands above your head."

Her eyes narrowing, Elina took a shuddery breath. The circlet on her head flashed and the android nearest to her swung around and shot the other android in the face. Just as quickly, R-17 leapt forward and slammed his fist into the remaining android's neck. Its head crumpling inwards, the android flew across the floor, landing against the wall with a crash.

"Follow me!" Elina cried. She ran back to the elevator and as they descended downwards, she hurriedly yanked off her jacket. Being careful to keep her face away from the camera, she handed it to R-17. "Put that on and pull the hood over your face."

"What are we escaping, Miss Elina?"

"The government."

"Are they the ones who took me?"

"Yes."

"You are crying, Miss Elina. I caution you to be careful. Excessive grief could endanger your child. There is a possibility of miscarriage."

"R-17," she whispered shakily. "We must run very fast when we get out of here. We have to escape the city before they catch us."

"You should not run in your condition."

"If I don't run, we don't have any chance of getting out in time! If that happens, the child is as good as dead. And so am I."

"Then we run, Miss Elina."

By now they had reached the bottom floor. On the floor above them, Elina could hear the violent thump of footprints. Further across the lobby, one of the elevator lights flashed. The androids from the other floors had been alerted of their presence.

"*Go, go!*" she cried. She and R-17 took off towards the front entrance, barreling through the doors and out into the street. A siren erupted from the skyscraper, stretching throughout every corner of the city.

"*Ow!*" A searing pain in Elina's abdomen cut her running short, and she collapsed to her knees, clutching her stomach. With both hands, R-17 helped her to her feet.

"You must let me carry you, Miss Elina. It will be easy for me. If I try to match your pace it will only slow us down. You should not hesitate to let me help."

The pain struck Elina again, and she let out a low moan. "Just get me to the house as fast you can."

R-17 looped his metal arm under Elina's and the other under her legs, lifting her off her feet. Then he raced down the streets, which had become more awake in lieu of the explosion and the ringing siren. People shrieked and dodged out of the way as R-17 flew past them, a blur almost impossible to identify to the naked eye. When they finally reached Elina's house, R-17 gently placed her on her feet. Still clutching her side, Elina staggered into the house and returned with the car keys. In her other hand was a tiny, black oval device.

"The car's behind the left side of the house!" she gasped. She tossed the device to R-17. "Put that on the door. It'll create a protective shield around the car." She let out a yell as another spasm of pain twisted in her stomach.

"You will let me drive."

"No! R-17..."

"If you persist this way, your condition might become critical. You will let me drive." Forcibly propelling her to the passenger side, R-17 opened the car door and gently pushed Elina inside. Fighting tears, Elina pulled the seat buckle over her shoulders.

Sitting beside her, R-17 started the car and backed out of the driveway. "What is our destination?"

"Nobiles. My aunt had a friend there. He's the only one I know to go to. I can't go to Renon's family." Moaning, Elina covered her face with her blood-crusted hands. "I would endanger them all."

"We will go to Nobiles."

"R-17, wait." From the side door, Elina pulled out a small camera that Renon had purchased in Phylidrum. Her trembling hands attached it behind R-17's neck. "Keep this on. It attaches to a screen sitting in the back seat. If we get separated, I can find you with this...maybe." Another moan escaped her lips as nausea twisted up her throat.

"Let us go." Backing out of the driveway, R-17 drove until they reached the city limits. A long bridge that stretched over a river deep within the ravine below came into view. Several robots stood guard by the bridge, one of them approaching as R-17 slowed the car.

Shaking all over, Elina's hands tightened around her seat belt. "Keep your head low," she commanded R-17. "Keep your head low and don't talk." She rolled down the window as the robot peered inside.

"We are enforcing a temporary lockdown. No one is to leave the city limits."

"Go and open the gate," Elina ordered, her circlet flashing as she spoke.

Straightening its shoulders, the robot turned and walked to a nearby booth, pulling the lever inside. The iron gates swung open as the other robots stepped forward repeating in unison,

"Stop! We are enforcing a temporary lockdown. No one is to leave the city limits."

"Drive quickly!" Elina ordered wildly. Pressing on the gas, R-17 sped past the approaching robots and through the gate. One of the robots aimed its gun and shot at the car. The bullet hit the car's protective shield and fell with a clang onto the road. Once they drove over the bridge and away from Votum, Elina let out a shaky gasp. "You know how to get to Nobiles?"

"Yes. I am already re-routing us so that we can get there as soon as possible. We should be able to make it before the car loses power. If there are no mishaps, it will take us approximately twelve hours to reach the city."

Too exhausted to say anything else, Elina nodded wearily and closed her eyes. The pain in her abdomen had slowed, and she wanted to cry again, but for some reason she no longer could.

"Do not worry, Miss Elina," R-17 continued. "Everything will be all right. I will ensure that you get to Nobiles safely."

Chapter 23
Welcoming Laeli

Elina tried to open her eyes but they felt incredibly heavy. For a moment she gave up, then tried again. As her vision cleared, she saw R-17 was sitting beside her on a stool and realized she was stretched out on a bed. A ceiling with wooden beams made a V-shape above her and the corner of the room was warmed by a small fire.

"Where am I?" Elina asked groggily.

"You are at your friend's house."

"Wait, what? What happened. I don't remember..."

"I helped you to his front door. He knew who you were. Then you fainted. I carried you inside, and he lit a fire. I washed your face for you while you were sleeping. I hope you do not mind."

"No..." Elina studied the ceiling, a fresh wave of remembrance hitting her like a stab in the heart. Tears spilled from her eyes and rolled down her cheeks. "R-17," she whispered. "The baby...?"

"The fetus is viable. Neither you or the child have suffered any damage. You are fortunate. You have admirable strength of mind, Miss Elina."

Elina closed her eyes, more tears spilling out of them. "All during the drive I thought to myself that I *must not* lose the baby. I *will not* lose the baby. It's the only thing I have left of Renon..."

"Besides this." R-17 held out the circlet in his hand. At the sight, Elina's eyes widened.

"You can't show that to anyone! We must hide it."

"Not now, Miss Elina. You need rest...for your sake and the baby girl's."

"*Girl?*" Elina gripped the blanket covering her. "How do you know she's a girl?"

"I am reading your hormonal levels, and they reveal that the fetus is female. Your chorionic gonadotropin and regulatory cytokine levels are high. There is no presence of Y chromosomes in your blood."

Elina closed her eyes. "He was right," she whispered. "Renon was *right*. The baby *is* a girl."

R-17 nodded slowly and inclined his head. "Will you be safe here in Nobiles, Miss Elina?"

"We'll be safe. Nobiles is run by Governor Tark. Dreadon can do nothing with both him and President Cair in office. Governor Tark will never know who I was in Votum. I'll use a different name here. Dreadon will not find out I that I'm in Nobiles. We'll be safe."

R-17 reached out a metallic hand and placed it on top of Elina's. "Then rest, Miss Elina. Be silent and rest."

***

"Are you sure you don't want to stay here, Miss Taren? It will be less expensive than living on your own. I won't charge you much."

"Thank you, Linus, but I need my own space. I want privacy, and I've got to hide R-17 until I can finish working on him. It will take me a long time before I will be able to afford the materials I need for his exterior synthetics." She placed a hand on her bulging tummy and sighed. "I also won't be pregnant for much longer. Please don't be offended. I'm so grateful to you. I can never repay you for all your help...and for keeping my secret."

"Don't worry. I understand. I'll never mention R-17 to any-one. But..." The old man hobbled forward, stroking his beard, "are you sure you can't tell me who the father is?"

"No. It's better if you don't know."

"Alright then. I'll let you go, Miss Taren. You said you picked out the place?"

Elina nodded. "I already bought it. Just yesterday. I also have you to thank for that. I was only able to get a job here as a robotics mechanic because of you and your connections."

"They say you're pretty talented!" Linus exclaimed. "So sor-ry, but I went in yesterday to the shop to ask about you. I'm pretty sure they'll keep you around for a while."

Elina reached out her hand. "Thank you, Linus. Thank you...for *everything*."

***

Opening the door to her house, Elina groaned and placed a hand on her back. The baby's weight, combined with working in the shop, had her completely exhausted. Placing her tool bag on the table, she sat in a chair and shut her eyes, wincing as a contraction shook her frame. Her boss's voice replayed in her mind.

You ought to rest. You're my best worker. I can save your job for you. Why don't you at least cut your hours?

Her mouth tightening, Elina shook her head and leaned back against the chair. She couldn't stop working. She *needed* to finish R-17, and it would take more money saved than what she had now. With great effort, she rose to her feet and entering a code into the side lock, opened the door of the closet where R-17 was.

"I have to finish you," she murmured. "I have a feeling my daughter will need you and...I don't know...but my body feels so *strange*." She pressed a hand to her heart. Its thump was steady now but lately it had been racing frequently, and she'd experienced trouble breathing. Swallowing hard, she reached out and activated the switch on R-17's back. He raised his head and spoke cordially.

Greetings, Miss Elina. How can I be of service?"

"Hello, R-17. It's good to talk to you after all this time."

"Do you need my assistance with anything?"

"No, R-17 I'm fine. It's just…" Elina paused, and her eyes grew round. She pressed her hand against her stomach and looked up at R-17. "My water broke!" In stunned shock, she turned and locked the door to her house. "I didn't think it would be today," she muttered under her breath.

R-17 took a step forward. "If your water broke than you should begin going into labor anywhere within the next twelve to twenty-four hours. I recommend going to the hospital so that you can receive adequate medical assistance."

Elina stubbornly shook her head. "No! I can't go to the hospital. I'll have to give birth here."

"That may be a risk, Miss Elina. I am scanning you as we speak and see that while the baby appears sound, your heart is weak. The blood vessels surrounding it are inflamed and the beat is irregular. I do not have the necessary equipment to help you should any complications arise."

"No," Elina repeated. "I stay here."

"I do not understand. Why do you not wish to go to the hospital?"

Elina faced R-17, her mouth trembling. "I'm going to die, R-17," she whispered. "I don't know when, but I can feel it. Maybe a year…a few years from now…but I *will* die." Her voice cracked. "Every night I get nightmares; every day is filled with horrible memories. I know my heart is weak. Grief is slowly killing me. I can't fight it. I can't unsee the things I saw." With a sob, she bowed her head. "I'm so ashamed! I feel so *helpless*. There are many days when I don't even want to live anymore.

If it weren't for the child, I would have committed suicide long ago." She shook her head. "I will try to fight it; I will try to live for my little girl...but in case I can't for long, I need someone who can protect her. That someone will have to be you, but you can't do that in your present state." Wiping her eyes with her hands, she began to pull the curtains over the windows. "I must save my money for both your sakes! I'm not sure if you can understand..."

"I understand." R-17 placed his hand on her shoulder. "I will help you as much as I can, Miss Elina."

Elina turned and pressed her hand against R-17's metal shoulder. "*Thank you*."

***

Elina gripped the edge of the bed, her knuckles white. With a muffled cry, she leaned over and gasped. Blood spilled down her legs and onto the towel rolled out beneath her on the floor. A violent contraction seized her abdomen. Pushing a strand of hair away from her sweaty forehead, she gave R-17 a pleading look.

"I want to lie down," she groaned. "It's been hours...*uhhh*." She cringed and let out another shout as another wave of pressure hit her like a balled fist. "Please let me lie down!"

"If you lie down it will be harder to push. There is a higher risk of tearing. I will help support you. Lean on me." Taking her arm, R-17 draped it around his shoulder while wrapping his around her waist. His eyes traveled over her abdomen. "Based on my scans, your labor will be over soon. Take small breaths. You are doing well, Elina. It will soon be over."

Suddenly, Elina began to experience a searing sensation. She let out a scream of pure anguish as fiery pain shot through her body. Her eyes dropped to the puddles of blood beneath her and flashbacks of Renon's mangled face filled her head. The memory, mixed with the agonies of labor, sent a new kind of ache throughout her body. With a gasp she closed her eyes, another scream erupting from her lungs.

"*Shh*," R-17 said soothingly. "It is all right...you will be all right. You are brave, Elina. The baby is coming out now. Just keep breathing...slowly, steadily." Still verbalizing soft encouragements under his breath, R-17 crouched down and held out his hands, catching the baby as she emerged from Elina's body.

With a stifled sob, Elina clutched the bed post. "She's not crying! Is something wrong? Is something wrong with her??"

"No, she is perfectly healthy," R-17 murmured, his voice filled with wonder. Titling his head in amazement, he cut off the umbilical cord and handed the baby to Elina. "She is simply observing."

Fresh tears of relief, joy, and sadness spilled down Elina's face as she gazed at her little girl. Big brown eyes stared back: brown eyes just like her own. The nose was a tiny snub and the chin and ears were small and round. A healthy sweep of dark hair covered her head. Elina choked on her tears. Once again, Renon had been right. Other than the mouth, which was elongated and delicate like his, the baby had all her features.

"Hello," she whispered. "My little girl. You are absolutely beautiful! I *love* you." She pressed the baby against her cheek and a tiny fuss came out of the girl's mouth. Bending over, violent sobs shook Elina's frame, her cries mixing with her child's. Once she was finally able to stop, she looked up tearfully at R-17. "*Thank you.*"

R-17 bowed his head. "You are most welcome. What will you call the child?"

Elina studied her baby's face. As a little girl she had once dreamed of this moment. All of her baby names had been picked out at age ten, stored in the back of her memory until the time came to use them. She had meant to leave the final decision with Renon but now that was impossible. As she gazed up at R-17's face, a terrible sorrow plunged over her heart. Closing her eyes, Elina bowed her head and whispered aloud the one that had always been closest to her heart.

"*Laeli.*"

Chapter 24
Ren's Promise

Two years later...

Elina walked through the house door and wearily closed it behind her. From the dim light of the room, a petite figure came racing towards her, arms outstretched.

"Mommy, Mommy!" it cried. "R-17 showed me how to count to...to *one hundred* today!"

"Laeli, darling!" In spite of her exhaustion, Elina reached down and swung Laeli up in her arms. "You learned to count to a hundred? In one day?"

"Yes, Mommy! It's easy. R-17 showed me."

"She is very bright." R-17 announced, emerging from the bedroom and walking towards Elina. "Her brain shows unusually high patterns of activity for her age. Her memory is photographic, and she remembers everything I show and tell her."

"Yes, Mommy, I'm bright." Laeli cocked her head, her voice becoming serious. "That's what R-17 said. Am I bright like the sun?"

Elina threw back her head and laughed. "Are you asking if you're sunshine?"

Laeli's lips drew in a small pout. "Mommy, *no*."

Elina hugged her tightly. "Well, you're *my* sunshine."

"Oh." Still appearing baffled, Laeli returned the hug and then giggled. "I'm *your* sunshine, Mommy and the sun is *my* sunshine."

"Yes, darling. That's very true."

"What's R-17?" Laeli grinned, then frowned again. "Seventeen is a number. Why's R-17 a number? He needs a name."

"What?" Laughingly, Elina gave R-17 a perplexed look. "But R-17 is his name. Why...what should we call him?"

"We can call him the name you say in your sleep!" Laeli slipped from Elina's arm and playfully flung herself against the android. "*Renon*."

Elina's face paled. Swallowing hard, she nodded and slowly turned away towards her bedroom, clutching the tool bag slung over her shoulder. "All right, Laeli," she agreed in a low voice. "We'll change his name. Not to Renon though. You can call him Ren."

"Yayy!" Laeli squealed, hopping up and down with her arms wrapped around R-17's legs. "Your name's Ren!"

"I am glad," R-17 exclaimed. "Shall you eat your dinner now?"

"Yes!" Rushing towards the table, Laeli climbed into the chair and straightened the spoon by the side of her plate. "Is Mommy coming?"

"Here." Taking her plate, R-17 filled it with food and placed it back in front of Laeli. "She will be out soon. Eat your food. I will go to her."

"Ok." Obediently, Laeli dug her spoon across the carefully separated serving of beef and vegetables. Leaving her to her meal, R-17 quietly entered the bedroom where Elina was sitting on the edge of the bed, facing the wall.

"R-17," she whispered as he drew nearer. "Do I really speak so loudly in my sleep?"

"Yes, Miss Elina. Sometimes you even scream."

Elina pressed a hand against her chest, breathing heavily. "I didn't know she heard. She never said anything so I thought...I thought she didn't."

"She once heard you scream. I comforted her and said it was her imagination and not to be frightened."

"But she's heard me say his name. How else would she have come up with the name Renon?" Elina groaned and covered her face with her hands. "What else do I say?"

"You warn him not to leave the house. You are often crying. You tell him to wake up. You curse..." R-17 stepped closer to her. "Miss Elina, you should not have asked me. I can see your heart..."

Coughing suddenly, Elina rose to her feet, leaning over and clutching her chest. "It'll pass," she gasped. When the pain finally subsided, she sank back down on the bed, closing her eyes. "R-17, you must say nothing to her. *Ever*. I don't want her childhood to be ruined. *Promise*."

"I promise. Will you tell her, Miss Elina?"

"No. I will never tell her. Neither of us will...unless a day comes when she *has* to know. I'll do my best to ensure that never happens. I don't want to see the light in her eyes die the way mine has."

"Miss Elina, you are..."

"I know." Elina's eyes dropped to the thin hand resting on her lap. "I'm getting worse. That's why it's so important that I finish my work on you. You *must* protect her...should I go." She sighed. "I have had to make you into the very thing I swore I wouldn't: a weapon." A tear slid down her cheek and onto her hand. "What choice do I have? How else will you be able to guard her if I don't?" Rising to her feet, she walked up to R-17, placing a hand on his arm. "Your primary concern will no longer be for me. I will alter your programming so that your only care will be for Laeli."

R-17 nodded. "It will be as you wish, Miss Elina. I will protect your child with my life."

Elina smiled at him sadly. "You will be her friend: the closest thing to a father she's ever had. With you she will be happy. I will make sure of it."

***

Laeli closed her eyes, more tears spilling down her already drenched cheeks. She opened her eyelids to see Ren still sitting in front of her. Her shoulders heaving, Laeli broke down into heavy weeping. It was no longer Ren, but her father's face staring back at her. The same brown eyes as his shone from Ren's countenance: the same mouth curved downward with the identical kind smile. Without hesitation, Laeli leapt from her seat and flung herself at Ren, wrapping her arms around his neck.

"You look just like my father!" she cried, burying her face into his shoulder. "Ren...*dear Ren*." Her voice mixing with bittersweet sadness, she looked up at him, clutching both his shoulders. "All this time...all this time you had my father's face, and I never knew." Another bout of violent sobs poured from her throat as she gave him a second hug. "Now it all makes sense, Mommy," she whispered. "Thank you, Ren...thank you for *everything*."

Ren carefully pressed Laeli to him, his strong arms holding her in a gentle embrace. "You are welcome."

Laeli reverently placed a hand next to the metal surrounding Ren's left eye. "Did Mommy...did Mommy make you this way because of my father?" she asked brokenly. "Because...because of his..."

"Yes," Ren replied soberly. "A design created to serve both as a separation from who I resemble and a symbol of what he lost."

Laeli dropped her head. "I *hate* Dreadon." Her voice was heavy with detestation. She looked at Ren again. "He took away my real father. He's responsible for Mommy's death. I won't let him take you away. I *won't*."

"I will not let that happen, Laeli."

Laeli leaned against Ren's chest, the tears continuing to fall freely from her eyes. A deeply-settled rage began to glisten in the back of her eyes. "*I* will never let it happen. Never, *never.*"

***

Javeer opened his eyes, wincing at the throbbing pain in the back of his head. Shifting his stiff frame across the bed, he raised his arm and touched the side of his face. He realized that a bandage had been wrapped around his forehead. Slowly, he pushed himself up with his arms to a sitting position. Swinging his legs to the side of the bed, he attempted to stand and groaned. His entire body ached and a wave of dizziness struck him. Gritting his teeth, he straightened and hobbled towards the door, opening it and peering out into the hallway. *Where'd Laeli go? I've got to find Laeli.*

Javeer inched his way through the dim hallway, leaning against the wall for support. He suddenly felt his leg bump against something metal and froze. As he glanced down, a bright light flashed in his face, blinding him.

"Ahh, Mimi!" he scolded, throwing up his hands to shield his eyes. "What are you doing in the hallway?"

"Hello, Javeer," Mimi's voice chirped. "You are up."

"Astute observation," Javeer snorted. With a sigh, he crouched down to face the robot. "Hello, Mimi...*aghh*. There's two of you." Grimacing, he pressed his palm against his forehead and squinted.

"No, there's only one of me."

"You're ridiculous." With a low laugh, Javeer lightly tapped Mimi's square head. "Where's Laeli?"

"Laeli is in the basement."

"I've got to go to her." Javeer carefully rose to his feet, just in time to see Lyon walking towards him.

"You feeling better, son?"

"Yes, Father. Just sore and dizzy. How long was I out?"

"Twelve hours."

"*Twelve?*" Javeer shook his head in disbelief, then lowered his voice. "Was I dreaming...or is that android thing real?"

Lyon took a deep breath. "It's real." With a mystified wave of his hands, he walked into the kitchen and sat down on a chair. With a sigh, he ran his hand down his face. "It's real, and I'm still trying to understand *how*. For something to look that human and not be human is...*unnatural*."

Javeer placed both hands on the table, leaning towards his father. "My mind is fuzzy," he began, "but we were attacked by something else that looked human and *wasn't*." Javeer sank into a chair. "That...that *thing* meant to take Laeli. It tried to kill me."

"Laeli told me." Lyon clenched his hands together. "There is something very sinister about all this. These *things*...they aren't found in Cuniculum. Whatever tried to take Laeli was sent by someone from one of the Five Cities. And they have ties to Malin." Lyon slammed his hand on the table, his eyes blazing. "Even this hell-hole is no longer an escape!"

A humiliated expression crossed over Javeer's face. "She would be gone," he muttered. "That thing would've taken Laeli, and I wouldn't have been able to stop it if...if it weren't for that android."

"That android," Lyon interjected sternly, "is a weapon. Whoever designed it created it to be one...and a deadly one at that."

"Laeli said it protects her..."

"Yes, but from what? Laeli still has not told us everything. You have been involved; it is now our right to know the rest. Bring her up to me. I wish to talk to her."

Javeer sighed. "Sure. I want to know the truth as much as you do." Getting up from the chair, he made his way to the door, then halted, clutching the door frame.

Lyon walked up to him swiftly, putting a hand on his shoulder. "Sit down, son. I'll get her."

"No, Father." Javeer clenched his jaw. "Let me go. I'll be fine."

Lyon nodded and removed his hand. Javeer walked through the hallway and cautiously made his way down the basement steps, clinging to the railing in case another bout of dizziness hit him. Once he reached the bottom of the stairs, he saw Ren was seated on a stool in the back of the room. In his arms, Laeli lay asleep, her shoulder pressed against Ren's shoulder. A nervous fluttering in his stomach, Javeer inched closer. As Ren raised his head, a shivery sensation shot through Javeer's limbs. In spite of the feeling, he kept on until he was standing right in front of the android. Glancing down at Laeli, he saw that her face was streaked with tear stains.

"What happened?" he whispered anxiously.

"She is exhausted," Ren murmured. "She has just learned a truth that will change her life forever."

"What do you mean?" Crouching slowly to his feet, Javeer gave Ren a perplexed look.

"There are many dark secrets from Laeli's past that have been kept hidden from her until now. The knowledge which she has acquired will be a great burden that she will live with the rest of her life."

"Is she in danger?"

Ren's eyes locked with Javeer's. "Yes. All her life she has been in danger. That is why I exist. I am her guardian."

Javeer gave Laeli a look of pure sympathy. "My poor girl." He turned again to Ren. "Do you know what the thing that attacked us was?"

Ren shook his head. "I am not sure. However, what I do know, I can tell you." He inclined his head politely. "Friends of Laeli are friends of mine." Now he smiled. "I've heard a lot about you, Javeer."

Javeer rose to his feet in surprise. "You have?"

"Laeli talks about you a great deal. It is good to finally meet. I am sorry our meeting had to happen the way it did."

"I can't say that I'm sorry. You saved my life...and hers. I'm very grateful. Let's uh...introduce ourselves properly this time, eh?" Javeer awkwardly held out his hand. "This is so weird to me but ok...I'm Javeer. Javeer Bellator."

Ren took Javeer's outstretched hand and shook it. "I am Ren. Ren, R-17. It is my pleasure to meet you, Javeer. I am glad we are friends."

Chapter 25
Kye's Shadow

The double doors of Kye's mansion creaked open, and Kye staggered through, his head bent. Grey liquid dripped around the knife in his eye and onto the floor as he shuffled forward, slamming the door shut behind him. Letting out a groan that echoed across the house, he made his way through the drawing room and into the red-mahogany hallway. Dragging his hand across the walls, he limped on and veered left, down the second hallway past rows of bedrooms, until he reached the very end. On the left side of the hall was a brown elevator door which he opened using his fingerprint. Kye kept his head lowered as the elevator slid deep below the surface of the house.

Once the doors slid open, Kye stumbled into what was a faintly lit laboratory. The silver-blue walls were smooth and glossy and in the corner of the room emerged a white robot, the very one Laeli had seen when she had visited the mansion. Its face was expressionless and the eyes unblinking as it stepped forward.

"Greetings sir," it began. Its monotone voice mimicked that of a woman's. "Your security system alerted us thirty minutes ago that a helicopter has been sighted. If it maintains its current speed, it shall reach us in approximately fifteen minutes. Do you wish to permit entry to this visitor?"

Kye's face twisted into a bitter smile. "He will enter whether I permit it or not." A cunning expression flashed in his good eye. "Let him in!"

Walking up towards a rectangular mirror stretching out along the right side of the wall, Kye leaned his head back and placed a hand over the hilt of the knife still embedded in his right eye. His hand tightened around the knife, and he slowly pulled out the blade. A stream of grey liquid squirted in all directions, spraying across the mirror and onto the floor. With a strangled yell, Kye removed the final tip and flung the knife against the wall. The wet blade fell with a clatter, fragments of Kye's eye and internal pieces clinging to it. Chest heaving, Kye tilted his head backwards and gazed at himself in the mirror. His one good eye stared at his reflection in horror. The right eye gaped back at him: a hideous socket of fluids and wires protruding from the hole in his face.

Turning away in disgust, Kye stormed out of the lab and back towards the elevator. As the elevator made its way up to the main floor, Kye paced back and forth before slamming his hand on elevator wall.

"What *were* you?" he ranted to himself. "What madness is this? If you are you...than what am *I?"* Exiting the elevator, he made his way to the dining hall, past the long table, and into the hallway behind the room. His one eye scoured the line of mirrors and staring into one of them, he flung his hand against the wall next to it.

"The longer I live the less I can see!" he bemoaned. "Why do you persist?" he exclaimed through clenched teeth at his reflection. "Why, *why?* You can understand nothing! There is only noise...*pain*. Broken memories...*broken memories*." With a moan, he clutched his head with both hands. "I cannot see what was and what is. So much is missing." Fiery rage ignited his one eye: a glowing flame of icy blue. "BROKEN...MEMORIES!" he screamed. With a hateful cry, he turned and flung his fist into the mirror. It shattered with an ear-splitting crack, glass flying in all directions. Like tiny crystal showers, they splattered around him to the floor. A large shard pierced one of the stuffed crows on the wall, embedding itself into its neck.

"*Laeli!*" Kye ranted. He began to pace feverishly across the scattered glass. "How could you be so *cruel?* How could you say no to me? It is because of *him*, is it not? That *man*...that man who has poisoned your mind. That man who you love! I *hate him*. He has replaced me. He is my enemy. He must not remain in our way. I will find him and kill him. Yes, I will kill him! *For us*. I will save us both." Kye halted in his steps. "Or...did you never love me?" His pace quickened, and he gripped his head again. "You turned that...that *creature* on me. That *thing* that I cannot overpower!" Stark terror flickered in Kye's eye. Then his eye narrowed, and his nostrils flared.. His hands dropped to his side. "No...I will find a way. Nothing can remain between us. If I am to ever to have peace, I *must* have you. You will never stay with me while that man you love is alive, so he must die. He *must* die. I will find a way. I *WILL* find a way."

Breathing heavily, fists clenched, Kye lowered his head and then slowly looked up. He could still see his reflection, appearing uneven and distorted against the broken glass. His sharp ears caught the sound of footsteps approaching from behind. In what was left of the mirror's right-hand corner, he noticed the jagged outline of a shadow. Kye turned his head slightly, his one blue eye gleaming bright with resentful hate. His words came out in a malicious hiss as he pressed his hand tightly against the wall.

"So...you have finally come." His lips curled in defiant mockery, a bitter smile extending across his face. "Well...*speak*. What do you want from me now? You...you who cause me unspeakable...*torment.*"

Thank you so much for reading this book! If you enjoyed it, feel free to leave a review on Amazon, Goodreads, and/or social media:) Your support means the world to me!

Author Website/Social Media

Acknowledgments

I have to first thank the people on Instagram who were following me when I was just starting out. This project literally came into existence because of your support and suggestions. Never in a million years did I think my first series would fall under the Sci-fi genre, but here we are! You all were really onto something when you said I should write a Sci-fi story. Now I can't see myself doing anything else.

Thank you, Mom, for the eager optimism you have for my goals and aspirations. (Thank you, Dad, for the laptop.) You might be a skeptic when it comes to my dreams of being a full-time author, but I hope to make you a believer soon;)

I wish to thank Gwen for the stunning artwork. I really got lucky when I stumbled upon your art page! You have the uncanny ability to create my characters just as I envision them.

Special thanks to Courtney. Being friends for 25+ years is such a flex, and our friendship has only been getting better. You listen to my endless story explanations and ramblings with such interest and patience. If that isn't true friendship, I don't know what is!

Last but certainly not least, thanks be to God.

Author Page

C. T. Berry is a Sci-fi/Fantasy author who loves creating stories filled with suspense, mystery, and plenty of romance. She began taking her writing seriously after graduating from Kennesaw University with a Bachelor's in English. When she's not coming up with dramatic plots, she enjoys drawing, music, movies, and spending time in nature.